Continuing in sight?

…An exciting science fiction told with a coherent protagonist. Would have liked to read the sequel right away - that ultimately decides the quality of the story, because there has to be something to come:).

— UMSTEIGER, AMAZON GERMANY

Harrowing, Thrilling Read

I read *Dark Eros* straight through in one sitting; I couldn't put it down. It's very well written, with a compelling heroine struggling to escape a horrible relationship and get her life on track against terrible odds.

— JAMES D., AMAZON US

Some things strange and sinister

Some authors have an uncanny knack for writing the dark and disturbed. H. Raven Rose is one of those authors. At the very opening of Dark Eros you want to clutch a can of mace, or a small 9mm handgun, before you continue going down this dark path.

— CYNTHIA VESPIA, AMAZON US

❧

PRAISE FOR EXU BOOKS

PRAISE FOR *MR. PSYCHIC: A NOVEL*

Funny and Entertaining!

He goes from being a person who avoids human connection, out of fear of being hurt or abandoned, to being a person willing to let himself love and be loved by a true Soul mate. An entertaining read, cleverly written and will bring a smile to your face. Five stars from me.

— SADSACK, AMAZON US

Mr. Psychic stole my heart

Mr. Psychic is a wonderful read! Dermot Davis and H. Raven Rose transform the main character, George, from a priggish elitist who thinks he has his life perfectly planned into Mr. Psychic, a soulful, open and loving human being. It's a fun journey and you'll love the characters.

— LINDA S. AMSTUTZ, AMAZON US

OTHER BOOKS BY EXU AUTHORS

Books by Dermot Davis and H Raven Rose

Encounter

~

Books by Dermot Davis

Brain: The Man Who Wrote the Book That Changed the World

The Younger Man: How Many Times Can You Take a Second Chance on Love?

Stormy Weather: A Novel: Are You Dreaming Now?

Fatal Eclipse

THE YOUNGER MAN: BOX SET (3 books in 1): How Many Times Can You Take Another Chance on Love?

CAGED: A Short Reads Novella

~

Books by H Raven Rose

Dark Eros: a Novella

Shadow Selves (Double Happiness)

The Big "O": A Romantic Comedy

Dread Zone

Bugocalypse: La Cucaracha V1

~

MR. PSYCHIC

A NOVEL

DERMOT DAVIS

H RAVEN ROSE

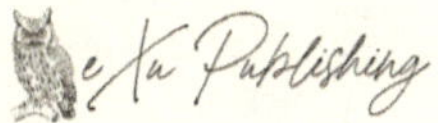

COPYRIGHT

This is a work of fiction. Names, characters, places, and incidents are a product of the imaginations of the authors or are used fictitiously.

Mr. Psychic: A Novel

Copyright © 2013, 2025 by Dermot Davis & H Raven Rose

All rights reserved. No part of this publication may be reproduced, distributed or transmitted in any form or by any means, including mechanical methods, without the prior written permission of the publisher, except in the case of brief quotations in critical reviews and certain other noncommercial uses permitted by copyright law.

Published by eXu Publishing
https://www.exupublishing.com/

ISBN: 978-1-957125-07-7 (trade paperback)
ISBN: 978-1-957125-12-1 (hardback)

eBook Edition: 2013
First Trade Paperback Edition: 2025
First Trade Hardback Edition: 2025

0 9 8 7 6 5 4 3 2 1

DEDICATION

For our parents... with great love.

CONTENTS

BOOK PREVIEWS

TO THE READER

Aite no nai kenka wa denkinu.
(One cannot quarrel without an opponent.)

— JAPANESE PROVERB

MR. PSYCHIC

GEORGE Beresford II COULD NOT BELIEVE his son's arrogance in telling him to get back out there and "find someone."

"There's more to live for in life than your precious roses, Dad," George III had said the previous weekend—as if the boy knew a rose from a rhododendron.

"Don't wait too long, George the second," his daughter-in-law had helpfully added in a joking tone. She was an attractive young woman with a pleasant demeanor, and it was hard to feel angry at her.

Her playful manner separated George, her husband, from George, her father-in-law, and always made George II smile. He couldn't help smiling now.

Her blue eyes twinkling, she smiled back and, flipping her long blonde hair, continued, "All the good ones get taken in their forties and fifties, after they've gotten divorced or been widowed. You don't want to end up speed-dating leftovers... women with issues who are incapable of love."

It wasn't the first time that this pair had bombarded their elder with unsolicited romantic advice.

George had ignored them both for months. A man of the world in his sixties, he had his career, investments, a beautiful home, and hobbies to enrich and sustain his soul. He didn't believe that he needed a woman in his life, much less a wife. Nobody had a dire need for romance, love, or communion.

He had everything and then some, and he knew that the idea of needing another half was a mad myth that ruined many a perfectly good life.

Yes, that's what he had, he decided, a perfectly good life comprised of satisfaction and select, cultivated pleasures.

~

George pruned his roses happily, enjoying the late afternoon sun and the pattern of light and shadow created by the golden sunlight and green plants on the wall behind the shrubbery.

He leaned close to a rose bush with lush green leaves and gorgeous reddish-pink, velvety blossoms, so fragrant and sweet-smelling. The scent made him dizzy for a moment. He closed his eyes and breathed in the delicious fragrance. The heavenly scent was the perfume of his perfectly good life.

He opened his eyes to gaze upon his prize-winning roses lovingly. What? He stared. He did a double-take. Then he looked closer. Phytophthora. A genus within the group of fungus-like organisms known as oomycetes had dared to settle upon his roses. The evidence was slight, yet he was sure that it was there.

He alternately examined the root and crown of his rose bush. He stared at the soil. Traitor. The treacherous Phytophthora species can infect a wide range of trees, shrubs, and bedding plants, and they sometimes lie in wait, persisting in the soil, for many years before settling upon a victim.

As he mentally debated whether the phytophthora had progressed enough to be diagnosable, knowing full well that chemical management of the disease was both impractical and uneconomical, he noticed Ed creeping about.

Ed was his forty-something-year-old neighbor. Or maybe Ed was in his fifties; it was hard to tell. Whatever his age, he was one of those men who perpetually looked pubescent and never seemed to age.

The man had retained his acne, gangly, awkward, overly fatty, immature-looking body, oily hair, smudged glasses, and surly teenage attitude throughout his life.

For some ghastly, unknown reason, perhaps boredom or jealousy (it's not just a myth that the married man with kids envies the life of a single man), Ed was constantly spying on George.

Watching from the corner of his eyes, he saw Ed pretend to check on an ugly and neglected bush growing on the side of his lawn; George grimaced internally while keeping his visage neutral.

"What a jerk," he muttered softly to himself.

There was a ginormous "Neighborhood Watch" decal on Ed's house window and a station wagon parked in Ed's driveway. George was surprised that one or more of Ed's snotty-nosed children wasn't clutching his pants leg or otherwise hanging off of his body, as was their wont.

He had a half dozen or so offspring of varying ages and levels of cleanliness, in addition to a wife who somehow managed to put up with Ed's annoying personality.

The man's inanity seemed irreparable to George, but he also knew that in life, you don't get to choose everything you desire for yourself, least of all your next-door neighbors. Other people, along with the family you are born into, fall into the "luck of the draw" category.

Ed ambled in George's general direction, as if he were strolling without purpose. There was nothing subtle about Ed, nothing ephemeral. Ed was, in fact, one of those on-the-nose humans, an oaf who was exactly what he appeared to be: difficult, obnoxious, and combative… the opposite of well-meaning.

"Morning, Ed. Special plans?" George asked, knowing full well that Ed usually had a singular purpose in mind.

Ed reached the far side of George II's front lawn and continued to walk toward his neighbor. Ed grinned and laughed loudly; his smile and laughter were mean and false. George stared at the front tooth gap in Ed's not-so-white toothy grin.

"Oh, you know… same old, same old. Spend some quality time with the wife and kiddies," Ed answered casually as George nonchalantly opened his garage with the remote.

"Guess you miss having little ones around," Ed said halfheartedly as he stared obsessively into the garage. As usual, once George II's garage was open, Ed was awestruck and nigh speechless. The man had a morally perverse, covetous appreciation of George II's belongings, specifically his cars.

Slobbering with desire, Ed stared, as he always did, at the beautiful antique roadster. It was parked right next to George II's Prius. George entered the garage and put away his pruning shears. He emptied the rose cuttings into the plant waste recycling bin.

Giving Ed a surreptitious glance, George took out his antique car cleaning kit and pulled out a blue surgical towel. Then, with Ed's eyes watching his every move, like a hungry snake might watch a mouse, George carefully wiped down his roadster with the cloth.

Ed didn't dare step inside George II's garage, or even on the intimate parts of his private property. The fallacy of their friendship didn't extend that far. Truth be told, they weren't friends at all. They had a simple relationship: George owned a few things; he had a lovely home with well-tended gardens and lived a carefree single life that Ed lusted after.

"What about you, George? Got plans?" Ed called to George II, from just out of his sight.

George smiled to himself and then carefully replied:

"Taking Miss Betty out for a ride in the beautiful sunshine." George heard a grunt and then footsteps and knew that Ed was returning to his own home. Smiling, George polished Miss Betty, his beautiful roadster, all the more slowly, the better to enjoy himself.

As Ed returned to the boisterous chaos of his family life, he looked at George II's manicured lawn and beautifully maintained home.

He was unaware that the gash of his toothy grin had slowly developed into a full-blown sneer. His mind was tight and bitter, weighted down and tired of the constant assault of raucous subconscious memories of the personal injustices that he had experienced throughout his life.

Unable to purge painful and unconstructive memories of his accumulated past, his thoughts were overwrought and began to verge on ruthless and hate-filled.

Thump. Thump. Thump. Crossing the edge of the yard and perhaps in an unconscious desire to rid his being of such unwanted negativity, Ed took wide, stomping steps.

With each reverberation, each angry footfall that boomed, the corners of Ed's mouth turned further down. He glowered and shook his head, disturbed by George II's apparent gentlemanly contentment and by the sounds of pandemonium made by four clamoring kids as he grew closer and closer to the inside of his dilapidated house of discontent.

Restless, filled with unhappiness and displeasure, which he had no way to cure, Ed paused in the yard to look into his residence. He looked through the plate glass window of his front room.

Inside, his four children ran amok. A couple of the rug rats shrieked and screamed with guttural laughter as the older siblings wrestled the younger ones with serious intent. The littler ones screamed with pain, tears streaming down their red, blubbering faces. Someone had punched or pinched, or otherwise assaulted, the two younger children.

Lindsay, Ed's very pregnant wife, appeared by the kitchen door and shouted at the kids, demanding fair play. Mocked by her children for her efforts, she unsuccessfully chased the older two kids, who only laughed and shouted in response to their mother's demands.

Ed, who really didn't wish to go back inside his own house, glanced back at George II. The wide open front door of George II's home revealed his quiet, tidy dwelling, a comparative bastion of peace and bliss.

George had finished polishing his fine-looking vehicle, which didn't need shining—it was pristine. He always kept it garaged and free of dust and dirt outside of brief weekend use.

George closed the door to his home, then got into the antique roadster and cranked up his beauty with one turn of the ignition key. As always, the sound of the purring engine elicited a satisfied smile as he backed her up, out of the garage, down his drive, and into the street.

To his great satisfaction, he noticed that Ed had stopped to watch him as he zoomed smartly out of the suburban neighborhood. A moment later, as George accelerated, the side of the street began to blur.

Shades of green and earth tones smeared in a hazy kaleidoscope as the car sped away. Checking in his rear-view mirror, George smiled as he watched a sad and envious-looking Ed slowly appear smaller and smaller and, finally, disappear from view.

~

George drove his Miss Betty leisurely through the beauteous, verdant suburban countryside. His windshield glass was immaculate and so clear he could see right through it. It seemed almost invisible.

The driver's side window rolled down; his left arm rested on the driver's side door. George drove with a single hand on the steering wheel, as casually as a seasoned cowboy might control the reins of his champion horse. Warmed by the golden midday sunshine, he luxuriated in the heat.

Sunshine streamed from the sky, and the simple act of driving in silence filled him with a deep peace. Thoughts of his son, George III, his only child, named after his father, as he was, were long gone.

George sighed with deep peace and surveyed the blue sky, with hardly a cloud, emerald grass, and newly leafing trees. In late

May, growing things were shades of green and beautiful. It felt like early summer as he drove: balmy, bright, and as if the day stretched endlessly before him.

George's weekends were sacrosanct. Truth be told, every detail of his life could be considered something of a ritual.

Over the years, caring for his home, cars, and other belongings had become somewhat ritualized. In addition to his household chores, grocery shopping, running daily errands, and indeed most details of his life, he followed a strict regimen designed to create a quiet, easy life based on routine safety.

Today, just like every Saturday, after caring for his roses and wiping down Miss Betty, he chose to do his weekly shopping.

Very happily, he shopped at three distinct stores: an ethnic market for certain staples, such as vegetables, meat, and rice (which were much less expensive there, even though the quality was the same); a dollar store for odd lots of brand-name items (which, for some reason, were sold at a significant discount); and an upscale health food store that sold whole foods, chic gourmet items, and other tasty foodstuffs.

Upon reaching the increasingly trendy upscale health food market, he happily parked his vehicle and went inside. He spent an hour carefully shopping for items he would need for tonight's dinner party with his friends.

Entertaining made him feel especially prosperous.

~

He perused the aisles of the natural foods market, singularly focused upon his task. He diligently avoided the gazes or other attempts by single women to catch his eye, such as the plump-looking brunette he was sure was following at a discreet distance. She most likely hoped to "bump" into him.

For a single male, the mere act of grocery shopping could be a hazardous affair, he had often noted to himself.

Having had years of experience in this endeavor (avoiding grasping females), George could instantly turn on an air of distraction and utter disinterest.

It wasn't that he would never be interested in a woman ever again. It was just that it wasn't a priority at this particular time of his life. A relationship was likely to be a distraction from the goals that were his primary concern.

It was all a matter of timing, he reasoned. A man needs to have his finances in order before considering adding a woman who needs looking after into the mix. Affairs of the heart would have to wait until he had his retirement package squared away; there would be no exceptions. So, he disciplined himself.

His marriage had been an utter fiasco, psychologically, financially, and in every other way. When George III was small, George II had determined to get his life sorted entirely before he even considered a serious relationship again. His mind hadn't changed since.

He pondered the merits of adding capers to the mixed greens salad in the gourmet section. Capers, artichoke hearts, and maybe some hearts of palm might go nicely on the evening meal menu.

He mused about the virtues of capers at length. This was partly because the brunette lingered overly close, and he knew he could wait her out. He was determined that way. George pondered the jars of capers before him. Real capers are the flower buds of a caper bush, Capparis spinosa (its large seedpod is called a caper berry), which was also called Flinders rose.

While young and green, the seedpods of nasturtiums look and taste a great deal like the buds of the caper plant. However, most cultured classes consider them "poor man's capers," so obviously, George was not considering those.

Naturally, the capers he was considering were the real deal, imported from the Mediterranean. They were picked, sun-dried, and then pickled in a vinegar brine. George glanced at the tiny yet beautiful jar in his hand. Would it be too much green? He wondered.

He planned to slice fresh tomatoes or red or orange bell peppers to add a splash of color to the top of the salad and then add pine nuts, lightly toasted with Celtic sea salt.

He would gently toss the salad in imported red wine balsamic vinaigrette with extra virgin olive oil. He would prepare and offer warmed, lightly breaded goat cheese medallions on the side of this salad.

Yes, he decided, looking at the tiny container of beautifully preserved capers. They would add extra texture and flavor to accentuate the salad's other attributes. He put two jars into his cart.

After a lengthy mental debate, George spent a fair amount of enjoyable time considering the wine choices. He chose a couple of moderately expensive cabernets and a single Californian Sauvignon Blanc for Marcus, the sole white wine drinker.

Of course, he had a completely stunning Le Cache European Country 5200 wine cellar, a free-standing furniture-style wine cellar with a chocolate cherry finish. It combined state-of-the-art wine storage technology with exceptional design artistry.

Made of premium cherry wood with crown and base molding, hand-carved wood trim, hardwood French doors, and digital temperature display and control, among other features, it was a highlight of George II's dining room. It was well-stocked with hand-picked wines, holding 544 racked bottles.

George did not like things to be empty. A place for everything, and everything in its place, was a motto he truly took to heart.

After paying cash for his groceries, he headed to the other two stores to finish shopping. A couple of hours later, the day still warm and illuminated by sunlight, he felt as satisfied as he had ever felt. The trunk of his car was stocked with luxurious, delicious, and sundry household items.

Sure, he had a perfidious phytophthora situation to deal with. Yet, thankfully, the rest of his life was blissfully perfect. Sure, he couldn't relax entirely until he was safely retired and living off the interest of his retirement fund, but he was on track to reach his financial goals in the next few years.

It would take more than phytophthora, that fungus of black death threatening his rose garden, to seriously mar his perfect life. With a sigh of contentment, he cranked his vehicle and seconds later was returning to his immaculate ordered home.

Everything about my life is on schedule, he thought happily to himself. Reaching his home, filled with an aura of satisfaction, he parked and unloaded his car.

~

He put the groceries and other items away inside his traditional, elegantly decorated dwelling. He then washed and pounded several chicken breasts and prepared a marinade with a bit of fresh rosemary, lemon juice, lemon zest, white wine, and garlic.

Leaving the chicken in the refrigerator, resting gently in the marinade, he carefully rinsed the vegetables needed to create a mixed salad. Preparing the veggies for the side dish, he washed and drained them in the colander and then left them on thick paper towels to dry naturally.

He had a few hours before he needed to prepare further for his guests, so he decided to check his retirement fund and other accounts just like he did every day (sometimes more than once).

It only took a couple of minutes. He kept his dinosaur of a computer in his home office, stripped of unnecessary programs so that it could run his financial investment software.

He continually tracked his personal banking, credit card, loan, 401(K), investment accounts, and personal balance sheet, not just to assure himself that he was on the right track but also because seeing his wealth accumulate gave him a great sense of inner peace and security of mind. The app on his phone was too small and induced too much anxiety for him to try and look at everything at once.

Most of his assets were investments, stocks and bonds, mutual funds, and other assets that formed part of his overall retirement plan. His liabilities were primarily the residual balance on his mortgage loan.

His parents were considered "well off," but they were young for their age, and even though he was their only child, he had never taken anything, much less money, from them. He had no intentions of starting now, not that he had the need.

George III and Georgie IV, his grandson, could inherit if his parents chose to choose heirs.

Settling into his home office desk chair, George looked at a computer-generated image of his current "real-time" retirement stock portfolio projections.

On screen, as thrilling as always, he was happy to see that the graph line on his portfolio was close to his $2M end goal. Obviously, $2M was barely enough to retire in the current fiscal environment in the United States.

However, it was a decent start and, when he reached that number, he planned to implement plan B, an aggressive series of investment strategies to seek to double his retirement fund.

He pulled out and glanced at his OMEGA 1932 Olympic pocket chronograph watch. A Rattrapante Chronograph in 18-carat yellow gold was powered by rediscovered unassembled movement kits that had miraculously been discovered in storage at OMEGA's headquarters in Biel.

The parts had been stored since 1932, when the watch brand first served as "Official Timekeeper" of that year's Olympic Games. In addition to being rare, the timepiece was a thing of great beauty.

The horological wonder of it all—an OMEGA product with mythological status—the 1932 pocket chronograph was impossibly seductive for him. When he learned of its existence, he had to have one. He had, at first, tried to resist his impulse to acquire one.

When he bought the watch, George was quite aware that, at upwards of $70K, it could not legitimately be perceived as an investment. Instead, when unable to resist his yearning, he justified it as a talisman to motivate him to create the future of independence he desired. It was a thing of beauty, and when he checked the time several times a day, he carefully held it.

Glancing at the timepiece, he felt wealthy and in control; the watch reminded him of who he would be if he industriously followed his financial plan. It gave him tremendous pleasure to check the time. Looking at it now, he got a quick fright as he realized he had barely enough time to shower and prepare for his guests.

~

George showered and dressed in his standard weekend attire, which he wore with such unwavering regularity, it could almost be considered his weekend uniform.

Putting on a pair of dark, cuffed slacks and a white linen long-sleeved shirt, he added a touch of after-shave and slipped his watch into his left trouser pocket. He noted with great satisfaction that his hair hadn't grown much since his most recent monthly haircut, taken care of the last Saturday of the previous month.

Sure, his clothes and suits were several years old, perhaps even a decade or two. Still, they fit perfectly as he meticulously watched his diet because it was cost-effective and so as not to succumb to that dreaded middle-age spread. They were freshly pressed, medium starch from the dry cleaner, just as he preferred, and nothing was worn, stained, or otherwise in obvious disrepair.

He felt very strongly that the compulsion to spend unnecessarily was a symptom of the dissolution and dissatisfaction rampant in the Western world, a debauchery which he found repugnant.

George was sure that his lifestyle choices would seem idiosyncratic to some, extreme even. Yet one doesn't become a middle-class self-made millionaire without generally being a very frugal person. He bought quality items, whether clothing or otherwise, and cared for them meticulously.

He did all the home and lawn maintenance himself, using a couple of books about how to do that. He only replaced clothing when it didn't fit, was irreparably stained or damaged, or was too worn to maintain its shape and hue.

He wasn't as well-off as his parents, being a self-made man. Truthfully, he jettisoned his work clothes first before getting rid of his at-home attire. He did this primarily because, for some idiotic reason, upper-level management increasingly seemed to think that clothes made the man.

Over the years, he had seen many a young upstart punk, with little to offer intellectually, yet inexplicably given an advanced degree, dressed in impeccable high-end attire, and with those and an arrogant, overbearing, and self-important attitude to match, get hired or promoted above their senior peers.

He felt content that all his promotions over the last forty years were based solely on merit. He was still at the same company, though the current president was now the son of the man who had initially hired him. Like his father before him, George was a man of rare employment longevity. And he hoped that he had passed on to his son his belief that endurance in service is akin to moral fortitude.

George was the current comptroller of the finance department for the Chief Financial Officer of Teleseismology Hub NS, a well-respected, small yet highly successful organization. Even though less than two years ago, George had previously been passed over for the CFO position—the job had been given to his younger direct report and former mentee—this time around, he expected to be promoted finally.

At first, getting used to reporting to a former direct report had been strange, yet he had managed. He was determined to do whatever it took to get promoted. He routinely spent hours and hours, above and beyond those worked by others in his department, doing whatever was required to provide timely, relevant financial data to support the company's planning and control activities.

If promoted, he would be responsible for directing the corporation's fiscal functions according to generally accepted accounting principles, which the Securities and Exchange Commission regulates, the Financial Accounting Standards Board, and other regulatory and advisory organizations.

He would finally be a Vice President and a bona fide senior management team member. The most senior and experienced—and, in fact, most loyal—member of the finance division, he had spent the last eighteen months endeavoring to show that he could handle any challenge.

Said challenges included being passed over for a promotion, working well with other managers despite that fact, and understanding and communicating technical financial data to others simply and straightforwardly. Thus, he was no longer worried about his competition.

George III, his ever-annoying son, loved to remind him, even though he had repeatedly asked him not to, that Teleseismology Hub NS was an anagram for "The Soulless Big Money."

George thought people who had time to play around with words were obviously irresponsible, possibly even lazy, and could lack drive. The SBM, as his son laughingly called the company, had made it possible for George to raise his boy. Alone.

Teleseismology was seismology that dealt with records obtained at long distances. The company had clients worldwide, from academics to government agencies. George dealt with the company's financial aspects and spent a growing amount of his time as an internal and external business consultant.

Long since liberated from the mechanical aspects of accounting and finance, he felt he was a trusted advisor and an increasingly capable intellect.

Despite being accused of micromanaging his duties and subordinates in the past, he felt that his research, analysis, reporting, and managerial skills were finally about to be recognized and duly rewarded.

Spotting outsourcing trends in other industries, he had recently submitted an unsolicited report to senior management detailing ways the company could immediately slash its bottom line and substantially increase its profits. Certainly, THNS had considered outsourcing years ago, yet other companies had lost business due to poor quality external hires. So, they had never leapt. George had found evidence that judicious outsourcing to language-tested, financial whizzes of the sort they could use would eliminate the hiring issues that reduced client or customer satisfaction and got such bad press.

Judging by some comments he had overheard through the office gossip grapevine, he felt certain that the report had struck a chord and, in private, was being very well received.

In contrast to the insinuation of his son's ignorant, almost slanderous, words, George felt that his company was not soulless. Naturally, they dealt with big and grand money concerns as befits any successful capitalist organization.

Thoughts flickered through his mind, like dust motes. Brushing aside thoughts of work, George switched gears and mentally prepared the dinner party meal in his head, then did an informal system check on the evening ahead.

*R*eturning to the kitchen, George's thoughts returned to the salad. Capers have a particular flavor; enjoyment of the garnishment could be considered an acquired taste. He loved introducing coworkers to this type of tiny life delight. You wouldn't get capers on the dinner party menu just anywhere.

He knew the capers' sharp, piquant, and salty taste would beautifully contrast with and complement the rest of the meal. After checking that the salad fixings were dry, he drained the sun-dried Mediterranean capers and set them aside.

The marinated chicken breasts were put into the oven, and he started brown rice in the steamer. His ex-wife had accused him of being obsessive, overly considering food and meal preparation, yet he found it so soothing, and life was so long and tedious. Really, what else was he to focus on?

He very precisely ripped beautiful green lettuce and sliced several fresh tomatoes, for the top of the salad, for a splash of color. After lightly toasted pine nuts with Celtic sea salt in a pan, he made red wine balsamic vinaigrette with extra virgin olive oil.

He put the salad together and then set it aside without dressing it. Then, he carefully poured the vinaigrette into a beautiful, tiny cut crystal decanter.

After steaming artichokes for the side and preparing an olive oil and fresh herb dip for them, he sliced up some pungent goat cheese and lightly breaded it in a rough-ground blue corn meal breading to serve as medallions on the side of the salad.

The white wine was chilled. He took two bottles from the wine storage and placed them in ice-filled clay wine holders. Then he took the bottles outside to the backyard patio. With great satisfaction, he noted the absolute splendor of his backyard. Looking around his garden felt peaceful, almost healing.

The setting sun cast an orange-gold glow over his award-winning roses, filling the backyard's air with a subtle, sweet fragrance in shades of red and pink. Greenery, vines, and precisely clipped grass and bushes created a deepening peace in his soul and being.

He placed the clay wine holders on a side table and returned to the house to get the red wines, candles for the tables, and place settings. He carefully created a beautiful arrangement of serving ware and settings for an intimate dinner for four.

With dusk rapidly approaching, he turned on the subtle outside lighting once back inside the house. Then he returned to the patio to light the candles and survey the table.

It was perfect. He hurried back into the house to make the final preparations.

Back in the kitchen, he warmed hearth-baked Bialy artisanal bread. The rich, hearty alternative grain bread, with black olives, thinly sliced sun-dried, caramelized, seasoned onions, and poppy seeds, would be delicious and taste almost cheesy in the middle.

Glancing at his OMEGA Rattrapante Chronograph, George sighed with satisfaction.

It was time.

~

With the dinner party in full swing, George stood back briefly to survey and assess his kingdom. George II's coworkers, Marco, James, and Bethany, chatted and laughed as they enjoyed the elegant backyard dinner party.

Due to George's diligent construction and organization, and despite the presence of the chatting and laughing party people, the garden and patio continued to be a haven of peace and elegance.

Verdant plants and blossoming flowers, including his beloved roses, exuded a delicate scent which increased the harmony. Flickering lit cream candles, inside Amber glass and wrought iron candle holders, cast a soft glow over the scene.

He smiled to himself to see Marco's face already a little shiny and red. He had swigged down a couple of glasses of wine as soon as he arrived. James had arrived first, though.

There had been a moment when, in a confidential tone, James had mumbled that he had something important to talk to George about, and it was clear that he didn't want the others to participate in the conversation. But then Marco arrived, and the opportunity to talk privately was lost.

Marco loved his wine and was an effusive guest. His general conviviality and appreciation of George's hosting efforts made him a pleasure to be around. He savored the food, the drink, the conversation, and the moment, and not being a shy type of person, he was always vocal with compliments and toasts.

James and he had been in the same division—the finance division —at Teleseismology Hub NS. George had tried to mentor him, to a certain degree, being that he had a good decade in years and work experience over him. They had an unspoken camaraderie that made work more pleasant.

Not too surprisingly, the guy had catapulted up the career ladder. So, oddly, he was now in a unique career position, having created his little department of one. He no longer reported to George because his department was an adjunct to finance. It was not an issue, George and he had much mutual respect.

Marco lifted his glass in a toast as if on cue and brought George out of his reverie. George refilled every stemless wine glass with more wine. He realized that he hadn't answered Bethany and strained to remember what she had just asked.

"Capparis spinosa..." George finally said to Bethany, pouring her another glass of red wine, "Its large seedpod is called a caper berry... but the plant itself is known as Flinders rose."

"Ah," Bethany remarked in response.

"Honestly, George, can't you invest in a decent bottle of wine?" Marco joked as he drank deeply. James frowned at Marco, obviously mistaking his tone.

"Pretentious much, Marco? You know George only has the best..."

Marco shrugged and laughed. He was amused that James didn't get the joke.

"That's right, the best..." added Bethany. Trailing off, she carefully sipped her glass of red wine. She then leaned back and luxuriated in the scene and setting.

"...the best retirement fund at this table," James added."So he has no intention of wasting his hard-earned Benjamin's on your beloved Syrah et Shiraz... French import or otherwise."

James laughed and gave George a conspiratorial wink. George knew that he knew that the one area where he didn't scrimp and save was on the wine and food.

"Well, I think it is lovely..." Bethany replied, lifting her wine glass carefully and uncharacteristically proceeding to guzzle her wine. " George's portfolio, I mean."

The guests and George laughed. More coworkers than bosom buddies, they were only half joking. George II's cell phone buzzed in his pocket.

He wasn't expecting a call, but—cautious man that he was—he would never irresponsibly leave his cell phone unattended or ignore his calls. Still buzzing, he pulled it out and checked the caller ID.

He sighed, stood, and motioned that he'd be right back to his friends, who were happily continuing their meals. Then he stepped away to take the call. George took several steps away, close enough to the patio speakers that played soft jazz music and near enough that he could still hear snippets of the conversation at the table.

~

"Hello?" he said into his phone. Hearing his son's normal voice, George sighed in relief, realizing there was no emergency. Even though the conversation behind him became more raucous, George could still hear every word on the phone.

Still unsure about the purpose of the call, George listened patiently as George III rambled on about having a family vacation.

"He can retire in five years or even less... and, I admit it, I'm a bit jealous," Bethany said and smiled. Her just audible words made George II smile just a bit.

"George is a saver. Big deal," Marcus said. George knew that Marcus would be waving his hands to punctuate his words. Bethany giggled and sipped her wine.

"Oh, admit it, Marcus, we're all a little jealous," James said good-naturedly.

Their voices faded away as George concentrated more fully on his conversation.

"Well, what do you think? You don't seem too excited about it," George III said.

Given his rising emotion, George quietly spoke as kindly as possible into his phone. His expression revealed uncharacteristic irritation.

"I told you, son, I have guests."

~

The master bedroom of George III's home was a mess. It wasn't dirty. It was just a jumble, the kind of disarray often seen in the house of a happy, harried family. Baskets of clean laundry, half-chewed dog bones, articles of clothing, a couple of tennis rackets, and baby toys were strewn about the room.

George III, patrician good looks, lay in bed, flipping channels on the muted television set while talking on the phone to his dad. A golden retriever lay on a dog bed on the floor.

Jenn wrangled their toddler Georgie IV into the bath in the adjacent bathroom.

"I want to nail down some dates for the family holiday... Don't you remember? You said you'd think about it, Dad," said George III.

George stood surveying his backyard patio.

"I said that because you wouldn't take 'No' for an answer, son," George finally said gravely.

"I'm sick of taking 'No' for an answer, Dad. Come on vacation with us. Don't you want to see your grandchild growing up?" George III said with apparent increasing exasperation.

Jenn, from the bathroom, looked at George III with apparent sympathy. He shrugged his shoulders, as if to say, "Dad is still being obstinate and driving me dotty." She nodded at him and scrubbed their child.

~

"*A*s I have told you repeatedly, son, wasting money on a holiday will prevent me from meeting my retirement contribution milestones and objectives in a timely fashion," George II said calmly. His face grew quite red due to some emotion that was not audible in his tone of voice.

He tried to understand why this was such a sore point with George III. He had virtually raised the boy alone after he was divorced when the child was three years of age.

They had both lost her, his wife and George III's mother, when the woman, a self-professed gypsy, had gone off to *find herself*.

Being a single father, raising a child on one income, and being forced to pay for child care when the boy wasn't in school, all by himself, required fortitude, self-sacrifice, and fiscal discipline.

He had raised his child to understand the value of a dollar and the necessity of planning one's life carefully.

He hoped these conversations weren't an indicator that the boy's mother's slacker genes were finally expressing themselves. Was there a genetic predisposition to laziness and profligacy? He almost shuddered.

~

"*D*ad, you've scrimped and saved for years. You don't enjoy life. You don't date. You hang out with a bunch of losers who eat your food and guzzle your cheap wine," George III growled.

Jenn, rinsing soap off of George IV, as he giggled and wriggled, and in an attempt to warn her husband to tread lightly, she shook her head, no.

Caught up in the call and the resoluteness of his position, George III didn't see her movements or get the message. Would he have heeded her guidance if he had?

~

*G*eorge stared at his friends. His coworkers were rapidly and quite rabidly consuming the meal he had prepared. They were also hurriedly imbibing the wine, which wasn't 'cheap' at all.

Unbeknownst to his guests, George had decided to treat them to a combination of his rare, special, and select private vintage. Perhaps only James would know the value of it.

As George looked at the group while gathering his thoughts to respond to his son, James looked up at him and gave him a genuine smile of gratitude.

James lifted his wine glass in a private toast. George immediately felt warmth in his heart at the gesture.

He thought of a couple of times when James, when the company was in a tight spot, had given him the heads-up about a situation at work when he didn't need to.

More importantly, probably, because of the risk to the guy's job security, he shouldn't have.

They weren't bosom buddies... but the younger man was a friend.

Despite his son's claim, none of them were moochers.

True, they didn't carefully craft intimate little dinner parties or other gatherings in their homes and invite George to partake.

Instead, they generally insisted on picking up his tab at any outing, luncheon, or other meal-related event.

Come to think of it, he rarely, if ever, had to pay for a lunch or dinner when he was out with any one of the three. Plus, he knew that Bethany had more than platonic feelings for him. She really and truly cared for him, as a man and a person.

Unfortunately, a romantic relationship was out of the question because he did not reciprocate Bethany's feelings.

Although they were merely platonic friends—and that was all they would ever be—he and Bethany were still relatively close. They exchanged holiday gifts, as a matter of fact.

Coming out of his daydream and realizing that his son was mid-litany and showed no signs of stopping his diatribe, George decided it was time to nip this irksome conversation in the bud.

"Georgie, you're out of line," George said sternly, and in a sharper tone than he could remember having used in a long time.

"My retirement fund is what will keep me from being a burden upon you and Jenn in my old age."

George III did not respond.

George II listened to the silence that followed. He half wondered if his son had actually had the audacity. Did George III hang up on him? Finally, his only child spoke.

~

"I'm sick of hearing about your retirement fund, Dad. Your grandson is growing up, and you... If you don't change your ways... you're going to end up a lonely old man with nothing to keep you company but an old hunk of metal and those stupid roses," George III barked.

Click!

George III hung up on his father and then flung the television remote to the other end of the sofa. Jenn, carrying their now clean yet sleepy toddler, entered the room.

George III took their son from her arms. Jenn sat near her husband and gently rubbed his temples. Neither spoke.

~

The city's white lights sparkled against the blue-black, darkening night sky. Disheveled from a night on the town, wearing a rumpled dark tux with the bow tie undone, George strolled down the sidewalk adjacent to an empty city street.

He was oblivious to an indigent homeless man and almost passed right by. The man grabbed George by the ankle.

In shock, George stared down at the dirty, sickly looking man. The man spoke:

"I used to have all the cards. Bet you have all the cards in your wallet."

"You used to have all the cards," George mumbled, almost incoherently. In a dead sleep, he tossed and turned, clearly dreaming —he was having a nightmare.

"What? What cards?" George responded.

"Saks Fifth Avenue, Nordstrom, Neiman Marcus, all of 'em," the homeless man gasped in a gravelly voice. Then the man coughed until he hacked something up.

George stared at the dirty, unkempt man with increasing horror and then, pulling himself together, managed to wrench his leg free.

He hoped that, whatever disease or malady the man might have, the fellow wasn't contagious. The destitute man laughed bitterly and stared at George with scorn.

"I used to have your life," the homeless man said, rubbing his eyes with a grimy hand. Then he whispered the words. "I used to have your life."

"You used to have my life," George muttered in his sleep, tossing his head from side to side, grimacing, obviously upset.

George pulled out his wallet. Progressively more upset, George wanted to find a way to shut the guy up and get away as quickly as possible. He slipped cash from his wallet and held it out.

As the sick, impoverished man stared up at him, George felt a wave of pity. Then the man wiped his oily hair out of his eyes, and George gasped.

The dirty, bereft, sickly man before him, the man who had once had a life like his own, had George's face. George stared in shock, and the blackness of the dark street and the bright white city lights in the distance seemed to melt.

The scene slipped sideways, and the homeless man's face and eyes stretched like a reflection in a funhouse mirror.

The man reached toward him, and George jumped back in panic.

~

George jumped in his sleep. He twitched and woke with a start. He looked around wildly.

The sight of his beautifully kept bedroom, masculine and ordered, a place for everything and everything in its place, was immediately somewhat calming.

He sighed heavily and yawned.

"A dream," he whispered, "it was only a dream."

Groggily, he rubbed his temples and closed his eyes. It wasn't real, he told himself. Yet the dream, it... he had been dreaming, hadn't he?

It had been so real. It had felt real.

It couldn't have been real, he decided, still not absolutely sure that he was in his bedroom or what had happened. Had he been truly dreaming?

Of course, he was, he decided, because he would never allow himself to be that disheveled in reality. Ever.

The thought of walking down a public street, unkempt and sweating after a night on the town, was horrifying.

But even worse of a shock was that the grimy, down-and-out man had his face, as if, in some way, he was the down-and-out, impoverished man.

Could this be an omen, he wondered? What he had just experienced was obviously a nightmarish dream. Possibly, he had caught something from one of his dinner guests.

Stumbling from his bed, George stood and headed straight to the bathroom.

~

A short while later, George II, immaculately groomed, towel wrapped around his waist, slapped Old Spice on each cheek and looked himself over carefully. He was again his controlled, calm, usual persona.

It had been a bad dream, likely induced by his son's telephone call of the night before.

After deciding to wear an older three-piece custom bespoke suit, he stood over his kitchen sink and carefully ate his regular weekday breakfast: a banana and a bran muffin. He leaned to his right and circumspectly sipped his tea.

He placed his mug on the counter, finished his fruit, and baked breakfast food. After disposing of the muffin wrapper, he obsessively picked up each errant muffin crumb with his index finger from the kitchen sink basin. When the sink was crumb-free, he rinsed it quickly and dried it with a kitchen towel.

Outside his home, George II checked his mail, as he did every morning. His peculiar habit was to check his mail daily before leaving for work.

Not checking after work (when he could be reasonably sure there would not be mail in the box) made him feel nicely restrained and in control. He felt sure that most people would not have the self-discipline to delay the pleasure of getting their mail overnight.

Once he had gotten his mail from the previous day, George got into and cranked his Prius and drove away.

George exited his parked vehicle and glanced around the parking lot of his Fortune 500 Company, Teleseismology Hub NS. He was pleased to note that, as usual, he was one of the very first employees to arrive at work that morning.

~

Seated in his immaculate private accounting department office, George finally relaxed. He looked over a stack of documents. Joe, a handsome young man in his thirties, dressed in the latest edgy, smart GQ business fashion, entered George's office without knocking.

George looked up in surprise. Although Joe was George II's current boss—the current CFO—it was unlike him to be disrespectful in that way. He always knocked first before entering.

"Can I see you in my office?" Joe asked brusquely, and it sounded more like a command than a request.

George managed to nod and answer in the affirmative. Before he could stand, however, Joe had turned and was gone.

George entered Joe's much nicer corner office; this was the same office that George expected would be his when Joe moved onto his new opportunity.

It was rumored that Joe, the younger guy who had previously surpassed George, would be moving on soon. George looked around in surprise.

The floor was covered with boxes full of files and papers. All kinds of forms from HR were spread everywhere. Joe's office was generally always tidy.

Joe sat behind his desk. He nodded at his subordinate, George, who sat carefully and uneasily. Joe looked at George II. Yet, for the longest time, as if mentally deciding how best to say what he had to, he managed not to say a word.

George grew increasingly nervous. His mind raced, filled with thoughts, fears, and questions.

What was going on? Was there an issue with his work or with the department? Was it possible that Joe no longer supported George for the CFO position?

"You know what BPO is, right?" Joe finally asked, after much sighing.

George breathed a sigh of relief. It was some kind of impromptu investigative meeting that Joe had called. Maybe the files were part of new research. George gathered his thoughts and replied calmly.

"Business Process Outsourcing. As you know, I just compiled and shared a corporate-culture-changing cost-benefit analysis and in-depth report on BPO… It's quite profitable," George said, and finally, he could relax entirely.

Perhaps he needed to consult on or explain some of the finer points of his findings. The report wasn't for finance at all; it was an overview of the benefits of outsourcing some Teleseismology Hub NS departments, primarily those involved in production or marketing. Joe nodded at him.

"Yes. Very, very profitable… So much so that they want to extend the program… to accounting," Joe replied drily. George stared. It was almost impossible for him to comprehend the turn of the conversation. Had he heard correctly?

"You're outsourcing accounting?" George asked dumbly.

"Don't take it personally… the entire department's going, plus that one-person on-site internal audit department guy, what's-his-name…" Joe added.

He stared at George for a long moment.

George was now gobsmacked and, therefore, speechless. He stared at Joe, his eyes wide. His throat felt tight.

After a long moment, Joe spoke the thoughts that explained the growing smirk on his face."It's pretty ironic, don't you think?"

George was still too shocked to answer or even consider what Joe might be referring to.

"I had forgotten that you wrote that report! Well done. You managed to demolish your entire department with one document." Joe laughed. Yet how he did so made the younger man sound sad, not amused.

"You're letting us go?" George asked querulously.

Hearing how peculiar he sounded, George forced himself to stop speaking, noticing that his throat had grown even tighter. George could barely swallow, and he felt a bit numb.

He stared at the walls and, for the first time that he could recall, noticed that the paint color was more gray than green. The décor suddenly increased his feeling of queasiness.

"As you stated in your report, George, it makes no sense to pay an American $55K annually when a guy in India will do the same job for $5500," Joe replied.

"You're not going to dispute your report, are you?"

George stared at Joe and then looked down at his hands. It was true. His report had conclusively proven that non-local, non-American hires' cost-benefit ratios and return-on-investments were significant… sometimes as much as 90% savings. He sighed heavily.

It had been one thing to be mathematical, logical, and brutal in his assessment of the bottom line when it involved other departments or divisions of Teleseismology Hub NS. He had no idea that his department, he and his friends, would end up on the chopping block, for which he now felt partly responsible.

"I like you, George, and you were quite good to me—when you were my boss—I appreciate your support of my new opportunities. I'm sorry you won't be CFO here; you would have done a great job. I mean that. Keep it quiet, for now, okay?" Joe added as George continued to stare at him.

"This isn't a formal meeting?" George asked.

"You're not firing me right now?"

Joe smiled even more sadly and shook his head to indicate no.

"This is me, giving my former mentor a completely hush-hush heads-up. Can I count on you to keep this to yourself?" Joe asked, entirely serious. George nodded slowly.

"Okay, then," Joe said, opening a folder on his desk.

At his obvious dismissal, George awkwardly stood and slowly exited.

~

George ambled, rather like a zombie, down the hallway. Being told that you're going to be fired is pretty much the same thing as being told that you're fired, he reasoned to himself.

What's the darn difference? A day? A week? Two weeks? He muttered to himself. He passed a doorway, then stopped and backtracked.

He stuck his head into a tiny office, almost like a cubbyhole.

It was an old supply office that had been appropriated for the on-site internal audit team, the solitary position, and the tiny department of one: James.

James sat at his desk. George, still numb with shock, walked in.

"You okay?" James asked.

George stood awkwardly. He looked around and then, on impulse, he hurriedly pulled the door closed. It was close in the space, with the door shut. The two men stared wildly at each other.

James was quite weirded out by George's peculiar behavior and the man's proximity. George appeared a bit breathless, and his eyes were bulging a bit.

"What?" James asked.

"I'm not supposed to say anything to anyone, but..." George struggled internally for a moment. Then he made an uncharacteristic decision: "But accounting is being outsourced to India... and so are you," George said quietly.

His friend's eyes widened. For a moment, neither spoke. George looked about nervously.

"Are you shitting me? When?" James finally managed to say, "Because I heard some rumblings on Friday. I wanted to talk to you about it on the weekend, but then Marco showed up."

"I know you value longevity... imminently, there won't be any of that here," George said in response, his tone strangely monotone.

He realized then that he was numb from the news.

"Shit-canned ain't going on my resume," James said passionately. George nodded.

James waved at George II, snatched up his telephone, and dialed as if his life depended upon it.

He looked at his coworker with such deep gratitude that George almost flushed. We truly are friends, George realized at that moment as he turned to exit the small space James had made his own.

"Georgie Porgie, I owe you, man," James said, his voice rich with genuine emotion. He quite obviously meant every word. George nodded mutely and left.

The afternoon was a blur.

First came the announcement of the corporate restructuring in a large group meeting.

Then came several smaller group and departmental meetings, with HR and an outside team hired to expedite and smooth the transition of all out-sourced workers.

Finally, and it seemed like a million years later, George exited the building at the end of the work day. He felt as if he had entered an altered universe.

Was it possible that an American company had purposefully chosen to outsource hundreds of jobs to non-Americans solely to increase its bottom line? A few dozen made sense. But hundreds?

It seemed un-American somehow.

George had nothing against non-Americans. He absolutely wanted people in other countries around the world to do well financially and otherwise.

He wanted Teleseismology Hub NS to do well, too, but he also wished he'd kept his job.

After all these years of expected employee loyalty, which he had given in spades, he was now discovering that such loyalty only went one way.

Was it naïve of him to expect equal loyalty from his employer? Apparently, or so he belatedly determined.

The late afternoon cloudless blue sky seemed uncharacteristically dismal.

Knowing that the sky was the same color as it always had been, George realized that he was feeling bleak.

Like everyone who was let go, he had been given pamphlets and other information about the transition, severance pay, and even re-entering the job market… but it didn't calm him.

This was a new feeling and an entirely new experience for him. He had never been fired or let go from a company position before. Being downsized or outsourced, whatever you wanted to call it, felt terrible.

Was it a good thing, even though it felt bad? Was there a hidden, yet to be discovered, silver lining somewhere? As a numbers man, he decided to consider his issue more logically. He pondered the situation of being outsourced as if it were both a company and a national concern that needed careful consideration.

Outsourcing was undoubtedly good for the company in the short term. It was probably even good for the country in a certain respect.

Outsourcing jobs would help US companies be more competitive in the global marketplace. Then again, he realized it also led to a large number of unemployed Americans and a further diminishment of the dwindling middle class.

As his thoughts drifted, his mind leapt to a new concern. It occurred to him that being let go would affect his retirement fund. Severance pay or not, he couldn't go on for long without income, and his investments would be jeopardized. Then he bumped into Marco and lost his train of thought.

Marco held four coffees on a tray. They both scrambled to stabilize the drinks and keep them from falling to the ground.

After the drink tray was stable, George took a step back. Behind the pair, other fired employees exited the building carrying boxes of personal items.

"Marco," George finally said.

"Hey, George," Marco said awkwardly.

"They fire you and then send you on a coffee run? What a nerve," George said.

"Uh, no. I got moved," Marco said, and his face flushed bright red with shame.

"You got moved?" George asked innocently. Then he quickly realized that what his coworker really meant was that not only did Marco keep his job, but the younger guy also got promoted.

"But I have seniority..." George said, and he was embarrassed to notice that his voice was squeaky and full of emotion.

Marco shrugged, his face still red, then looked at his watch and turned away, carefully leveling the coffees to ensure they wouldn't fall.

George felt his heart fall. They had passed him over... again. Another case of style over substance, he said to himself.

"Gotta fly. I'm late. Call me," Marco said in a faux-friendly, cheery tone and hurried away.

George II, truly shocked by this betrayal, stared after Marco.

*D*azed, George drove the Prius home. He nervously tapped his fingers on the steering wheel. He found himself uncharacteristically tense.

Looking around as he drove, he felt he hardly recognized the world around him. He struggled to name his emotion.

Indeed, he felt a bit, maybe a lot, numb some of the time. Right now, however, he felt shocked and upset.

Believing that his usually manageable life had just gone off the rails, he felt out of control. I'm like an accident victim, he realized. I'm in shock. It's as if I've been involved in a wild, unplanned, tragic event or experience, and I'm traumatized.

George noticed that, unlike before, when he had driven on the weekend, he wasn't comfortable driving with a single hand. He gripped the steering wheel tightly with both hands.

Arriving home, the man felt that he needed guidance. In the past, in those rare events that George felt distraught or confused, he would open his Japanese proverb book and seek a relevant philosophical saying.

He wasn't quite sure what Japanese philosophy was all about, but he found that the Japanese view of life was very soothing and reassuring to him in a way that Western philosophies were not.

He flipped through the pages randomly without looking at them, and after staring into space for a time, he stopped and focused on a quote from the book:

Aite no nai kenka wa denkinu.

The English translation was:

One cannot quarrel without an opponent.

George sat down and tried to divine some meaning from the quote that would be pertinent to his current situation. On initial reflection, it didn't seem relevant.

He didn't wish to quarrel at all. He had no quarrel with his company. He didn't feel Teleseismology Hub NS was an adversary or a rival. As far as he knew, he didn't have any opponents at all. Well, maybe his neighbor Ed was a foe, but Ed had no real effect on his life.

Unable to find a way to make meaning of the proverb, George was sorely disappointed. His random quote method had never failed him in the past.

In the comfort of his beautiful home office, George sat down slowly in the desk chair before his computer and punched several keys on the keyboard. He needed to understand what would happen if he removed his current income factor from his retirement portfolio.

Tapping some buttons, George deleted his six-figure income and then typed in $0 for income. He shuddered involuntarily as he typed in the number.

He pulled up the output screen at the push of another couple of buttons.

George stared, and his face grew pale as his once-beautiful retirement graph tanked. To his increasing shock and horror, when he typed in the short-term and paltry, to his way of thinking, severance pay and its end date, it hardly affected his bottom line.

There was a brief bump up and a short flat line. But then, once the brief severance pay period ended, his retirement fund dropped off a cliff.

George rubbed his forehead. All of a sudden, he had a pounding headache.

Numb and uncertain, he stumbled from the room.

Dressed in elegant, slightly threadbare, quite out-of-fashion gentleman's pajamas, George II sat on his bed and stared into space. His cell phone rang. He sighed and checked the caller ID. Seeing that it was his son, he ignored the call.

He thought that perhaps he should get up and read through the pamphlets and other information that he'd been given during his one-on-one restructuring update meeting. Finally, exhausted, he turned off his bedside lamp, pulled up the covers, and finally managed to fall asleep.

*B*eside his driveway, in the soft gray light of early morning, George checked his mail. He was dressed like normal, in an out-of-date custom-tailored three-piece suit, as if ready for work.

He didn't seem to know what to do with himself. Finally, looking over at his neighbor's house and seeing Ed staring out the window at him, he got into his Prius and drove away.

George drove to his office building and parked. The parking lot was emptier than usual, though there were always fewer cars parked there at this hour. He stared at the building with yearning and then slumped over his steering wheel, defeated.

George drove aimlessly around the city. Then, passing a large billboard advertising an employment website, he suddenly became quite invigorated. He drove straight home.

George trolled various job websites on his computer in his home office. With each click, uploading documents and applying to positions listed online, he grew almost frenzied with excitement.

He had a brief few minutes of frustration when the computer screen seemed to freeze.

He applied for job after job. Finally, when the light outside had shifted—clearly the day was approaching early evening—George stood and stretched happily. He then went to his bedroom and did calisthenics for half an hour.

When finished, sweaty and even more energized, he went and showered. After he got out of the shower, he checked his cell phone. Nothing. No calls. He looked at his watch and shrugged. Give it a little more time, he thought.

George sat alone in his pristine dining room. He took comfort in the pale green painted walls, which were adorned with tiny shelves. Each delicate wooden shelf held beautiful Japanese netsuke carvings. Collecting netsuke was a meditative and almost spiritual experience for George II.

He ate his meal, periodically glancing at his silent cell phone, which lay on the table before him.

Why was he getting no calls?

He slowly and carefully ate a small green salad, skinless, boneless oven-grilled chicken breast, and a side of broccoli. Night had fallen while he showered.

"Guess I shouldn't expect to hear anything until tomorrow," he said as he finished his meal. Then he almost laughed in relief. Of course, people weren't hiring at night.

Standing, George picked up his plate. Making certain that he had left no crumb or detritus on the dark cherry wood of his dining room table, he picked up his cutlery and cream linen napkin and left the room.

George tossed and turned all night. He woke once, sweating, and lay for some unknown period of time.

He stared at the ceiling. He tried to count sheep, but his mind was too active, and it kept drifting elsewhere. In the wee hours, exhausted, he managed to drop off and stay asleep.

Sometime in the late morning, George awoke slowly. His mood was neutral. Aware that it was well past his regular waking hour, he sat up. George looked around.

Grabbing his cellular phone, in a state of near panic, as if he might have missed an important call, he checked his email and messages. His face fell. Disappointment threatened to crush his soul.

His mood went straight past concerned to just plain upset.

George couldn't understand why his multiple resume submissions hadn't gotten a single response. He slipped off his bed to the bedroom floor.

His expression was one of defeat. Then, with great determination, George lay on his back. He bent his knees, with his back flat on the floor, and placed his feet a foot and a half, or so, away from his tailbone. He put his hands behind his head and exhaled.

He curled up toward his bent knees and did sit-ups. Each time he sat up, he said: "Positive." Sometimes he alternated the word "Positive" with "Relax," or "Stay calm."

It appeared to be working. The more sit-ups George did, the

more relaxed, calm, and even "positive" he seemed. He grew more energized. A sheen of sweat appeared on his face.

Breathing in and out, slowly and with great control, he did set after set of sit-ups.

He kept the bottom of each foot, his back, and tailbone against the floor and continued to do sit-ups until, covered in sweat, the sheen on his forehead slick and wet, he was physically unable to do one more set.

Something about his current state reminded him of the homeless man from his nightmare. He shuddered at the thought and went straight to the bathroom.

~

George did his regular shower routine. He didn't bother shaving because he lacked motivation and told himself that one day wouldn't make a difference.

He stared at himself in the bathroom mirror.

He rubbed his forehead to try and prevent what felt like the possibility of a migraine.

Despite it still being early in the day, he looked tired.

"Pull yourself together, old man," he told his reflection in a serious tone. He laughed in response, finding humor in the oddity of the moment.

The laughter seemed to help. Immaculately groomed, except for the salt-and-pepper shadow covering his jaws, he stood with a towel wrapped around his waist.

Nearly dry after his shower, he vigorously slapped Old Spice on both cheeks. He smiled at himself and suddenly seemed resolute and relatively upbeat.

Now dressed in his usual Monday suit, George II entered the kitchen.

~

He looked in the refrigerator. There was a packet of bran muffins, with two missing. He stared at it. He sighed and slowly closed the refrigerator. He looked at the beautiful basket of fruit in a hand-carved wooden bowl, which sat on his polished black and gray granite kitchen counters.

Free from any apparent blemish, the bananas and apples looked perfect.

George picked up a banana. He sniffed it. Realizing that he wasn't even hungry, he gently placed it back in the bowl.

Rather than focusing on the bleakness of his situation, George decided to try to enjoy and appreciate the gift of being given time off, which was very rare in his history of work and incessant toil.

He pondered the Japanese Proverb yet found he couldn't relate it to his current situation.

George rummaged in the kitchen cabinets until he found his fancy, imported coffee maker, which, although it made the best tasting coffee, he didn't normally use.

He did not often like to spend the inordinate amount of time it took to brew even just a small pot of coffee. Now, however, was the perfect time to use it. He opened a new tin of his favorite coffee grounds and sniffed. Yum.

Buoyed by the luxury of having zero time pressure, he made a pot of fresh coffee and poured himself a large mug. He added milk and sugar to the coffee and stirred slowly with a spoon.

He stared into his mug of coffee for a few moments, as if there were some kind of information or message in the pattern as the creamy milk swirled and mixed with the pitch black, robust coffee.

George took a sip and sighed with deep satisfaction. This was a vice, an old daily ritual that he had developed in his college years, but had given up the very first day that he started in his first grown-up job.

It was a simple pleasure that he would allow himself again, at least until he found a new job. George took his coffee to his home office.

~

Feeling a bit calmer, after wiping away a little dust from the side cabinet, George placed his coffee on a coaster with a picture of a sixteenth-century tall ship.

The first thing he did, having powered up his laptop, was to check his email.

His inbox was teeming, and he was thrilled to see dozens and dozens of unread electronic mail. It had worked. Submitting to numerous open positions had led to results.

Scanning the unread emails in his inbox, he was horrified that very few communications were from either companies or recruiters. He deleted the mostly junk emails.

It was a bunch of digital trash from numerous financial institutions selling their wares or others with which he had existing accounts. The latter were attempting to upsell him to a range of other financial services that they were sure he would be interested in.

I wasn't before, and I'm certainly not interested now, he thought to himself.

There was no hopeful email in the bunch; no professional or other responses to his resume submissions, and not one of those that he clicked on to open was personal. It did seem like he had way more junk email than usual. Was it possible that he had opened himself up to spammers by applying for jobs online?

How could it be that, so far, he had not had a single response to the job listings that he had submitted? It boggled his mind.

He opened a resume attached to an email in his sent email folder to check if he had included the correct email address for himself.

Perhaps a contact omission or a typo might have confused an HR person. He became further puzzled when he realized his resume and submissions were correct and error-free. Had no one even the decency to respond to his applications?

Even if he wasn't right for the positions for which he had applied, whatever happened to common courtesy and a polite, "Sorry, but no thanks," or something?

Were companies so inundated with resumes that they would cherry-pick a handful of possible hires to whom they would respond and interact further, and simply ignore everybody else?

I'm so out of touch with modern recruitment in this electronic age, he thought to himself.

Perhaps his resume wasn't appropriate for the current job market or needed some improvements.

He decided to update his resume, research job hunting in the current financial climate, and make a to-do list.

George searched the web for modern resume templates and samples and then began editing and adding to his resume. Looking at his curriculum vitae objectively, he knew that it was good.

From a future employer's point of view, his ultra-stable employment history alone—he had been with his employer for decades—suggested not just years of knowledge and experience in the industry but also loyalty.

His resume conveyed that he took his employment commitment most seriously. There was no indication here of jumping ship every two years or so to a different employer, as so many of the most recent batch of workers were wont to do.

Not used to sitting in his home office on a work morning, George noticed how quiet everything was.

Looking out the window and past the tree on his front lawn (which he now noticed could use a judicious trimming), beyond the occasional passing car, he didn't see much movement at all.

Does everyone out there have a job, except me? He wondered.

Looking down at his cell phone, which he had placed prominently on the desk—not wanting to miss any calls—he willed the dark screen to light up with an incoming call.

The mobile telephone sat motionless, dark and silent.

He checked again to ensure it was on full volume and not set to silent or airplane mode.

Not sure what to do next, he got up to walk to the kitchen and see if anything in the fridge would serve as a mid-morning snack.

*T*ime seemed to pass more slowly than it had during his entire life.

Staring into the fridge for what seemed like an age, he realized that he wasn't a mid-morning snack kind of person.

Patting his still-slender belly, he decided that just because he was now spending his mornings at home was no excuse to begin any bad habits. Selecting a ripened purple plum, he washed and dried it and returned to the office.

Rechecking his emails, he was still disappointed not to have received any.

Deciding that it was time to change tack and apply for a new job, George approached corporations directly—whether they were hiring or not—and entered some keywords into a search engine, hoping to find suitable companies within or compatible with his industry.

Apart from a handful of companies that he discounted (knowing that they were struggling and hence wouldn't be hiring), the number of companies he came up with resulted in a tiny list.

He stared at the minuscule list. He probably knew people at most of the companies, and for a quick moment, he discounted any embarrassment he might feel when anyone who knew George recognized him. He needed a job—period, and fast—he told that part of himself.

Even though he considered it a long shot, he sent his resume and a cover letter to a select group of corporations, fewer than a dozen, outlining his interest in working for the business. If there happened to be an opening and mutual interest, he would be ecstatic. The endeavor took less than an hour.

He glanced at his desktop computer and considered firing it up to check his retirement plan. That would be a total waste of time since he knew nothing had changed without a salary to enter into the plan.

He then had a completely new thought. I suppose I had better look for any job to earn some income, even if the job doesn't use my skill set and isn't in my industry.

He felt a small burst of energy at this idea. He was an intelligent, honest guy with a good work ethic: who wouldn't want to have him as a model employee? Within reason, it didn't matter what kind of industry he worked in. Every company in the entire world, large and small, needs an accounting department or an accountant. He would find something for now, while he sought the ideal long-term option.

However, after numerous fruitless searches and many hours later, George realized he didn't know how to find a new position.

How does one find out if employers are hiring? George wondered. Noticing that the carpet in the office needed a good vacuuming, he decided to maybe talk to some of his buddies later and see what tactics they were employing.

For the rest of the day and late into the evening, George vacuumed all the carpets in his house. Then he thoroughly cleaned the main bathroom and washed and dried all the bed linens.

When his home was immaculate, despite being exhausted, George determined to do one more thing.

eorge went to the dining room and selected a tiny netsuke—one of his carvings—to hold. He leaned back against and slid down the dining room wall.

He knew that this would cultivate a greater sense of peace and calm.

He gently held the miniature sculpture and closed his eyes. The longer he sat there, holding the netsuke, the calmer he felt. It was as if he drew strength from the object, and in a way, he did.

He sat holding the tiny carving for hours.

Not feeling particularly hungry, he chose not to prepare an evening meal. Instead, feeling unusually tired and afraid that he might be coming down with something, he went to bed earlier than usual.

~

Sleeping fitfully, he roused ever now and again to find himself awake in late-night darkness, facing the now eerie silence of the empty house.

George woke to the noise of a neighbor's leaf blower feeling shitty and, upon seeing his reflection in the mirror hanging inside his wardrobe closet, looking even shittier.

It's an adjustment period, he thought to himself. Of course, things will seem very unsettled. It would probably be like this until he started a new job and returned to a familiar routine. "Must have patience," he whispered to himself.

Deciding that it would make him feel better—to feel more himself—George dressed in one of his smartest, newest suits. As he straightened his tie in the mirror, he realized that clothes did indeed make the man.

Standing more erect, his head not bowed, he considered himself eminently hirable.

What employer wouldn't hire him on the spot if he walked into their office looking as he did right now? George asked himself.

Realizing that he hadn't checked his mailbox in the past few days, George smiled and thought about what a sunny, pleasant morning it was.

He determined to go outside.

~

Trying not to be hopeful and not deflated by disappointment, George opened his mailbox and extracted what exclusively appeared to be junk mail.

"Hey, George. Late for work?" George turned to see Ed.

His neighbor had snuck up on him, as usual.

Many thoughts ran through George II's mind simultaneously, as he contemplated what or how much information to give his neighbor. He quickly considered that, if the man didn't know already, Ed was sure to find out sooner or later.

He had better own up now, or else he would have to fake going off to work until he got a new job. Realizing that Ed might happen to know someone, an individual or company perhaps, that was hiring, George realized that he should use the opportunity to update Ed and also network.

"My company..." began George, who then stopped, wondering

what the best phrase to use was apart from "let go," "early retirement," "forced out," or "downsized," and so on.

All of the phrases, in his mind, now seemed so entirely negative. It wasn't as if George had done anything wrong, after all. His entire department had been let go. It wasn't personal… yet it still felt crummy.

"Yeah?" asked Ed, tired already of the protracted silence.

"There was a…"

"There was a what?"

"Uh…" George could not find the words. His cheeks pinked as he stared into Ed's eyes. Ed's eyes widened, and his typical mean grin grew sharper and toothier.

"You got shit-canned?" Ed quickly volunteered. The man almost sounded happy about it.

"My department was let go. The work is being outsourced… overseas."

"That's horrible, George. Does this economy suck rocks or what?" Ed said with gravitas, yet inwardly seemed delighted. His reaction would have been more appropriate if George had been promoted or given a raise.

"Yeah, it sure… sucks," agreed George II, trying desperately to avoid sounding despondent.

"Hey, this will cheer you up," Ed said excitedly, as he quickly tried to remember a joke he had recently heard.

"What's the difference between a recession and a depression?"

Without waiting for George to answer, Ed delivered the punch line.

"A recession is when a neighbor loses his job. A depression is when you lose yours!"

Ed laughed and laughed, and George thought he sounded like a drunken donkey braying. George did not see the humor in the joke, but, so as not to offend, managed to give a weak smile.

"Get it?" asked Ed, as if George were somehow lacking both intelligence and a sense of humor.

"That's... funny," replied George as he turned to enter the comfort and safety of his own home. A wave of fatigue hit him. He suddenly felt the urge to be inside, maybe have a cup of tea or, better yet, lie down and take a nap.

"Chin up. You'll find something," Ed said, sounding as if he didn't believe his own words, and almost gloated.

He gave George a cheery wave, returned to his driveway, and then got into his beat-up station wagon. Ed cranked the vehicle, which growled to life, the ragged engine sounding like the scream of a metal wildebeest in mechanical pain, and then pulled out and drove away.

George stared after Ed, and he couldn't be certain, but it appeared that Ed had flipped him off. Perhaps the man had merely been lifting his hand to indicate farewell.

Overcome with an intense feeling of despair, still pondering Ed's terrible joke, George turned and trudged back into his home.

~

Once back inside, George loosened his tie and threw a wad of junk mail into the recycling bin next to the kitchen trash. He stared morosely as he failed to score a three-pointer, and some junk mail fell onto the kitchen floor.

He had separated several bills from the pile, and, still holding those in his hand, decided that a glass of wine would go down nicely.

He didn't feel like facing the bills without it. It didn't occur to him that there was anything wrong with imbibing wine at such an early hour.

Pouring himself a glass of white wine from a bottle in the fridge, he added a splash of orange juice. He then took his drink and the remaining mail and went to sit, open the bills, and assess the damage. Flipping through several bills (that typically gave him no pause), he felt worse than ever.

He downed his drink, stood, and returned his glass and a few empty envelopes to the kitchen.

Looking around, out of sorts in a way he couldn't remember he had ever been previously, he stuck the bills into the fruit bowl on the kitchen counter. The bananas and apples in the bowl were now overly ripe, and one or two looked spoiled already.

He didn't even give the fruit a second glance or bother looking for a bran muffin.

Feeling peckish yet not wanting to cook anything for breakfast, or eat his usual bran muffin and a piece of fruit, he stood at the kitchen counter and ate dry cereal straight from the box.

Then, instead of boiling water for his former customary morning cup of tea, and deciding the idea of coffee didn't inspire him, he decided to have a soda.

Choosing not to dirty yet another glass or piece of crockery, he drank the soda straight from the can.

Unaccustomed to drinking carbonated beverages, or anything

else, in this fashion, he popped the top and accidentally sprayed himself with dark soda froth.

He stared down at the dark beverage, which was seriously threatening to stain his light-colored suit and white shirt.

"Crap!" he shouted out loud and grabbed a sponge from the sink to try and mitigate the damage. As he dabbed the stain on the clothing that covered his torso with the wet sponge, he realized that the sponge still had a red substance, possibly tomato sauce or jam, on it.

He stared down at his shirt. To his horror, he realized that his efforts to clean off the soda had made the situation much, much worse.

In frustration, he quickly stripped off his shirt. He turned on the kitchen sink faucet, thrust the shirt under it, and immediately tried to scrub the stains out under the stream of water. He felt like screaming, but didn't. It was as if the fates were conspiring to dampen his formerly positive mood.

Abandoning his suit, he glumly changed back into casual clothes.

Feeling exhausted and purposeless, he sat at the end of his bed and stared into space without any overt thoughts. He found life to suddenly be without meaning.

He could have sat like that for many hours, but a short time later, he did manage to gather his thoughts and force himself to take action. He entered his office to check his email. There had to be some good news, somewhere, George thought.

Soon, discovering nothing but spam in his email inbox folder, he followed a random thought. As a curiosity only, he checked out some used automotive sites to get current on the value of roadsters.

He idly looked to see what he could get for a car of a similar model, make, and year to the one in his garage.

That way, in a worst-case scenario, he would have an idea of how much cash he could expect from disposing of that particular asset, not that he was considering such a drastic option just yet.

George was surprised to discover that his beautiful car, Betty, which meant so much to him, had not held its value very well.

The automobile had fallen out of favor with the public. It had to be the economy, he decided.

Despite being considered a classic and in mint condition, the car was no longer worth what he had paid.

George fell into a sort of fugue state, as a melancholy mood overcame him.

Somehow, the day slipped away, and, at the end, George had no idea how he had spent his time.

One moment, he was checking his emails, wandering to get a drink or snack from the kitchen, and making lists related to the job market, and the next thing he noticed, the day was over, and it was time for bed.

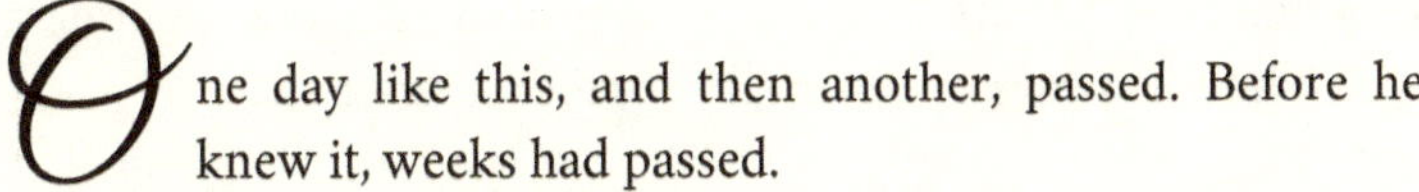

One day like this, and then another, passed. Before he knew it, weeks had passed.

Thankfully, he had unemployment from the state and was managing to scrape by on his bills.

He was embarrassed to do it, but he forced himself to return any bottles of wine or other non-perishable grocery items he had bought in the thirty days before being fired.

If he had a receipt, and an item hadn't been opened, George returned it.

He had a larder and freezer full of good food, and the wine cellar had more than enough wine.

As the days turned into weeks and the weeks quickly turned into months, George began to wonder if he would ever work again.

His unemployment was almost drained, and things were getting quite desperate.

He had to work again, he insisted to himself.

He did not yet have enough money for retirement, even if he opted to live very frugally and skip plan B altogether.

Even worse, if something didn't change soon, he'd have to contemplate selling his house and perhaps moving to a smaller home or even a rental apartment.

He felt that he was on a slippery slope and if something didn't change, he could only expect to stand helplessly watching on as everything he'd worked so hard for gradually slipped away... entirely.

He reasoned that it wasn't beyond the realm of possibility that he could actually end up on the street.

He shuddered at the thought. It appeared that the nightmare which he'd had days earlier might come true, after all.

For the first time in his life, he was honest enough to admit it to himself, George felt terribly, terribly lonely.

Perhaps he had always felt this way, and his daily visit to his place of employment and the false camaraderie of his office colleagues were but distractions that masked his true feelings.

To make matters even worse, he felt it necessary to avoid all calls from and contact with his only child, George III.

He couldn't bear the humiliation of sharing his current state of affairs. However, he wouldn't mind sharing the news with his boy if he could find another position first.

~

His house began to look as he did: gradually more unclean, unkempt, and in a serious state of neglect.

Staying up late, eating ever-increasing amounts of junk food, not exercising, and failing to bathe and shave for days on end, George felt himself seriously sliding down that slippery slope toward homelessness.

One morning, looking at his wooly face in the bathroom mirror, George gave himself a talking to.

It was an apathetic and half-hearted talking to, yet a talking to, nonetheless.

"If you do not, in fact, end up homeless," he told his reflection, "yet, you continue to look like this, pretty soon you will be perceived as destitute." He believed it.

If he were to leave his house and walk among the living without first spending hours cleaning himself up and grooming, he would likely be considered destitute.

Something had to happen, and happen soon, he was wise enough to realize.

In a desperate summoning of will, George got into the shower still wearing all his clothes: a worn bathrobe and a pair of ragged and dirty sweats.

The desperate act brought him to his senses. He removed his soggy clothing and, after showering and getting cleaned up, he grabbed a telephone book and riffled through it.

Finding what he was looking for, he dialed his cell phone madly and set up an appointment with an employment office that he found listed in the yellow pages.

Although he shaved carefully, cleaned himself up, and wore one of his old smart suits, his under-eye circles and overall aura of desperation made him look less than professional.

He drove like a man possessed, desperate to reach the appointment on time and unable to stop thinking about the cost of maintaining his vehicle.

~

Sitting across from Bertha Reynolds, a large, beautiful black woman who ran the small office, George composed himself. He forced a smile and arranged his seating position into what he considered perfect posture.

"You know what a recruiter does, right?" Bertha asked as she scanned his resume. She spoke again before he could speak.

"You work, I get paid," she answered her own question."What are you looking for?" she asked, looking up for the first time.

"Accounting. I'm an accountant."

"I know that, honey, but beggars can't be choosers in this economy. And you're no spring chicken, know what I mean?" Bertha said very directly, yet entirely kindly.

George knew what she meant exactly, but he secretly didn't want to admit that his age would prevent him from having the job of his dreams.

Although he had been planning his retirement for years, George never wanted to consider aging and all its ramifications.

Getting old was not something George ever wanted to think about.

Unfortunately for him, whether he liked it or not, it now appeared that age would be the number one topic in his search for a successful life change. He would have to consider his age to better transition from unwanted and unemployed to being a successful and rewarded member of society again.

George realized—deciding that he was as desperate as he'd ever been—that he would do just about anything to be gainfully employed and get back on track.

Bertha nodded and made noises, rife with meaning, as she read his resume and looked it up and down.

"Uh-huh," she said to herself, and George desperately wished he knew what she was thinking. As if she had been waiting for George to inform her of something, the recruiter prompted him:

"Let me put it this way," Bertha continued, "what kind of work would you not do?"

"Ms. Reynolds—"

"Bertha. Everyone calls me Bertha," she said sweetly, yet firmly. He coughed and tried again.

"I was two or so years away from retirement. Everything was... everything was perfect. Along with the company severance and pension, the 401K, the IRAs would be maturing..."

"I have to stop you there, George," interrupted Bertha.

"You're not going to talk about all this at a job interview, are you?"

"No, I'm just saying... I need to get my retirement plan back on track, that's all," George said a bit defensively, even though he immediately recognized that she was right.

"So, what I hear you saying is that the job doesn't matter as long as you can retire in two to five years?" Bertha asked, obviously seeking to clarify what George wanted.

He sighed in relief. She got him, she understood, and she wanted to help him achieve his goals so that she would get paid. He nearly wept.

"I guess that is what I'm saying," George rambled, thinking out loud.

"Two to five years, give or take."

"Good. I'm glad we know where we stand," Bertha said drily. George didn't catch her drift.

"Good. Yes," George replied, wondering if it could really be as easy as all that.

"Well, don't you worry a bit," Bertha said kindly, knowing full well that the man would better understand the lay of the land, of reality, once he'd gone out on a few interviews.

"Jobs we got. I'll send you for interviews. Before you know it, you'll be back to the old grind. How does that sound?"

"That sounds... amazing!"

George rarely, if ever, used the word "amazing," but that was precisely how he felt when he left Bertha's office.

Renewed, filled with energy, and uplifted, he drove home with a broad grin on his face and the radio playing upbeat music. He should have done this earlier, he decided.

He felt like chastising himself for the delay in seeking employ-ment assistance.

Everything was going to work out just fine. He had nothing to fear, all along.

It was a new world, he realized, what with headhunters, recruiters, and the like.

Indeed, he'd had calls from a couple over the years, each time sharply reprimanding the aggressive upstarts for daring to try to poach a valued employee from an upstanding company.

They had naturally stopped calling. It had never occurred to George that he would need job placement assistance.

~

The following morning, Bertha called George and gave him the details of his first appointment. It was a day in the future, and he was terribly excited. To occupy himself, he got his home and clothes in order.

The next day, he returned to his old, employed self routine: up early, calisthenics, a shower, a bran muffin, a banana, and tea.

George arrived for his interview energized, early, and well prepared.

He had extensively researched the company on the internet and had all the expected answers prepared.

The interview was being held across town in one of the few office towers whose architecture George liked. He could get used to the morning commute, he decided, and it would be an absolute pleasure to work in such a light-filled and clean environment.

Driving over, he was ecstatic over his good fortune. After securing the position, he would be more frugal than ever and get his life and retirement back on track, if it was the last thing he did.

Checking in with the receptionist, George was surprised to see many other applicants, so many that they filled nearly every available seat in the large reception area. He smiled at the one or two who made eye contact with him, but most were uninterested in being friendly, at least to other applicants.

All of the other people waiting were impeccably groomed and put together, and they all looked younger than George, most by a considerable amount.

He thought that if you ever wanted to feel old, walk into a room full of young graduates. Looking around, he wondered if they were all applying for different positions. It was thrilling; maybe the company had an entire department to fill.

One by one, George watched the other applicants be called in for their shot at the grand prize, desperately desired and oh-so-necessary gainful employment.

The longer he sat there without being called in for his scheduled time, the more his good humor flagged. He began to feel disrespected by whoever was in charge of the interviews.

Despite arriving earlier than his appointed time, it was now a considerable amount of time past his agreed-upon interview hour.

Was it possible that he had gotten the time and date wrong?

His thoughts, about whether he should "suck it up" or mention how he felt when he did eventually get the meeting, were interrupted when his name was called.

A cold chill of nervousness ran through his body as he entered an office with a name plate on the door that read Rupert Ringleder, CEO.

Rupert was a grizzled-looking, larger-than-life character who appeared to be in his seventies. Sitting behind a large modern desk, smothered in files and paperwork, the man barely looked up from his reading to acknowledge George II's entrance.

George was instantly uncomfortable.

"Good afternoon," George said as he sat down.

Rupert finally looked up from reading George's resume and, with brashness that George was unaccustomed to, simply said, "You are over-qualified."

George was stunned on many fronts and waiting—hoping against hope—at the very least, for a " but" which did not come.

Rupert Ringleder stared at George expectantly and didn't continue. Finally, George managed to squeak out the beginning of a statement:

"Well, I, uh, could—"

"What? Be less qualified?" Rupert interrupted and looked down again at George's resume. His attention appeared to, in particular, be hung up on the section that outlined past and expected salaries.

"You wouldn't be happy with the pay," Rupert said, looking coldly at George to gauge his response.

"I'm... salary is negotiable," George finally managed to utter.

Rupert didn't respond, nor did the man look like he was going to. His grizzled, scraggly eyebrows went up, as if he found George's statement a bit ludicrous or unbelievable in some way.

"I need a job," George admitted and then coughed, as if he were choking on the statement.

"Everybody needs a job. Everyone in that waiting room is hoping to be hired for this position," Rupert said brusquely.

Then, when George obviously failed to understand that he was being dismissed, Rupert spoke again.

"You're not the man for us. Thanks for coming in. I suppose you have to try for anything at your age, huh?"

George stood and slowly left the office, holding onto his dignity and his folder full of resumes. He was horrified to realize that all those people, many much younger than he, had been interviewed for the exact same position.

He wondered what was on their resumes. He felt compassion for them, for many of them were at the beginning of their careers. They likely had no savings or retirement.

If George was traumatized at his first real interview in the harsh world of modern recruitment, he softened the blow by commiserating with himself.

He told himself that the harsh treatment and disrespectful manner in which he had been received were an anomaly, an exceptional occurrence, and not at all typical or common.

He told himself that one rotten apple doesn't have to spoil the barrel. He continued a running mental patter, all positive self-talk, until he got home.

~

*R*eeling with emotion, he made it into the house and went straight to bed. The next morning, he resolutely got up, refusing to allow himself to sink to his previous low.

It was comforting to him that it wasn't more than a couple of days before Bertha arranged his second appointment. He prepared even more carefully for this interview than the first. Others could choose to be unprofessional or slack, yet he would not stoop to their level.

Expecting his following interview to be a lot different, he only had second thoughts upon driving to the interview.

His GPS directed him to a rundown building in an unfamiliar warehouse district, a particularly sketchy part of downtown.

Still, he parked the car, gave himself a pep talk, grabbed his briefcase full of resumes, and went into the building. Having given his name to the man behind the window, George sat in a grimy open seating area filled with cheap metal furniture and a fake green plant.

He thought, This hardly qualifies as a reception area. Workers in overalls and work boots came and went, quite obviously collecting their paychecks from the man behind the glass window.

George wondered if he could even work in such an environment. Then again, he decided, a paycheck was a paycheck was a paycheck. He would be overjoyed to stand before the window and collect wages today. The office emptied.

Taking advantage of a lull between workers coming to collect their pay envelopes, Al Greenhops came out from behind the glass window to greet him. He was the man George had previously given his name to, and George belatedly realized he was likely the office manager.

"You must be George," Al said, reading from a resume he had placed in a manila folder.

"Yes," replied George II, getting up to shake Al's hand.

"Don't get up," instructed Al, who plopped down on a cheap gray metal folding chair beside him.

"You got yer degree, huh?" Al said, as if letting George know that at the very least, he had looked over his resume.

"Yes, sir," George responded uncertainly. Was he about to hear that he was over-educated? Perhaps he should keep his mouth shut, respond minimally, and see where Al led things.

"Huh," said Al, as if not quite sure how to proceed.

"Uh... yes," said George II. George wondered if this was an initial meet-and-greet. Or, had the interview started? Was this guy seriously conducting the interview in the waiting area? Several workers arrived and stood anxiously and awkwardly awaiting their paychecks.

"Well, here's the thing," continued Al. Then he paused for a long moment before blurting out, "My brother's kid done been offered the job."

"Oh," replied George. He was so shocked by the sudden revelation that he couldn't think of a single additional thing to say.

"If'n he don't work out, after a few months' trial period, I may call you. All right by you?" Al spat out.

George could barely respond but just about managed to nod in agreement. Al stood.

Taking their cue, the trio of waiting, grimy workers stood in front of the glass window. Al shook George's hand and ambled away to resume the task of giving his workers their weekly paychecks.

Dazed by the experience, George II stared after Al for a few quick moments before quickly shuffling off.

*L*ater that day, George had another interview. He was most excited about the position, or so he repeatedly told himself.

Bertha had managed to procure an interview at a small company looking for a full-time bookkeeper.

George agreed that it was well below his pay grade and expertise, a job he could do blindfolded, yet he also decided that, as Bertha had said, "A job is a job."

At this point, he was beyond desperate.

Sitting across a desk from a young woman, who looked like she was still in her twenties, he struggled to sit still. A petite redhead, almost as wide as she was tall, the female introduced herself simply as "Cherry."

George wondered if she was the one with the power to hire or if she was merely an initial applicant screener to weed out inappropriate candidates.

"I see you're a CPA?" Cherry said.

"Yes," George replied calmly. He took a breath, happy to suddenly be back upon what felt like solid ground. For the first time in his job hunt, he was on an interview that actually felt like an interview.

"Do you know BizBooks Pro?" Cherry inquired.

"Uh, no, not firsthand. I didn't use BizBooks Pro... in my last position. That wasn't in use when I, uh, started. I, uh, my focus has been on other... tasks," George managed to reply.

He didn't want to add that he'd supervised accountants in actual bookkeeping, that he hadn't done such mundane bookkeeping tasks in quite some time.

"What did you do in your last position, George?" she asked, surprised by his previous answer. He supposed that his response would wow her.

He chose to go back a few years in his employment history and include things that he had done in the distant past, which he could do again, as needed, to get hired.

"I did cost and general accounting, monthly general ledger close, balance sheet and income statement analysis and prep, reconciled account balances, prepared monthly, quarterly, and annual financial reports... reconciled inventory to general ledger... things of that nature," George said.

He did not want to disclose that he'd mostly been doing research, analysis, and writing reports for the last several years. It didn't matter anyway; he still knew how to do all of those other things.

"You don't do BizBooks Pro?" Cherry again asked, this time making notes. Judging by her incessant harping about BizBooks, it was obvious to George that she had no knowledge of accounting principles and hadn't understood a fraction of what he'd said.

If she had known accounting, she would have known that his work experience was way more advanced than the elementary bookkeeping data entry nonsense required for BizBooks Pro!

Aside from her ignorance and lack of suitability in hiring for the accounting department, George felt humiliated by her failure to maintain a modicum of eye contact.

The young woman, whose skirt was too short and tight and sliding up her huge thigh, wouldn't look him in the eye. Instead, she obsessively focused on her pad of paper and notes.

I'm a person, he thought to himself. How could I be reduced to this?

"I'm one hundred percent confident that I could pick it up. I'm a quick study," answered George, more calmly than he felt inside. What he really wanted to tell the young woman was that his skills were light years of complexity beyond the relative child's play of learning a software program like BizBooks Pro.

"We need a full-charge bookkeeper with direct, hands-on experience with the latest edition of BizBooks Pro. We're willing to consider someone with experience in the last version of BBP if they can get up to speed with the new release," Cherry practically read from her notes. He figured she'd been given those by her boss or their accountant.

"Honestly, George, you just don't sound qualified."

She sighed heavily as if he had purposefully wasted her time. Then she sneered and gave him a mean look, as if she were deliberately trying to annoy him.

Shocked by this Cherry employee's ignorance and overall incompetence, George quickly concluded that he wouldn't accept the position, even if it were offered (and it obviously was not going to be).

"Thank you for your time," he said, standing and speaking with remarkable restraint.

Perhaps miffed that George would end the interview right there and then rather than sit through her ignorant, verging-on-insulting interrogation, she spoke under her breath, yet audibly, apparently for George's benefit.

"I cannot believe this, why on earth would Bertha send me this bozo?!"

George couldn't prevent a hot blush from turning his cheeks bright red as he turned to leave. Although his face crumpled, he managed not to lose it.

He had to bite his lower lip to prevent himself from telling the young woman exactly what he thought of her rude, stupid, and offensive behavior.

Cherry stood and extended her arm. His heart softened momentarily as he thought she was trying to shake his hand.

Then he realized she was trying to return his resume to him, holding it out as if it were a used hanky or other objectionable item. He ignored her and didn't take it.

"Good day," he said, and turned heel and left.

~

Sipping a glass of wine, or two, while watching late-night TV soon became a habit for George.

At first, he was amazed, if not a little shocked, by the low class, outrageousness, and inferior quality of late-night TV shows. Over time, they became amusing to him. He could appreciate their entertainment value, in a "slumming it, there's nothing on television so I'll watch anything," kind of way.

One TV show that he developed an affinity for was called *Scrip for Scrap.*

It was a yard sale show on one of the lesser cable channels. On each episode, different people would put out their unwanted storage items and miscellaneous junk and, guided by experts, sell it all for good old American cash.

Watching the show that night gave George an idea.

At this point, he was almost numb with fear each morning, yet he had to do something. He had lovely things, but they were meaningless to him if he couldn't pay his bills and then lost everything, anyway.

He figured a garage sale might help slow down his financial free fall.

~

The next morning, George set out on his driveway and lawn a number of items he had accumulated over the years (whatever he felt like he could let go of, that is).

As he did so, his neighbor Ed decided that it was a good time to wash the station wagon parked in his driveway.

"If I didn't know you better, George, I'd think you were having some kind of yard sale," Ed remarked loudly, in a somewhat insulting tone.

"Yeah. Thought I'd declutter," George said carefully, hoping that he didn't sound defensive.

"Job hunt's not going so well, so you wanna make some old cashola, huh? Earn some boffo, get some wherewithal, increase your fortune, earn a little chump change," Ed said loudly, in a sing-song voice.

It was as if Ed thought that he were some kind of well-known comedian or star. Then he laughed. Whatever, George thought to himself and didn't respond.

"Fleece some suckers for some filthy lucre, build a wad, grab some wampum, make some sawbucks," Ed continued.

"Yeah. You nailed it. Boffo!"

George forced himself to answer brightly, through clenched teeth, purely to end Ed's very annoying, over-the-top, and fairly nauseating routine.

Ed stared at George II. George was sweating and setting his jaw as he arranged items on the immaculate folding table.

Realizing that George must be close to despair or some kind of breakdown, if his nerves were so easily rattled, Ed changed his tone to one of apparent, compassionate-sounding calm.

"Hey, you wanna come by the store? We got a couple positions open. Low level, but it's something," Ed offered casually.

George looked up at Ed. Was the guy serious? George didn't think he could survive another shitty interview.

Ed smiled at him, and his expression made George believe that the offer had been genuine. Surprised at the turn of events and Ed's apparent sincerity, George actually considered the offer.

Would it be weird to work with his neighbor? But then, if George was working in accounting and Ed was working... whenever it was he worked, they wouldn't probably even see each other. Then again, George decided, it didn't even matter.

"You have some vacancies? Sure, I could come in," George said, willing himself not to sound pathetic.

"You come by, first thing tomorrow morning... say around nine? Sound good?" Ed added. George nodded. Ed waved and grabbed a bucket, and pulled a garden hose toward his parked vehicle.

"Yeah, okay. I'll be there," George said and felt his heart lift.

Maybe things were going to work out. I have to be kinder to Ed, he decided.

Things happen for a reason. Maybe he and Ed would patch their relationship up and even become friends. I should cultivate a more humble attitude, George considered.

George went into the garage and pulled a lightweight yet sturdy portable covered storage closet out onto the lawn.

He usually kept his winter clothing in it. He had sorted through his clothes to find well-kept duplicates or similar items of any value so that he could sell them for quick cash. Going back into the house, he grabbed the clothing items, suits, shirts, sweaters, and such from his bedroom that were marked for his yard sale. Finally, after bringing out items, he tagged everything carefully with tiny stickers that he typically used to label file folders.

To his surprise, several browsers had already arrived to check out George's stuff.

"How much is this?" an overweight man asked, unzipping the covered storage closet, pulling out and holding up one of George's suits.

"That's a custom bespoke suit. A hundred," replied George.

"A hundred? One hundred? Dollars?" the browser asked incredulously.

"Firm," insisted George, knowing that the suit was worth several times that amount.

"He's out of his mind," the browser whispered to his wife.

"How much for this?" another stranger asked and held up a tiny sculpture.

George had managed to convince himself to part with some of his collectibles.

Eating came before art appreciation, he decided.

"That's an antique netsuke figurine... Quite rare, signed by the artist," George said. He desperately hoped that the person was a true connoisseur of art and had recognized the value of the item.

"I'll give you three bucks for it," the man barked, holding out three dollars as if he expected George to take his offer. George's face grew stiff, and his expression hardened.

"It's authentic Japanese... It's worth hundreds of dollars," George said. He could not entirely mask the shock evident in his voice. He hoped that his tone of voice didn't sound snotty.

"Japanese? Gimme a break. Everybody knows that everything's made in China nowadays," the man said huffily. He replaced the figurine with a light thud.

George stared. He hoped that the rest of this experience wasn't going to be this obnoxious scrabbling for, what was the word... oh, yes, for bunko.

"Yeah. We can get one just like it for a buck... at any dollar store in town," his female companion stridently chipped in and tried to pull her companion away from George's table.

"How about ten bucks for the suit?" the original shopper, the overweight man, haggled as he tried to force the jacket onto his portly upper torso.

"I won't let it go for less than a hundred," George insisted, thinking to himself that this yard sale was not a good idea, after all.

The so-called "reality" TV program was probably all scripted and manipulated to make you think that people actually made money from having yard sales.

He groaned to consider that the people who rushed to those TV sales might be all paid background extras.

George began to perspire a little as he watched the guy with the jacket continue to struggle to fit into it. These yard salers would probably lynch him if he mentioned that the suit shopper was far too obese to fit into that particular size jacket.

George could hardly bear to watch the man and hoped against hope that he wouldn't damage or leave sweat on his suit.

"Your yard sale prices are bonkers, dude," the suit guy concluded, finally giving up and replacing the jacket on its hanger.

"How much for this?" an older woman asked while holding up a Japanese woodblock print of a country landscape.

"I can let that go for fifty dollars," George said, giving her a bargain because of her age and elegant demeanor.

"This loser wants top dollar for the cheesiest crap," the lady declared to the others as she glared at George, making him blush. He was aghast at how quickly the woman, who had resembled a pleasant granny moments ago, morphed into a wicked, witchy-looking crone.

George wasn't aware of how little patience he held in reserve as late.

As each day of increasingly humiliating unemployment passed, although he was unaware of it, he became increasingly ill-tempered.

He was no longer at all his usual, agreeable self. The tendons on his neck stood out, and George flushed.

"Japanese?" the figurine shopper harrumphed, "Targét has nicer stuff... stuff that's new with a warranty... and you can return it with a receipt, and the clerks there don't treat you like you're low class for browsing."

Then the man stared at George, and it was as if he had thrown down the gauntlet.

The other yard-salers glared at George, ganging up on him, as if he could be persuaded to mark everything down to a dollar or less.

They appeared to believe that they could shame him into dropping his prices so they could buy everything at bargain basement discount prices.

Two more cars pulled up and parked on the street. Several people with young children got out of the recently arrived vehicles and hurried toward George's yard sale.

Without any attempt at discipline from their parents, the unruly children ran amok through his stuff. They picked up the more expensive of his objets d'art and played with them as if they were discarded toys.

George felt a burst of rage.

"That's it," he snapped."Get out! All of you, the yard sale is over. Get off of my property before I call the cops on the whole cheap lot of you."

The approaching assembly ground to a halt. Several people took a step back, obviously fearful that George was deranged and might harm them.

A baby began crying, which only added to the misery that George felt as he alternately rushed at the figurine guy and the suit man. Red, sweating, and enraged, George chased off the cheap-ass yard salers.

In a huff, they returned to their respective vehicles.

With a weighted weariness, George packed up his belongings and took them back inside. When the yard was restored to its former pristine state, George was sad to note that the front lawn grass was noticeably trampled.

That's the last time that I'll watch that dumb TV show, he muttered to himself as he repaired his lawn. They must obviously stage everything from the higher-class neighborhoods, the pleasant shoppers, items that are a great value, though discounted, and sold at a price that pleases the seller.

George looked around and was pleased to see that Ed was nowhere in sight. Knowing that Ed had witnessed the yard-salers insulting George and his belongings would have been an indignity too difficult to bear.

George spent some time caring for his roses. It was a small comfort to him when he realized that the hint of phytophthora that had appeared to threaten his rose bushes earlier had not fully manifested.

After caring for his roses, George went inside.

~

George took a long nap, didn't eat, and, after getting up to take a brief shower and check his email, went right back to bed.

In the morning, after tossing and turning most of the night, George slowly got ready for his interview at Ed's company. He made sure not to overdress, as he didn't want to give Ed any reason to criticize him.

When he was ready, George took the Prius and drove to Ed's grocery store.

He timed it so that he would arrive right on time. A young clerk, wearing too much make-up and tight clothes, showed George to Ed's office.

George sat anxiously across from Ed in the cluttered office at the rear of the store, who was looking over his resume.

"Says here you're a highly qualified Senior Staff Accountant, George," Ed said.

"That's right," agreed George, feeling weird. It was odd being interviewed by his next-door neighbor, who had been told on numerous occasions what George's occupation was and what he did.

"Sweet," replied Ed, making a checkmark on the resume.

"What kind of salary were you getting?" George thought about his for a moment. He couldn't very well lie. Ed would probably check anyway, plus it was ethically wrong to lie. George coughed and then managed to get out an answer:

"With salary, bonus, and profit sharing, I ended up around, uh, about a $100K."

Ed almost turned green but managed not to throw up his recently rushed breakfast.

"A... a hundred K? A hundo? A bean?" Ed stammered.

George nodded and took a deep breath. Talking about money to strangers was so awkward.

"Yeah. But of course, right now, I'm earning zop. I mean zip," George added nervously.

Ed frowned. Then he smiled, except his smile was no longer friendly.

Ed again resembled a grinning shark, as he had for most of the time that George and Ed had been neighbors.

Had he really stooped so low as to allow himself to be interviewed by his obnoxious neighbor? George wondered to himself.

"My father-in-law would say a man earning zed, zip, nada, nothing... is a man who's ready to work," said Ed finally, with false enthusiasm.

George sighed with relief. Ed seemed to have accepted his resume and realized that he was ready to work.

"I'm ready to work," answered George as he uncrossed his legs. He felt a moment of excitement; all of his struggles could be over soon if Ed really did just hire him, as it appeared.

"Well, let's see if you can do the job. Shall we?" Ed said ominously.

"Like I say. I'm ready to work," George said and stood.

"Excellent. Which do you want first? The good news or the bad news?" Ed quipped.

"Uh, good news, I guess," George responded and sat down again.

"Good news is we have accounting positions open," Ed admitted.

"Okay," said George, tentatively. Something about Ed's tone made it clear to George that he shouldn't get excited, just yet.

"Bad news is we have a policy of hiring internally. For you to get into accounting, you'd have to start where we all start," Ed said meaningfully.

When George obviously didn't understand, Ed added, " At the checkout." George stared and tried to process this new tidbit of information.

"You mean, as a checkout clerk?" George finally asked. Ed laughed contemptibly.

"You wish," Ed finally said and laughed once more. Then he spoke again.

" No, I'm talking entry level, lowest rung on the totem pole... bagging groceries."

"A grocery bagger?" asked George, not sure that he could have heard right. He was an older man, didn't they give that job to boys and girls?

"Just to start. Then, as you work your way up and I can see that you're a fast learner, bop, bop, bop, next thing you know... you're in accounting," Ed responded.

George felt too stunned to reply. Bagging groceries? Seriously?

"I understand. It's too low level, and probably too menial to boot. I guess it's beneath you, Mr. Fortune Five Hundo," said Ed as he handed George his resume.

"I was just trying to help a neighbor out, that's all."

"I'll do it," George gasped, standing once more. Ed stood and grinned at George.

"Then follow me, George," Ed said gleefully and left his office and headed toward the front of the store. George followed and desperately hoped that he could accomplish whatever tasks were set before him.

He couldn't imagine that Ed wanted him to prove his ability to be a successful grocery bagger. Still, as Ed quickly grabbed some random grocery items from the shelves, it seemed as if that's exactly what Ed expected George to do.

At the checkout stand, Ed stood imperiously surveying the scene as the elderly clerk, Lee, cheerfully rang up the chosen items and put them onto a barely functioning conveyor belt.

"So, is this a test?" Lee asked her boss as the grocery items rode down the conveyor belt toward the bagging area.

"I'll void the entire sale once the test is complete, Lee. Pretend that I'm the customer and he's the new bag boy," Ed answered, giving a friendly wink to George.

George managed a smile back but felt strangely nervous despite the idiotic simplicity of the task which awaited him.

"Go ahead and ask me," Ed said to George. Unused to such role-playing games, George racked his brain for an appropriate response.

Was he supposed to ask Ed "the customer" something? He couldn't fathom an appropriate question. Finally, when it became clear that Ed was not going to help him out with specific instructions, George coughed and then spoke.

"Ask you what?" George inquired.

"Whether I'd like paper or plastic, of course," Ed said, his tone implying that George should have known that. George sighed.

"Oh, yeah. Paper or plastic… sir?" George asked.

"I'd like paper, thank you very much, grocery bagger boy," Ed said, putting on what he considered to be a snobbish accent.

"I'm a snooty customer," he said as an aside to George. "We get lots of those here."

"Sure," agreed George, as he struggled to open a folded brown paper grocery bag.

Lee frowned and shook her head at him, as if to communicate, "No."

George assumed that Lee meant that he needed to double-bag it, instead of using a single grocery bag. He struggled to open another brown paper bag and place it inside the first.

Feeling tense, George couldn't seem to make his hands cooperate. He ripped one of the bags. Giving up on the idea of using double bags, George focused on carefully opening the remaining bag.

Ed smiled in a conspiratorial, "Relax, man," kind of way, which caused George to laugh nervously. He then stuffed, willy-nilly, the groceries into the paper bag.

It was challenging to fit everything in the bag, and he had to sort of squish a loaf of bread between a box of cereal and some canned goods, but finally, he managed to fill the bag and leave nothing on the conveyor belt.

Emotionally exhausted, George waited for Ed to speak.

"How did I do?" he finally asked.

"George, I'm sorry," Ed said and paused, his expression thoughtful, before continuing with what sounded like phony sorrow.

"Your bagging approach was just a little too... inconsiderate of the items."

"I was nervous. It looks easier than it is. I'm sure if I practiced— " George said desperately. Could he really have failed a bag boy test? George's self-esteem plummeted further.

"I'm sorry, George. You must trust my years of experience in grocery store management... Even though I've never earned a bean as an annual salary... I do have a certain expertise... You just wouldn't cut it as a grocery bagger," Ed stated imperiously.

Humiliated, George could barely remain standing. Ed extended his hand.

"At least we gave it our best shot, old man. No hard feelings, I hope. I was just trying to help."

Although George took Ed's hand and they awkwardly shook hands, George couldn't help but think that his neighbor had never intended to hire him in the first place.

As Ed cancelled the register transaction, the clerk returned the food items to the proper shelves.

Feeling ancient, as if his very soul had been bled nearly dry of his essence, George trudged back to the parking lot. He got into his car.

~

*H*e sat there for some time, staring idly around the grocery store parking lot, watching shoppers drive up, park their cars, and go in to shop.

It took him a long time to develop enough energy and motivation to crank his vehicle and drive the few short blocks to his home.

As much as he hated to, George was forced to take desperate measures. He called his investment broker, Frank.

"That is seriously unfortunate, man," said Frank, a slick, handsome broker who ran his own office, even though he was still in his early thirties.

"But no worries, I can get you the cash."

"I hate to sell any of it," George said.

"I don't know what else to do." He looked at his OMEGA 1932 Olympic Rattrapante Chronograph pocket watch. He was probably going to have to sell it. He very nearly broke down.

"You could leverage your current assets..." Frank replied. When George didn't say anything in response, Frank spoke again.

"You can borrow against your portfolio, Georgie," Frank said. "It'll get you some cash in the short term, and I can look for a transaction where you can reinvest and make up the difference."

"Do you think that's possible?" George inquired nervously.

"Sure, it is possible," Frank replied confidently, "But it's up to you. Margin investing isn't for everyone, obviously. There is a risk potential. Not everybody has the psychological tolerance for it."

"What's the worst that could happen?" George asked.

"Best case scenario would be that you multiply your gains. Worst case scenario, you get a margin call," Frank said.

"I'm presuming that the margin call is if the stocks depreciate below the maintenance margin requirement? Then I'd have to cover the difference, right?"

"Correct."

"In which case, how long would I have to cover it?" George asked, only slightly shocked with himself that he was actually considering it.

He didn't like high-risk investments or high-risk investment behavior. But then again, desperate times call for desperate measures, he thought to himself.

"You'd have five trading days to deposit funds or liquidate to cover it, and, obviously, I would liquidate your position to maintain the minimum account equity," Frank said.

George nodded. He wasn't sure, but he had to have the cash, and he hated to consider selling stock seriously.

Without his customary research, analysis, and pontification to the Nth degree procedure, the approach he usually engaged in for investment decisions, he made his choice. There and then, George decided to take the risk.

"I'll do it," George said with confident aplomb.

~

After a nap and a meal, which consisted solely of black coffee, George showered and prepared to meet with Bertha.

She had left him a voicemail in the morning (during the grocery bagging fiasco) and had mysteriously said she had something that might be a good fit for him.

When he called her back, she had insisted that he come in and speak to her in person before she would divulge any details.

George felt no anticipation, excitement, or positive energy whatsoever about the meeting. The job interview process had quickly become a source of new and increasing indignity.

After waiting briefly in the waiting room of the employment office, looking more than a little beaten down and depressed, George sat himself down across from Bertha. She smiled kindly at him.

"I have a feeling about this one, George. I could practically see your name when I got the listing," Bertha said with genuine excitement as she looked him over.

She was sorry to see that, although groomed, showered, and dressed for an interview, George seemed subdued. He was a different person from the one who sat in the same chair at their very first meeting. He seemed muted somehow.

"What kind of position is it?" George asked without even a hint of excitement in his voice.

"They want someone with a little life experience, someone wise..." Bertha said judiciously.

"That's what they wrote on their listing?" George asked.

"Wise accounting person with a little life experience needed?" He grinned bitterly. The totally insane audacity of people was beginning to sicken him.

"Don't you get snippy with me, mister. You've had a rough couple of weeks, and I know the slippery slope you're on. Each time you come in, you look a little less groomed. You're obviously in a funk, eating and drinking too much, staying up late, caught up in negative thinking... isolating. Oh, I've been there, honey," Bertha chided gently.

"This is life, and it's time to put on our big boy pants and keep moving forward, until life gets better. You need to chin up, George, and know that it will all work out. Have some faith."

George stared at Bertha, who had never been anything but kind to George and who always uplifted him.

From the look on the black woman's face and in her eyes, she was still being kind. Bertha was trying to help him and meant well.

She was right. Life wasn't always easy, even if it had previously always been easy. He determined right then to grow up, or do whatever he needed to do, to keep moving forward. If he couldn't be optimistic, then he would be neutral. He would do what he had to do to be a man and keep moving forward.

"It sounds terrific... whatever it is," George responded, feeling quite mollified.

"Oh, it is…" Bertha said,"…if you keep your mind open and follow the opportunity."

~

George stood outside a red brick office building and kept staring at the lone business sign that read, "The 3rd Eye."

The word "Eye" had some kind of mesmerizing Egyptian symbol around and above it.

He double-checked the address against the one Bertha had given him and realized that this was indeed the correct building. The Egyptian symbol uncharacteristically unnerved him.

No self-respecting financial or accounting institution would use such a tacky symbol for a logo, he reasoned.

He took a moment to repeat Bertha's recent words, "Keep an open mind and follow the opportunity."

With a deep breath, George entered the building and stepped into the open elevator on the ground floor. He punched the button that would take him to the third floor.

After getting off the elevator, George was led straight from reception into the office of Burton Houser.

Burton was an attractive, either gay or metro-sexual, man in his forties.

After the initial pleasantries were exchanged and George quietly offered a folder with his resume inside, they both sat. Burton sat behind his desk, and George pulled up one of the two elegant chairs facing the man's desk.

Burton continued to give George one hundred percent of his attention. Expecting him at least to refer to his resume and ask relevant questions, George waited.

Burton, however, continued to look at George and smile. George nervously looked around the office. It was beautifully decorated, in a warm, new-age, spiritualist style heavy on muted purples, teals, and earth tones.

"So, tell me something, George..." Burton finally said and then stopped.

"What would you like to know?" George prompted.

"Tell me something about me," Burton said as he relaxed back in his chair.

"About you?" asked George, not comprehending Burton's meaning. He had anticipated that he would be questioned about himself, his motivations, or what he could offer, and some such.

For the first time since beginning his job hunt, he had failed to research the company that was hiring. He had no idea what the offices of "The 3rd Eye" did. George was now regretting his inability to make himself care and his decision to instead "wing" it. The world had changed in the last several years, and so had job hunting. It was almost astonishing how different the job search was now compared to forty years ago.

"Look at me. Really look at me and tell me what you see. Gimme George wisdom. Speak your mind from your gut, but... say it with heart," Burton encouraged.

Unaccustomed to such an avant-garde interview technique, George was unsure how to answer. If this were some kind of psychological aptitude or personality test, not having the inclination or even patience for such a routine, George was sure he would fail.

He closed his eyes for a moment.

"Okay. What do I think about you?" George asked, opening his eyes, willing to give it his best shot. Burton didn't answer but just sat back further in his chair and smiled beatifically.

George looked more intently at Burton. He noted the colorful way that the man was dressed, his comportment, indicators of his sexuality, and most importantly, he looked into his eyes and got a sense of the kind of person that the man was.

George suddenly relaxed, knowing that Burton was a really good guy and that, whatever this test was, Burton was in no way trying to trip George up.

"I believe you may have been misunderstood most of your life," George began gently, speaking as kindly as he would to a young child.

"You were probably teased a lot at school by other boys."

Pausing to test Burton's reaction and hoping that that was the end of that interview segment, Burton nodded and seemed to react with sharply remembered pain, as if what George said was so, so true.

Burton nodded to indicate that George should continue.

"Taunted, beaten up..." George added, encouraged by Burton's positive feedback.

Was Burton even going to attempt to restrain his powerful emotions and avoid tears? The man's eyes appeared to be watering.

Burton nodded again for George to continue. So he did.

"Your parents had a hard time understanding you; you weren't terribly good at sports..."

George paused, thinking that he had gone too far.

Burton merely signaled for him to continue, and grabbing a tissue, he sat poised to wipe away imminent tears pooling in his eyes.

George was surprised by how much compassion he was feeling for Burton in this moment.

He felt as if he knew and really liked, or maybe even loved, the guy. He wanted to help him understand himself, if this was what the guy truly wanted.

"Your father had a hard time communicating with you… The last thing you wanted to do was follow him into the family business, or be very like him at all," George said forcefully, yet kindly and gently.

Really enjoying the exercise now, George sat forward in his chair.

However, as tears began rolling down Burton's face, George hesitated. He didn't want to hurt Burton's feelings. Should he stop? "Please continue. I need to hear this," Burton said tearfully.

"Going away to college was your great escape," George continued.

"Yes!" Burton exclaimed, his outburst surprising them both.

"You finally broke free of family restrictions and the small-mindedness of your hometown and found people that really got you..." said George, enjoying himself.

He grinned at Burton.

"You have no idea," agreed Burton, nodding happily and wiping away a tear.

"It was there, at college, that you finally found yourself..." George said.

"It was!" Burton agreed and, for a long moment, seemed caught up in a reverie of his youth.

"For the first time in your life, you could be truly yourself, among like-minded people... people that accepted you for who you really were," George added.

"They really did," agreed Burton, cheering up as George continued.

"You came out in college," George continued, on a roll. At Burton's frozen reaction to his words, however, he froze.

"I'm sorry. I went too far... please forgive me," George apologized.

"Oh, my God," Burton announced breathlessly, crying and laughing, feeling a mixture of shock and relief. I've never told a soul. How did you know?"

"I don't. I didn't. I don't know what I'm talking about. You told me to go with it," George blurted.

"Do you know what you are?" Burton asked enigmatically.

"No... I..." George said, shaking his head wildly, wondering if he was passing or failing the interview.

"You've no idea what you are, do you?" Burton asked again.

He shook his head in apparent astonishment. George was totally unsure of any kind of sensible response.

"You're a natural, is what you are!" proclaimed Burton, smiling broadly.

"What you have is so rare... You have no idea, do you? I felt it when I held your resume... and I was right. You have the gift!"

"The gift?" George echoed. The room seemed to shift around

him. He slowed his breathing down to try and calm himself so that he could better understand what was happening here.

"Absolutely! Like the seventh son of the seventh son, you're that good! You're hired! When can you start?" Burton said, wiping his tears away, and sat up straighter.

Stunned by Burton's words, "You're hired!" George almost jumped up with shock and excitement.

"Really? I have a job? I mean, I got the job?" he asked, unsure that this was all truly happening. How could he have aced the interview when the man hadn't even looked at his resume or asked him any hard questions?

"You can start today, if you like. Right now, even. I don't care," Burton said ecstatically.

"That's great! That's wonderful!" George stood up with joy and shook Burton's hand with gusto, "Oh, boy," he said with great relief.

"Oh, boy, oh, boy, oh boy," he repeated with joy.

"Congratulations and welcome to the team!" Burton said, still vigorously shaking George's hand.

"You just made my day, mister," George said jovially and finally took his hand away. "You have no idea."

"You're going to be a tremendous asset to our company, George."

"Okay!" said George, resisting the urge to fist-pump the air. "What exactly would my title be?"

"We'll need a good one for you," Burton considered.

George frowned and wondered how that worked. Had he been interviewed for a position without the hirer determining a job title in advance?

"I've got it!" Burton delightedly said, as if having a lightbulb moment, "Mr. Psychic!"

George stood motionless for a few seconds, as his mind caught up with what Burton had just said.

"Mr. Psychic?" he said. George frowned as he spoke, as if he had to say the words aloud to understand the implication fully.

"I know what you're going to say," Burton continued, "too corny, right? But I think for you, it's appropriate. Old-fashioned yet elegant. Absolutely trustworthy. Mr. Psychic. Yeah, I like it. You don't like it? I hope you do like it because right now I feel lighter. I feel happier, I feel healed, and other people desperately need to feel this way. You're going to be huge."

On a scale of one to ten, George's mood deflated to below zero.

"You want to hire me as an... as a... as a... as a psychic?" George asked in disbelief, hoping against hope that it wasn't true.

How could he work as a telephone psychic? He was a finance guy. What would people think? Seeing Burton's expression shift to serious and sober, George sat back down again fast.

"I thought you needed a financial analyst or senior accountant... or something?" George said aloud.

"Are you kidding?" insisted Burton, and then the man spoke again without pause:

"Don't sell yourself short like that! No more boring, wanna blow my brains out at the end of the day, crunching numbers in a cubicle for you... You have a gift!"

George became so suddenly depressed that he couldn't respond. He barely managed a polite smile.

"I'll let Bertha know that you are perfect... You're the one," Burton said as he made some notes on his day planner. Despite George's palpable near-suicidal mood, Burton remained ecstatic.

"Bertha deserves a little bonus on this one. She's going to be so pleased," Burton said as he continued to make some notes.

George, in a daze and not knowing how to respond, simply walked to the door and exited.

~

Extremely drowsy, George channel-surfed late-night TV.

An empty wine bottle on the floor nearby, he slipped back onto the sofa. His eyelids closed and opened as he struggled to stay awake. Slumped backward, he paused from switching channels when he saw an infomercial for the 3rd Eye Psychic Hotline.

A fairly dreadful actor addressed the camera, attempting to sound casual and friendly, as if he were advising a friend.

"Do you wonder if you are on the wrong life path?" he asked meaningfully.

"Do you wonder if he, or she, is cheating on you? Do you need to know when things are finally going to change?"

Another actor, presumably depicting a clean-cut Average Joe, addressed the camera.

"I was in asset recovery for twenty years. That's right. I was that guy who repossessed people's cars and speedboats. I hated my job. In fact, it got so bad that I got suicidal and called the people at the 3rd Eye. Based on my reading, I quit the job I hated. Now I play sax in a jazz band. The folks at the 3rd Eye changed my life."

The Average Joe smiled and lifted a saxophone to his lips, then played a few jazzy notes.

"Thank you, 3rd Eye," he said as false tears streamed from his eyes.

George, half-asleep, laughed at the corniness and ridiculousness of it all.

"Of course you were unhappy, jerk face," he said to the TV.

"You were a repo man!" George flipped channels. Losing his battle with fatigue, he finally slipped all the way down on the sofa and nodded off.

~

It was a typical work morning in the business district. Assorted business people made their way to work. Some stopped for coffee or to buy newspapers.

A homeless man, with a cup extended, went from person to person begging for some loose change. Not a single person put coins in his cup, so the homeless man decided to rummage through trash cans and check vending machines for loose coins.

It became clear that the homeless man was George. Not finding anything of interest in the trash cans, George II squatted down in a doorway.

Furtively taking out a hidden stash of gourmet chocolates, which were concealed in a paper bag, he munched on them with obvious glee, savoring each bite. One by one, people from his old life passed him by and avoided looking at him: Ed, Marco, Bethany, and finally James.

Bertha walked past and did a double-take. Recognizing him, she stopped to fumble in her purse for some cash. Holding back tears, she gave him a bill and then reluctantly moved on.

George III and Jenn, pushing baby Georgie in a stroller, were strolling down the sidewalk toward George II.

George III stopped in his tracks upon seeing his father squatting and unkempt in the doorway of a building. Seriously ashamed, he couldn't look at him. A cell phone somewhere rang.

"Dad? Dad?" George III called out.

~

George bolted awake and opened his eyes. Late-night programming, a poorly lit old black-and-white movie, cast a strange glow over the living room. Stretched out on the sofa, George saw his cell phone ringing as it lit up the darkness.

"Hello?" George II said as, still flustered, he answered the portable telephone.

"Dad?" George III asked.

George looked at his watch. It was four AM.

"Hello, son. Is everything okay?" George asked, his voice filled with some concern.

"Sorry it's so late... but I just had the worst and weirdest dream about you, Dad. You were in the city and... well, really messed up. Are you okay, Dad? Please tell me that you're all right," George III said.

"Yes, of course. I'm fine. It's... It's very late," George said, after a long moment.

The alarm and evident love in George III's voice touched George's heart.

It was strange, too—had they actually been dreaming the same dream? He was not certain if he had ever heard of such a thing. It would be better to say nothing about the shared dream to his son, as the young man already sounded concerned about him.

Tears fell from George II's eyes. He struggled not to burst into guttural sobs.

"I'm worried about you. Why don't you come and stay with us for a while? Jenn and I would love to have you, and it would be good for little Georgie..."

Unable to respond for fear that his son would hear his sobbing, he met George III's suggestion with silence.

George III subsequently changed his approach.

"Or I could lend you some money, Dad. It wouldn't be any trouble."

George found the disquiet in his son's voice so profoundly moving that he struggled to stop his tears.

"That's very generous, son, but trust me, I'm doing okay... really," he finally managed to answer. A little ragged catch in his throat was the only indication of his shaky emotional state.

"Did you get a job yet?" George III asked hopefully. George II was speechless. His son knew. Somehow, his son knew that he was unemployed.

"Grandfather heard through the grapevine that Teleseismology Hub NS closed the finance department and, well, I didn't want to say anything. I figured you would bring it up when you felt like it. But my dream was so awful. I just had to call you..."

Georgie III's voice trailed off. He hoped that the question, though asked at this late hour, sounded casual enough not to alarm his father or cause the man to become defensive and shut down.

George was surprised that his parents and son, and daughter-in-law were abreast of his situation.

He had avoided most, if not all, contact with them in the last few months. He'd begged off of family dinners, avoided their telephone calls, and generally isolated. He preferred to solve his problems by himself.

"Did you get a job, Dad?" Georgie III asked again.

It was funny to George II, but his son now sounded like the young child that he had fond memories of raising. Recognizing the enormity of the casually presented question, George paused and gathered himself.

"Yes," he replied gently.

"Yes, as a matter of fact, I did. Finally," he cheerfully smiled, hoping to disarm his son of his obvious worry and concern.

"That's great! Congratulations," George III said, sounding genuinely relieved and pleased.

"You didn't call us..."

"No, I just got the offer today, actually," George loosened in his delivery, satisfied in the knowledge that he wasn't totally lying to his son.

"Nothing has been settled yet, salary, benefits, and stuff. It's been busy around here," George added.

"Well, thank goodness. You have no idea how relieved that makes me feel," George III said. Then his father heard him whisper to his wife, "Great news, honey, Dad got a job offer today!"

"Me too. I'm relieved too, son," George said, holding back his tears.

It was palpable and exceedingly endearing, the love that his son obviously felt for him. George pressed the phone to his ear, even more tightly, sensing that the call was coming to an end.

"Dad, I'm sorry I pressured you to go away with us. I hope you'll forgive me," George III said softly.

When his father didn't say anything, George was somewhat dumbstruck by the healing occurring between himself and his son. George III spoke again.

"I should let you get some rest now, Dad. Congratulations again! Call me with details when you can."

"Thanks, son, I will," George said, hanging up.

He then dropped onto the sofa and, placing his hands to his face, sobbed. He felt like he had no choice now. He'd give Mr. Psychic a try.

~

So excited that he was almost jumping up and down, Burton escorted George through the 3rd Eye offices. Wearing a custom, slightly dated, bespoke suit, which he was glad he hadn't sold at his yard sale, George looked sharp, well-to-do, and extremely capable.

Feeling quite nervous, though it wasn't at all apparent, George returned the smiles of other employees. Many of them were looking over their cubicles, most of them on phone calls.

They're a colorful and varied lot of workers, he thought to himself. He had never seen such a vibrant and out-of-the-ordinary collection of employees in a professional work environment before.

Does that guy have a feather in his hair? George squinted to try to get a better look as he passed a woolly, disheveled man whose outfit resembled the traditional garb of a Native American.

Even these people's cubicles were individually and colorfully decorated, each presumably expressing its individual personality. He struggled to repress the thought, which popped up unbidden.

It filled him with a particular anxiety to think that he didn't fit in, not one little bit.

"Everybody," Burton announced as he and George reached the center of a large open space in the midst of the cubicles.

"I want you to give a warm 3rd Eye welcome to... Mr. Psychic!"

George smiled and feebly waved as people who weren't on calls came out to greet him. He looked around at what appeared to be an office filled with smiling kooks.

A young Goth girl in her twenties approached and introduced herself to him as Star Child. She had thick black eyeliner and blackish lipstick on her face and wore black and white striped tights, black Doc Martens, and a black dress that was half ribbed knit T-shirt and half black tulle ballet skirt.

"That's a lovely name," George told her as the fairly unkempt, very hairy man dressed in Native American-inspired garb approached them. The man extended his hand and announced himself as Sacred Rainbow Feather Walking Man.

"How do you do?" George asked as he shook the young man's hand. "I'm George."

"Namaste, George," Star Child said as she pressed her hands

together, placing them in front of her forehead, and bowed to him.

"The Divine in me recognizes the Divine in you," she explained in response to George's puzzled expression.

George nodded respectfully and quickly pondered what an appropriate response might be.

"Ah," he said, mentally scrambling to get it right, "Nama... Namasty, to you, uhm... and peace." She smiled happily in response.

"Be good to Sacred Rainbow Feather Walking Man," she said after a moment.

"My guides say that you and he will be very close buddies." George tried to absorb and process this fairly flabbergasting info.

"Oh, excellent," George nodded his head in exaggerated friendliness, noting that this was a brand new defense mechanism that had cropped up in his personality. "Very good. Thank you," he added.

"How, Ahab," whispered Sacred Rainbow Feather Walking Man to George, raising his hand in salute.

He spoke again, a little more loudly to George, "My wigwam is your wigwam."

"Thank you, Feather Man, uh, Walking Sacred, uhm, Rainbow, I'm very honored..." George replied. Then, desperate to find an amiable topic of conversation, to be friendly, he inquired, "What tribe are you?" Everyone suddenly laughed.

George flushed bright red and wondered what he'd said wrong.

"Just jacking around with you, man," Sacred Rainbow Feather Walking Man said.

"I'm from Utah. My parents are Latter-day Saints. Welcome to our humble bit of heaven, dude."

"Oh, good one," George responded with false laughter. It's a little bit of new guy hazing; I get it."

"Come over here and meet Mimi," Burton said, pulling George toward a colorful cubicle. A sexy, effervescent blonde beauty in her fifties, Mimi was an especially vivacious hippie chick.

"Hi, George... or should I say, Mr. Psychic?" the woman, Mimi, said to George in a low, throaty musical voice. Something about her presence made him instantly feel warm inside.

"Welcome to our little family," she added and extended her hand.

Instantly smitten, George took her hand and shook it slowly and very gently. He stared at her just a bit longer than most people would for a first-time introduction.

"I feel as if I know you," he said, although he was very sure that he had never met her before.

"We have been together, many lifetimes," responded Mimi happily, her bright blue eyes shining.

"I love you, George," she then said, and it was as if the room spun around the two of them.

It was just the way he had read about it in books with a romantic plot, or the way he had seen this moment, the meet-cute, often shot in romance movies using a camera on a crane. He grew giddy with excitement, and it made him feel decidedly lightheaded.

"Oh, terrific, I... It's great to meet you," he babbled, dizzy with feeling and clearly thrown off guard.

For a moment, the rest of the world dropped away, and Mimi and George stared happily into each other's eyes. Without noticing what he was doing, he grabbed her hand and held it.

She laughed and smiled and squeezed his hand, and boom! It was like a warm electricity shot right into his heart and spread outward. He flushed bright red, and his face grew hot. The moment was exhilarating, so pure and delicious; it was almost celestial.

"Wonderful, then," announced Burton, after giving a little cough to get both of their attention. George broke his eyes away from Mimi to see that everyone but her and Burton had drifted away.

George's new boss grinned. Then Burton checked his watch and spoke again.

"I'll leave you in Mimi's capable hands. She's the best... except for, possibly, you."

The former accountant looked down to see that he literally was holding Mimi's 'capable' hands. As casually as he could, confused to remember that he'd grabbed her hand moments earlier, he let go.

George smiled sweetly and awkwardly at Mimi as Burton drifted away. Mimi stared at George as if she were meeting up again with a long-lost friend. Then, flushing, George nervously spoke.

"Will you excuse me for a moment? I'll be right back," he said.

Mimi nodded. George hurried to go to the restroom, which he had seen on the way in when Burton had guided him to the cubicle area.

When he finally arrived at the restroom, after taking several hurried steps, he sighed with relief. He hadn't needed to go but rather felt a need to escape.

Instantly taking a mass of deep breaths, he splashed his face with cold water from the tap.

What on earth am I doing here? He asked himself.

There was no doubt in his mind that he didn't belong among these very strange and mystical, perhaps mentally challenged, people. Perhaps he should find a good excuse to leave and never come back.

Then again, a foot in the door might not be a bad thing. Perhaps there was an opportunity to find more suitable employment within the organization here; after all, every business needs an accountant.

They seem to like me, he reasoned. Perhaps when they realized that he had no aptitude for the job he was hired to do, they would simply transfer him to the accounting or, considering the company's small size, the bookkeeping department.

They probably use BizBooks here, he considered and kicked himself for not brushing up on the accounting program after that disastrous earlier interview.

George determined to mention that he was an accountant each time that he was within earshot of Burton.

He was already an employee, after all. It would be an ingenious plan if it worked, because if he played his cards right, it would be their idea.

He could even appear to hesitate and thereby be in a better position to negotiate a higher salary. It was a good plan, he considered, as he dried himself off.

~

Then he hurried back to the warm and welcoming smile of the vibrant and appealing Mimi.

"Would you like to trade readings?" Mimi inquired upon his return.

"Sure," George agreed, not knowing what she actually meant. Mimi took his hand and led him to what was obviously her cubicle. It was prettily decorated in an exceedingly subtle, uplifting style.

"Will I go first, or will you?" Mimi said, gesturing to indicate where each of them should sit. She sat in what was obviously her desk chair, and he slipped into a similar adjacent chair.

"I don't really know how to do a reading," he replied.

"Oh, you did in another life," she said, then thought a moment.

"There's a technique that you can try. I use it to help me remember things from the past. You give a command to your unconscious mind that you will remember this skill from your past."

"Uh-huh," said George, wondering just how scatty this chick was.

"You better go first," he suggested.

Mimi beamed at George again. Becoming more radiant by the second, it seemed that she really liked being in his company.

George was secretly flattered, yet on another level, he questioned her sanity. He wondered if, perhaps, she was like this with everyone. Was she a woman who fell in love at the drop of a hat?

Mimi shuffled a tarot deck and placed some cards carefully face down in a particular arrangement on the desk. Although skeptical, George was aware that he was more than a tad curious.

"Do you remember France?" Mimi asked George sweetly, as she turned over one of the cards to reveal the four of pentacles: a man, wearing a crown, was seated.

On the card, the man's feet rested on two golden pentacles, or coins, set on solid flat ground. He cradled one pentacle or coin in his arms. On his crown was a fourth pentacle.

"France?" answered George, and almost laughed, "No, I've never been."

"You were a woman then, and so very beautiful. I had never seen a more beautiful woman... but you were just like the four of pentacles," explained Mimi curiously.

"A woman? I don't really... remember," responded George awkwardly.

"Tell me about the card."

"The four of pentacles is known as the card of the miser. A person who stops having fun because they're so worried about how much it costs them. Preoccupied with money, they don't like change..."

"We were in France?" George asked, trying to get his head around all of this, and not at all liking where Mimi was going with the miser thing.

He flushed, thinking about how some people might consider him to be preoccupied, maybe even obsessed, with money, but life was hard.

It was every man for himself, and no one but he could properly prepare himself for retirement.

"France in the Middle Ages, remember?" encouraged Mimi in her soft, sweet voice.

George wasn't thinking about France at all as he found that he couldn't stop thinking about the word "miser." Mimi looked at George; it looked like he wasn't racking his brain too hard to remember.

"Your parents were merchants. You had saved all this money... But you wouldn't marry me. You died alone, in a shack, with gold under your mattress, remember?" Mimi asked.

Then it happened. In a flash, to his complete and utter shock, George did remember.

He got flashes—images, color, sound—and saw gold. He could practically smell the moldy hay and the earthen floor of the shack. He felt the ache of loneliness and heartache so deep that he felt it must transcend multiple lifetimes.

"No, I really don't recall," answered George, not lying exactly, as he didn't remember the entire storyline.

Instead, he was getting disparate bits, flashes, really, of information. None of it made a complete story, and it was entirely humiliating to boot. He wondered if his imagination was making up some story in response to her vivid descriptions and suggestions.

"I was so sad," continued Mimi, looking genuinely sad and bereft as if it had just happened yesterday.

"I loved you so much… I threw myself off a cliff, finally. The pain was just too much to bear."

"Oh," responded George, really not knowing what to say. Should I apologize? he wondered.

"I'm so sorry," he finally said, passing her a box of tissues, noticing that she was weeping.

"So very sorry," he added.

"Is this what I have to do for people?" George asked, thinking to himself that he definitely wouldn't be up for it.

He already felt sad, drained, and almost disappointed in himself. If this were what working as a psychic would be like, it was entirely too depressing. He'd never be able to do this every day, he reasoned.

"No," replied Mimi, almost instantly changing back to a business-like demeanor.

"Not unless you find it helpful. Some of us find that tarot helps us as an aid, but no, it's certainly not a requirement. And past life readings and healings are not the primary type of reading that we do here."

"Good," George automatically said, feeling great relief. He felt even more relieved that her anguish and sorrow over some imagined life in France that they shared seemed to have entirely, near-instantly disappeared.

He took a deep breath and relaxed.

"Let me show you what you'll be doing," Mimi said, sweeping away the tarot cards.

"We can always get back to the cards and our karmic connections another time," she added.

George stared with acute concentration as Mimi expertly pushed buttons on the telephone and video console to show him how his 3rd Eye telephone headset and Video Chat interfaces worked.

"Is it usually video chat?" George asked, wondering if he should be taking notes.

"Mostly it's on the phone," answered Mimi.

"Video chat is at a higher rate. You'll also get a higher commission for those, but don't stress if you don't get that many," she said and smiled.

"So what do I do, exactly?" George asked, still unclear about the precise work description.

"It's straightforward," answered Mimi in a warm and calm voice.

"People call in, and you answer. You do the same thing that you did for Burton, you know, in the interview process. Tune into the person and tell them what you see, feel, and think. If you're getting inner audio, clairsentience, then share that."

"What? You mean, hearing voices?" George asked, with alarm.

"Your guides, or intuition, or your higher self may wish to share unique information with you... Naturally, you should really tune into the frequency so that your sub-personalities, or dark forces, demons, or other attachments, or the like, don't influence the reading," explained Mimi, very matter-of-factly.

George grew wide-eyed with a mix of shock, horror, and amazement.

Did she really say dark forces and demons? he asked himself.

As Mimi talked on about the ins and outs of the job, George saw her lips move but didn't hear another word.

Already, his head was reeling from information overload. Tarot cards, alleged reincarnation, and now guides, hearing voices, and the need to make certain that the voices weren't demons, threatened to send George over the top totally.

His head pounded, so he rubbed his temples to try and stave off a headache.

"I can't do this," he admitted.

"It's… I'm not that type of… It's not something… I really can't do this, I'm sorry."

George felt pure panic and, shaking like a leaf, wondered if he should leave that very minute. Mimi took his shaking hand in hers, and instantly, George felt peace and calm spread throughout his being.

"Sure you can do it," Mimi consoled him.

"You're a natural. You just don't know it yet. Burton can see it, and I can see it. You just don't know who you really are yet, that's all," she added.

Mimi's voice and demeanor were so deeply reassuring and soothing that George allowed himself a few deep breaths. He managed to abate his terror.

"Just give it a try," Mimi reasoned softly.

"What have you got to lose? If it's not for you, it's not for you. At least you will have given it a shot, right?"

"I guess," answered George, incapable of countering her logic with any kind of meaningful or reasonable objection.

"I guess I can try it out."

"Monday morning is always quiet, so why don't you put my headset on and take the next call. I'll be right beside you, okay?"

"Sure," George agreed.

"How hard could it be?" He would do just what he'd done for Burton during his job interview.

When he noticed a bit of tension in his body and mind, he reflected upon it.

He pointed out to himself that the fact that he had stayed and not listened to the part of himself that wanted to run out of there at the first opportunity proved that he was being a good sport. It was also evidence that he did have an open mind, after all.

He noticed that while he was having a dialogue in his mind, Mimi sat patiently waiting.

He reminded himself that he was still on the clock and getting paid and that, if he began to take phone calls, he would have something to show for the day's efforts.

So what if it turned out to be an embarrassing disaster that he would later prefer to forget? Feeling settled mentally, George turned to face Mimi.

"I'm ready, now," he said, smiling. She stood up, and he looked at her in surprise.

"Can you cover me while I take a restroom break?" Mimi asked.

"Oh, sure," he answered, and she excused herself to go to the bathroom.

~

As soon as she left, George heard a tone and looked around. The gentle tone sounded again.

George anxiously stared at the console and headset. Hearing the tone a third time and seeing a red button lit up, he realized that it indicated an incoming call.

He looked anxiously around. There was no sign of Mimi, and he realized that he was on his own.

He put the headset on his head and answered.

"Hello, this is... Mr. Psychic," he answered apprehensively. A woman spoke.

"Hi, I asked for my normal psychic. I usually use a woman, but I believe in providence... So, this must be a good thing, right? My getting connected to you?" she said. George didn't have time to reply before the woman spoke again.

"My name is Doris, I'm hoping you can tell me about my love life," the woman, who sounded like she was in her forties, said. George was determined not to overthink things.

"What seems to be the problem with your relationships?" asked George, deciding to wing it.

"They always start great..." Doris began and paused to bite into something. She was clearly eating, and George got the definite impression that she was consuming a piece of chocolate.

"But then they get busy or start seeing another woman. They stop calling. I guess I'm too intense. I love too much. I have such a big heart, and it scares them off," Doris added.

"I see," said George, unsure about how to proceed. Listening to Doris chewing loudly, he was thankful to see Mimi now returning from the restroom.

"I've got a middle-aged woman named Doris looking for relationship advice," George whispered to Mimi when she entered the cubicle, his hand placed over his mouthpiece.

"Sparkly," replied Mimi, cheerfully.

"What do I say to her? She's telling me all this... bullshit," George exclaimed in a panic.

"Well, you should tell her that," answered Mimi serenely.

"What? That she's talking a load of bull crap?" George asked. He was really shocked that Mimi would suggest such a thing.

"Certainly, if that's what your instinct tells you, you should go with it. Be yourself and tell the truth, George. That's the only way this will work."

~

A fairly clinically obese woman, sitting on the couch in front of the TV, which was on but muted, pressed the telephone tight against her ear.

"Hello?" Doris asked. Her double chins were smeared with dark chocolate. I may ask for a refund, she decided, when the male psychic didn't immediately answer her.

She was surprised. The 3rd Eye was usually excellent. She opened another chocolate bar while waiting for the psychic to respond.

~

"*Y* es, I'm here," George answered and then improvised, "Please bear with me… while I consult the oracle."

"Tell her that she's talking crap? Seriously?" George asked Mimi, his hand again tightly covering the mouthpiece. He couldn't believe what he was hearing.

"Won't she feel offended? Or hurt?"

"What if she does? We're not here to tell callers what they want to hear, George. We're here to tell them the truth," Mimi explained.

"Huh?" he gasped out, eyes wide with surprise.

"This is the service we provide. The truth may hurt, but if that's what the caller needs to hear to actually make a change in their lives and move from pain to clarity... what greater gift is there? Be loving and be kind... But don't hold back. Give it to her straight, Mr. Psychic."

"Okay," agreed George, with reluctance. He took a deep breath to center himself and tuned back into the call. To his surprise, he had visuals and a strong sense of Doris, even though he couldn't actually see her.

~

*D*oris bit off and chewed a piece of the chocolate bar.

"Hello? Hello?" asked Doris, wondering if she had been cut off.

From her living room, she could see into her kitchen. The blue and orange bag of Cheesy Puffs on the kitchen counter seemed almost to beckon to her.

She sighed. It seemed like she was always hungry, but what could she do? Fat or not, she was sure that she was hypoglycemic. She needed to eat real regular like.

~

*G*eorge sat back in his chair and relaxed as best he could.

"Yes, Doris. I'm still here. I've consulted the oracle," he began, giving Mimi a knowing wink, which she returned with a lovely smile.

"Well, go on," Doris said. It sounded to George like she was standing right next to him. She had an almost peeved tone in her voice.

"Doris, I think we both know that you're lying to yourself," George blurted out.

~

"What?" asked Doris, dropping her chocolate. She quickly sat upright in her chair. Her face turned beet red, and her eyes teared up. She couldn't believe that her psychic had just accused her of lying.

~

George felt an expansion of energy as words rapidly spilled from his mouth and flowed from his heart and inner knowing.

"You don't love men, you hate them. You fear that they're just like Daddy. And you won't find love, or love men, until you forgive him for all of the terrible things he did to you..." said George.

It felt easy for him to spill it and absolutely tell it like his intuition told him to.

Standing next to him, quite taken aback, Mimi's mouth became a little "o" of surprise.

Fortunately, George was adjusting his headset and didn't see Mimi's horrified expression.

~

The foil wrapper squished, and the chocolate bar pieces inside broke as Doris squeezed her candy bar so hard that it broke into tiny bits and melted in her hot hands.

"You... I can't... Of all the... I called to find out why I haven't met the one yet... and you insult me? You're a horrible person. I'm not going to pay for this, crap. You can't blame me for what's happening to me, you asshat," Doris practically yelled.

She slammed down the telephone and was shocked when her white-hot rage combusted into a full-on meltdown. She sobbed into her hands.

~

George gripped the headset and wondered if that had gone as badly as he thought it might have.

"She hung up the call?" Mimi asked, seeing the light on her telephone console go dark.

"That's no biggie," she hurriedly added. "It happens when the truth is too much for someone to take in. Every psychic here gets hung up on some of the time if they're any good."

"I was too harsh?" George asked, fearful that whatever he had said, and he actually couldn't even remember it all, had been too much.

"Well, maybe a little. But don't worry, you shared a hard truth, and that's the most important thing. Over time, you'll get the hang of the best way to deliver those insights. You have to do many calls to actually develop a good telephone manner, know what I mean?" Mimi said nonchalantly.

"No, but thanks for the vote of confidence, anyway," George said as he took off the headset. He shrugged and shook his head. She smiled down at him.

Maybe it hadn't been that bad. If Mimi wasn't worried about him getting in trouble with Burton for causing a client to hang up on him, then it was probably okay.

"You'll get the hang of it. And when you do, there isn't anything else you'd rather be doing, trust me," Mimi said.

George looked at her beautiful face and realized that her effervescent personality was entirely charming. He could get used to spending time with this woman. George stood and stretched.

"I think I could use some coffee," he said. Mimi smiled and stood up.

"It's the perfect time for me to show you the break room, then. Let's grab a cup, and then we'll set you up in your cubicle. Unless you'd rather quit and run home to hide?" She grinned as if she really could read his every thought.

"No, I'll give it until the end of the day," George responded. "An accountant never quits until all the books are balanced."

"Sparkly," Mimi responded, not falling for his bait.

George looked into her eyes and wondered how it was that she had gotten the gist of his recent thoughts.

"Then… I'll run home and open the best bottle of wine I have left in my wine cellar," he decided. He hardly realized that he had spoken aloud.

"Oh, now that sounds delightful," Mimi said with such envious delight that George wondered if she was angling for an invite. He blushed and immediately desired to invite her over for dinner.

Before he could respond to her last words, Mimi grabbed George's hand and pulled him out of her cubicle and took him to the staff break room.

*O*nce inside the employee lounge, George looked around. The walls were painted in rich colors, and it was a pleasant place decorated with plants and crystals. There was just enough floor space for three bistro tables, pairs of chairs, and a few large potted plants.

There was a full coffee pot on the counter near the sink, yet Mimi used what looked like a high-end espresso machine to make each of them a specialty coffee drink.

"She called me a name and hung up on me," George said, as he went over the phone call once again in his head. He felt a sense of shock. He hadn't experienced anything like that in his entire work history. Sure, people got angry or upset in professional situations, but his coworkers generally kept their cool.

There had been no name-calling at Teleseismology Hub NS.

"Don't beat yourself up about it, sweetie. Everybody gets clients like that… people that don't want, or can't handle, the truth. It is hard to see ourselves clearly and change, right?" she said. He nodded.

"I guess. Thanks, Mimi. I appreciate your help and support," George replied. He patted her hand, without noticing that he had initiated physical contact.

"Of course, George. I love you," Mimi said, and he suddenly felt a bit breathless.

George blushed when Mimi handed him his special drink. He sipped it carefully and then looked around the break room more carefully.

He determined that the coffee, a cappuccino, was incredible. While he sipped his delicious hot drink, Mimi showed him where he could store his lunch and the selection of healthful snacks that the 3rd Eye offices stocked and provided.

"Are you ready to get back, or do you need a few minutes?" Mimi asked after she had given him the full office tour.

"I do have…" began George, and then reconsidered.

"What, sweetie? Is there something on your mind?"

"Well, it's just that… I really don't fit in around here, do I?" said George, looking down at his business suit. He immediately felt better for expressing his doubts.

"Well, of course you do, George. That's like saying that you don't fit in… in the big wide world, out there, isn't it? It takes all kinds, right?" Mimi said.

"What I mean is… this whole psychic thing. I mean… I guess what I'm wondering is, why did Burton hire me when I'm not one bit, you know, psychic? I really don't understand," George said.

"Let me tell you one thing about Burton," Mimi said, leaning closer and lowering her voice. George leaned forward, the better to hear her, and became almost entranced by her aroma as if she smelled like some kind of amazing flower.

"He may act a bit, well, you know, over-the-top, but, trust me, he always knows exactly what he's doing, when he's doing it. He runs a successful business, after all, so he must be doing a few things right… right?" Mimi practically purred.

George tried to focus on her words and not on her voice, because she was just so sexy.

"I guess," agreed George finally, his agreeable response concealing his underlying concerns.

"Look," Mimi said, in a more serious tone, obviously not fooled by George's answer.

"He hired you to do a job… so he must believe that you can do it. Just suppose that you are as gifted as he believes you are? Would that be a disaster? Would you feel like less of a person or something?"

"No. No, of course not, it's just that… I've never done a psychic thing in my life, you know?" George said. "So, naturally, I'm not used to thinking of myself in that way."

"Then maybe it's time you loosened that old tie of yours and got to know yourself a bit better. Maybe you could open up. Try something new, and see if your life improves. What do you think?" Mimi said.

"You may have a point," agreed George, feeling somewhat chastened.

"Admittedly, Burton has wanted to extend the business into a more… professional arena; he wants to attract clients from the professional classes, for instance, and maybe hiring you might be part of that. But if I were you, I wouldn't second-guess everything and overthink yourself out of a good job with benefits. You know what I'm talking about," she said, looking around to make sure that they were still not being overheard.

"I do know you're talking about," agreed George, feeling much better.

"More than you know."

Mimi looked George up and down, and it was clear that she liked what she saw.

"You want my advice? Have fun. The only way this is going to work for you is if you don't care about what you're saying or whether you're hurting anybody's feelings and just tell it like it is. When you relax and talk from your intuition, your hunches, your gut... whatever you want to call it, you have to be loose and allow yourself to sound off-the-wall. Because, let's face it, what we do here is very off the wall, thank God. Sound good?" Mimi smiled.

George thought about her words and managed to crack a smile in response.

Despite Mimi's apparent hippie vibe and appearance, George considered that her perspective was actually very freeing. She made some very astute and salient points. So what if he angered clients? So what if he got fired? So what if he didn't feel like he was a real psychic?

Burton was a successful businessman and could have hired whoever he liked. George had bills to pay. Did it really matter how he paid them, as long as his work was aligned with his ethics and morals? No, it really didn't.

"Yes... Mimi," George added her name awkwardly with a broad smile.

"It does sound good. What you said makes sense. I feel ten times better. Thank you."

"You're welcome, sweetie. Ready to go back in, or do you want to walk around, maybe a bit, and get a feel for the place and how everyone else works around here? Because we all have different ways of working. There is no one right way, and it may take you some time to find yours. Wanna grab another cup of coffee and meander around for a bit?" Mimi inquired.

"Yes, actually, I would. That sounds great, thank you. For everything," George said and meant it.

"You're welcome, Mr. Psychic," Mimi said playfully and winked.

"Come join me when you're ready."

~

*A*s Mimi returned to her desk, George remained in the break room and poured himself a cup of regular coffee. Taking a quick sip, he considered that the brewed coffee was as good as the cappuccino.

Both were fresh ground, and the beans were rich and dark, just the way that he liked them. He was indeed feeling ten times better, and his smile confirmed his more relaxed state.

Cup of coffee in hand, he walked around the call space, familiarizing himself with the general layout. He occasionally waved to someone on the phone who caught his eye and smiled or otherwise greeted him.

He watched Star Child handle a call and noticed how relaxed and totally present she was while listening to what her caller had to say. She was aware of George, yet she gave him just the slightest hint of her attention.

George really liked the way Star Child seemed devoted to her caller. He figured that the person on the other end of that call would indeed feel listened to and cared about in a unique way.

Sacred Rainbow Feather Walking Man smiled a big smile and gave George a "peace" sign. George smiled and awkwardly made a peace sign in return. He almost went over to visit with the man, but then the guy got a video chat call, and George was quite happy to stroll away.

After getting a sense of how the other psychics used their space and handled calls, George went back to his workspace.

~

*H*e was happy that he was only a short cubicle screen partition away from Mimi. Mimi was on a call but gave him a broad smile and a thumbs-up sign.

George smiled back and relaxed into his space. Something about Mimi made him feel very accepted and secure. George sorted out his desk, placing the phone, stapler, pen, and notepad just the way he wanted them.

"Just say the word, George, and we'll start putting your calls through," Mimi said as she stood and leaned over the partition.

"Bring it," George said and smiled.

"That's the attitude, Mr. Psychic," Mimi encouraged. A minute or two after she sat back down again, his phone line blinked. George quickly put on his headset and flicked the switch to engage.

"Thank you for calling the 3rd Eye, this is... Mr. Psychic," he answered self-consciously.

"Oh, Mr. Psychic, thank God. My name is Nigel, and I desperately need your help. I'm devastated..." the male caller sobbed.

"It's Ferdinand. I'm absolutely certain the bastard's screwing around on me. So, is he? And tell it to me straight, I can take it..." Nigel said, and sounded as if he couldn't bear it, despite his statement that he could, if Ferdinand were actually cheating on him.

Unaccustomed to grown men crying on the phone complaining of man problems, George drew a blank. He had no idea what to say at this point.

He heard a shrieking, crying noise and, after a moment of intense listening, was sure that the sounds were over the phone and not some line interference. George had no idea how to handle or even if he should interrupt the caller's wailing.

"I know I'm fragile, vulnerable, and alone," the man then continued.

"But I have to know the truth. God help me, I just can't take it anymore... what do you see?"

"Just one minute," replied George. "Let me get clear my... focus. I, uh... I have to tune in." Seriously freaking, George stood up and leaned over the partition to get Mimi's attention.

"It's a guy," he whispered to her.

"And he's crying..." he continued. Mimi shrugged at him.

"...about another guy," George said meaningfully.

"What do I do?" he asked when she said nothing.

Before she could speak, Mimi's headset rang. Giving him the "thumbs up" sign, she took her call.

Realizing that he was going to have to handle this on his own, George sat back down and took some serious deep breaths.

"Relax. Just have fun," he said to himself.

Listening to Nigel whine and sob on the other end of the phone actually made George a little nauseous. Nigel's voice rose in a crescendo, as if he were some kind of tormented screeching jungle bird. Finally, it was more than George could take.

"You must pull yourself together, Nigel," George admonished.

"You know very well that Ferdie's not cheating on you. You're just lonely; your heart and soul are desperate for a creative outlet. You're completely bored... with life," George continued sternly.

There was sudden silence on the other end of the line.

~

earing silky robes and stretching out on his plush sofa in his large, exquisitely ornate, and tastefully decorated apartment, Nigel held his phone to his ear, as if taking stock of what had just been said to him.

He lay motionless for a few moments before he quickly sat up and beamed a broad smile.

"Oh, my God, you are fabulous, Mr. Psychic," he said.

"I am lonely. I'm bored and of course Ferdie wouldn't cheat on me, the sex is too fabulous... You're so right, I am cheating on myself by not honoring my art. I thought I needed a holiday after finishing my last project. But no, I must create. Today."

"And stop torturing Ferdinand," George added.

"He loves you so much. You remind him of his mother, and that's not always a good thing. So cool down the whole... Diva routine. Ferdinand's a keeper."

The caller burst into tears.

~

igel cried, but he no longer sounded like a tormented bird. Finally, his sobs became sniffles, and he eventually stopped crying altogether.

Then he laughed out loud.

"Mr. Psychic, you're a Godsend. I feel so healed. It's as if I were a bubble made of light. I must go now, I have to make... art." Nigel hung up and was in such good spirits that he almost floated off the sofa.

~

George chuckled and smiled as he took off his headset. That was kind of fun, he thought as he rubbed his temples. He realized that Mimi had finished her call before he finished his. Standing, she had been listening. This time, she gave him two thumbs up. Her smile and the weirdness of the phone conversation made him laugh out loud.

George took another five calls in quick succession, his confidence growing with each. The more calls he took, the more he realized that, with this job, there were no wrong answers. All he had to do was simply listen to the caller's concerns and then give his opinion.

It was the first job he had where there were no exams to pass, professional qualifications required, or, indeed, anything to prepare beforehand. Nor was any training required. He was being paid to share his feelings, thoughts, and intuitions; having a broad encyclopedic understanding of the world of the caller and how it worked was not required.

He soon learned that people's concerns and preoccupations were very narrow indeed. People's fears and anxieties were generally restricted to love, career, or money, and health, with love taking up the lion's share of people's mental and emotional energies.

Even though his initial panic had eased, and he was beginning to enjoy himself, he was still secretly waiting for the boom to drop. He felt like he'd receive either a pat on his shoulder from Burton or be told that it was all a mistake… and he was not the right fit for the position, after all.

Until either of those moments happened, however, he was pleased to be on the clock and get a day's pay for his troubles. It would be the first paycheck he would have earned in several months.

After he hung up from his last caller, he considered it curious just how much people enjoyed talking.

He had spent several hours on the telephone, yet, in truth, he talked for very little of that time and mostly listened as the callers unburdened themselves of their cares and worries. In some ways, he felt like he was acting as an alternative to a therapist. And who's to say that what he was doing was any less effective than traditional talk therapy?

In between calls, he liked to stretch his legs. George would wander to the break room to get a beverage and nibble on some of the dark, delicious chocolate he found there.

Looking at the wall clock, he realized that he had time for another call or two. He hadn't discussed time particulars with Burton, so he guessed he'd knock off around six.

Upon arriving back at his cubicle, he was surprised to see that the video chat program on his desktop computer was lighting up. He had an incoming video chat call.

Shock and panic immediately ran through his system; he sat up so quickly that he almost fell off his chair. Jumping up, he popped his head around the partition to alert Mimi to his dilemma.

"It's the video thing," he announced with alarm in his voice.

"Answer it, honey. That's top rate," Mimi answered casually as she made notes in her work journal.

"How do I look?" he asked with such adorable insecurity that it put a smile on Mimi's face.

"You look marvelous, darling," she said. It occurred to George to wonder if she was saying that for real or in jest. Then he immediately realized that he needed to take the call without further delay.

~

George sat back down, straightened his tie, and faced his cubicle webcam. As he clicked "answer" on the screen, the face of a businesswoman in her fifties appeared.

She seemed a tad impatient. In the background, George could see that she was obviously calling from a high-rise, executive office suite.

"Sorry for the delay," said George."Thank you for calling The Third Eye, my name is—"

"Okay, here's the deal," the woman interrupted.

"All my advisors are saying to move forward, buy, acquire, diversify. They're preaching optimism, saying that the economy is generally sound..."

"Okay," said George to let her know that he was listening and understanding, so far.

"So, why am I calling a psychic?" she asked, "Because I don't get it. Obviously, I must have some doubts, right? There's a little voice in here," she said as the woman tapped her gut.

"And that little voice is telling me it's all BS; we're heading toward a cliff and that I should retrench and circle the wagons before the shit hits the fan. I can't get a straight answer from my people, so I'm calling you."

"I appreciate the call," began George. When she said nothing in response, he launched into sharing from his inner knowing.

"The truth is… and you know this, you are almost always right. Listening to that little voice has gotten you to where you are today. This is no time to stop listening, even if everybody else says that you're going off the rails or wrong."

"You're right," said the woman and waited expectantly for further information.

"In the future? Don't hire guys like your father... guys who don't listen to you. They don't understand what you're capable of and are so intimidated by you that they feel compelled to try and beat you down."

The woman stared at him. She was dumbfounded.

"Wow, you're good," she said as if everything now was crystal clear. "What did you say your name was?"

"They call me... Mr. Psychic," George answered, trying not to cringe.

"Well, Mr. Psychic, or whoever, this has been brilliant. To show my appreciation, I'm giving you a bonus, and if I call again, I'll ask for you. Got to go. I've got shit to handle, deals to back out of... and people to fire," she said and winked knowingly.

When the screen went dark, George let out a massive sigh of relief. All of his pent-up anxiety finally left his body. He had made it through his first video chat... and it hadn't been so bad.

~

Moments later, in the break room, George grabbed a bottle of water and some nuts. Mimi ate a raw food snack of some kind and drank a fresh juice.

"She gave me a bonus!" George excitedly told Mimi with the enthusiasm and energy of a little kid.

"It just flowed, the information was right there, and she gave me a bonus when it was already top tier for video chat." His smile was so broad that he felt like his face might crack.

"That's terrific!" responded Mimi."You were really busy there for a while. How are you finding it?"

George took a moment to reflect on the calls. He was flooded with new energy and emotions, and his experiences and thoughts emerged in a stream-of-consciousness declaration.

"The first call was horrible. She hated it, but you knew that already, but the rest were okay. I don't understand it. I've been doing what you told me, you know, relax and have fun with it. It's the weirdest thing… stuff comes to me."

Mimi silently waited to see if he had anything else to add.

"Whereas before," George said, "I'd censor myself, right? Here, I just let myself go. I mean, I make stuff up. Or rather, I use my imagination, that's probably a better way of describing it. The bizarre thing is that it seems to make sense to people. Plus, I feel close to them… I like talking to them."

"You're a natural, George," said Mimi, touching his arm with affection.

"I don't know. How come I didn't have it before?" asked George.

"Have you ever tried before?" asked Mimi.

"No, true enough…" answered George.

"You probably always had it but never tapped in. Also, fear blocks the channel. If we're afraid, the heart chakra tightens. It could close up almost entirely, and so… no flow. No flow, no info, right? Maybe the challenges you've been having lately have helped to open you up. Like, what have you got to lose? You know?" Mimi offered.

As George mulled over what Mimi was saying, Burton popped into the break room and beckoned to George. George gave Mimi a little wave goodbye and went over to his boss.

~

*T*he former accountant looked at Burton.

"Got a minute, George?" he asked. George nodded, and he couldn't help himself. He felt fear flood him. George's heart sank, and he figured there was a fifty-fifty shot that he was about to be fired.

As George followed Burton to his office, he grew more certain that this was the talk he had been expecting all day. As he walked, he took stock of the time and mentally computed the number of hours he had actually worked.

He wanted to be prepared with the figures, should Burton wish to draw up a check for his day of labor. Burton sat behind his desk and motioned for George to take a seat.

"So, Mr. Psychic. How was it?" Burton asked in a friendly tone.

"Honestly?" George asked. He wished to preempt his firing and save face by being the first one to say that he had no aptitude for the position.

"You really need to be a people person for this job, have a soft touch, or something. It's not me. It doesn't feel like a good fit..." George added.

"Well, then, that's perfect!" exclaimed Burton. George gave him a puzzled look.

"The fact that you think you don't fit in is exactly why you do fit in," said Burton, as if that made perfect sense to him.

"I'm not sure that I follow," replied George, struggling to understand.

"You go out there and ask every one of my psychics if they feel like they fit in. They'll tell you the exact same thing..." Burton stopped and looked expectantly at George.

"Do they not feel like they fit in?" George asked, trying to make sense of it all.

"Bingo," concluded Burton as he grabbed a printout of a spreadsheet. Placing it on his desk and turning it so that George could also see, he pointed at a column of numbers.

"There you are," he said.

"Where?" asked George, looking to where Burton was pointing. "What exactly is this?"

"This is a printout of today's calls by the operator. This column is you. You were on the phone just under two hours, total—right in the middle of the bell curve, which is a bit above average for a new hire. So don't worry if you have a bit of a drop off later," his boss said.

George tried to comprehend the data.

"We'll deal with that if and when it happens. Your cut is three bucks a minute, plus video chat bump, and three delighted customers, who definitely know that tipping is not a town in China... they each gave you a bonus!" Burton talked quickly and excitedly.

George's pupils instinctively dilated as his eyes followed the numbers to the figure in the total tally column.

"I made nearly $400 today?" he asked with amazement.

"I'd like to schedule you for 6-hour days," Burton wrote in his notepad.

"Feel free to go home once you hit or exceed your quota... does $400 a day work for you?" he asked.

George stared at the numbers as he computed some math in his head. He smiled giddily as he concluded that $400 a day and six-hour days would do very nicely indeed.

If he worked five days a week for fifty weeks out of the year, he could very nearly approach his old salary. It boggled his mind.

~

George spent the weekend catching up on chores like grocery shopping, deep cleaning his home, doing laundry, and getting in some good gardening work. While out caring for his rose bushes, George noticed Ed arrive.

Ed parked his station wagon on his driveway and, after getting out, sidled over to George's yard.

"Hey there, George," he said casually.

"Ed," greeted George, without turning his head. He could hardly believe the man's audacity. What the heck was Ed doing coming over to chat, after purposefully humiliating him a few short weeks ago?

"How're things on the job front?" Ed inquired, as if he genuinely gave a damn.

"Really good, as a matter of fact," George responded coolly.

"Oh, yeah? Found something?"

"Yeah. I... uh, I'm doing a bit of consulting," George said.

"Consulting? Really? Like business consulting? For accountants?" asked Ed, seeking clarification.

"Not so much for accountants," answered George, beginning to enjoy himself.

"Some business people, certainly. Different people. All kinds, I guess."

"All kinds, huh?" Ed repeated, confused yet determined to get some clear answers.

"What kind of consulting did you say it was? Being that it isn't accounting or business based?"

"It's different for everybody, depending on what people need," said George, relishing Ed's discomfort and being purposefully obscure.

The busybody squirmed, not getting the info that he desired.

"Yeah. Different consulting for all kinds of different people..." Ed summarized, hoping for further elucidation from George.

George coughed and continued to avoid looking at Ed.

"We'll see how it goes," said George, deliberately still vague.

"That's great, George. Good goin' neighbor," Ed stood waiting, hoping for something further from George.

Realizing that nothing would be forthcoming, Ed sulked and went inside his own home. George smiled to himself, and from the corner of his eye, he saw that Ed was peeking out at him from inside his home.

George did the math in his head again and realized that he could potentially make even more than he'd been making in finance and have way more fun doing so if he could meet or exceed his quota regularly.

*L*ater that evening, George sat at his home office desk and crunched actual numbers based on Burton's printout and projections of continued 3rd Eye employment. His retirement portfolio graph shot way up. It astounded him.

He could work less, have a lot more fun and less stress, and make the same money as he did in finance. Maybe, in the future, he could work a bit more and reach his retirement goals sooner. George smiled and allowed himself another glass of one of his very special Pinot Noir reserve wines.

*E*d stared out the window of his living room. That son-of-a-bitch was up to something. Ed knew it. It made him sick. Guys like George always come out smelling like roses, while the rest of humanity struggles and suffers.

For the love of Moses, he and his family hadn't been able to go on a vacation, a simple holiday, or much else in years. His kids needed after-school activities and summer camp.

It was the same old story—the "haves" and the "have-nots"—and he was sick of it. He determined to find out about George's new situation.

Did the guy really have a job at all? Maybe he was up to something criminal, those bankers, finance, money men types always are, he considered.

Ed's face grew tight and red with anger. He could hardly pay his damn cable bill on time, or feed his kids. Forget about extras, Ed had a beat-up POS car. The other guy had it all, including a big fancy house that one person could practically get lost in.

The jerk had not just one but two cars; one of which was a really sweet, expensive, beautiful car that Ed would almost trade one of his children for (one of the younger ones, who didn't have much personality yet).

He may be stretching a little in offering his kid, yet what would he give to own a car like Miss Betty? He could see himself driving in the sunshine, everyone on the road pointing, staring, and waving as he sailed past in that spectacular automobile.

Where does he go every day? Ed wondered. Isn't he smiling more now? I've never seen him like that, Ed decided. He has to be up to no good. It's probably crime, or drugs… or worse.

Well, no matter, Ed thought: I'll get that smug bastard no matter what I have to do. Ed, lost in thought, shrieked and nearly jumped a mile high when his wife clamped a claw-like hand on his shoulder.

"What you starin' out that window fer, Ed? Help me git the kids' supper. My ankles're swelling," Ed's very pregnant wife, Lindsay, drawled.

When she was exhausted, she spoke with a more pronounced Southern accent even though she and her family hadn't lived in the South in years.

She rubbed her protruding belly and wondered what to feed the four kids who were literally climbing up the walls, trying to see who could first reach a framed print of The Last Supper.

"Something's up with the neighbor, I know it," Ed said, as he continued to spy through the front window.

It occurred to him that, for several hours now, only one room was lit in George's house, the upstairs home office, which was a room George never usually visited at night. Oh my Lord, was George upstairs next door cooking meth?

Ed grinned evilly, thinking about how embarrassed George would be if he were busted for drugs. He could easily imagine the guy arrested by several policemen in the middle of the night, with all of the neighbors watching.

Everyone in the neighborhood would look out of their windows, as the police car lights created patterns of blue and red on George's lawn.

"That George has had a smug smile on his face the last couple of days," he continued. She grunted softly in response, yet said nothing.

"An unemployed man isn't smug, Lindsay, not unless he's up to something." Ed looked at Lindsay, expecting her to agree with him. Surely his wife would be worried about having a criminal type next door.

"Honestly, Ed, this obsession you have with George ain't healthy," Lindsay proffered as she picked up the kids' discarded toys.

"You don't understand. Something's going on, I just know it. I think he's into drugs," Ed said, and then Lindsay rolled her eyes at him, like he was an idiot.

He desperately added, "Yes, drugs or, maybe, gone all white-collar criminal on us. Next thing you know, it'll be the FBI using our house for a real stake-out."

Lindsay punched his shoulder lightly and shook her head no, like he was being brainless. Ed felt saddened that his wife was so downright disrespectful to him. George could be a criminal.

"Well, if the fibbers wanna use our house for a stake-out, they better pay. Now, you either help me git the kids some pork-n-beans or I divorce your sorry ass, right now. I mean it, Edward Shortall," Lindsay threatened.

There was something in her voice that made Ed nervous. Lindsay didn't joke about things like divorce. He sighed.

He knew that his wife was tired of trying to feed the family on love and good intentions. Try as he might, Ed couldn't seem to make his salary stretch.

He'd be damned if he'd crawl back to Lindsay's father, who thought they shouldn't have so many kids, and ask for yet another salary increase. The old man was as stingy and tight as they came and entirely disrespected that Lindsay was a good Catholic.

Lindsay's father and Ed didn't really get along. His father-in-law felt that Ed managing a single grocery store was enough, and Lindsay's daddy wasn't about to put his son-in-law in charge of enough stores to earn a real payday.

He wouldn't even give Ed more than a cost-of-living raise each year. Ed didn't know what he was going to do. They were church mouse poor, but he didn't see a way to rectify things.

Truth was, he didn't know what he'd do without Lindsay and the kids. The thought of losing his family, when he really had nothing else, made him feel sick.

As Lindsay stalked off to the kitchen, Ed peeked out the window one last time. He'd have to be sly in catching George, he reckoned.

"I'm gonna get you, old boy, just you wait," he said under his breath.

∼

*T*aking in the balmy night air, George paced in his beautiful back garden while he talked with his son on his cell phone. He breathed deeply, enjoying the scent of the flowers.

"It's kinda like personal consulting, son," he explained, not wanting to disclose his full hand.

~

*A*fter helping his wife prepare the meal, Ed finally joined his family for supper. He sat uneasily and looked distracted as he watched Lindsay and their four kids devour plates full of pork and beans.

After quickly finishing, Ed put his paper plate in the garbage bin. He then surveyed his family and got an idea.

"I'm taking out the trash," he declared. The man went and stood in front of the dirty white bin with the flip lid on it, which was next to the fridge.

"Got tired lookin' at it and waitin' on you to do it for me. We ain't got no trash, no more. I took it out earlier," Lindsay said harshly. Ed looked at her. Her feet were definitely swollen, and she looked drained.

Ed looked around desperately and grabbed two empty industrial-sized bean cans from the kitchen counter. Lindsay's eyes narrowed, and she shook her head slightly.

Luckily for Ed, one of the little ones started screaming about the fat piece in their pork-n-beans that their brother had stolen from his plate and eaten.

"This is trash," Ed said as he threw the empty bean cans into a garbage bag.

Lindsay looked at him and suggested that he might just be nuttier than a jar of peanuts, but then she was forced to intervene with the kids, who were now slugging each other. Ed took the trash bag with him and stepped outside.

~

$\mathcal{E}$d walked across his drive and stood in the darkness by George's trash cans.

He looked up at George's home office window to see if he could see George's silhouette, but he couldn't. Using his cell phone as a flashlight, he quietly snooped through George's trash and, apart from regular household trash, didn't find anything incriminating.

He figured that standing on the trash cans would give him enough height to spy through the window.

When he tried it, he quickly realized that he didn't have enough height. He missed a clear view through the window by less than a foot.

Grabbing hold of the window ledge, he tried to pull himself up. Desperate to maintain his balance, he feared that he was making too much noise.

~

$\mathcal{A}$t the rear of the garden, still on the phone to his son, George turned when he heard a noise.

"Let me call you back," he told his son, hanging up as he hurried around the side of the house to investigate.

In the semi-darkness, George saw what looked like a man's figure. A figure who appeared to be trying to break into George's house through the second-floor office window.

"Who's there?" he bellowed in an uncharacteristically deep and threatening voice. Looking around for a makeshift weapon that he could use, he grabbed an empty wine bottle from the recycling bin.

He lifted the wine bottle and strode toward the intruder.

"That you, George?" Ed called down, nonchalantly. He was just barely holding on to the window ledge, the fright of hearing a deep voice at first causing him to lose his footing on the trash cans.

"Ed?" George asked as he squinted his eyes to get a better look.

"I was just taking out the trash," Ed said as casually as he could, which totally belied his uncertain predicament.

Instantly out of breath, from clinging to the window ledge and speaking at the same time, Ed's feet pedaled air. He desperately tried to hold on and explain the situation at the same time.

"I was taking out the trash, and I thought to myself, does George have double-glazed windows? So I came to check," he added.

Realizing the ridiculousness of Ed's excuse, George's eyes narrowed. What is this idiot up to? He wondered.

"Are these double-glazed windows?" Ed asked again.

"Yes, they are," answered George, "So, to clarify, you're checking out the glazing on my windows? In the… dark?"

"The wife, she's, uh… for the kids, she thought we'd be better off getting double-glazed glass… for safety and to save on the electric, with the winter coming and all," Ed replied. His voice was now shaking with the strain of hanging onto the window ledge for all he was worth.

"My windows are, in fact, as I've just mentioned, double glazed. Reduces my winter heating bills by up to 7.2%. I can show you the numbers if you like," George answered. Ed was sweating now as he hung on for dear life.

"Are you… Do you need help?" George asked, now seeing clearly that Ed was practically swinging precariously from the window ledge.

Unable to hang on any longer, Ed fell to the ground and landed sorely on his bottom. Bouncing up as quickly as he had fallen, Ed stood with a grimace.

"Are you okay?" George inquired, genuinely concerned. Ed was standing strangely, as if he might have fractured or sprained something vital, or even strained his back.

"Oh, sure," answered Ed, as if everything was perfectly normal.

"I'll go tell Lindsay she was right… about the windows."

"Seriously, are you okay, Ed?" George insisted. "That was quite a fall."

"I'm fine," Ed answered as he turned. He hobbled, holding himself, back to his house.

George stared after Ed as his batty neighbor retreated to his house.

"Up to 7.2%? Wow. That's significant. I'll go tell the wife," Ed called loudly over his shoulder. Then he vanished from sight.

George shook his head and wondered what the heck Ed was thinking. Idiot.

~

*M*imi stepped into the 3rd Eye elevator wearing eye glitter and a diaphanous, incredibly flattering outfit. Wearing shades of lavender and teal, with sparkling crystal jewels, she looked more gorgeous than ever.

George had seen her in the parking lot but had been unable to catch up with her.

George sped up to the elevator before she could get away, and he stuck his hand in the door just as the doors were closing. The elevator doors bounced open again, and George got in.

"That was close," he said, and smiled.

"You almost got away."

So happy to see him, Mimi smiled in delight. Blushing like an adolescent schoolboy, George grinned goofily.

"Good morning, Mr. Psychic," the woman said as she successfully balanced a to-go cup of tea, her scarf, sunglasses, a set of car keys, and a handbag while putting on a very sparkly headband.

"Good morning, Mimi," George responded."How are you today?"

"I had a great weekend, and I am feeling the love this morning, George. How about you?" She looked at him and smiled. Accidentally dropping her keys, she juggled her other stuff as she bent down to pick them back up.

"It's a beautiful day. Things are definitely looking up," George said, and he reached down to retrieve her keys for her. As he leaned down, he was struck again by her radiance.

"You're looking very… sparkly… today, Mimi," he said. Their eyes met, and George's heart melted.

George grabbed the keys before she could, and he and Mimi stood up together.

She wobbled a bit on her strappy, delicate metallic heels as she straightened back up again and struggled to handle all her possessions.

George reached out and held her shoulders to steady her; she fell against him, upright and in no danger of falling, yet they were touching. He nearly swooned. She really was lovely, he thought to himself.

She seemed very happy that he was touching her, and he smiled. She grinned. It was a sweet moment, if not a little awkward for George, who felt himself get inexplicably nervous. He could smell the scent of her perfume or some kind of body product.

Was that her hair that smelled like flowers or strawberries?

Mimi regained her balance and could now stand on her own. George blushed as he realized that he was holding her a tad longer than he should.

Taking a step back, he peevishly put his arms back to his sides.

Even though he had gotten nervous being so close to her, he felt irritated that they were no longer touching. He took another deep breath and tried to guess what perfume she was wearing.

"Thank you, George," Mimi said sweetly. George struggled to think of something clever to say.

Ding! The elevator stopped with a jerk. Star Child got on, as George and Mimi held the door for her, and the two of them got off.

George realized that psychics must work all hours. Star Child was clearly finishing a shift or else on her way to her lunch.

"Good morning, Star Child," Mimi said.

"I have those three crystals to help balance out your aura and give you some protection."

"Thanks be to heaven," Star Child said.

"I haven't been sleeping... flipping abductions."

George tried to process their exchange. Star Child had been very nice to him the other day. He wanted to be helpful and congenial with his new coworkers.

"If the, uh, the crystals don't work for some reason... I have an outstanding physician that I can recommend," George finally suggested helpfully.

"Your doctor can stop ET abductions?" Star Child asked, really quite surprised by the possibility.

"Oh. No," answered George, now feeling quite embarrassed.

"I thought you said obstructions. You know..." The elevator door closed, and Star Child, who was by now bent-over laughing, almost hysterically, over what George had thought she'd said, had vanished.

~

*M*imi giggled softly, yet tried to hold herself back, to avoid hurting George's feelings.

George, wide-eyed, replayed the conversation in his head as he walked with Mimi toward their cubicles.

ET's? Had she really meant extraterrestrial abductions? "Was she serious?" George finally asked Mimi.

"Unfortunately for her, yes," replied Mimi.

"I hope this particular combination of crystals does what they're supposed to do and helps her out. Poor thing."

George didn't know what to think or even where to begin to respond intelligently, so he didn't. The two of them reached their workspace.

George immediately noticed how bare his cubicle looked compared to Mimi's, which was colorfully decorated and, well, sparkly. Curious, he picked up a clear pink crystal from her desk.

"Where'd you get all of this?" he asked.

"Oh, different places. That one came from Sedona. Some were presents. Around," Mimi replied casually.

"Do you ever worry that people might think you're weird, Mimi?" George came right out and asked.

"Why would I worry? I know that people think I'm weird. People always perceive anyone who isn't very much like them as a weirdo. Don't you think?" answered Mimi, unfazed.

"I guess that's about right," George responded, not quite knowing what to ask or say as a follow-up.

Mimi's headset rang for the first call of the day. She settled into her chair to answer it. George gave her a little wave, popped around the divider, and sat down at his bare-looking cubicle.

~

George took about twenty calls that day. As the day wore on, he began to relax and enjoy himself thoroughly. It greatly helped that each of the callers was courteous and expressed gratitude for the advice he imparted.

Even though he later discovered that the industry he was working in was considered "entertainment" and not something believed to be or offered as legitimate, he did genuinely feel that his occupation had value beyond mere amusement.

When he looked up the meaning of the word psychic, he discovered that the origin of the word was Greek and that it meant of the mind or mental.

Interestingly, to the ancient Greeks, the word also meant soul, and in their mythology, Psyche was the Goddess of the human soul.

All things considered, he still felt very reluctant to disclose his new profession to his family and friends. When they asked what his new job entailed, he would not fully disclose what he was up to.

He did fret about his decision a bit. George wondered to himself exactly why he wasn't forthcoming with full disclosure. Something about his reluctance didn't feel quite right. Was he ashamed to tell them?

He felt that it might be that he knew his family well enough to know exactly what their responses would be.

His friends and family wouldn't understand, he reasoned. Invariably, they would give him a very hard time about it. At best, they would say that it was not a "real" job. They would look down on him for taking the job. They might think that he was a failure because he couldn't get a better job. Their shame would become his shame.

At worst, they would probably consider him as being involved in some kind of con job, or perpetrating a hoax upon innocent people based on greed, opportunistic business practices, akin to the sort perpetrated by rascals and unethical conmen.

George decided that there was no way that he could ever tell his conservative, proper, classy, educated family about his new job.

The week passed quickly. Every day was relatively pleasant.

Sometimes, he had a caller who didn't like his brand of "reading," and he would recommend that they try another psychic.

Burton and he had a short conversation about it. His boss assured him that, at any time, he could tell a client that they weren't a good fit, energetically or otherwise, and that they could consult with someone else, if they so chose.

As he settled in, George found that the work itself was enjoyable.

It was a laid-back, creative environment, and people were quite social. George didn't believe that he'd ever had a work week pass so enjoyably or indeed, so quickly.

He was still keeping mum about the details of his new job and telling no one any of the details. Still, George had yet another highly successful and surprisingly satisfying work week. He regularly exceeded his quota and really loved his new job.

Yet he was exhausted and ready for the weekend when it came.

~

Friday night, he relaxed. Saturday morning, he did chores and caught up at home.

When he was invited to an outdoor BBQ at his son's house, George hated to deceive and yet decided to remain vague about his position. He'd avoid specifics until they got fed up asking and stopped inquiring. In truth, it was none of their business, anyway, he considered.

"I don't understand why you're being so evasive about what you do?" George's son expressed his frustration.

He and his father drank imported ale and manned the outdoor grill. In the background, Jenn chased little Georgie IV around George's backyard.

"There isn't much to say," responded George II as he flipped a burger.

"I can't say much, anyway. Client privacy and all that. It would be pretty boring to you anyway."

"You've never been employed as a consultant before. I'm just curious. What's a typical day?" his son dug deeper.

George realized that there was a lot that he could share, without giving it all away.

"I'm on the phone all day, sometimes video conferencing. Clients call with specific questions in mind; they're looking for solutions. I do a great deal of listening. Periodically, I give my two cents' worth," George answered very casually.

"And you're making better money?" his son asked, as Georgie IV ran over and grabbed George's leg.

"Well, for now, it's about the same, sometimes better, and better in the sense that I'm working fewer hours," George answered honestly.

"Of course, with consulting, like being a freelance operator, you never know for certain what the sales will be." At a thump to his lower leg, George II looked down.

Georgie IV clung tightly to his grandfather's leg. Reacting awkwardly to his grandson, George patted the head of the sticky-fingered child.

He wasn't quite sure what to do. Pick him up? Throw him a toy? Chase him away? His throat got tight, and he felt awkward and uncomfortable. Fortunately, Jenn came to George's rescue and scooped the toddler up into her arms.

"You're looking great, Jenn," George commented. It was true. Jenn was fit and strong and obviously happy with his son. George felt a pang that he almost couldn't identify.

Then he realized that, for the first time in quite a long while, he was feeling happy. Although he was pained that his child had been brought up in a broken home, he felt joy that the boy had managed to make a good marriage himself.

"You look pretty good yourself lately," Jenn replied and stared at her father-in-law. George blushed a little and automatically stood up straighter, tucking in the slight bulge in his tummy. He was finally looking more like his former fit self, except more relaxed and happier.

"Are you seeing somebody?" she asked while looking him up and down speculatively. As the man looked much happier than he used to, Jenn instinctively knew that usually meant one thing.

"Yeah, Dad. It's been years. When are you going to get back out there?" George III asked, as if he thought his father couldn't possibly already be seeing someone.

"I've been alone so long I wouldn't know how to do all that dating stuff... plus, I'm just too busy. I have a lot on my plate with my new job. Being unemployed really affected my finances," said George.

Even as he was saying all of those things, he realized that he didn't entirely mean them. He actually felt like he was almost ready to ask Mimi out.

She didn't really fit in with his family, but then he didn't have to introduce them to each other. Heaven forbid, he couldn't see Mimi meeting his parents. That would be way too odd.

"You've gotta stop being such a cheap bastard," George III whispered to George II, but not so quietly that his wife didn't hear him. Jenn duly punched her husband in the shoulder.

"Language, mister," she chided.

"And don't be so mean to your father. He'll introduce us when he's ready, right, Dad?"

George thanked the heavens that Jenn had interrupted, although her intuition was so accurate, it was disconcerting.

He'd about had it with George III's impertinence, and he didn't want to fight with his son. He could hardly believe that George III had called him a cheap bastard.

George IV squealed and tried to escape his mother's arms.

George II quickly escaped to check out the meat on the grill. Ah, perfection, he almost said out loud as he scooped up the beef patties.

"You'll both be the first to know," replied George II casually to Jenn and his son.

"Now, who's ready for burgers?"

~

Wearing his headset, on a call, George paced his tiny office space.

"That's right, you can. The past... is in the past. It's time for you to stop looking backward, trying to heal what is over, and focus more on the present. Be honest with yourself. Take action from where you are now, not where you think you should or ought to be. You can only play with the cards you were dealt and not the cards that you think you should have been dealt, right?" George said.

Then he listened for a long moment.

"Determine your goals and dreams and move toward them..." he added and waited.

"Of course, thank you for calling Mr. Psychic and the 3rd Eye."

George ended the call and popped his head over the cubicle wall.

Mimi looked up at George and smiled. She had a tarot reading spread out in front of her on her desk as she talked into the phone. He grinned at her.

She smiled and rotated her finger, indicating that she was wrapping up in just a moment. George draped himself over the cubicle separator and watched Mimi work.

"There is deception in the cards. Either he's lying or you are. You don't have to tell me what's really going on, I don't want to know more than what you've already said... but at least be honest with yourself." She listened to the caller for several minutes, nodding her head.

"Right action requires honesty, honey... Okay, sure. Thanks for calling," Mimi added.

Mimi ended her call and took off her headset.

"Come and see something," George said and smiled warmly.

Mimi walked around to George's cubicle. He waved to indicate the framed photographs of antique cars that hung on the walls and the car models that lined his desk. Mimi looked carefully at his art and the cute little car models.

She smiled up at him.

"When did you start liking antique cars?" she asked.

"It was my father's hobby. He used to take me with him to classic car shows when I was a kid. I own a pre-war Buick," he said proudly.

"It still runs?" asked Mimi.

"Like a dream."

"Then who owns the Prius you drive to work?" she asked, a little confused.

"I do. I get 60 M.P.G. In the city," he said, obviously boasting.

George caught Mimi smiling to herself as she checked out his new artwork.

"What? You don't like it?" he asked.

"They're lovely, George. But I'm just wondering what the real George likes."

"The 'real' George?" he repeated. When she said nothing, he spoke again.

"What do you mean? I don't get it."

"You're not your father's little boy anymore, George. It's okay to be you, now."

"This is me," George replied, "who else would I be? I don't understand."

"This is the safe, George. This is predictable, smart, left-brained, dependable, nicely turned-out George. This is George, who pleases and is like his father. This is George on display for the world," she said, sweeping her arm to indicate the new arrangement of his space.

George looked around and tried to take in her words.

"I want to see authentic George. Not good, perfect, polished George... in his three-piece custom suit, doing everyone proud. When is the real George going to show up?"

"I'm George. There's only one of me... and this is me," he repeated, baffled and feeling miffed that she didn't seem to be listening.

"It is lunchtime. Let me take you to lunch?" she asked. George nodded begrudgingly, still peeved. What did Mimi mean by 'real George'?

George drove slowly, conservatively, in his Prius while Mimi fluffed her hair and checked her makeup in the mirror on the passenger-side sun visor.

Arriving at Mimi's favorite Japanese restaurant, a hostess led them both to a cozy, almost intimate seating area at the rear.

Mimi removed her shoes, and George followed suit, thinking that it must be the correct etiquette. They then stepped up to a raised platform and sat on the floor next to a raised, traditional table.

"This is fantastic," George remarked, impressed by the décor and overall authenticity of the restaurant.

"It's probably one of my favorite places to eat, and I knew that you'd like it," Mimi admitted, as she settled her position.

"Tell me about yourself, George. Something you don't normally tell people."

"I do have a secret... vice," George confided in a low tone.

"Do tell..." Mimi whispered and leaned in closer.

"I collect netsuke," George said proudly.

"A what? You collect what?" Mimi whispered.

Her eyes were wide, as if George had said something quite sexy and more than a little mysterious. George pulled a tiny dragon netsuke figurine from his pocket.

"It's a miniature sculpture. Originally, they were used as little toggles or fasteners to close something, like a tobacco case or pouch for holding money. Traditional Japanese garments didn't have pockets. Look at the precision... the artistry," he said, passing it to her gently.

"Oh, my, that's beautiful," the blonde beauty said as she carefully examined the piece of portable art.

"It takes a lot of precision and true artistry, and skill to create netsuke. From ancient times, the Japanese have been blessed to create wonderful, delicate, detailed, and exquisite works of art. The netsuke may be animals, insects, human figures, or mythological creatures, or the like," George instructed.

"That's interesting," Mimi said, meaning it.

"The netsuke are really diverse... aristocratic to working-class, celestial to terrestrial, the sublime and the vulgar. Sometimes they are meant to be taken seriously, and sometimes more as a joke."

"They sound like people," Mimi supposed and smiled.

"They are citizens of my world," he acknowledged.

"It's beautiful," shared Mimi, looking over the delicately carved dragon in her hand.

"That's my favorite," George admitted. "Even though it is hard to tell what it is meant to be."

"Thank you for sharing it with me," Mimi said and touched George's hand. He flushed slightly and, without second-guessing himself or thinking about it, took her hand in his own.

"You have others just like it?"

"It would take me months to tell you all about the ones in my collection," he said.

"I'll look forward to that," Mimi said, shamelessly flirting with George. She looked closer at the dragon.

"It's a dragon changing form. You're changing form, too," she mused aloud.

"I suppose I am," he said. Then George looked again at the netsuke.

"It's a dragon?"

"It sure looks like a dragon… to me," Mimi said, holding it at an angle.

"I can see that," George said, somewhat surprised that he had never noticed it before.

"I knew it was a mythological beast of some kind," he confirmed, still squinting at the figurine.

"Did you know that in some cultures, Dragons represent manifesting dreams into reality?" she asked.

George shook his head to indicate no, as Mimi continued, "And also a dragon totem indicates a need for strength, courage, and fortitude… It's a message of balance and magic, and the messenger itself suggests that we tap into our psychic self and perceive the mystery and wonder of reality."

"No, I didn't know that. I just know what I like," he confessed. "I guess the real me likes to collect pieces that draw out deep peace and contentment."

"That's what the netsuke makes you feel… or think?" Mimi asked. He nodded slowly in response.

"That sounds fairly Zen, George," Mimi said, leaning into him.

"How so?" he asked.

"Zen is all about attaining enlightenment. Zen Buddhists seek peace and contentment, to experience that altered state, through meditation," she replied. George thought about her words for a moment.

"I like to hold my netsuke, look at them—well, really contemplate them. I suppose it is a form of meditation… it definitely puts me into a state of peace and contentment," he replied.

He then paused to think before adding, "I never thought of myself as religious, per se, but what you've just told me about Zen Buddhism… it feels like me." Mimi nodded happily, truly interested in George's thoughts.

George was quiet for a long moment, holding and looking at the little dragon netsuke, which indeed, now that he looked at it more carefully, did appear to be changing form.

George looked into Mimi's eyes. She smiled. He put the dragon netsuke into her hands and gently brushed her eyes closed with his fingertips. Mimi giggled; the sound of her laugh made George smile.

"What does it make you think… or feel," George asked her.

Mimi tilted her head sideways and, after a long moment, spoke.

"In happy hours, when the imagination… Wakes like a wind at midnight, and the soul… Trembles in all its leaves, it is a joy… To be uplifted on its wings, and listen… To the prophetic voices in the air… That calls us onward," Mimi said, pausing meaningfully, to punctuate the deeper meaning of the poetic words.

When she was finished speaking, she finally opened her eyes.

"That was beautiful," George said. The tenor of his voice revealed that he was fairly astounded.

"Henry Wadsworth Longfellow," Mimi replied softly.

George nodded and grabbed Mimi's hand, holding it tight. He looked happy and upset, near tears, simultaneously.

Mimi's smile slipped away, and her own bright, shining eyes became luminous, as they also filled with tears. Neither of them spoke. This… this moment, George thought, is living in truth.

He wondered to himself how being around Mimi could, so rapidly and easily, make him a more real, honest, and authentic man and person.

On their way out of the restaurant, George and Mimi stopped in a gift shop annexed to the eatery. It was filled with exceptional and unique gift and décor items. There were silk kimonos, tea sets, an array of exquisite origami papers, some marbled with metallic colors, sake sets, stationery, and other items.

"I know that I don't have to tell you this, but a certain amount of office decor is probably tax deductible," Mimi said, laughing.

"As if I need an extra incentive," he replied.

George was enthralled. He touched silk, picked up and put down chopsticks, checked out bento boxes, pottery, teas, lanterns, plush stuffed animals, and more.

George purchased several items, including a desktop Zen garden, scented candles, and incense.

~

That night, George found himself angry. At first, he didn't know what was wrong. He felt tired and irritable in a way that he normally did not. It wasn't work fatigue.

He really enjoyed his new job and wasn't tired at the end of the day, unlike in his previous job.

He lay on his bed and closed his eyes. In his mind's eyes, he saw Mimi's face, and then he felt the pinch of anger, almost rage. His throat tightened.

How dare she? His face and chest got hot. He felt like punching something or crying. How dare she say he didn't love old antique cars? How dare she suggest that he was a... a fake.

Hot tears slipped from his eyes, and no matter how tight he scrunched his eyes and face, he couldn't stop crying. Then he felt rage over being fired from Teleseismology Hub NS.

He thought about the years, the decades, of showing up early and leaving late, and the challenge of garnering the respect of higher-ups.

He'd had to grovel and bust his ass to get a very average salary.

In retrospect, he felt sickened by the disrespect of his former peers, the arrogance of, and the irritation of dealing with, fucking incompetent young MBAs. They had no experience or know-how, yet wanted to earn high salaries while expending the minimum effort possible.

He was the opposite. Yet he'd pissed away a significant chunk of his life, and now his house of cards was tumbling down around him, while he desperately tried to grab onto and save the individual cards… the components of his life.

He tried not to feel hate for Mimi and immediately got so angry that he sat up.

He punched his pillow and shouted the word angry, repeatedly. He was shocked when his thoughts suddenly flipped from his love interest to his father.

He clenched his jaw and cried and punched his pillow as hard as he could. For a while, after he felt nothing but pure, unadulterated rage, he laughed and cried at the same time.

He felt a strange, curious alternating mixture of fury and grief, and at the same time, things had begun to seem more than a little comical.

Within fifteen minutes of sustained anger expression, he stopped crying. The feeling was gone. Remarkably, his insides felt empty of rage and anger.

He laughed out loud, and his laugh felt new and different. Thoughts rapidly skittered through his mind. It was exhilarating. He felt connected to his emotions and thoughts in a way that he hadn't previously.

As he held his awareness on his thoughts and emotions, contemplating them simultaneously, as if they were a beloved netsuke, he had a series of revelations. He wasn't always honest. He often said or did what he thought was right, not what he felt like saying or doing. It was a habit.

He had a habit of trying to be appropriate. He had a habit of saying and doing the right thing. He had mistakenly thought that there was only one correct way of doing things. He didn't always say or do what he wanted, or at least he hadn't in the past, for most of his life.

In a way, in that sense, he was a liar. A person who behaved in a certain way, trying to be something, striving to be a particular type of person, a pretentious, approval-seeking human, was inauthentic.

He felt sick over the fake, dishonest person that he had been. What a bull-shitter he generally was. He had always been so afraid of upsetting people, of alienating people, of somehow, in some way, being imperfect.

He thought about Miss Betty. Was she a wonder of early auto genius? Most definitely.

But did he genuinely love classic cars?

Would he have loved vintage vehicles if his father hadn't taken him several times each year in childhood to see classic cars, men sitting smoking and drinking around their vehicles parked in the sunshine, on display, on a Sunday afternoon in summer?

In the thoughtscape of his mind, he was a boy, in the golden sunshine and pleasant heat of summer, spending rare time alone with his father. In the background, happy families looked at cars or ate picnics while sitting on the green, soft grass, vendors sold brightly colored balloons and delicious-smelling snacks, and people were laughing and talking happily.

Looking around, he saw shiny, bright open hoods propped up, glistening creamy paint jobs, pristine engines, and immaculate leather seats. He could feel his father holding his hand, pulling him along, describing the attributes of each vehicle in great detail.

In hindsight, George recognized that he had perceived the attention from his father—a rarity in his youth—and the shared experience of the old cars as an expression of the old man's love.

It was practically the only time that George Beresford II was alone with his father, George Beresford I. Emotionally energized and understanding himself in a way that he never had, George opened his eyes, got up, and went outside. He then went into his garage to look at his antique roadster.

He felt the urge to polish the vehicle, and as he did so, he appreciated the glimpse and scent of another era she offered, an era in which he, for once, had felt his father's love.

In that moment, George realized that, although the car was truly a thing of beauty, it was his father's attention and love that he truly craved.

The realization stunned him. He kept considering the idea. He turned the thought over and over in his mind as if it were a piece from his netsuke collection.

He went back into the house and fell into a deep sleep from which he woke more rested than he had felt in months.

~

The next morning, upon reaching his cubicle at the 3rd Eye, George removed all his antique car prints and miniature models from inside.

He then extracted the beautifully crafted desktop Zen garden that he had purchased and several of his Japanese netsuke sculptures from a cardboard box. Taking time to tune into the ideal placement of the objects, he carefully placed the items around his space.

He arranged and rearranged until he felt entirely satisfied.

The last thing he did was pull out and place a zazen meditation cushion on the floor, then he arranged a vase of lucky bamboo.

A few moments later, Mimi poked her head around the cubicle partition. She immediately noticed and smiled broadly at his new arrangement. He grinned happily.

"What do you think of the real me, now?" he asked, and George spread his arms wide to indicate his new decor.

"I like it very much, Mr. Psychic," Mimi said and smiled.

George motioned for her to come closer. She opened her eyes wide as if to ask, Who me?

George nodded, and Mimi came all the way into his cubicle. As soon as she was close to him, George grabbed her into his arms and hugged her tight. Mimi hugged back.

"I really like you," he whispered into one of her ears. She squeezed him tighter and giggled against his chest. He looked down at her bright and shining, pretty face.

"I really like you," she admitted. George blushed and felt happy. An influx of energy and emotion made George feel like he could jump over the sun.

Then both of their headsets rang, and they separated. Mimi went to her cubicle, and George sat down and answered his first call of the day.

~

George sat in his home office and smiled approvingly as he input updated figures from the latest work printouts into his computer. Somewhat distracted by the task at hand, he noticed and answered his ringing cell phone.

"Frank, what can I do you for?" he cheerily asked.

Frank, his investment broker, was on speakerphone.

"Georgie, I am loving the figures you're making in that new job," he began, "and I know that you'll be back on track soon, but that margin call looks likely. So get ready."

George immediately gripped his cell phone more tightly.

"How much and how soon?" George asked, giving the call his full attention.

"When I know, you'll know," Frank responded.

"The maintenance margin is just about to hit 40% of your equity. Obviously, I have no way of knowing when, or even if, it'll happen. Just wanted to give you a heads up, so you could plan. Keep up the good work. Gotta go. Cheers."

Frank hung up. He was, quite obviously, not remotely concerned with how what he'd just said to George might affect his client. In fact, Frank was already thinking about his upcoming golf game.

George hung up the phone. His forehead creased with worry. He had no way to come up with that kind of cash. There was no way on the planet that he would ask his son or parents for the money.

It made him feel a little sick: so much change, so rapidly. Well, he would have to figure a way out of this, somehow.

The only way he knew of increasing his income immediately was if he worked longer hours. However, he was not too keen on doing so. That might prove too exhausting and could end up with him resenting the work that was so fun and fulfilling. Also, too many calls might reduce the quality of his work.

So far, clients had been entirely happy with his psychic readings. Yet he had to find some way to get that money.

Another possibility was to request more video chat calls. Those paid top dollar, although he had been reluctant to take many of them up to this point.

He knew that his lack of enthusiasm for video calls stemmed from his discomfort presenting himself over the webcam. He had an impossible-to-shake fear that he would be one day recognized by someone he knew or someone who knew someone he knew.

George pondered the problem. There had to be a solution that would allow him to take the higher-profit calls and eliminate his fear of being discovered as a psychic reader.

Perhaps if I were to disguise myself in some way, he thought.

~

The next morning, George poked his head into Mimi's workspace. He still wore his customary suit and tie, but today, for the first time since he'd taken the job, he had skipped the vest. George looked a bit more relaxed as a result.

"Hey, handsome," Mimi greeted him playfully.

"Hi, Mimi," responded George.

"You look terrific, as always." He looked her up and down and wondered how she was still single. She was so pretty, positive, and sweet. She charmed him. He smiled into her eyes. She spoke.

"Thank you," Mimi said softly. Something about the way that she spoke and the look in her eyes almost distracted him. It definitely made his heart skip a beat.

Forcing himself to concentrate on the matter at hand, and since she didn't have a client just then, he entered her cubicle.

"I need your help," he said, lowering his voice as he got closer to the blonde.

"Of course, Georgie. Help what with?" Mimi asked.

"I've added my name to the video-chat roster," he said.

"Sparkly," Mimi said.

"It's about time you got on board that gravy train. Video-chat is where the big money is."

"Exactly. Except, I didn't expect to be here long, so I didn't think things through," George began, adopting a more confidential tone.

"What if someone I know calls and recognizes me?" He waited for Mimi to respond.

"That happens more than you would think. My advice would be to… remain professional," Mimi answered casually.

"The way that you would if you ran into your therapist or doctor out in public."

"No, you don't understand. I don't want people I know to recognize me at all," George finally admitted.

"Why not?" Mimi asked, her voice filled with genuine surprise.

"I don't have to explain why not," George replied, somewhat testily.

"It's a personal preference. I do not wish to be recognized. Ever. Period."

"O-kay," answered Mimi, looking at him more closely now. This was obviously a sore point of contention for him.

"Are you ashamed of what—"

"Mimi," George interrupted."I don't want to… this isn't a discussion. I was hoping that you would guide me, your professional opinion regarding an ideal solution, not give me a discussion of whether or not you believe that I need or should want a solution. So, will you help me out or not?"

"Of course I'll help you, George," she said warmly. She placed her hand upon his.

"You're my best friend. I could never deny you anything. You can use anything of mine that you want."

She pulled off her glasses and a neck scarf and held them out.

George removed his suit coat and put on Mimi's artsy eyeglasses. Thinking a moment, he took off his tie and wrapped it around his head like some funky bandanna. It kinda worked.

Looking at himself in Mimi's makeup mirror, he smiled at how goofy he looked. He looked like a semi-deranged, New Age, hipster guru.

He thought no one would recognize me now, but just to be sure, he tried on a carved Japanese mask that completely obscured his face.

He decided that wearing the mask was going a bit too far and made him look like a comical kabuki actor from an over-the-top Japanese melodrama, so he removed it.

He looked at himself once again in the mirror. On the verge of being satisfied with the disguise, he examined his reflection while tilting and turning his head at several angles and poses.

"How does this look?" he asked Mimi. She looked him up and down and suppressed a smile.

"If I were your medical doctor, I wouldn't recognize you," Mimi replied, answering the primary question underlying the entire charade.

Just then, a tone rang, indicating that George had a caller initiating video chat. His eyes widened. Mimi laughed and sparkled at the call's obviously Divine timing.

"Perfect synchronicity," Mimi said.

"Take the call and test it out."

~

George hurried to his cubicle, nervously faced his webcam, and clicked his mouse to answer the call and allow the caller to see him on full-color HD video.

To his utter and complete surprise, Frank, George's smooth-talking, very polished, handsome young broker, appeared on the computer screen.

"I'm told you're the best," Frank said nervously.

"Frank?" George said in a shocked tone.

Frank acted dumbfounded, truly stunned, and yet terribly pleased.

"Wow, you're good! Damn! I didn't even use my real name with the operator," Frank finally said, after a long moment.

George leaned almost off camera to hide and altered his tone of voice, speaking more deeply than he normally did and faking a vague, indeterminate accent.

He mysteriously waved the Japanese mask, as if he were conducting some kind of purposeful spiritual ritual, and then put it on to add to his disguise.

"What can I help you with... Frank?" George asked.

"I'm going to make this real simple. No details. Is the portfolio in question going to go up or down?" Frank blurted out, his voice fraught with tension and fear, which he was also conveying well with his body language.

"It's going to tank," George blurted out, and was as surprised with his answer as Frank was.

"I'm not going to say that didn't hurt, but I like a straight shooter," Frank said.

"Question number two. Dyno Tech. Sell or buy more?"

"You understand that I'm not a stockbroker and I can't give— " George began.

"Yeah, yeah, save the disclaimer. If I thought I'd get a straight answer from a broker, I wouldn't be calling a psychic, would I, champ?" Frank said and laughed.

"Guess not," George said.

"So. Dyno Tech?" Frank said.

Mimi was standing, out of Frank's sight, yet leaning over the cubicle partition, listening in.

"They had a patchy start, a weak IPO, but products are strong... plus they're about to get a serious cash injection from an unnamed source. Then, boom... the stock'll explode... maybe go into triple digits before the end of the next quarter. So buy, buy, buy," George said, without thinking about it.

Again, George's own words surprised him.

Frank peered at George closely, yet still didn't recognize him.

"You're not a broker? I'm not saying I buy into this psychic hocus pocus, but if even a tenth of what you say is true, you can safely regard me as a repeat customer. Nice head piece, by the way, and thanks," Frank said, meaning it.

The man clicked off and disappeared in an instant. George sighed with relief.

~

*M*imi peered at George and came around the partition.

"How'd you know all that stuff? Is it true? About Dyno Tech?" Mimi asked George breathlessly. George shrugged, his eyes wide, making him look a bit like a helpless little boy.

"I've never heard of Dyno Tech in my life. All that info... it just came out of nowhere. That was Frank, my actual financial advisor IRL. See, that's exactly why I wanted the disguise, in case somebody I know calls me! What did I just say?" George said nervously.

"You just gave away the biggest stock tip since... since Google went public. That man's going to make a fortune," Mimi said excitedly.

"But what if it wasn't true?" George asked.

"Of course it's true, George. It felt like the truth, I got chills. We keep telling you you're a natural," Mimi said, still quite excited.

She then spoke so softly that George had to lean toward her to hear her well, her voice now filled with concern.

"But, here's the thing, you'd better be careful. I mean it," Mimi said.

"What?" George asked and looked around nervously.

"This psychic stuff isn't something to play around with. The universe isn't your personal piggy bank. People have a destiny, a life purpose..." Mimi replied.

"Okay. And?" George asked, not getting it.

"Our job is to guide people, to help them in a time of spiritual crisis," Mimi clarified.

"Not to help them financially, you mean?" George asked.

"If you help them spiritually, help them connect with their heart and better understand how to heal their issues... to guide them into stepping firmly onto their Soul path... they'll usually get in touch with their abundance," she added.

"Oh," George said and thought hard, trying to take all of that in. Mimi then smiled and hugged him.

"Your job isn't to give people the information they want... It's to give people the information that their hearts and Souls need," she whispered.

George nodded as if he understood... but he really didn't. Then they both got calls and had to pause their conversation.

~

Mimi and George had an ongoing dialogue, in between each of their client telephone and video chat calls, throughout the rest of the day.

When she and he were both free, Mimi leaned on the edge of George's desk, and they discussed the nature of the soul, the purpose of life, and other subjects of a philosophical bent.

Despite the serious nature of their discussions, they still managed to find some levity and humor. At one stage, both George and Mimi laughed so hard that they had to be shushed by Star Child, whose cubicle was all the way at the back.

If George's headset or video chat rang, Mimi headed to her cubicle.

Then George would talk into his headset or video chat with a client.

Sometimes he paced his tiny space and talked on the headset, finding that he could feel the difference when he was moving versus when he was sitting still.

It seemed to him that, when he was moving, he felt more open and information flowed more freely.

Sometimes Mimi would get a call or video chat and dash off to answer it in her cubicle.

When Mimi left, if George had no calls, he sat in meditation on his zazen cushion.

As the day passed, George looked and felt more at peace and comfortable in his cubicle.

He looked around his office space and realized that his day had actually been even more pleasurable than previously.

George's headset rang, and he noticed that he was pleased—in fact, entirely eager—to answer the call.

With every client call or video chat, his voice naturally became more soothing and loving.

Near the end of the day, he was on a call, entirely present to the caller, listening raptly as the caller wept in response to his counsel. At times, he interjected, sharing additional information.

George finally finished the call and disconnected. It was surprising to him how increasingly energized he was by this work.

He wasn't even truly hungry, and it was almost time for dinner. He stood and stretched, noticing how terrific it felt to use his body.

George went to the restroom and returned to his cubicle several minutes later.

~

When he returned to his space, Mimi was sitting on George's desk playing with a Japanese mask.

"What's up?" George asked happily, very happy that, yet again, she was back on his side of the relatively close quarters they practically shared.

"Was that a date?" Mimi asked curiously.

"Was what a date?" George replied.

"Our Japanese lunch thing," Mimi said and smiled.

George felt his heart tighten when she smiled like that. She was really attractive—dazzling, in fact—and he still wasn't used to being in such proximity to any woman, much less an extremely friendly, earthy, beautiful woman who said that she loved him, that they had shared many lifetimes together, and made it clear that she liked to be physically close to him. Phew. It made him dizzy.

"Did you want it to be a date?" George asked when he caught his breath.

"Did you?" Mimi asked.

"What are we talking about?" George asked, seriously backpedaling because he was experiencing a fear that had become more like terror.

His throat grew tight, and he struggled to breathe normally. Calm down, he told himself. To distract himself, George picked up and then decided not to eat a piece of gourmet dark chocolate.

"About when are you going to ask me out on a proper date?" Mimi asked and giggled. Her bell-like laugh, pure joy, and the sexy way she looked at him melted his fear and his heart.

He found her quite adorable and entirely alluring at that moment. His heart skipped a beat. In his mind, he replayed what she had just said. He considered appropriate responses, then spoke.

"How about this Friday night?" George said.

"Really?" Mimi said, ebullient.

"I'm hosting a little dinner party for a few close friends. Will you be my date?" he asked.

Mimi smiled hugely, and her eyes sparkled even more.

"I'd like that very much," Mimi said and leaned toward him. George felt his cheeks grow warm at her proximity. He nodded.

"Very well, then," George said. Mimi gave him a quick kiss on the lips and turned to leave.

George blushed, entirely stunned by the kiss.

Then a thought flitted through the edge of his mind, and he found himself asking her a question, partly because he didn't want her to go just yet and partly because he felt a burning desire to know the answer to his query.

"How was your doctor's appointment?" George blurted out.

Mimi turned and stopped, surprised.

"My... my doctor's appointment?" Mimi repeated.

"Didn't you say— " George began to clarify.

"No, I did not," she replied firmly.

"And especially not to you. How did you know?" Mimi asked, her eyes wide. George was perplexed and tried to remember. Didn't she mention it to him sometime?

"I don't know," he finally said.

"A lucky guess? Chance, maybe," George added.

Mimi said, as she was departing for real this time, "If I've learned one thing in life, there's no such thing as chance, handsome."

He blushed, surprised and pleased that she just called him "Handsome."

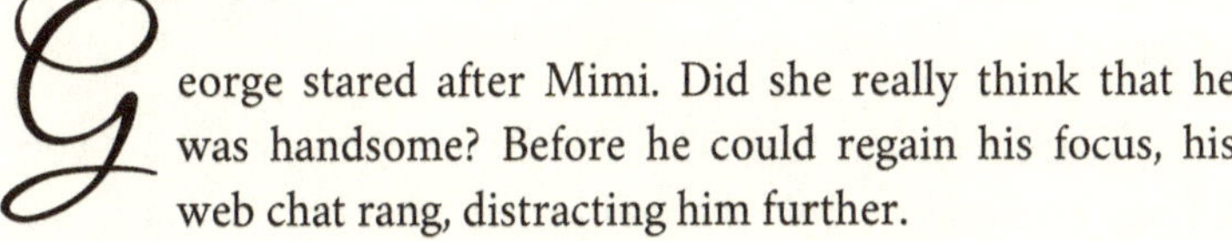

George stared after Mimi. Did she really think that he was handsome? Before he could regain his focus, his web chat rang, distracting him further.

He hurried into disguise and managed to get himself together before the caller hung up or returned to the operator. George faced his webcam and clicked his mouse to answer. On video was Jellie, a skinny Goth girl in her early twenties.

"Thank you for calling the 3rd Eye. You've reached Mr. Psychic," George said calmly.

Jellie spoke incredibly slowly and paused for long periods, forcing George to be extremely patient. He smiled pleasantly and breathed deeply.

"Mr. Psychic... thank God..." Jellie said breathily, "I'm Jellie."

"Hello, Jellie," George replied.

"Hi," she said and gazed at him raptly. Her eye makeup was thick and black; it made her look a bit like an angst-ridden teenage Cleopatra.

"How can I help you?"

George finally asked when it became clear that the girl wasn't going to launch into a story about her issues. Jellie bit her fingernails and stared at him for a long, awkward moment.

"It's my... parents," she finally admitted dramatically and then fell silent again.

Jellie stared at George. George waited patiently.

"Yes?" George finally said encouragingly when it seemed like no additional information from Jellie would be forthcoming. She dreamily gazed at a spot above her head.

"They... don't get me," Jellie finally admitted, her voice becoming a whisper.

"They're from another generation. Of course, they don't get you," George said and smiled. She nodded, focused on his words, and tried to comprehend what he was saying to her.

"You remind them of their flaws, their ignorance. They're also probably a little afraid of you, but mostly they're afraid for you. They're afraid of their future and of... dying. They're worried about when they'll die and won't be there for you, since you're an only child," George added in a constant stream.

His eyes were firmly locked on those of the girl. Jellie's eyes widened, and then she dropped her gaze.

"Really?" Jellie asked, with her eyelids half-closed, in her dreamy, breathy, child-like voice.

"Really," George confirmed. Her eyes opened, and she stared at him.

"Is that why... they keep telling me... what to do? Trying to... control me?" she managed to get out.

Although she still spoke quite slowly, it was obvious that she was managing to interpret George's words and extract his meaning. George nodded. She bit her lip and tilted her head.

"They know what worked for them. They want things to work for you," George added.

Jellie paused for a long moment. She got lost in thought, and George did his best to let her take the time she apparently needed to process these ideas fully.

"That is so... just so... entirely helpful," Jellie finally said, and her eyes were shiny as if she were truly and deeply emotionally moved by the concepts that George had just shared with her.

George intended to remain quiet and give Jellie all the time she needed to reflect, yet he found himself speaking again, saying words that weren't in his mind and which came out without effort.

"When your mom wants you to wear something besides black? It's not about you. Just means she's afraid," George said quietly. Jellie leaned forward and took in every word. He spoke again.

"Black reminds her of depression, and your mother doesn't process these ideas fully, having struggled with death and funerals. She knows that, bar some disaster or unexpected incident, one day you'll be attending her funeral and she'll be dead and unable to help or protect you anymore. Both of your parents are terrified of leaving you alone."

Jellie was horrified and amazed by these utterly new concepts and ideas. The awareness of these startling and upsetting insights illuminated her face.

She began to cry. At first, she cried quietly and quite softly. Then she cried loudly, sobbing, gulping in great breaths of air.

George looked around nervously, even though he was the only person who could hear her since he was wearing his headset. But her eyeliner—her black Egyptian-looking eye makeup—was smearing down her red face.

Her face on screen, covered with tears, was wailing and in obvious, terrible pain.

To George's great relief, no one paid the slightest bit of attention to his call. He realized with some great relief, although he hadn't really noted it before, that the background was filled with a fairly loud babble as psychic advisors spoke to clients.

All of the other advisors' attention was riveted on their clients (whether on video chat or a telephone call). The advisors who weren't on calls were drinking water, resting, or doing other things, heading to the break room or bathrooms, and paying no one else the slightest bit of attention.

A short time later, Jellie had finished crying. She was radiant and appeared truly happy. She let George know that she would call him again.

She thanked him so profusely that he felt almost embarrassed by her appreciation and compliments. He had mostly shared common sense, he thought.

Time passed rapidly for George. His headset rang, or his computer signaled a video chat call, and he would answer. Mimi was equally busy. George sometimes paced his tiny cubicle space while talking.

He always wore his evolving Mr. Psychic getup, which now included funky eyeglasses, a bandana, and a half-cut Japanese mask.

Time passed in a blur of calls, and truthfully, he didn't always remember everything he had said when he was on a call. He began to love his job even more.

On Wednesday, Mimi and George snuck a real kiss in the break room. It happened quite by accident.

One moment, he was eating his snack, standing up to chat to Mimi as she made herself a cup of herbal tea, and the next, he was grabbing her around the waist and kissing her.

She snuggled against him in response, as if it were the most natural thing in the world.

There was a certain kismet in the flow of their interactions. Often, George and Mimi would arrive at work at the same time or find themselves leaving their cubicles and walking to the elevator side-by-side—all completely unplanned.

At home each afternoon, after a day of giving readings, George gardened, meditated, listened to music, or exercised. He felt and looked better than he had in years.

On Friday, George concluded a video chat and then put his head on his desk to rest for a moment. He was so happy. It felt strange. He didn't trust it. He took a deep breath. It helped.

He got up from his desk and sat on his zazen cushion. George had begun meditating regularly in between client calls.

Sometimes he held a netsuke, and other times he just sat. The effects of the meditation attempts were cumulative. He began to feel a deep sense of peace almost immediately after sitting down. He sat, focusing upon his breath, aware of the air going in and out of his lungs, as he breathed slowly and deeply.

His headset rang and he took a call. He was relieved that it wasn't a video chat.

His head itched; he scratched it. He was definitely ready to get his kooky getup off his head. The voice of the caller began to squawk in his ear, and in one moment, he was entirely mesmerized by the caller. He listened carefully and waited until it felt right to respond.

Burton strolled the floor and surveyed his psychics. Passing by, he joyfully watched Mimi and George work. His smile and being were radiant. Call volumes were up. Profits were up. Morale was up.

The entire organizational vibration was up. Happy-making it was, for all.

~

Yet again, Ed stood at the window in his living room. Exhausted from a long and utterly boring day at the grocery store (training a new clerk who entirely lacked ambition, drive, and initiative), he stared out into the darkness of the evening.

Lindsay, mixing bowl in hand, joined him.

"Now what, Ed?" Lindsay, her belly even larger, said petulantly. She really wished Ed would pay more attention to her and the little ones. His obsession with the neighbor was downright weird.

"That car… that car in George's driveway," Ed sneered and indicated with his head. Lindsay looked at George's drive.

Mimi's car, a VW bug, was parked beside George's Prius.

"What about it?" Lindsay said, a moment later. It was just a car. Ed was so weird.

Why hadn't she noticed this about him before they were married, when she had a passel of guys interested in dating her?

"I've never seen that particular vehicle before," Ed said quite ominously.

Lindsay was now thinking that her husband had gone totally demented.

"You gotta be joshing me," Lindsay said and laughed at her husband. Ed ignored her laughter.

"He's got a woman in there... or worse. I'd put money on it," Ed said, and his voice was hard and mean.

~

In George's home office, Mimi watched George prop up a mirror and sit at his desk. Mimi admired a color printout of George's retirement graph.

It revealed the upward climb, and ultimately the apex, of his old plan, which was framed and hanging on the wall. She mistook it for artwork.

"I like this," Mimi said, analyzing it.

"Life is full of peaks and valleys, but eventually, we all get ahead." She smiled. Turning to George, she added, "I love how modern artists trust their inner visions and express them in their work." George frowned.

"Oh, that's not art. Those are my financial projections... Well, they were my old projections, from my other job. I was doing very well before," George corrected.

"Still, I love the colors," Mimi said. Then she looked at the computer screen. She saw a similar graph, with current projections, based on George's new job.

"Mr. Psychic seems to be doing very well, as well," Mimi noted.

"Only as long as I can keep up the disguise," George said.

"I was hoping you could help me with that... again."

He sorted through a magician's costume kit on his desk. It included a mustache, a black cape with a red lining, a black top hat, a black wand with a white tip, a black vest, and a red bow tie.

"Mr. Psychic doesn't really need a disguise, does he?" Mimi said playfully.

"The glue first... and then the mustache?" George asked and, at Mimi's silence, added, "You did say that you would help."

"And I will. Haven't I been helping you since day one?" Mimi replied. Then she took a peek into George's box of stuff, "Let me see here."

~

*E*d peered out the window of his living room, using a ginormous pair of high-powered binoculars. His oldest child, a daughter, Edwina, about ten years of age, watched him curiously.

"What are you looking at, Daddy?" Edwina asked. He smiled at her, and the gap between his two front teeth was especially evident. Edwina was his eldest child and his namesake.

"Neighborhood watch, Sweetie Pea. Daddy's on the lookout for anything suspicious. Gotta protect my offspring, and your mama," Ed said.

Lindsay entered from the kitchen. She had obviously been stuffing a chicken; she held the lifeless creature in one hand and some herbs in the other.

"You got a pair of binoculars, now?" Lindsay asked. Her voice was filled with irritation. Here she was going without any help at home, and Ed was wasting hard-earned dollars on expensive boy toys.

"Just keeping the fam safe, Lindsay," Ed whined in a tone meant to placate his wife.

"Can I see?" Edwina asked.

Ed put the binoculars in front of his daughter's eyes.

"Tell me what you see," Ed said to his daughter.

"I don't see nothing," Edwina said petulantly.

Ed directed the binoculars so they are pointed at Mimi's VW bug.

"Check out this car. Tell me about the owner," Ed instructed.

"I don't see anybody!" Edwina said, already bored.

"That's why we have to do some detective work," Ed said, "Now, look very closely."

"Now, Ed, don't be infecting our Edwina with your mental issues," Lindsay said. She wasn't sure if she should shoot her hubby down.

Although she was partly freaked out that he might be giving their daughter unhealthy ideas, she was partly happy that her hubby was finally spending time with one of the children.

Edwina stared through the binoculars at Mimi's VW bug. Ed leaned over her shoulder and pointed. Lindsay headed back to the kitchen. Ed was weird, but he was the only father Edwina had.

"See... The car's clean," Ed said to his daughter.

"There's a pink fluffy steering wheel cover and a flower. So, the owner is a woman."

Edwina nodded and tried to understand their detective work.

"Should we call the police?" Edwina asked. Her tone was hopeful. It would be pretty exciting if the neighbor got arrested, and maybe she and Daddy could be special witnesses like that show on TV. Maybe the whole family would have to go into the witness protection program and could move somewhere exciting.

"Not yet, sweetie. Let's find out more about her first. Out-of-state plates mean she's not from around here. See the bumper stickers?" Ed said.

Edwina looked at the bumper stickers on the VW Bug. One read "Greenpeace," one read "Free Tibet," and another had a strange but kind of nifty series of symbols that read "Coexist."

"She's a leftie..." Ed said, his voice dripping with hate.

"She's left-handed?" Edwina said uncertainly.

"Worse. Much worse," Ed said ominously, "she votes Democrat. See the sparkly things hanging from her rearview mirror? Crystals..."

"It's a sparkling angel. She has a crystal angel, daddy," Edwina said, her voice filled with excitement as she jumped up and down.

"Yes, she does. And what does that tell us?" Ed asked his child. Edwina stopped peering through the binoculars and looked up at her father, her eyes wide.

"She's really cool and good?" Edwina said happily and smiled.

"Could be..." Ed said.

"But it all adds up to a young woman, maybe late teens, early twenties, if that..." Ed's words trailed off as he had a profound thought.

"Oh, my God," Ed said and ran out of the living room. Edwina stared after him.

Inside the kitchen, Lindsay mixed cookie dough in a bowl. Ed stormed in, with Edwina trailing quickly behind him.

Lindsay had just opened a bag of chocolate chips and was measuring some out. Then she poured them into the bowl and stirred them, all the while looking at Ed. Ed stood, breathing hard, wildly staring around the kitchen.

"Guess what? You'll never guess, honey. George has an illegitimate child, a secret daughter... that he's never told anyone about. After years of searching for him, she has finally tracked him down and she's confronting him right now, this very minute!" Ed said. He spoke in an overly dramatic voice, as if he were tattling on George.

Lindsay rolled her eyes and shook her head, like Ed was a maniac. Lindsay finished stirring in the chocolate chips.

She began dropping spoonfuls of chocolate chip cookie dough onto a well-worn cookie sheet. Edwina came over to beg for a taste. Lindsay tickled her and gave her a chocolate chip.

"Honey, don't be a dip-" she said and mouthed the last word, so that only Ed could hear, "shit."

Ed frowned at his wife. What was it with women? Why'd they have to be such harpies, always trying to control a man? Sometimes he could entirely understand why the divorce rate was so high.

"Now you go get them kids ready for bed, right now," Lindsay said in her "I mean business" voice. Edwina covered her mouth to hide her grin. It was hilarious when Mommy told Daddy what to do.

"Oh, to be a fly on that wall," Ed said, as if Lindsay hadn't spoken.

"I mean it, Ed," Lindsay added in a warning tone. She was getting sick and tired of Ed's near psychotic obsession with their neighbor George.

Lindsay wondered if maybe she ought to speak to her father. If her Daddy gave Ed more work to keep him busier, maybe he could give him a raise, too.

"I'm going, I'm going," Ed finally said, as if he were a childishly sulky teenager talking back to his irritating, overbearing mother. He took Edwina by the hand and they left the kitchen.

"Kids," Ed shouted from the living room, "It's bedtime." Lindsay smiled to herself and put the baking sheet full of cookies into the oven.

~

Inside George's home office, Mimi put the finishing touch on George's disguise. He was now entirely unrecognizable.

Dressed all in black, he now had a mustache, sideburns, a swami hat made of shiny material, and wore the black cape with the red lining. He looked imposing and mystical.

"There, George. All done," Mimi said. George scanned his face in the mirror.

"You are truly amazing," George said. After looking himself over more carefully, he turned to Mimi and asked, " Are you sure the turban is better than the top hat?" She nodded.

"No question. You are much less recognizable and much more interesting in the turban," she said.

George nodded, and Mimi beamed at him. He leaned toward her, her eyes widened, and she grinned. The doorbell rang just before their lips met. George pulled back, sighed, and checked his watch.

"Somebody's early. Be right back," he said, irritated to have lost the chance to kiss Mimi.

~

Still in full disguise, George hurried down the front hall toward the front door. He opened the front door and was quite surprised to see his neighbor Ed.

"Oh, I was looking for George," Ed said awkwardly.

Realizing that Ed didn't seem to recognize him, for fun, George impulsively decided to experiment a bit and see if he could really and truly get away with his disguise. He faked a French accent.

"George... he ees not here... at ze moment," George said and struck a dramatic pose in the doorjamb.

Ed took a step back and flushed bright red. Dear Lordy, he hoped that George's "friend" wasn't gay. Maybe George was gay. Maybe that's why George's wife left him.

Was this guy hitting on him? The dude was standing somewhat suggestively in the doorway.

"Uh. I'm sorry, we haven't met. I'm Ed, George's neighbor," Ed mumbled awkwardly, blushing and backing up hurriedly. I had better get out of here, right now, he thought to himself.

"Oui, Ed," George said and batted his eyelashes at Ed. Ed blushed and, standing as far away as he could, while remaining in proximity, proffered a hedge trimmer.

"Just came to return this," Ed said awkwardly. George fingered his mustache and gave Ed a peculiar little smile.

Ed gulped and prayed that he wouldn't crack up, lose it entirely, maybe punch the guy, right then and there. He coughed.

"I vill give to George… upon his return," George said. He took the lawn tool and, with a quick scuttling movement, grasped and kissed Ed's hand.

Ed gasped and yanked his hand away.

"Uh, yeah," Ed said and then quickly scurried backward. George gave Ed a little wave goodbye and smiled to himself as he saw Ed gag. Then George closed the door on Ed, who appeared a bit sick and very puzzled.

~

*E*d, very disturbed, furtively tried to get a look at the interior of Mimi's car as he walked down the driveway. He couldn't see anything of interest in the vehicle.

Maybe, he thought, the car belonged to the weirdo. Good Lord, he thought, it would make total sense if George were gay and that guy were his secret lover.

Ed felt sick. He was fairly positive that he had thrown up a little in his mouth when that freak kissed his hand. Then he walked back to his home, mumbling to himself all the while.

Ed entered his home, continued to grumble, and headed straight for his barcalounger. To distract himself, he flipped television channels for a while, yawned, and finally fell asleep in his chair.

~

Mimi approached George in the front hall. He was peering out the front door through a tiny peephole. She put her hand on his shoulder. He jumped and gave a tiny little shriek. Mimi laughed and laughed.

"I'm so sorry, George, I didn't mean to scare you, oh my..." she said. Obviously, terribly amused, she had a hard time stopping laughing.

"Was it an early dinner party guest?"

"No. He's just a very nosy neighbor, and guess what?" George said and gave her a big smile. He didn't know me from Adam!"

George whooped and picked Mimi up and whirled her around.

"The disguise totally works! Even my next-door neighbor doesn't recognize me!" George proclaimed.

"George est mort," Mimi said, giggling and kissing George's neck, "vive Monsieur Psychic!"

"Monsieur Psychic!" George repeated and laughed.

"I like that!"

George let himself go for a moment and kissed Mimi thoroughly. Pulling himself together, he checked his OMEGA Rattrapante Chronograph. It gave him the same thrill that it always had. It was time, he decided.

"Okay, let's get me out of this getup. They'll be here in an hour," he said. Mimi nodded.

~

An hour later, in the living room, George offered appetizers while Mimi moved around pouring wine for Marco, James, and Bethany.

They stared at Mimi, who, in her inimitable way, radiated goddess-like good vibes. Her apparel was sexier than usual. Her sex appeal was partly due to the low-cut neckline of her deep pink blouse, the fit-and-flare patterned lavender faux snakeskin ruffly long skirt, and the strappy high heels that she wore.

Her long blonde hair was shiny, curled, and hung in soft waves. Her makeup, in pale glittery lavender and pinks, was delicate yet shimmering.

The woman also looked like she felt sexy. Mimi had the look of a woman who did yoga often and got regular massages. The way she looked made George wish they were spending tonight alone in his home.

She sparkled in a way that George had grown accustomed to; his friends, however, could not take their eyes off of her.

"Where did you find this marvel, George? She is so not your type," Marco said slyly.

"How would you know what George's type is, Marco Polo?" Bethany asked Marco.

"I don't think anyone here could be so presumptuous to know George's type, considering none of us have ever seen him with a woman," James said drily. Mimi laughed happily.

"What I mean is... Mimi is so... colorful. You all know what I mean," Marco said defensively.

"I don't know what you mean, Marco," Mimi said, and her laughter pealed like bells ringing. Her laughter was so spontaneous and happy that George almost hugged her. He had to stop himself.

"No offense, but—" Marco began.

"Go ahead and put your whole foot into it, Mr. Polo," James said.

"George is just so... starchy," Marco said, fumbling to find the right words.

"Perhaps you don't know him as well as you think," Mimi said. No one said anything, and she spoke again.

"You probably haven't spent time with him in a while."

Marco shrugged. It was true: he hadn't seen George much lately. None of them had.

"Not lately," Marco admitted. George gave him a look as Marco sounded a little sad.

"Meaning?" Mimi inquired kindly. James and Bethany exchanged a glance.

"In Marco's defense, George hasn't been George very much, of late, and we've all been busy... sort of gone our separate ways," James said quickly.

George coughed. Mimi and the others looked at him.

"You do all know that I am very much here... in the room?" George said laconically.

"You think this is bad? You should hear what we say behind your back," Bethany said and giggled.

Off the guys' looks, she added, "Joking. But, not really."

James laughed, and Marco rolled his eyes.

"I didn't get how you two met?" Marco said. He sounded genuinely curious.

Mimi looked at George. He smiled at her and shrugged.

"We met at work," Mimi said.

"You're colleagues?" Bethany said, incredulously. She had to hear this story. Mimi didn't at all look like the type of woman who worked in finance.

"That's right," George said.

"Tell us about your meeting," James said.

"Yeah, Mimi. Your 'How I met George' story. We wanna hear it, we're all ears," Marco stated.

Mimi looked to George for direction. How much was George comfortable in revealing?

"I wish it were a magical, wonderful 'our eyes met' story..." Mimi said delicately, then immediately saw that George was more than a little hurt by her words.

"...but it goes much deeper than that," she added, and he relaxed. Now she had everyone's attention. She moved around, making eye contact with each of them. Mimi looked deeply into James' eyes as she began the story. He was captivated.

"Have you ever looked into someone's eyes so deeply that you can see their very essence? I'm talking about looking beyond their ego and personality, into their very soul itself?" Mimi asked him.

Riveted by her words, James didn't reply. She turned to Marco, who squirmed.

"Looking so deeply that you see all lives and expressions of who they've been? The hurts, disappointments, the pain they've endured for eons, their desire to love and be loved?" Mimi added.

She turned and addressed Bethany, who was as transfixed as James.

"Have you seen another so clearly that you see not just the many masks they wear but what they are capable of? What they are evolving towards, their true nature, their journey, potential, and destination? Maybe even their life purpose? Seeing their heart and soul in all its beauty and splendor?"

Mimi, now breathless, was overcome with intense emotion. She remembered the moment as if it were happening again, exuding love and devotion.

She gazed at George. He didn't blush or look away. He met her gaze, and it was as if they were alone. The others held their breath.

As if suddenly stripped bare of their artifice and pretentiousness, James, Marco, and Bethany hung on Mimi's every word and looked back and forth between George and Mimi.

An incredibly sweet, yet sensual, energy created lines of static electricity between George and Mimi. After a long moment, an entirely pleasurable eternity, Mimi turned to face the three.

"And that's what it was like... when George entered my life, and our eyes met," Mimi said.

George did blush then, as Mimi raised a glass to him.

Bethany brushed a tear away, and Marco and James finally took a much-needed breath.

"To an amazing man... the tenderest of souls, my soul mate, George," Mimi said. Everyone raised their glasses and drank silently, bereft of words.

The rest of the evening was spent in more casual conversation.

For the first time, George felt a little awkward around his friends and genuinely different from them.

There were moments when he didn't have anything to say. He caught up on what Bethany, Marco, and James were doing, yet he found he didn't feel too comfortable talking in-depth about how things had been for him when they asked pointed questions.

It was clear that whatever friendship the four of them had shared previously, something had changed.

Their superficial banter was the same, and they didn't try to engage him deeply at all. Much of the evening was spent in friendly patter, eating, and drinking.

~

*L*ater, George and Mimi cleaned up.

"And these are your closest friends?" Mimi asked pleasantly.

"You didn't like them?" George said defensively and shoved some leftovers in the fridge.

Realizing that she had upset him, Mimi took some time to think carefully about her response.

"More relevant is whether they like you or not. And clearly, they don't seem to, at least not very much. They seem to have trouble accepting you for who you are," Mimi finally responded.

George was hurt but knew she was speaking the truth. Mimi walked back into the living room.

"Selfish? Pretentious? Arrogant?" George asked, following her.

"For starters," Mimi agreed.

"That describes nearly every human... on this entire planet," George growled.

"No, George. It does not," Mimi said softly and looked around for something to pick up.

"I mean that if it weren't for the people whom you imply are self-obsessed and pretentious... I wouldn't have any friends," George said, like he actually believed it. Mimi stared at him, entirely horrified.

"Present company excluded," he added as an afterthought.

She picked up a trio of empty wine glasses and walked with them toward the kitchen.

"I'm just saying, you could connect with people more aligned with your soul," she called over her shoulder to George. He shrugged and rolled his eyes as she left the room.

"Maybe. Honestly, I don't even know what my soul is," George thundered to be sure that she could hear him in the other room.

"Maybe you could meditate on that," Mimi responded in a quiet voice as she walked back in.

He looked at her and nodded. He realized that part of him was terrified. Would Mimi reject him or his love if he wasn't "spiritual" enough, or totally in touch with his soul, or something? The thought horrified him.

Then he wondered, and the thought was even worse: Did she think he was selfish, pretentious, and arrogant? Before any of those fears could take root and become beliefs, Mimi had traveled across the room and was in his arms.

"I'm sorry for saying anything, George," she said breathlessly.

"It's rude and judgmental of me; it's just that I love you so much and want you to feel free to be yourself."

She was really and truly sorry; it was apparent. He could literally taste her positivity, joy, and love for him. He melted with relief into her love and held her tightly.

~

*L*ate that night, inside his bedroom, George tossed and turned before settling into deep sleep. Starlight shone silver on the thick carpet of the master bedroom.

It grew later, and with a soft sigh, George deeply entered REM sleep, his eyes moving rapidly back and forth underneath his closed eyelids.

Sitting inside his cubicle, wearing his headset, George was deeply and intently focused on giving a reading when he heard a noise.

Looking up, he saw that his cubicle was surrounded by practically everyone that he knew in real life: his parents, his son and daughter-in-law, his neighbors, his old boss, broker, and colleagues.

Like a distorted, whacko fun house experience, George's family and friends pointed and gestured, made disapproving faces, were embarrassed, angry with, and/or laughed hysterically at him.

George turned bright red with shame. He began to shrink fast, first becoming a small boy, until he was tiny.

The smaller George shrank, the more the people around him laughed and laughed.

He turned to run away, and his tiny feet, scrambling for traction, made scratching noises on the desk.

Scratch. Scratch. Scratch.

His tiny feet couldn't get any traction on the surface of his clean and shiny desk. The harder he tried to run away, the more the distorted, warped, and terribly frightening faces of his friends, family, and coworkers laughed and laughed.

Scratch. Scratch. Scratch.

The wind blew, and a tree branch scratched against George's bedroom window. The dappled silver starlight on the carpet disappeared as clouds covered the sky, and it began to rain.

George bolted awake and sat upright, terrified. He looked around wildly. He was both shocked and relieved to realize that he had only been dreaming of an intense and very public shame.

Scratch. Scratch. Scratch. He looked at his bedroom window and realized that the sound of a tree branch rubbing against the house and window had woken him. He smoothed his covers and lay back down to try and return to sleep.

~

The next morning, George, in his new "Monsieur Psychic" disguise, took the elevator up to the 3rd Eye offices. He met Star Child in the elevator. Sipping a to-go cup of hot coffee, it took her a moment to recognize him.

"Oh, George, it's you," she said.

"Did you get the message? Burton needs to see you in his office first thing." George, already uncomfortable, didn't even bother trying to explain his disguise. Shaking his head to indicate the negative, he looked like a deer caught in the headlights.

Burton wants to see me first thing, he repeated mentally. That can't be good news.

"Uh, how are your... are the...uh, did you stop the abductions?" He finally managed to blurt out nervously. Star Child couldn't help but giggle at his innocence, coupled with his disguised demeanor.

"Oh, my Goddess, you won't believe it, but Mimi's crystal combo really worked," she said.

"Oh, thank... thank goodness," George said, and he gave her a little wave as they got off the elevator and went their separate ways.

When it rains, it pours, George thought to himself as he walked towards Burton's office. This is it. Burton is going to fire me and everything: my life, my savings, everything that I've worked for is going down the drain. He felt numb inside.

eorge got to Burton's office and saw through the open door that Burton was meeting with two men and one woman who appeared to be higher-ups.

Too far away to catch Burton's eye, George entered and tried to act nonchalant. He wasn't sure if he should stay.

"You wanted to see me, Burton?" George said when Burton finally acknowledged him with a look.

"Come in, come in, George. Take a seat," Burton said happily.

Everyone stared at George. He grew more uncomfortable, knowing that, in his turban, cape, and heavy makeup, he must have looked ridiculous to the smartly dressed business people.

Burton's smile grew huge as he pulled up a chair for George to sit in.

"No, you're not being fired," Burton whispered cheerily so softly that only George could hear.

George almost imperceptibly sighed with relief as he sat just to the side of the two men in suits.

The business people whispered to one another, and one of them looked at George and smirked. George paid them no heed, but he was still concerned about whatever it was that Burton wanted from him.

"Quite the contrary," Burton continued, and smiled.

"Guess what I've cooked up for my newest star psychic?" Then Burton looked at one of the business gents, Ben. George looked first at Burton and then at Ben.

"Ben, why don't you set it up?" Burton asked nicely. George remained flabbergasted. What was happening?

Ben stood up and promptly gave a multi-media presentation, accompanied by images showing a grand mix of housewives, teenage girls, some frazzled, unkempt, or overweight, and other quirky-looking females.

Everyone in Burton's office, including George, paid rapt attention.

"We've looked at the extensive data on typical 3rd Eye clients for the past three years. Sure, there are outliers of all kinds, including the incredibly wealthy persons who are of every orientation and gender, yet the trends outside of those outliers are clear. We discovered a large distribution of lower class to lower middle class, left-leaning artistic types, most of whom are primarily female and often monetarily and love challenged," Ben stated. Everyone present, including George, nodded.

It made sense to George. Most of his callers were women in need of relationship, life purpose, or other advice.

"Until now," Ben said. At the click of a button, the presentation revealed a businessman in a power suit with a briefcase. This final picture stayed on screen.

George stared at it, perplexed. He sure hoped they didn't expect that, just because he had a background in business, he could somehow change their demographics all by himself.

"What we haven't had are highly successful, right-leaning, sharp, put-together business types with serious disposable income. But, since Mr. Psychic came on the scene, that has all changed, quite rapidly and dramatically..." Ben said.

George was flabbergasted. Could that be true? He was changing the company demographic?

"Ally," Ben said, pointing to the woman in a red suit. Ally stood to speak.

"Not to label or judge anyone, we've all been there, right? But for the purposes of this meeting, we'll refer to these two different categories of clients as loser types and winner types," Ally said.

Unable to stop himself, George actually slapped his hand against his forehead. Sheesh, that was rude, he said to himself. It's like these business people are clueless that we are all souls on a human journey. There is no failure, no loser, in this journey.

Ben picked up and waved around a large graph revealing that "Winner Types" were now outnumbering "Loser Types." Everyone in the room, except for George, applauded enthusiastically.

"The times they are a-changin', people," Ben said. "And it's happening all by itself."

"Mr. Psychic appeals to the conservative, logical, rational-minded winner type that most psychic hotlines would give their eye teeth for. We weren't seeking them out, but rather, they were drawn to us, to him, Mr. Psychic, by an undeniable, like-attracts-like… energetic force. And it's a game changer, people," Ally said, dramatically.

"Thank you, Ben and Ally," Burton said, standing and smiling at everyone. Ben and Ally sat down.

"And to Mr. Psychic," Burton said, sweeping his arm wide to indicate George. The business people, including Ben and Ally, applauded George heartily. He blushed.

"You ready, Sam?" Burton asked and nodded at the other consultant. Sam stood.

"We envision a national ad campaign aimed at attracting our newest and highly desirable client demographic… 'Winner Types,' the crème de la crème of potential psychic clientele," Sam said.

Sam clicked through various concept print ads, all of which featured George without his new disguise. George squirmed in his seat.

No, this wasn't going to be possible, he thought to himself. Anyone who knew him would immediately recognize him. This would not suit. This would not suit at all.

Sam adopted an announcer's voice as he spoke, "Mr. Psychic's the new kid on the psychic hotline block… and he understands professional and world-class problems all the way from the general office room floor to the exclusive penthouse office suites of the captains of industry. He'll tell it to you straight, in language you can understand. He will almost never use words like "energy," "vibration," or "feelings" because he's just not that type of guy."

"He's like you," Ben added, as he stood up to join in or help out. George wasn't quite sure.

"He knows the score. He understands your need for a terrific Return On Investment and just how critical the bottom line actually is... He wears a suit and he shaves every day... just like you."

Sam nodded at Ben, who sat down. He was extremely pleased with himself.

"We're still working on the actual copy, that was just to give you an idea," Sam concluded.

"Of course," Burton replied, "I think George totally gets the idea. Don't you, George?"

Oh, George got it all right, but he swore to himself that it was never, ever, going to happen. He wouldn't allow it. George couldn't believe how corny the entire pitch sounded, but then again, late-night infomercials weren't known for their slickness and intelligence. Deciding to keep his thoughts to himself, for now, George forced a smile and reluctantly nodded.

"Okay, everybody, terrific work," Burton said, ending the meeting.

"Now, leave me with my superstar financial-whiz-kid psychic, already," he said, jokily.

The trio of suits was extremely excited and chattered amongst themselves while they gathered their to-go lattes, folders, briefcases, and other items and left the room.

Once alone, Burton and George proceeded to hold a staring contest where neither of them seemed willing to talk first or even be the first one to break eye contact. After what seemed like minutes when it was probably only seconds, George won.

Burton looked down and then finally broke the silence between them.

"I really don't see what your problem is, George."

George frowned as he spoke. He tried to speak kindly and carefully, but his ire was obvious.

"The problem is having my face pasted on billboards and the sides of buses and God knows where else. No. I won't do it. I won't allow it. It's out of the question," George said.

"Are late-night infomercials completely out of the question?" Burton inquired.

"Especially late-night infomercials," George replied, his voice unusually high-pitched.

"I thought you were happy here, that you loved your job?" Burton said, and he meant it.

"I do love the job... as Mr. Psychic. I do not love the job as George Beresford the Second! I'm sorry; it's a step too far. I'm glad for the boom in business, but I can't be your... your... 3rd Eye spokesperson," George said.

He could just imagine his mother and father's reactions. The old man would literally die. What would all their country club friends say? George felt mortified just thinking about it.

Burton stared at him. They were at an impasse. With nothing more to say on the issue, George stomped out.

George vented to Mimi for a while. She said nothing as he rambled. He began repeating himself and justifying and explaining when, to his utter shock, she leaned and grabbed a fairy wand. George was continuing to talk, saying why he couldn't do what Burton wanted when Mimi thwacked him between the eyebrows with the thing.

George stared at it and Mimi for a long moment. The wand had a bejeweled shining star on it. From underneath the star, shimmering curling ribbons streamed down.

"Why'd you do that?" he asked her.

"It seemed like a good idea at the time," she said. At his frown, Mimi spoke again.

"No, seriously, it's to help you see better, with your third eye," she replied in a serious tone. He rubbed his forehead even though the thwack hadn't actually hurt.

"Uh-huh," George said and went to talk to Sacred Rainbow Feather Walking Man.

~

"Surrender control?" George said and stared at Sacred Rainbow Feather Walking Man.

The two of them were sitting on the steps leading into the building that housed The 3rd Eye.

The dude looked so strange today, stranger than usual, that is. The hairy man had metallic bird feathers woven into his hair, an odd vest, and some kind of shiny silver leggings instead of slacks or pants or jeans. Shaking his head, George II forced himself to return to the conversation at hand.

"Yeah, man," George's coworker said.

"Huh," George said and tried to decipher the wisdom that might be found in the two-word phrase.

"You're a major control freak, Mister P. It's written in your aura," the big hairy man said.

"Anything else?" George inquired. He hoped that there would be nothing else. Nothing that Sacred Rainbow Feather Walking Man said made sense to him. He secretly wondered if the guy had done a lot of drugs, either recently or in the far distant past.

George II didn't know anything about drugs. Yet, he vaguely remembered hearing that people could have experiences, trip out, up or over themselves, or something like that, many, many years after they'd taken drugs.

Maybe that was why Sacred Rainbow Feather Walking Man was so strange. The dude might be tripping over himself.

"I'm not strange," Sacred Rainbow Feather Walking Man said, and George gasped.

"And I didn't do a lot of drugs, Dalai drama," the big hairy man added.

"Uh, oh, sorry," George said. His face got hot with embarrassment. This was all going terribly. Why had Star Child said that he and Sacred Rainbow Feather Walking Man would be close friends? His relationship with this dude was a trainwreck.

"Dude, I hope that I can call you dude," said Sacred Rainbow Feather Walking Man, "seeing as how you keep thinking of me that way. I genuinely like you. I'm not any more of a freak than you are, by the way, and judging by your self-identity torment, I may be considerably more normal. I have no relationships that I would term a trainwreck."

It was then that George finally realized that Sacred Rainbow Feather Walking Man was reading his thoughts and had been for at least part of the conversation.

George didn't know what tripping felt like, yet it had to be a little like this. He'd slipped from regular reality to not knowing when something was really happening or where his imagination ended and reality began.

Maybe I really am a major control freak, George thought to himself.

"Bingo," said Sacred Rainbow Feather Walking Man with great satisfaction, "control freak, dude, majorly. You could benefit from some time to contemplate, meditate, and to peace out. You're so frozen, dude, that you cannot possibly flow. Everything good comes from flow, peace, joy, and love. Keep in mind, regarding meditation and seeking flow, you might have to wade through some serious control freak shit before you get to the good stuff."

George nodded and tried to take it all in. Next thing he knew, Sacred Rainbow Feather Walking Man was standing, patting him on the head, and walking away. Seconds later, George's friend turned back. The man smiled a big smile and, like the first time that they'd met, he flashed George the peace sign.

George sighed with relief. The dude didn't hate him and, despite his unlikely garb, Sacred Rainbow Feather Walking Man was very much a wise man.

George was determined to meditate and get some answers.

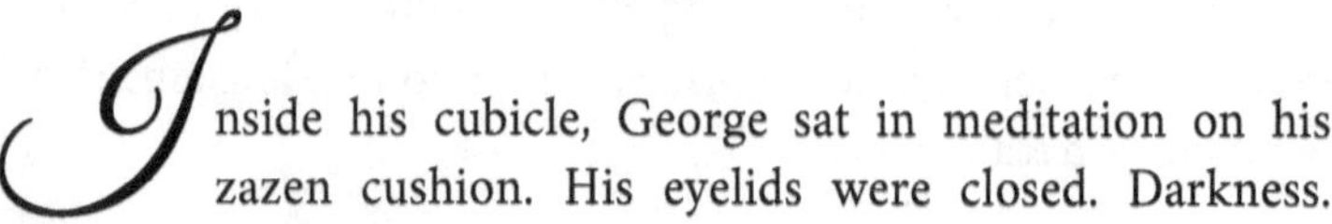

$\mathcal{I}$nside his cubicle, George sat in meditation on his zazen cushion. His eyelids were closed. Darkness.

Against the blackness, in his mind's eye, a cobalt blue sphere appeared in front of George's third eye area.

The blue faded, and it became a garish, colored light that grew blindingly white.

George shook his head, yet managed to keep his eyes closed.

"Surrender, George," said a heavenly voice which sounded bell-like. George jerked and opened his eyes, terrified.

Was that a voice in my head? He asked himself and looked around in shock.

Before he could become obsessed by what had happened, George got several back-to-back calls. The hours passed happily.

~

George and Mimi ate lunch together in a nearby Thai restaurant.

"It was kind of scary, actually," George said.

"So, George Beresford the Second has actual psychic ability. Is that so bad?" Mimi asked gently.

"As New Age hippies raised you, you couldn't possibly understand," George replied.

"Try me," Mimi said drily. George thought hard.

"My parents always wanted something better for me..." George said and stopped. He tried again, "With my education and upbringing... they expected more of me. In many respects, I am a disappointment."

"You're a disappointment to your parents?" Mimi said, barely managing to hide her horror.

"To them... but mostly to myself, I thought I'd be somebody by now," George said and looked truly sad.

Mimi sat quietly and listened, without saying a word, until he spoke again.

"I thought that I'd, I don't know, be more successful. I could see myself successful in my head, I just was never able to make it happen out here, where it counts," George said sadly, and gestured.

"In your head, are you something other than an accountant?" Mimi inquired.

George didn't slow down or stop to think about her questions; he continued to speak.

"At first, I was just a bean counter counting other people's beans, but then I was part of something larger. At Teleseismology Hub NS, for many years, I was an integral part of an important multi-national. I was a promising accountant headed toward being a CFO. Now I'm not even that," he replied.

"Don't you think that you are better at this... than you were at being a bean counter? Maybe you were following the wrong career path all along," Mimi said gently.

"They want me to be some kind of performing monkey. I can barely look people in the eye as it is," George said, not answering her question at all.

"Why don't we go away this weekend? Get out of the city," Mimi spontaneously suggested.

"I can't this weekend," George said dolefully. Mimi was disappointed. George hurriedly clarified.

"My son's baby... my grandson is turning three years old. They're throwing some kind of little birthday bash at my parents. Just family and some close friends," he said.

George paused and didn't say anything further. Mimi looked at him expectantly, clearly hoping for an invite. He didn't speak.

He looked at her; she looked away to avoid crying.

She wondered if he was ashamed of her. She reflected on their conversation and his treatment of her.

George sensed her upset. He really didn't feel a hundred percent comfortable taking her into his family situation, but the idea of hurting her or upsetting her in any way was unbearable.

"Would you come with me?" George asked. He might regret it later, but he would deal with that then, he decided.

Mimi looked at him in surprise, and her smile was huge.

"Really? To your parents?" Mimi asked.

"I'd love for you to be my date," George answered.

The joy on her face made him happy that he'd asked her.

~

George drove Mimi to his parents in his beautiful antique roadster. He looked nervous. He looked at Mimi and, without noticing what he was doing, gave her the once-over.

She was so busy enjoying the ride in the beautiful vehicle and admiring the scenery that she didn't notice that he was inspecting her.

As much as he cared for her, he realized that Mimi wasn't what you would call a classic beauty. Her style was sort of Bohemian-love-goddess, girly chic.

He wondered what his mother would think of Mimi. He realized that what his parents thought was quite important to him.

"You know, I've never seen your hair up. Do you ever wear it like that?" George asked.

Mimi thought about what he had asked for one second and then pulled a hair clip from her purse and put her hair up.

"I used to wear it like that all the time. How do you like it?" Mimi said, turning her head this way and that to tease George.

With her blonde updo, she looked quite classy and prettier than ever.

George, still incredibly anxious, looked pointedly at her glittery, jangling bracelets.

"You are prettier than ever, but... those bangles... they are a bit noisy, though," George replied.

"Oh, I guess I don't have to wear so many," Mimi said, taking some off.

"Better?" she asked hopefully.

"I like it. It's simple," George nodded happily. Mimi looked down at her outfit.

"I probably don't need all these necklaces, either. Lose them all or keep just one?" she asked.

"Keep the pink one. Pearls are nice," said George thoughtfully. His mother would definitely like the pearls, even if they were pink.

George took a deep breath and tried to relax. His hands clenched the steering wheel of his beloved car. Mimi looked at his hands and spoke.

"How're you doing? Nervous about introducing me to your folks?" Mimi asked softly.

"No, it'll be fine," George said, barely keeping his voice even. His cell phone rang. He looked at it.

"Mind if I take it? It's Frank, my broker," George said.

"No, take it," Mimi replied casually. She wondered why George was behaving so strangely. It was clear that he was afraid, perhaps fearful of introducing her to his parents or maybe frightened by navigating two worlds at once.

She knew that he was undergoing tremendous personal change, so she decided to do her best to support him.

George put the call on speakerphone and drove with one hand. "Frank, what's going on?" George answered the call.

"That margin call? I'll have exact figures in a couple of days, but you should prepare yourself for something larger than fifty," Frank said nervously.

George's mouth fell open. It couldn't be possible. He must not have heard Frank correctly.

"Grand?" George said quietly.

"Something in that neighborhood," Frank responded.

"Okay," George finally managed to gasp out. George was stunned.

The influx of money had tided him over until he started generating income again, but it had all been for nothing. He would be forced to sell his house or belongings and take whatever he could get for them.

"Sorry to ruin your weekend," Frank added and clicked off.

George hung up, clearly shaken. Although he had known that trading on the margin was speculative and had also known the risks generally, he was still taken aback.

"Are you okay?" Mimi asked.

"Where in the world am I going to get fifty thousand dollars?" George asked himself aloud. Mimi lovingly stroked his tense neck. George was almost out of his mind with upset.

"I'll give you a reading at home," Mimi said soothingly.

"It may offer some advice or guidance."

"Great. Thanks," George said, not listening to a word that she was saying.

For the rest of the drive to George's parents' house, he seemed lost in his own world.

Finally, they reached a residential neighborhood containing palatial homes on fairly grand estates, each piece of land consisting of several acres. George pulled up on the large driveway of his parents' home.

George and Mimi got out. George became even more nervous, whereas Mimi was secretly impressed by the grand house.

George looked at Mimi. Her eyes were wide and childlike. He smiled to himself.

"You'll be fine," George said, and took her hand, finally forgetting his problems and realizing how much she meant to him and how nervous she might be at meeting his family.

"I'm more worried about you," Mimi answered truthfully, as was her wont. Holding hands tightly, they approached the front door of the house.

~

George I and his wife, Meredith, were both in their 80s, still fit and healthy in appearance. They wore clothes and jewelry that suggested they were well-to-do and entirely proper to the point of conservative in their appearance. The pair, George and Mimi, plus George III, Jenn, and little George IV, ate ice cream and cake at their leisure. They sat in the sunshine on a large patio decorated for a genteel toddler birthday celebration.

All afternoon, Mimi gradually gravitated towards being the center of attention and was now mid-story.

"Are you a Buddhist?" Jenn asked Mimi curiously. Mimi smiled.

"No," Mimi replied smoothly and didn't elaborate.

"So, what happened next?" George III asked Mimi excitedly. George cringed, though he tried to hide it, in anticipation of Mimi's response.

"I told the Dalai Lama that from that day forth, I would meditate on impermanence, as well," Mimi replied. Jenn and George III nodded.

George was apparently embarrassed by Mimi's story. Everyone else seemed genuinely interested in the woman and the little bit of personal history that she'd revealed.

George's mother, Meredith, seemed especially taken by the personal anecdote.

"Impermanence... how beautiful. If there is a single thing I've noticed in the last eighty years, it is that things change, either constantly or eventually," Meredith mused.

Mimi nodded. Georgie IV, sticky all over with frosting and ice cream, got up from the table and ran away from the patio. George III and Jenn got up and followed their child. George, his parents, and Mimi sat quietly watching the trio.

After what seemed to Mimi to be an interminable length of time, George stood. "Well, mother and father," George said, "we'll be going now."

Mimi stood and smiled. They both said their goodbyes to everyone.

~

George and Mimi walked back to the car. There was tension between them that had never existed before. George appeared to be so angry that he was on the verge of tears.

"What is going on with you?" Mimi asked gently.

"I just wanted them to like you," George said truthfully.

"What makes you think they didn't?" Mimi asked.

"It was awkward. None of those people know anything about Buddhism," George said after a moment.

"No, George. They were lovely. You were the awkward one," Mimi countered.

"They're not used to weirdness. They were nice to you, but in truth, I think my family was freaked out," George insisted.

"Do you understand the meaning of projection?" Mimi asked, not a hint of sarcasm or meanness in her voice. George shrugged uncomfortably.

"I don't want to talk about it," he said as they reached the car.

"Projection is when you think someone else is having a certain experience or thought, but it's what you are experiencing or thinking yourself," Mimi specified. George didn't respond. The blonde looked at him and smiled. She waited for him to speak.

"You talk a lot," George said finally. Mimi gasped and fell silent.

George and Mimi drove the rest of the way back in silence. George pulled his car up outside Mimi's apartment building. Night had now fallen. George sat silently and kept the engine running.

"Aren't you coming in, George?" Mimi asked.

"I'd really—" George started to reply.

"I can give you that reading. Trust me. It'll help," Mimi interrupted firmly.

George reluctantly parked and turned off the engine. Inside Mimi's apartment, in the darkened living room lit only by candlelight, Mimi sat across from George. She dealt a spread from her tarot deck.

George was preoccupied and strained to force himself to pay attention.

He found himself replaying the conversation with Frank in his mind. Perhaps he hadn't heard Frank correctly. The margin call couldn't possibly be fifty grand.

Struggling to focus, George looked down at the tarot spread. Mimi was staring at the cards.

"What do they say? Is it good?" George asked desperately.

"The cards are neither good nor bad. They simply give a picture of what may lie ahead if one continues on the path that one is on," Mimi stated calmly. She continued to study the cards.

"So, how does it look?" George asked again.

Mimi and George both looked at the seven tarot cards spread before them.

"The cards reveal a crossroads, George. You're facing a decision or point of choice. You can do what you've done all your life or take the road less travelled... in a new direction," Mimi said.

"Which one is best?" George asked.

"It's not a question of what's best... It's a question of the path of the heart, of course, because that is your soul's path. Until now, you've followed the head path, the way of the logical mind," Mimi replied carefully.

George couldn't wrap his head around the idea. Heart versus logic? Logic was all he knew. Logic had saved him from the day that his wife left. Logic had brought him everything in his life.

"Could you be any more obtuse?" George said as if he were joking, yet he was really quite serious.

"It only sounds obtuse to your mind. Your heart knows what I'm talking about," Mimi said calmly.

"I take it that the path of the head is finance and the path of the heart is, what, Mr. Psychic?" George said.

There was a disagreeable tone in his voice which Mimi chose to ignore. Mimi quickly put several of the cards back in the deck.

"Okay, so the path of finance... what happens if I..." George said.

Mimi held up the Tower tarot card. George stared at the card. It was a disturbing image. Two people were falling from a burning tower that had been struck by lightning.

"It's a major arcana card," Mimi said meaningfully.

"It means several things: disaster, destruction... the end of everything you know. Obviously, sometimes that could be good."
George stared. He looked around the room. He rubbed his eyes,
which felt dry. He realized that he had a slight headache.

For a few seconds, he closed his eyes and leaned back against the
soft velvet couch.

"And the Mr. Psychic path?" he asked, after a long moment, and
opened his eyes.

Mimi held up the Lovers card. He stared. It was definitely a much
prettier card than the Tower. There was some kind of angel
behind a couple, and the sun was shining down.

"Union. True love. Happiness like you've never known," Mimi
murmured.

"It represents relationships and choices, and usually indicates
that something must be sacrificed in order to gain this new state
of being or reality."

"You wouldn't happen to be projecting here, would you?" George
asked skeptically. Mimi laughed.

"I cannot discount completely that I may be affecting things, but
these are the cards and, ultimately, you must decide what it
means to you. This isn't about a romantic relationship, necessar-
ily, though it could include that. It's about making a choice, and
being careful in the choosing," Mimi replied.

George looked at both cards. He felt more confused than ever.
The night sky was dark, and the room, lit only by candlelight,
somehow seemed too dark, almost ominous.

"It's late. I should get going," George finally said.

Mimi's smile waned and then disappeared. She was obviously
disappointed.

"Okay. Thank you for introducing me to your lovely family," Mimi said. George stood and pecked Mimi on the forehead and, before she could even stand, let himself out of her apartment.

~

*I*nside his home office, George poured himself a nightcap and looked at his retirement portfolio projections on his laptop. He entered a margin call of $50,000. The graph dropped vertically, the line representing his investments going down, down, down.

"Oh, boy," George said to himself. Not coming up with the cash would be far worse.

Frank would liquidate stocks left and right to gain the minimum margin requirements. His portfolio might go off the rails entirely. As bad as things were right now, they could get much worse. Much worse.

George lay awake in bed, tossing and turning in the bedroom's near-total darkness. He realized that the night sky was dark tonight. He longed for the light of the stars, but the cloud cover was obscuring their twinkling beauty.

He felt sad at the thought. Wiping away a tear, he wondered angrily what his problem was. Everything changes, he told himself. It's like the Dalai Lama said to Mimi. Impermanence. He thought about his ex-wife. He hadn't seen her in almost twenty years. He wondered if she was happy.

All this time he'd thought she was an irresponsible bitch.

What had his responsibility gotten him? He wondered. Sure, George III was a good kid and happily married now with a wife and child, a son.

But what have I made of my life? He asked himself.

He thought about how nebulous and fragile his reality was.

Everything—the darkness, the lack of starlight, the house, the 1500-thread-count Egyptian cotton sheets that he was lying upon—felt precious and insubstantial.

It was as if everything in his life could slip away forever.

He tried to force himself to stop thinking. He refused to let himself lie awake all night, wasting time, growing more depressed and upset, possibly harming his immune system and health. He would figure out a way to deal with whatever happened, he decided.

As he dropped off to sleep, thoughts he had never had flitted through his mind.

He realized that the world was filled with men and women in circumstances much like his own. They'd all been downsized or outsourced, or maybe even fired, due to forces outside of their control or, quite possibly, incompetence. Whatever.

What he was left with, though, thinking of the vast numbers of people in the same or a similar situation, was compassion.

In that moment, his heart really and truly opened, and he wept.

He wept, not for himself, but for all of those who still had little ones at home; those people who didn't have belongings of value to sell, and the people who might not even own their own homes.

He cried to think of people who needed food to eat, or a place to live, yet didn't have the money or credit to pay for it all.

He felt such compassion and concern for these total strangers that, cheeks damp with tears, he was instantly exhausted. George fell into a deep and dreamless sleep.

~

he next morning, George took photographs of his antique roadster. He wasn't terribly shocked when he heard a voice disturb the silence and peace of the morning.

"Don't tell me. Miss Betty's going on your Christmas card this year?" Ed said, and his voice dripped with jealousy and sarcasm.

George turned to face Ed; dressed for work, the man wore his typical managerial outfit: dark slacks, a sports coat, a white button-down shirt, and an overly wide striped tie.

Ed had his arms crossed and was sneering at George. George sighed. What had he ever done to earn such hatred and vitriol from Ed? He wondered if he might have accidentally, deeply offended the man.

"That's a great idea, but I doubt she'll be around at Christmas," George said.

"I'm putting the little beauty on the market," he added when Ed raised his eyebrows in surprise.

Ed was so shocked that he had no response. He couldn't imagine what might have caused his neighbor to sell his much-loved car. George suddenly felt deeply disturbed, and he couldn't discuss it further.

Without notice or any further gesture of any kind, George simply went back into his house.

Ed stared after his neighbor. Well, that was just plain rude, Ed thought to himself.

~

*I*t was a scenario that, up to several hours ago, George would not have thought imaginable. The first thing Monday morning, George found himself in Burton's office, sitting across from his boss.

"Let me get this straight. You want to go ahead with the commercials, but only if you're wearing a silly disguise so that no one you know could recognize you? And you want fifty thousand up front?" Burton said.

"It's my guidance they want, right?" George said defensively.

"They only want to confer with Mr. Psychic, not take him home to meet their parents," George continued. Burton nodded slowly, trying to understand where this apparent turnaround was coming from.

"True," Burton agreed, realizing that George was being earnest and not trying to be funny.

"It shouldn't matter what the guy looked like... the stats don't specify that Mr. Psychic has to look like a businessman to attract that specific type of clientele," Burton said as he sifted through the marketing proposal.

Many of George's calls had been over the phone, with no visual whatsoever. He'd worn various disguises in video calls.

He thought to himself, perhaps the "Mr. Psychic" personality and George's natural ability would be enough.

Waiting for Burton to respond further, George was lost in his thoughts. How else was he going to come up with the cash that he needed?

Thoughts raced through his mind, but none of them solved his problems. If he didn't come up with the cash for the margin call,

Frank would liquidate more of his stock, and his losses would be greater than ever. He felt tired and anxious.

He had to find a way to get the cash. He planned to sell his car and anything else that he could part with, hopefully through an easy, fast online auction site.

Realistically, he knew that his desperation to come up with quick cash was a negative factor. The secondary market for belongings was at least as dismal as the secondary relationship market, if not more so.

George hadn't the time to ponder the strange and fairly negative directions that his thoughts were traveling in because Burton finally spoke.

"I think we can come to some agreement about the advance or bonus, or whatever. Do you have to do the voice?" asked Burton.

George breathed a sigh of relief. They were on.

~

Inside a TV recording studio, George, as Monsieur Psychic, faced the camera. He was dressed in an updated version of his home-made disguise: a silk vest and black silk shirt, and an enormous yet realistic-looking mustache made of fake facial hair attached with gum adhesive.

George stood on the set before the young director, the production team, and two rolling cameras as Burton watched from the side.

George stared at the edgy director. The guy was obviously driven and appeared to be barely thirty years old, yet he had the self-confidence of a much older man.

"And action," the director said.

"Are you worried? Concerned about your job, your loved ones, or the state of the economy?" George asked smoothly, delivering his lines to the camera.

Even with his phony, comical-sounding accent, George sounded as polished and slick as a used car salesman.

Burton winced, however. That unctuous, smarmy, and superficial man, with the pseudo-European accent, was not at all what he'd had in mind when he'd decided to take the company in a new direction.

He prayed that he hadn't been wrong about George and the new promotion plan. This was a preliminary commercial, a little test shoot of sorts, but these kinds of screen tests cost serious dough.

"You have questions. Monsieur Psychic has answers. Call me now. 3rd Eye operators are standing by," George said, sounding like a smooth operator. The director had George run through it several more times.

George never flubbed his lines and was practically unrecognizable in his Monsieur Psychic getup. Still, no matter how many times he did it perfectly, Burton just didn't love it.

Inside a dressing room, George had just taken off his disguise as Burton entered.

"Smooth delivery, George," Burton said, trying to find something positive to say about George's act.

"You hated it," George said flatly.

"Not what I had in mind exactly, but let's see how it plays. Are you okay?" Burton replied.

"I'm fine. Why?" George answered.

"You just don't seem yourself this week. You know you can always talk—"

"Just some financial stuff. Might have to sell my house. No biggie," George said brusquely, "I'll figure it out. It won't interfere with my work, I promise."

"Fine," Burton said and nodded, not really knowing how to respond to George's shocking attitude and obvious predicament.

~

*A*rriving home, George decided to check the mail and his email, only to be disappointed when it was junk mail and bills.

There continued to be no job offers. There were no "Thank you for your application, but we've decided to go with a better-quali-fied candidate" notes. There was absolutely nothing related to his old identity and former line of work. It was like his former career, like his retirement fund, was rapidly disappearing entirely.

He looked at the envelopes and fliers and felt only despair and defeat.

He had turned to return to his house when he saw that Ed, who had arrived home moments before him, was staring at him curiously.

Turning away, George touched his upper lip and realized that, although he'd changed back into his regular clothes, he still wore his fake mustache. He hurried inside.

Ed stared at George. Had the guy grown a mustache? That was so weird.

George had always been the clean-cut type. Plus, Ed thought he'd seen George sans facial hair just yesterday.

~

George watched his computer screen inside his cubicle. Mimi brought him his newest favorite afternoon beverage: organic coffee sweetened with stevia and a splash of Irish Cream syrup.

"What's so engaging?" Mimi asked, when he grunted a thank you and quickly put the drink aside.

"In less than sixty seconds, some happy bidder will be the proud owner of my antique roadster. Fifty seconds..." George said glumly. Mimi placed a reassuring hand on his shoulder.

"I'm so sorry, George. I know how much that car meant to you," she said softly.

She and George watched the counter tick down... 5... 4... 3... 2... 1.

"Sold! To LuckyPlucky, the biggest bargain that lucky bastard ever..." George said and almost broke down. Mimi remained silent and unmoving, for which he was extremely grateful.

Any kindness from her would have brought him beyond tears to full-out sobbing. He collected himself and closed the online auction site. As he rubbed his forehead, he had a surprising thought. He realized that, in a way, it was a tremendous relief.

His money anxiety was almost over. He had managed to gather together the 50G he'd needed for the margin call, but most of it was sleight of hand. He'd gotten cash advances from two recently acquired credit cards and had also taken some cash from the line of credit available on his mortgage. Sure, the 3rd Eye was arranging the advance that he'd insisted upon, yet he knew that trading on the margin had been a terrible investment and business decision.

Realistically, he'd just bought more time. Pretty soon, he would have to scramble to sell everything that he had of value in order to pay off the practically usurious cash advance credit card debt, which had a terribly high interest rate, before the snowball of financial calamity destroyed everything that he had worked years to amass.

He felt like his entire reality became a precariously balanced house of cards, on the edge of tumbling down around him, in front of his very eyes.

With a click, the intercom on his cubicle wall came on.

"Call for Mr. Psychic, line two," the receptionist said. George realized that he had mistakenly turned his headset off after the last call. It was the first time that reception had needed to contact him via intercom. He'd had no idea what the box on the wall was, and his face flushed red, realizing he had been a bit irresponsible during working hours.

Mimi looked at him. George was still staring at the intercom. She realized that he was in no condition to answer the incoming call, so Mimi spontaneously grabbed his headset.

"I'll take it for you. Take as much time as you need," Mimi said.

"Hello, thank you for calling the 3rd Eye," Mimi said and walked out of George's cubicle.

George slumped over and held his head in his hands. He couldn't remember ever feeling this low in his entire life.

Where would it end? What would his bottom be? Homeless? Unemployable? Was his nightmare coming true?

~

George worked days as Monsieur Psychic, being as responsible as he could. He genuinely listened to and was honest with clients and spent his nights liquidating anything he owned of value.

It made him sick when he finally sold his 18-carat yellow gold OMEGA 1932 Olympic Rattrapante Chronograph. He was only able to get twenty-five grand for it.

Stinking economy. Or maybe he'd been foolish to invest in objects that purely had subjective value. It made George sick. Every precious thing that he owned, costly and of value to him, was worth very little on the secondary market. Used, quality goods, at least at this point, weren't worth much of anything.

Partly, people seemed happier with brand-new, low-quality goods made in other countries. The other half was that people could shop online and find almost anything they wanted, including older, original items, at cut-rate prices.

His periodic restlessness at night, nightmares, and difficulty in falling asleep became full-blown insomnia.

Rather than lie in his bed at night, George began sleeping on the couch.

He channel-surfed and watched old black and white classic movies and TV shows until he was exhausted enough to fall asleep.

Every day, however, he woke a little more tired. He wondered when things would turn around for him. Things couldn't continue the way they were. He wouldn't make it.

That night, George lay stretched out on his living room sofa, wearing an old bathrobe. He was channel-surfing when he flipped past something that caught his eye.

What was that? He clicked backward. It was him, on TV: the commercial he had shot weeks before was now on the air.

"Are you worried? Concerned about your job, your loved ones, or the state of the economy?" Monsieur Psychic asked the world. His delivery was slick and smooth, and he didn't look much like George.

George watched with embarrassment. He was almost relieved when his front doorbell rang. It didn't occur to him to wonder who would be calling on him at this time of night: 9:30 PM.

No one ever visited him without notice, especially at this hour.

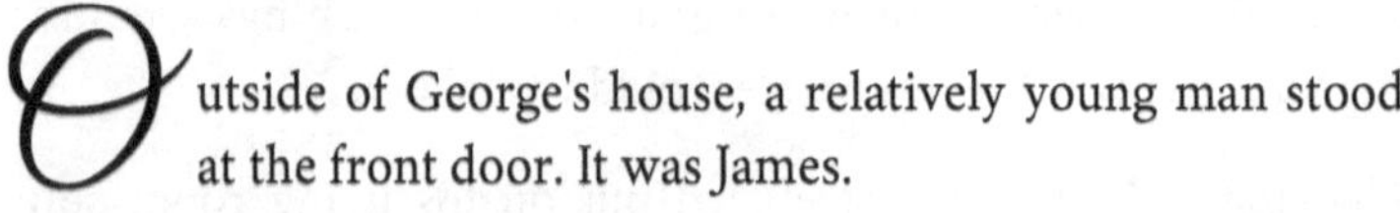

*I*n the living room of Ed's house, Edwina, binoculars to her eyes, peered out the window. The young girl coughed and gave a little shriek. Her father, Ed, sat up.

"Dad, movement next door. The suspect has a visitor," Edwina stated.

Ed dropped the remote, left the TV, and rushed over to his offspring.

"Good girl, Edwina. Let me see," Ed said, snatching the binoculars from his child's hands.

*O*utside of George's house, a relatively young man stood at the front door. It was James.

"James?" George said, opening the door.

"I was in the neighborhood," James said self-consciously.

"Come in, come in," George said.

George was a bit embarrassed to be caught in his bathrobe, yet it was close enough to bedtime that he figured it wouldn't matter.

He was incredibly grateful that, despite his insomnia, his home, including the living room, was spotlessly clean. He could only imagine a reaction of horror from his former peer if George hadn't previously resumed keeping up his home.

James followed George to the living room, where George poured them each a drink.

"We could have talked on the phone, but... I wanted to see you," James admitted.

"What's going on?" George asked.

"It's only good, George. Actually, it's unbelievably good," James said and smiled happily. Then he punched George lightly on the shoulder as if they were celebrating some kind of team win.

"I'm intrigued," George said, feeling his spirits lift. James never exaggerated, George thought to himself.

James was indeed a friend, whatever Mimi and George III thought. His appearance tonight and words proved it. The fact that he had stopped by with good news was exciting.

"I need your utmost confidentiality on this one, George. No speaking of this to anyone, not a single soul, especially Marcus. I'm not bringing him in on this. That prick knew that I was getting the chop, and he never said a word. And the punk had to have known because he was promoted before we got laid off. Mei in HR confirmed it." James said.

"You got canned before you could find something else?" George asked, and the thought made him feel sick.

"Forget that, because I did get employment: twice the opportunity and double the salary. In this economy, it's a freaking miracle," James said.

"Terrific, James. Congratulations," George said, and he meant it.

He was incredibly relieved that his pal wouldn't have to endure the financial strife he'd gone through and, in truth, was still going through. It was so intensely stressful not to be able to make ends meet.

But it was the words that James spoke next that fairly floored George.

"I wanna bring you in," James said quietly.

"What?" George wasn't sure that he'd heard correctly.

"You had my back, George. You were there for me. You always have been. I need to surround myself with people I can trust. I know you've been trying out this consulting thing, but trust me, this is a major opportunity. It's a Fortune 500 with perks like you would not believe. You should see my new ride. Think about it, for me?" James queried.

George didn't stop to think.

"What do I have to do?" George asked.

"Nothing, for now. It'll take me a few weeks to assemble a team. I'm the 'Project Leader.' Who'd have thought? Just stay clean, no controversial blogging or tweeting, not that you do any of that stuff. They'll probably do the usual background checks, Google you and shit. We caught a break, buddy! We're going to be okay," James said.

George almost cried when he heard the phrase, "We're going to be okay." He'd felt so all alone. He'd felt so very close to being unable to go on. He'd felt nearly at the end of his rope. He had a friend. He had a different possible future.

What a sense of relief he felt as he smiled broadly. He couldn't believe his good fortune. This opportunity must be what the cards had predicted, he decided. His psychic job was The Tower tarot card. This moment was the point of choice that the tarot cards revealed. Mimi must have been projecting about which path was right for him and so gotten it just a bit wrong. The right cards, the wrong interpretation. This new opportunity was clearly the path that he should take.

"Thank you, buddy," George said, and then, even though he thought his emotions were under control, his voice broke with emotion. James patted his back. He practically pounded James's back in return.

He and James each had a short drink, a finger each, of his best whiskey. He didn't bother telling James about the libation. It was pure pot-stilled Irish whiskey made at the Tullamore distillery, which closed in 1954. The elixir was bottled three decades or so later, in 1987, for the Knappogue Castle label.

If it weren't already open, he would have sold it.

Knappogue Castle 1951 whiskey was worth roughly a grand a bottle, so he only drank the fiery spirits on rare occasions. The last time he'd had it was with his son when his grandson Georgie IV was born.

The amber uisge beatha, as the Irish would say, the ancient Celtic phrase meaning 'water of life', warmed George.

James and George sipped their whiskey and talked about the future. It felt right to George.

If George could trust his inner knowing, the feeling in his bones, and what James believed, they both had something significant to celebrate.

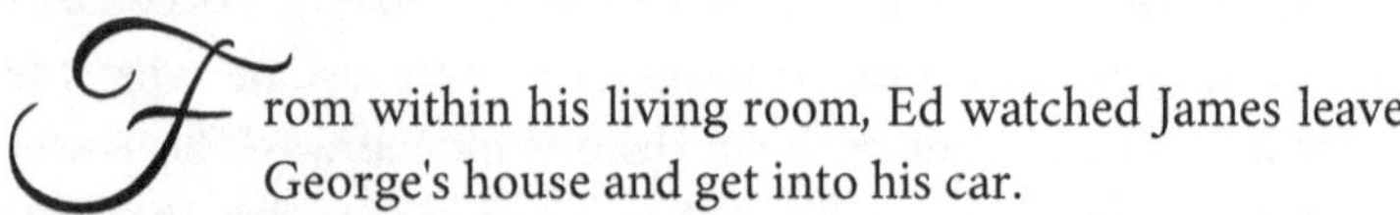

From within his living room, Ed watched James leave George's house and get into his car.

"That's interesting," Ed said snidely.

"What, Daddy?" Edwina asked curiously, knowing full and well that she was now officially up past her bedtime.

She could hear her mother with the twins and realized that her father was so distracted by the neighbor that he had forgotten to tell her to go to bed.

"George, uh, I mean the suspect, is hurting for money. But his late-night friend's got a spanking new car. What fiendish business are these guys cooking up?" Ed speculated.

Edwina knew the drill by now. Her father would trash-talk the neighbor, using grown-up words she wasn't supposed to understand and making wild speculations about the man who lived next door. All the while, her father would get more and more upset, and she got to hear everything, as long as her mother wasn't in the room.

"Is it drugs, daddy?" Edwina asked.

"Could be, but not enough clues, yet, little Ed," Ed said and patted her head.

"Maybe drugs, maybe insider trading, maybe illegal stock manipulation, but it all stinks like three-day-old fish." He said.

"Real, real bad!" Edwina said enthusiastically.

"Yes, it's bad. Real, real bad," Ed repeated dumbly. He was lost in thought, staring at George's house, when his daughter took his hand.

"Maybe the police'll come and bust the suspect, and we'll be watching," the little girl added and giggled.

Then, as if waking from a deep sleep, Ed looked down at his daughter. He realized that he would be in big trouble if Lindsay came back in and saw them scheming together.

"You'd better get into bed before your momma catches you," Ed said, conspiratorially.

Edwina grinned and ran from the living room. Ed settled back into his barcalounger. He flipped television channels for a while and yawned.

He was falling asleep in his chair, his eyes closing and his head jerking backwards, when he happened to see the Monsieur Psychic commercial. The sight instantly woke Ed up.

"Well, well, if it isn't George's mysterious French friend," Ed said to himself.

~

Inside his home office, officially tired and ready for sleep now, George sat before his computer. He input the money earned from his car sale into his retirement projection. The graph made a minor correction. He sighed.

It wasn't enough. George needed to make a massive financial correction to be sure that he could hold onto the house and pay off the rest of his debt. Even the $50K from the 3rd Eye wasn't going to fix everything. It was clear. Going with James was a chance to course-correct and get onto the right path. The psychic thing must have been meant to be temporary, a gift from the universe or soul path deviation, so that he could meet Mimi, or for other unknown reasons.

The universe was guiding him toward the new job and away from the 3rd Eye.

He had no choice, he decided. He had to be responsible, pay his bills, and prepare for retirement, and the new job, if it panned out, would allow him to do so.

Burton and Mimi would have to understand the facts. George sighed with relief.

~

*E*d watched the "Monsieur Psychic" commercial with a sneer on his face.

"You may fool everyone else, including your fancy, schmancy criminal-type friends, George, but not me. No, sir, Bob, you never fooled me for a second," Ed snarled to himself.

Then the man laughed maniacally for several long moments. He didn't stop until his wife entered the room and glared at him.

"What?" Ed asked.

Lindsay said not a word. She just stared him down until he shrugged sheepishly and clicked off the TV.

~

*G*eorge entered the 3rd Eye offices' cubicle area. The psychics were all standing around Sacred Rainbow Feather Man's cubicle, watching his computer screen and laughing.

"What's going on?" George asked.

"Hey, George. Check it out. You're famous, man!" Sacred Rainbow Feather Man said as he punched a key on his computer keyboard and replayed a video on YouTube.

It was a version of George's "Monsieur Psychic" infomercial edited into a hilarious rap music video. The psychics cracked up all over again.

"Who put that up there? You guys?" George gasped with outrage, not at all amused.

"I wish. Nobody knows who put it up. It's gone viral, half a million hits in three hours. Hilarious," said Sacred Rainbow Feather Man. George stared in shock. Viral?

"And the phone lines are blowing up! It's totally cosmic!" Star Child shrieked, quite joyfully.

~

*U*pset, George returned to his cubicle. To his shock, his headset was already ringing. He entered his cubicle and hurriedly fixed his Monsieur Psychic disguise.

He took the call and soon was in the zone. An hour later, as another call ended, Mimi approached.

"Want to talk about it?" Mimi asked as George pulled his headset off.

"Who would do something like that?" George asked.

"It's cute," Mimi offered.

"I'm this close to being outed," George said, gesturing with his hands.

"What? You're not straight?" Mimi said, displaying a mock disbelief. George was not amused.

"In addition to being a dumb joke, this is terrible timing. James, you met him... he's going to offer me a job... in a few weeks, after he works out some stuff," George said.

"Are you going to take it?" Mimi asked incredulously.

"I don't know. Obviously, I have a commitment here..." George said and indicated his cubicle. His computer rang. He had a video chat call coming in for Mr. Psychic.

Looking peeved but trying not to succumb to the emotion, Mimi exited his cubicle.

"What?" George called after Mimi, picking up on her mood.

"Take your call, George," Mimi called back, over her shoulder.

George reluctantly took the call. It was Ed on the screen.

"You've got to be kidding me," George said to himself under his breath. He leaned off-screen as much as he could and then spoke.

"Oui, 'ello? Ow may I help you?" George said in his fairly terrible fake French accent.

Ed stared George down.

"I didn't quite catch your first name, Miss... Your... Psychic. We met before... at George Beresford's. I'm le neighbor... Edward," Ed said drily.

"Naturallement, Ed. Ow can I help you today? Your question, monsieur?" George asked.

"Oh, uh, yeah. I'd like to know general stuff, about my future and all," Ed stated.

George closed his eyes and dug deep.

"The future, Ed... she is not good," George said sadly, meaning every word.

"What?" Ed gasped. Ed's face reddened, and he rubbed his head, freaking out.

"The path you are on is no good. You need to be on le path with heart," George said.

"Okay. Hokey, but okay. How so? What does that even mean?" Ed asked.

"You work in the market because of your father-in-law, not because you love grocery market work," George said carefully, after tuning in to his neighbor.

"Who would wanna work in a grocery store if it wasn't their first choice?" Ed asked bitterly.

George felt his guard slipping. Was it possible that he was truly making a heart-and-soul connection with his neighbor, Ed?

Despite Ed's true, ulterior reasons for calling the line, perhaps he could be of real service to Ed. George felt his heart swell with compassion and love for this relative stranger.

"Exactement! It ees easy for you, because you are capable but your heart ees so sad. It make you angry and... what is the word... jealous. You are a veddy jealous man, Ed."

~

*E*d got riled. Who did this freak think he was, telling Ed that he was jealous? The thought enraged him. And sad? A sad heart? Why, he wasn't unhappy.

A loving wife and family surrounded him; he was important. His father-in-law depended upon him. He had everything, while this obnoxious idiot George had nothing.

"This is a bunch of damn hooey, George... I mean, Monsieur Con Artiste," Ed said nastily.

George felt his heart tighten. He suddenly found it difficult to swallow. Did Ed just call him a con artist? Did Ed recognize him?

George was so focused on the connection between himself and George, and the information flowing, that he wasn't entirely sure what Ed had just said.

"Your, uh, uh..." George struggled to find words, yet finally managed to get deeper into the reading. "Your heart grew sad when you stopped of the singing."

Ed's eyes grew wide, his mouth fell open, and he forgot to close it. He looked like he had just gotten hit with a brick. He flushed red and started to sweat.

"How do you know about the singing?" Ed asked suspiciously.

"Every day you do not sing, your heart grows harder and harder. One day it will break. You will become too bitter for this life, and there will be no going back," George said as kindly as he could.

As if George had just hit a nerve, Ed grew close to tears. He swallowed repeatedly and willed himself not to cry in front of George.

"I never ever told anyone about the... who told you?" Ed demanded.

"Even when no one listens to you, you must sing. Sing in the shower. Sing in the car. With practice, once again, you will sing to people. That is where you will find the love that is missing. You will not be sad, angry, or jealous; your heart is full when you sing and connect with the people," George said quietly yet firmly.

"The love that you seek will only be found in your heart... when you sing."

Tears now streamed down Ed's face.

"I have to go," Ed managed to whisper.

"Bye."

With a click, Ed hung up, and George's screen went dark.

George clicked a button on his keyboard to end his side of the call. His normal screensaver returned, and he put his head in his hands. This was a terrible turn of events.

The only thing that could be more terrible than his neighbor Ed calling would be if a family member or a peer from Teleseismology Hub NS decided to call.

George sat and stared at his computer. The turbanned man tried to figure out how to get the video removed from YouTube. He had gone back to the site earlier in the morning, but the video had already been copied and was all over the web on different video sites and blogs.

George stood resolutely. He would go and speak to Burton. Surely there was some legal protection that they offered him.

People couldn't just take his likeness and make a loopy video from a privately owned commercial. He hadn't given permission for his image to be used in this manner, nor had he been paid.

Burton should get quick legal advice and have every copy of the video removed from every web hosting site— stat!

George hurried down the hall to Burton's office. Preparing

mentally for what he was going to say, he slowed his pace down to a crawl.

He realized that he couldn't tell Burton of his real concerns about the video because George would then have to explain to Burton about the possibility of the new job. For many reasons, he was not yet ready to have that conversation.

He would need to feel out Burton first. George determined to find out where his boss stood on the issues of plagiarism, legality, and ridicule.

~

George knocked lightly on Burton's open office door and poked his head in. Burton looked up and, from the broad smile upon his face, was genuinely happy to see him.

"Come in, come in, George," Burton said and happily waved George into the office.

"What's up?" Burton asked as George entered, looking morose and not at all a happy camper. Sinking into one of the chairs facing Burton, George picked up a heart-shaped rock off of Burton's desk.

"It's that YouTube video," George admitted, hardly able to make eye contact with Burton.

Burton laughed and flipped his computer screen around so that George could see it. The video in question was on the screen. Burton unplugged his headphones from his computer and pressed a button.

"You mean this?" Burton asked. George looked on as the YouTube video replayed.

"You can't buy genius advertising like this," Burton said, laughing, entirely delighted.

George felt himself shrink inside himself. This was terrible. Burton quite obviously loved the video. George looked at his hands. They felt larger than normal.

He realized that he had never contemplated his hands before, and so he really didn't know if they were or weren't larger than they had been.

"I can't do this anymore," George gasped out, giving up on examining his hands. He did wonder if he was going just the tiniest bit whacko. He looked around Burton's office. Everything seemed brighter and bigger.

I must be finally losing it, he decided. That video is definitely the last straw.

"What?" Burton said, staring at George.

"Look at me. I'm a joke," George said and looked down at his outfit.

"The disguise was your idea," Burton said, entirely missing the point.

"I had no idea what a farce it would all become. I can't spend my life talking in a fake French accent," George said.

"It was a stupid idea. I can't believe you let me do it."

"Hmmm, I thought your accent was Russian," Burton said. His expression changed as if he'd had a sudden realization.

"You want more money?"

"It's not the money..." George said and then added, "Well, it was the money. But that's not it, now."

"You have the gift, George," Burton said firmly.

"In all honesty, Burton? I really don't. Every time I get on that phone, I make the whole of all that shit up," George said.

"Don't turn your back on your gift," Burton said.

"I'm sorry, Burton. I tried. I just can't do this," George said, then he stood and left.

~

George hurried down the hall to his cubicle. Mimi knew what it meant as he rapidly packed his things, throwing his stuff willy-nilly into a large cardboard box.

It made him feel ill, and he kept flashing back to being fired from Teleseismology Hub NS.

Mimi reached into her desk and handed him back the netsuke dragon. He took it without looking at it or realizing the significance of her offering.

In her heart, Mimi knew that George was leaving not only his job but also their fledgling relationship behind.

"So, that's it, then?" Mimi said pointedly.

"That's it," George said, again without thinking, as he put the netsuke in his pocket.

"We had some fun, right?" Mimi asked as if she were asking George something else entirely.

George felt terrible. Leaving the 3rd Eye suddenly felt very hard, much harder than he had imagined. He felt like he wasn't just leaving a job; perhaps he was also walking out on Mimi.

Stopping to look into her sad eyes, briefly, he realized that his world was unlikely to intersect at all with hers in the future.

"Yeah. It was fun," George said sadly, yet so much in emotional and mental pain that he was almost in tears.

"I don't want to lose my house," he said, slowly.

"I know, George," Mimi said sympathetically.

She wanted him to stop what he was doing, put down his box of belongings, and take just a moment for them to gaze into each other's eyes.

She felt sure that if he did so, he could finally see what was important to him and, for the first time in his life to make his decisions from a place of love instead of fear.

George hefted the cardboard box tightly to his chest and avoided making eye contact.

Heartbroken, Mimi watched him as he took one last look around his space, ready to walk out the door, and perhaps out of her life, forever. It really hurt her heart, but she knew that there was nothing she could do or say: it was his choice to leave or stay.

"Will you call me sometime?" Mimi asked softly, sounding terribly sad, as George nodded at her and left his cubicle.

When George didn't even bother to answer, a single tear slid down her cheek.

~

George entered the sports bar and instantly spotted James, Marcus, and Bethany sitting at a booth. Having left his current employer earlier than he had planned and anticipated, George felt nervous.

Nothing seemed to have worked out for him. Despite his brief interlude working at the 3rd Eye, he really felt that since getting fired, things had gone from bad to worse. He was now right where he had started: unemployed and possibly, because of his age, unemployable.

What if James hadn't gotten him an offer? What if Mimi was right and these people didn't honestly care for him? What if they had seen that pathetic viral video?

George braced himself, pasted a smile on his face, and strolled over.

"George!" James greeted him warmly.

"The man of the hour," Marcus commented.

"Congratulations, George. I knew you'd land on your feet," Bethany said and really meant it.

"What'll you have, George?" James inquired. George hesitated. What was going on?

"Champagne all around, hey? We'll have Cristal... or whatever passes for bubbly or a celebratory drink in this joint, to celebrate George's terribly good fortune," Marcus said.

"They are lucky to have you, George," James said.

"Truly," said Marcus.

"It's rather cool," he added, although he sounded suspicious and jealous, "That you and James both got a gig at the same place."

Although he didn't show it, upon hearing those words, a wave of joy and relief swept through George's body; they had invited him here to celebrate his new job!

George felt like shouting and caterwauling with joy. Instead, he played his cards close to his chest and allowed the good news to filter in and decompress every fiber of his being. For the first time in such a long time, he could finally and utterly relax.

The group chatted idly while they waited for their waiter. When he didn't come, Marcus went to find him. George immediately turned to James.

"Did you and Marcus make up?" George asked.

"Not exactly," James said.

"Keep your friends close but your enemies closer," Bethany said and grinned slyly. George laughed.

Marcus came back with the waiter, and they placed their orders. Bethany updated them on the happenings at Teleseismology Hub NS.

George was terribly surprised to realize that he didn't care. He didn't wish ill for the company and his former peers, but he didn't feel interested either.

What he did want to hear were details about his new job and his new company. He wanted to know what his title and job description would be.

Based on his earlier conversation with James, he expected the salary and perks to be generous and more than enough to bail him out of the financial hole he had dug for himself.

As anxious as he was to hear further details and, more importantly, to receive a written and official job offer, he decided to be patient and accept everything in good time.

If he had learned anything from his sojourn at the 3rd Eye, it was that it was essential to allow rather than to force. This was how the universe seemed to operate, and despite his desperate need to know and to be in control, he would be respectful of that.

Their orders came. Bethany and Marcus made a toast to George and James. Before long, they were bantering lightly and laughing together just the way that they used to.

George felt so happy to be back, and that's exactly how he described his feelings to himself.

"I'm back," he said to himself, giddily, "And it feels so good to be back!"

~

Late that night, inside his bedroom, with the closet doors fully extended, George sorted through his suits and dress shirts as he talked on his cell phone.

"I just thought I'd give you the news, Dad," he said and then listened for a long moment while George I spoke.

"I know... it is a great job, better than anything I could dream up. Thank you. I hope to nail it down tomorrow. You never know, though… I kind of don't want to get ahead of myself," George said, and then listened.

"Okay, all the best," he said, signing off.

George hung up just as another call was coming in.

"Hello, son," George said, with a big smile."Yeah, it's terrific. Consulting? No. Wasn't my thing, after all. Guess I'm a real nine-to-five, work for the man, get a solid paycheck, type of guy," George added and paused to listen.

He picked out a suit, a tie, and the perfect shirt, and hung them on his valet.

His outfit for the next day picked out, George sat on his bed.

"We'll know tomorrow. I hope it's just a formality," he said and listened to George III's response.

"Thank you very much, son. That means a lot to me." George teared up a bit. He could feel his son's love, and it was very heart-warming.

"Give my love to Jenn and little Georgie. I'll let you know as soon as I know. Okay then, goodbye," he finished and hung up the phone. Exhausted, George finally got ready for bed.

~

George walked on the sidewalk outside a downtown office building. He looked up at a forty-two-story glass and steel building shimmering in the heart of the financial district. It was impressive.

He entered the lobby and, after passing through security, got into the elevator. He pushed the button for the 21st floor.

Well-dressed, George appeared to fit perfectly into this setting. When the elevator doors opened on the 21st floor, James stood waiting for him. James was obviously happy to see him.

George felt unusually emotional, considering the business setting. He felt warmth for James in the center of his chest. It filled his being. They shook hands.

To George's surprise, over James's right shoulder, as if superimposed over his body and being, George saw a series of images. They were pictures of him and James, though the people in those images didn't resemble him or James in their current bodies.

He saw himself and James in other lifetimes. They were in different bodies, and neither of them was always male. He realized that they had been father and son, brothers, husband and wife, and priests in the same order, among other relationships.

It was a peculiar experience, and it would have been much more frightening if he hadn't recently been working as a psychic. He didn't try to interpret his experience but instead allowed it. What a trip. He and James had a pretty deep soul connection, which explained a lot.

An increasing sense of joy and gratitude meant that soon his entire body was tingling.

The sensations and flood of images finally stopped. Well, that was weird, he thought to himself. Yet, it wasn't really what had happened that had felt familiar and right. He shrugged the experience off as rapidly as possible and saw that James was indicating for George to follow him. So he did.

~

James led George down the hall and through a maze of busy cubicles. The office space was more luxurious than the Teleseismology Hub NS offices and would have dwarfed the offices of the 3rd Eye.

George was terribly impressed. The carpet, the paint on the walls, the furnishings—everything was well-appointed and extremely high-end. No expense had been spared. He wondered about the company's bottom line.

"Your office is on the other side," James said to George.

"I get an office?" George asked, surprised. James smiled, his expression resembling that of a happy shark.

"With a view," James said. They continued down the hall, hung a left at the end, and with another turn, trod down the plush carpeted hallway about a third of the way down.

James waved his arm toward a doorway, as he was a herald introducing a royal person.

The two of them entered George's new office. The furniture was made of highly polished cherry. It wasn't antique, more sleek and modern, yet it was exquisite. The carpet, even more plush and thicker than the hallway carpet, was a pale green color.

Practically speechless, George marveled at his lavish office. James grinned.

"We share a secretary... Muriel," James said, and waved toward an older woman in her early sixties. The woman appeared friendly yet entirely professional in demeanor and appearance.

She was seated outside George's office, at her desk, in an anteroom just off the hall.

James turned to George; the guy couldn't stop grinning. Clearly, he wanted to surprise George.

"What do you think, buddy?" James asked, his voice bubbling with the enthusiasm of a small child.

"I'm... speechless," George said, clapping James on the back and giving him a half-hug.

James, obviously delighted, squeezed George's arm.

"You ready?" James asked. "We've got an appearance to make."

"Thank you," George said quickly, "I will remember this."

James flushed with pleasure. "I won't let you forget it," James said, and laughed.

"Come on."

James turned, and George followed. James led him through a maze of hallways. They reached a conference room, entered, and took seats among the others present. George was nervous. He hadn't realized that the interview was a group interview. It was always harder to track that type of experience.

"Everybody, this is George. My newest team member," James said.

George was flabbergasted. Wasn't there some kind of interview process? He'd been prepared to be put through the ringer, questioned about his past, and forced to perform to get hired.

Instead, the other people present simply said, "Hello," or gave some form of greetings, waved, or nodded at him. Winston, an impeccably dressed, imposing man in his seventies, took his seat at the head of the table.

George was immediately aware, by the man's elegant clothing style and appearance, that this was the person responsible for the tower's beautiful décor.

"Welcome aboard, George. I hope you're ready to help us shift our numbers this quarter," Winston said, looking George square in the eyes.

George smiled and spoke, surprising himself as much as anyone else.

"Not going to happen until the end of the fourth quarter... next year," George said firmly.

George's mouth almost fell open, as shocked as some of the others by his statement.

"Excuse me?" Winston said.

"That's how it's looking... from my preliminary analysis," George said, trying to salvage the conversation and the impression that he was making upon Winston and the group.

"Thank you for the welcome... I'm glad to be here," George added.

"I haven't shown you any reports yet," James whispered to George.

"You haven't? Oh," George said softly, then added, "I guess I took that away from my research."

"Let's get started, then," Winston said. The lights dimmed, and a multi-media presentation began.

George did his best to focus, but the facts were terribly boring. He noticed that, even though he wasn't meditating and his eyes were open, there was a blue color between them, in his third eye area.

Winston clicked a remote to pause his chart-heavy PowerPoint presentation. He looked around at the group. He noticed George, who appeared to be almost nodding off. He frowned.

"These projections are suspect. D&B says they're low... S&P says they're high," he paused a moment, "Questions! Feedback! Analysis, anybody?"

Winston looked at the blank faces around him, scanning them yet avoiding eye contact.

"How about you, George? You seem to have opinions. Too low or too high?" Winston asked. He had seen the new guy's eyes fluttering, maybe drifting off, and he didn't like it one bit.

All eyes focused upon George. He knew that he didn't have enough factual data to comment. He also knew that his body and being, most particularly his spirit, had thoughts, feelings, and opinions. He could feel it in his gut. Here goes nothing, thought George.

He breathed deeply and got quiet. He opened his eyes more widely and looked at Winston.

"I understand it's too—" Winston said, when George didn't immediately respond.

"They're both right," George blurted out.

"How can that be?" Winston asked. He didn't say it meanly, yet his disbelief was evident.

"S&P is using the long form spread and extending the analysis over the long term, in which case, they are currently too high. D&P are using Bronstein's short-term analysis in which context the numbers are below the initial starting threshold... if that makes sense," George said.

The others watched for Winston's reaction. He very slowly smiled.

This guy hadn't been falling asleep at all. He must have been entirely focused on and tuned into everything that Winston had been saying. Winston felt terribly pleased. There was something special about the new guy.

"You got all that from my presentation?" Winston inquired.

"Sure," George said slowly, "and it's the only way it can make any sense."

Winston was impressed; because of that, others paid more attention to George.

"Right or wrong, I like your spunk," Winston admitted. Then he turned to James.

"You got a live one, here," Winston said and winked at the younger man.

"Yes, sir. It's why he's on my team," James replied happily. Winston resumed his presentation and, when the attention was back on the front of the room, James gave George the tiniest little nudge.

George hid his smile, yet he knew that James was very, very pleased with him. An hour or so later, everyone broke for lunch.

~

James and George made their way back through the downtown tower hallways, toward their adjacent offices, reaching George's office first. James, excited, followed George into the space.

"I've worked with you for fifteen years. I've never heard you talk like this before. The D&P Bronstein index? What the frack?" James asked and gave George a little shoulder punch. George smiled and shrugged his shoulders.

"Man, I hope you're right," James said."Plus, that was a stroke of brilliance, setting the old man up for slower growth. He's steamrolling to see improvement by the end of next year. That'll take the pressure off."

"It's just how I see it," George said.

"We'll work just as hard, either way, but certain subjective market elements are entirely outside of our control and so will naturally make it harder to achieve certain goals and milestones. It's really about aligning with market flow."

"You are like a fine wine, George," James said happily.

"You just get better and better with age. It's inspiring, buddy."

James waved his arm, indicating that George should settle in.

"I'm having lunch brought in for the two of us," James added, "that way you can get a feel for the place."

George sat down at his new desk and looked around. James gave him a little wave and headed to get some work done.

~

George worked for a few hours. It felt great to be back. He could hardly believe how quickly his luck had changed. It was a head-spinner, for sure.

Maybe there is something to the tarot and the whole psychic thing, he thought.

In the late afternoon, George left his office and, after getting directions from Muriel, headed to the break room. He planned to grab a gourmet coffee quickly.

He was terribly impressed with the ability to get freshly ground gourmet organic espresso at the push of a button. He made his drink and sat at a little table.

Within earshot of George, a couple of young suits, Steve and Ray, chatted.

"So, I said, go ahead. Walk out. Disappoint your parents, your relatives, and two hundred of your closest friends," Ray said.

"It's not like I care if your daddy loses his many deposits."

"Good for you, Ray," Steve said, although as he was checking his iPhone, it wasn't clear that he was listening all that well to his friend.

"I was so like, call my bluff, sweetheart. Make my day," Ray said, obviously wound up and more than a little bitter over his relationship with the woman in his life.

"Think she will?" Steve asked, sounding as if he didn't care one way or the other.

"Of course not," Ray said smugly.

George, mesmerized by the light and color of the nicely appointed break room, a bit wired from the espresso that he was sipping, and entirely high on positive energy from his new job, could not help himself.

He addressed Ray, without considering whether or not they would find him rude.

"But she will," George said.

The two guys looked up at George.

"What'd you say?" Ray asked, incredulous.

"She's going to call your bluff because she met someone. It's what screwed things up, to begin with," George said.

Then, realizing that he had quite likely overstepped the bounds of polite company, George got up and hurriedly exited the room.

"Who was that guy?" Ray asked Steve.

"George something. New guy, lots of attitude. He was downright sassy to Winston this morning. He'll probably be toast by next week," Steve said and checked his social media feeds.

Ray was deep in thought about his relationship.

"He's not right, is he?" Ray inquired, hesitantly.

"No. Of course not," Steve said.

"But what if he is?" Ray fretted.

"How could he be? He's never even seen you before today, and he sure hasn't met your fiancée."

~

Four weeks into his new job, George looked like the happiest worker bee alive as he entered data into his laptop. His new office walls were now decorated with framed vintage car pictures.

Vintage car models were lined up on his desk, alongside George's dragon netsuke. Winston stood silently in the doorway, watching George work.

"Question!" Winston said to get George's attention. Startled, George wondered how long his boss had been standing in his doorway.

"The proposed merger with Link Star... Good idea or no?" Winston asked. George looked up and gave him the thumbs down sign.

"Gotcha," Winston said and left. A moment later, Steve entered.

"Hey, uh, George. Got a minute?" Steve finally said when George didn't look up.

George smiled and waved Steve into his office.

"What's up, Steve?" George asked. Steve fidgeted.

"You were right about my ex. I guess I didn't love Kelly the way I thought I did because, uh, I met a girl..." Steve admitted.

George was shaking his head no before Steve could get the words out of his mouth.

"Bad news," George said, and continued to shake his head no. Steve's face fell. He immediately looked disappointed and more than a little sad.

"Not the one, huh?" Steve said, dejection filling his voice.

George shook his head and then shrugged.

"It's really your choice, but here's what I see. Sex, fun, and games… at first. And lots of it, an enjoyable phase. But then you'll be bored and ready to break up with her, but before you can tell her, two months from now, she'll be pregnant. You do the right thing… and then start to hate each other, and that phase lasts a long, long time… if you go down that road," George said.

"Thanks, George," said Steve. He sadness was quickly turning into relief.

"That's a shame, but not a road I wanna go down. It's just that I get so lonely... You know? I really want to have a deep connection with someone."

Mimi's face flashed in front of George's eyes, and he nodded. He almost teared up because he was so instantly filled with real longing and deep emotion. He missed her company and their unique connection so profoundly.

"Wait for the next one, Steve-o. She's a keeper. You'll be so happy that it will be hard for you to accept it, seeing as how all of your past relationships have been pretty bad," George said.

"That's true, I've had shit relationships," Steve said.

"It's why it's so easy for me to settle, I guess. You're right, I should spend some time and… what was it you said before… meditate on feeling worthy?"

"That's it," George said solemnly. I oughta try that myself, he thought.

"Thanks, George," Steve said and left.

George took stock of his office. Something was wrong. It took George a minute to figure out what was bothering him. He laughed at himself. All it took was the thought of Mimi. Just her face, and he was suddenly more honest.

He stood and took down his vintage car prints and scooped up the car models. He put them on the floor by the door. That version of George is dead, he reminded himself.

~

Returning from work, George pulled into his driveway and parked his flashy new convertible. He got out and looked at his prize-winning roses.

Was that some kind of beetle that he'd seen on the bush at the end by the mailbox? The thought horrified him.

Gently touching the green leaves of the bush, he realized that he'd imagined the beetle.

He was thrilled to note that the Phytophthora, if that was what it had been, had disappeared entirely.

Ed drove his beat-up station wagon, singing his heart out, as he turned the corner towards his house. To his shock, a brand new, terribly expensive sports car was parked in George's driveway.

Ed parked the wagon on his driveway and got out.

"Hey, George. What's that? A rental?" Ed managed to get out, struggling to be polite.

"Not a rental, Ed," George said modestly and smiled kindly at his neighbor.

"A loaner? Your Prius in the shop? I've heard those things are trouble," Ed sneered, unable to stop himself.

"Sold the Prius, which was a fantastic car by the way. Highly recommend them. Bought this bad boy on impulse. Beauty, isn't she?" George finally admitted.

"I'd put her in the garage, but I'm going out for a bit of fun later."

George walked toward his front door, using the remote on the keys to lock the sports car. The car security alarm chirped a beautiful little tone to indicate that it was now armed.

~

*E*d was entirely astounded. He was unable to beat down his typical jealous response. It was totally unfair, he thought to himself. Does this guy have some nerve, or what?

It sickened him thoroughly that his "goody-two-shoes" neighbor was actually a white-collar criminal and he was making a complete mockery out of honest, hard-working folk like him.

Ed knew many people who were laid off and couldn't find a job to save their lives, yet Mr. Slick here comes out of the same situation smelling like roses.

He needed to be stopped, and someone should turn him and his accomplices in to the authorities. Ed wondered how he was going to finally going to take the guy down.

"What kind of mileage that get?" Ed finally managed to cough out.

George gave a " thumbs down" sign while making a raspberry noise. Ed was aghast.

Mister tight-ass now doesn't even give a damn about what mileage he gets? Is this the same guy that knows exactly what his energy savings are using double glazed friggin' windows?

What a duplicitous SOB, Ed thought to himself and frowned.

"See ya, Ed," George said with a big grin as he went inside his home.

~

Retiring to his home office, George sipped a brandy while listening to soft jazz music. Deep in thought, he stared at his laptop screen, which showed his financial portfolio on an upward trend.

He knew that he should be feeling happy, but for some strange reason, George was feeling sad.

He suddenly realized that this was probably the first time he had looked at his healthy financial portfolio and felt down.

What is happening to me? He wondered to himself.

~

Ed sat at his computer in his cluttered den and downloaded Monsieur Psychic's commercial into his editing software.

Then he held up a recent photograph of George.

"The jig is up, Miss your Psychic, my ass. You may be fooling some of the people with your devious, sleight-of-hand con games, but I know who you are, George, old boy," he said to the image on the screen.

"I don't exactly know what your new scam is, mister, but you ain't gonna hurt no one ever again. Why? Because I am taking you down!"

He then scanned in the picture that he'd secretly taken of George and smiled happily.

Still sitting, staring at his screen, focused on his current and projected financials, George was at a loss. He could not understand precisely why he was feeling so lonely and sad.

He had always been content with his own company. In fact, he preferred solitude to socializing with others.

Yet, here he was, not for the first time in his life choosing jazz, brandy, and solitude, and yet—for the very first time—feeling downright miserable.

He felt an urge to connect with Mimi. He knew that seeing her face and listening to her soothing voice would make him feel happier, but he hesitated.

He hadn't called Mimi like he'd said he would, and what if she was feeling hurt or disappointed? If he called her, she would misconstrue his motivation for telephoning.

He didn't want to resume their relationship or whatever it was they had shared.

They may have casually dated for a while, but he was sure that they both understood that it was just a loosey-goosey kind of connection, where both of them were feeling lonely and perhaps a bit curious about each other.

They were so different in every way imaginable that an ongoing relationship was laughable, and any idea of a long-term romance was out of the question.

He was sure that she must feel the same way, especially as she had this whole "going with the flow" thing going on. Yet, he so dearly wanted to talk to her as a friend.

He decided not to call her directly and instead chose a more devious plan of action.

So as not to be seen, he placed a strip of masking tape over his webcam.

He then put on his headset, called the 3rd Eye hotline, and requested Mimi.

~

George's face entirely lit up when Mimi appeared on his 17-inch screen.

When she smiled and said, "Hello," he felt a pain in his heart, soon followed by a warm gush of joy.

"I know you requested a video," she said, "but your picture isn't coming up on my screen. Can you see me?"

"Yes," answered George, disguising his voice.

"My webcam's broken, but I want to pay for the video. I can see you, and the audio's better."

"Okay, then. Thank you for calling the 3rd Eye. This is Mimi. How may I help you?"

George suddenly felt lost for words.

He realized that he didn't so much want to have a conversation with her but rather just look at her as she talked about anything and listen to her voice. Mimi remained quiet, however, waiting for a response.

"I... I might need money help. I can't seem to figure it out. No matter what I do, it goes wrong," George finally said.

Mimi became quiet for a few seconds and tilted her head to the left, as if she was listening to someone or something else.

"Perhaps you need to let that go," she then declared.

"Let that go?" asked George, forgetting to disguise his voice.

"Let what go?" he then asked, his real voice now hidden. He had thrown a problem out there, not really thinking about it.

"Sir, are you controlling your money... or is your money controlling you?" Mimi asked pointedly.

"I don't know what that means," said George, now feeling unsettled but not knowing why.

"What about my future?"

Mimi looked more deeply into the lens.

"Are you living in the present or just surviving in the present to try and get some... ultimate, future fantasy?" she asked.

"What about you?" George asked, his undisguised voice sounding high-pitched and vulnerable.

"What about me, George?" Mimi asked.

Feeling shocked at being so quickly unmasked, George wondered for a split second if he should deny his subterfuge and continue his charade.

"I know so little about you," he heard himself saying in his normal voice.

"You never asked," Mimi replied, her voice quivering a bit and sounding a little less confident.

"I'm asking now," George said.

"Tell me about your parents."

"For starters, they weren't New Age hippies," Mimi replied as if correcting a glaring error in his thinking.

"My mom was a psychologist, and my dad taught engineering at a university. They were lifelong, registered Republicans, actually. Really good people, ethical, moral, and old-fashioned in a good way."

"Looks like I got you all wrong," George said weakly, feeling now a bit lost.

"Can I ask you another question? Completely unrelated."

"Of course. This is your dime," Mimi answered, a little thrown by George's change of direction.

George stared at Mimi's face and suddenly felt like weeping.

Oh, God, he thought.

I've been a complete ass. Am I so utterly stupid as to throw away my only real happiness, the only deep, mutual connection that I've ever had, to throw away the precious love that I found in the autumn of my life? He wondered if he would really be so stupid.

"What is your question?" Mimi asked.

"I make a lot of mistakes," George admitted.

"I've been a fake and a phony all my life, and so I struggle with what's real and… what's right for me. I guess I'm wondering… do you think I could get back with my girlfriend?" George asked softly.

"I kind of blew it."

Mimi paused and seemed to soften.

She reflected for a long moment, and her expression changed rapidly as she cycled through different emotions. At first, her face looked vulnerable, sad, a little angry, and then hopeful before switching back to her professional persona.

"I'm sorry, but I can't comment on that. That question is really for you to answer. However, thank you for calling the 3rd Eye. We do appreciate your business."

George stared as he heard a click and the video faded.

~

Mimi quickly hung up. The blonde made sure that her screen went dark before allowing the tears in her eyes to flow freely down her cheeks.

~

George sat staring at his blank computer screen for an inordinate amount of time before his brain even concocted a cogent thought.

"Well, that was a bad idea," he decided. George realized that he now felt ten times worse than before he made the call.

"Stupid, stupid, stupid," he yelled to himself, resisting the urge to slap himself on the forehead repeatedly.

~

George couldn't help but admire the glorious view from his downtown high-rise office window as he raked his tiny Zen desktop garden, which he had placed by the window.

Soothing Japanese music played as he surveyed his office décor: netsuke figurines and bamboo art.

Before attacking the day, George decided that he would get a cup of coffee.

After calling Mimi the night before, he hadn't slept well.

Making his way to the break room, George got a sense that his coworkers were making comical gestures and gossiping about him behind his back.

He didn't react. He figured that, as he was still relatively new, it had to be some kind of typical "new hire" office hazing behavior.

As he made his selection from the generous choices of gourmet coffee, James entered the break room and sidled up alongside him.

"Hi, George," he greeted cheerily.

"James," George greeted in response.

"Are you okay?" asked James.

"Why do you ask?" George asked, scrutinizing James' facial expression and demeanor for clues to his meaning.

James didn't seem upset, but then he didn't seem particularly happy either.

"I don't know," answered James.

"Maybe it's the Zen garden you have in your office and the strange way that you're acting lately."

"Oh," pondered George, looking over James' shoulder. It was Ray, Muriel, and a group of unknown employees who seemed to be gossiping about the new guy.

"Nobody likes me here, do they?"

"It's not that people don't like you, George," James responded as he waved to indicate that they should take their coffee to a vacant table.

"They just think you're... a little offbeat, I guess. You've got opinions about everything, and most of what you say, strangely enough, seems to come true. Quite frankly, I think that you intimidate people."

"I see," George replied, mulling it over.

"And what about you, James? Do I intimidate you, too?"

"Well... I don't think. It's really not about what I think," James fudged.

"I'm not the George you used to know, am I?"

"Want to tell me what's going on?" James asked, feeling now a sense of relief and freedom.

"Are you hungry?" asked George.

"We could go grab some lunch?"

"Now?" answered James, looking at his watch, "Isn't it a bit early?" George said nothing, and the younger man shrugged and spoke. "Oh, sure, what the hell. Let's go to lunch."

George took James to what had become his favorite Japanese restaurant. He had warm memories of his visits there with Mimi.

Upon entering, he was surprised that the restaurant looked and felt different to him. He thought that perhaps it was the time of day that had changed things. The eating establishment, now, in some disappointing way, felt less cozy, warm, and intimate.

James followed George's lead by taking off his shoes when they were ushered to a table near the front.

"Seriously?" James grumbled when he looked down at the barely off-the-floor table.

"You don't like Japanese?" George asked.

"Oh, I love sushi, but I'm not so nuts about having to practically undress and sit on the floor to eat it. Besides, these people freak me out. They keep bowing and smiling so much that they make me feel like I have to be on my best behavior."

"I'm sorry if this makes you feel uncomfortable," George apologized.

"I just thought it would be a nice change from someplace like Hooters."

James gave a brief giggle.

"They smile at you in Hooters, too, but at least you can act like a badass there and still feel good about yourself. Don't worry, though, this is good. Let's just order," James said.

Then he tried to get into a comfortable sitting position, stuffing cushions beneath his large bottom.

As a smiling and bowing Japanese waiter arrived to take their order, James quickly and unsuccessfully looked up and down the menu for something recognizable that he could safely order.

As George ordered the same sushi and Tempura dish that he'd had before, James put down his menu in defeat.

"I'll have the same," James conceded to the smiling waiter.

"Very good," the waiter said and left.

"So, cut to the chase, George," James said after taking a sip of water.

"What's with all this Japanese shit in your office and now this? Are you dating an Asian or contemplating a mail-order bride from Japan or something?"

"No, I..."

"Hey, get me right, I'm not a racist or anything. You can tell me. I hear the Japanese make the best wives. Very compliant and... supportive of the male, am I right?"

"No, it's got nothing to do with Asian women, James. I just like their culture... it speaks to me, you could say," George said, thoughtfully.

"Yeah, okay, I get it," said James.

"First time I went to London, I felt like I had just come home, you know? Like the English people were my people. Which they are, as a matter of fact. We Millers can trace ourselves right back to the Mayflower and across the pond, isn't that something? Of course, there are a lot of Millers, the whole country is full of them, and there were a whole bunch of them on the Mayflower, but I'm kinda sure..."

Either realizing the irrelevance of his thought or figuring out that he sounded a little dumb, James stopped talking.

"You were saying?" he prompted George to continue.

"I guess something happened to me in my... consulting job," George began to explain.

"What happened?" asked James as their meals arrived.

"That was quick!" James gestured to the waiter, who smiled and bowed

James looked at his meal, not recognizing any of it: it looked to him like some fried food with octopus and other curious seafood.

"I don't know what happened, James. I wish I did know."

"You've lost me," replied James, poking his food with his chopsticks.

"It's hard to explain, but it's like a switch went on. Or off. Some inner me I never knew about got switched on..." George said, his peaceful facial expression belying his inner confusion.

"So the George we all know and love got... switched off?" James asked, taking a mouthful of food.

"It's more like he faded and merged with this other George. The really bizarre thing is... I don't much like that other George," said George.

"You're scaring me, George," James said, dropping some food from his chopsticks.

"You sound a bit like a screwy person. Maybe you should see somebody. You could have multiple personalities."

"I love this music," George announced as if now hearing it for the first time. It was traditional Japanese music, orchestral court music, in fact.

He was surprised that he had not noticed the lovely music on his previous visits. Feeling deeply at peace and at home, George dug into his food.

James stopped struggling with his food and pushed his plate away.

"I can't eat this crap," he said. "You know I don't go in for all that psychology BS, but I only ask one thing, George."

"What's that?"

"Don't embarrass me at work. Weird stunts you pull in the office reflect poorly on me. Act daft as a loon on your own time... after hours. During work hours, be professional. Be nice and polite to everybody. Don't get into people's business. That guy Steve, from finance? He swears that you're some reincarnated guru or something. It's embarrassing."

"I just told him what I thought," George replied calmly.

"Sure, sure... about his personal life," James said.

"As far as I know, you're not qualified to counsel or give advice on personal matters. Do what we were hired to do: finance and accounting or related consulting."

George was taken aback but, appreciating James' candor and honesty, maintained his composure.

"James, I appreciate you offering me this opportunity," he replied in an even tone.

"You didn't have to bring me on board, and I'm grateful. I'll do my best not to embarrass you."

The rest of the lunch passed mostly in silence. James drank his tea and ate some rice while George relished his meal and sipped his tea.

~

*B*ack at the offices, George walked past the busy cubicles to his own office. Some coworkers were less covert in their sniggering and their gestures as he passed.

"George?" Muriel called.

"Yes?" answered George just as he approached his office door.

"Winston needs to see you, ASAP," she said, barely looking up from her computer screen.

"What's going on?" George asked quietly as he approached her desk.

"You don't know?" she asked.

"Know what?" he asked, now a little concerned.

"It's not good," Muriel said, preferring to err on the side of nondisclosure as she returned to her work to signal, "this conversation is over."

George popped his head around Winton's open office door, knocking on it politely.

"You wanted to see me, Winston?" he asked.

"Come in, George. Close the door," Winston said. He removed his eyes from his computer screen and gave George his full attention.

"Have you seen it?" he asked, as George shut the office door.

"Seen what, Winston?" asked George.

"It's all over the internet. How have you not seen it?" Winston asked, looking closely at George to detect any subterfuge. Winston punched some keys on his laptop and swiveled it around so that George could take a look.

The large screen loaded a YouTube video.

Winston clicked on the full-screen option. The video played another edit of the "Monsieur Psychic" infomercial.

Instantly recognizing it, George sat down and braced himself for inevitable embarrassment and humiliation... and the strong possibility of being let go.

This particular edit was different from the one he had seen before and showed George's animated face on top of Mr. Psychic's body.

Winston, who had already watched it many times, did not look at the screen but seemed more curious to see George's reactions as it played.

George watched at first in abject horror and embarrassment. However, as the video continued to play, he actually began to find it very funny. Before long, George found himself laughing.

Puzzled by his reaction, Winston looked back at the screen to see what was happening and make sure that the video was still playing. It was.

"What's so funny?" Winston asked.

Unable to answer right away, George laughed and laughed almost like he was out of his mind.

"This is you?" Winston asked, referring to Mr. Psychic on the screen.

Still laughing hysterically, George managed to nod, yes.

"You are Monsieur Psychic?" Winston asked, beginning to get annoyed now.

"You think this is funny?" he barked at George.

"I've been outed!" George said, tears of laughter rolling from his eyes. He couldn't stop laughing.

"Darn right you're outed," Winston said, not sure what the heck was going on.

"The phone hasn't stopped ringing since lunch." Unable to understand what George was finding so funny, he looked at the screen and then back again at George.

"Wouldn't a normal reaction be to feel ashamed and humiliated?" he asked George.

"You have to understand," George said, sobering up and wiping his eyes with a tissue.

"I've been dreading this for months. I've had nightmares about this moment. I gave up a job I was destined for... and the love of my life..." George didn't finish his thought, but suddenly became very sad and very elated all at the same time.

"Pull yourself together, man. You're acting like a lunatic," Winston said, not knowing if George was going to cry or continue to laugh.

George's expression now looked closer to that of pain, however.

"That's correct, Winston," George said in a more serious tone of voice.

"I have been acting like a lunatic. What on earth was I thinking?" Before Winston could answer or further question the man, George quickly rose from his chair.

"I'll vacate my office immediately," he said and exited without even a cursory glance back at a baffled-looking Winston.

~

*W*inston was left pondering. He couldn't understand what had just happened. He decided that maybe if he played the video again, he might understand George's bizarre behavior.

Clicking play once again, he watched the video from the beginning to seek any hidden clues that it might contain.

Reentering his office, George quickly packed his netsuke and whatever else would fit into his briefcase. Looking irritated, James entered the open door.

"Are you nuts?" James said without any preliminary greeting.

"Monsieur Psychic, was your consulting gig? Buddy, do you know how bad this makes me look?"

"I'm sorry, James," George responded, continuing with his packing.

"It wasn't ever my intention to make you look bad or foolish. I was so ashamed about the whole thing, I never told anybody."

"That doesn't make me feel any better. I thought we were friends," James complained and stormed out of the office when he saw Winston approaching.

Winston entered George's office and closed the door.

"I didn't say that you were fired," he said to George.

"You're not firing me?" George asked and turned to face Winston, a framed bamboo print in his hands.

"Honestly, you've been right about so much... The firm has bene-fited from having you here," Winston admitted.

"Here's the deal," he continued.

"It's a YouTube video, so what? Right? Folks around here may treat you differently for a few days, but... people get bored, they move on to the next thing... it will all blow over in a few days or weeks... one month tops."

"If that's your way of saying I'm not fired and that I still have a job... I appreciate it," George responded.

"However, although I absolutely need this job... I really don't fit in."

"That doesn't matter," argued Winston.

"Coworkers are coworkers. They don't have to be your friends. Do they?"

"Question," said George as he paused for dramatic effect.

"Will I control my money or will I let my money control me?"

Practically scratching his head with puzzlement, Winston realized that he would never figure this guy out.

"I don't know the answer to that," Winston admitted.

"I know the answer," said George as he passed Winston with whatever of his stuff he could carry.

"I'll have to come back to get the rest of my personal items."

Winston watched George leave. The older man's expression was baffled and helpless. The head of the firm was at a loss for how to reach this quirky guy and make the situation make sense.

"Is it the money? I can give you more money," he called after George, but the man was already out of earshot.

~

George wandered by the side of the road in his neighborhood. A car screamed past him and narrowly avoided hitting him. George quickly looked to see who was driving.

The driver, who happened to be Ed, ducked down out of sight before George could get a good look.

As the shock of nearly being run over wore off, George realized that the car that had almost mown him down was the beautiful antique roadster that he used to own.

The vehicle drove off in a cloud of dust.

The next morning George made some decisions. He knew what he wanted to do. After a quick trip to an office supply store, George was ready. The changes might be scary, but he would deal with that.

George placed a "FOR SALE" sign in his new car window and then promptly hammered a "HOUSE FOR SALE" sign into his lawn.

Ed exited his house and mug of coffee in hand, and walked over to George.

"You're moving out, George?" he asked.

"I guess," replied George, not feeling like he needed to be hospitable.

"You bought a bigger place?"

"I lost my job, Ed. Both of them," George responded coldly.

Ed, for a moment, looked genuinely shocked.

"The YouTube videos?" he blurted out.

"You saw those?" George asked, not really interested in how his obvious enemy might respond.

"Yeah," Ed responded as nonchalantly as he could.

"Someone e-mailed me... I'm so sorry, George." Ed didn't sound sorry.

"Ah, forget it. I'm sorry about the bad French impression," George said, smiling to himself. He laughed to know that Ed did not realize that he knew who had made the videos.

"I knew it was you," Ed admitted.

"Didn't know you had a sense of humor. You were funny. The videos, I mean, they were pretty funny," Ed said, without much conviction.

"Yeah," sighed George. "Why'd you do it, Ed?"

George finally faced Ed straight on. He knew by Ed's facial expression that he had caught him entirely by surprise.

"The videos, Ed... I know it was you."

Knowing that he was caught, Ed didn't bother trying to deny it.

"You don't remember me, do you?" Ed said coldly. Ed was as angry as he'd ever been. He was surprised to realize that he didn't at all care that George was losing everything. It served the creep right.

"Remember you from where?" George asked tonelessly.

"Summer camp," Ed responded with serious resolve, his face and body becoming tense.

"Summer camp?" George couldn't really process what Ed had said.

Did the guy really say "summer camp?" Maybe the old boy had a screw loose, a big one.

"You were there, don't deny it," Ed answered, his steely eyes fixed on George's gaze.

"I've been to summer camp once in my life, but that was way back..."

"I'm not surprised you don't remember," Ed replied with a chilly note of derision in his voice.

"I was a runty little snot-nosed poor kid. Some charity paid for me to go to that camp. You and the other big kids, the rich punks, ignored me the whole time. Wasn't good enough for you, was I?"

Surprised at this turn of events, George racked his brain to recover any relevant memories that he might have from that time of his childhood.

"Ed, I honestly have no memory..."

"I didn't go to a posh school like you and your snooty pals. My father was a roofer all his life. So, to you and your stuck-up little brat friends, we were inferior?! I didn't have money... but I had feelings. Your kind makes me sick."

Looking as if he might cry at any second, Ed stormed off back to the sanctuary of his house. George stared after him.

Was that Ed's problem with him? Something that happened forty-plus years ago continued to torture Ed, and his response was to torture George?

~

George stood by the open door of his home office and wondered where to begin to strip it down. His first stop was to rip his retirement planning graph from the wall. Then he tore it into several pieces.

Placing pieces in his shredder, he hesitated just briefly before pressing the shred button. Years, months, and days of past collated data and future projections, as demonstrated on the colorful graph, slowly got swallowed up by the sharp and powerful cross-cut blades. As he watched the last graph disappear, his phone rang.

"Hello, son. Nice surprise," George II said when he answered.

"Is it true?" George III asked angrily, in lieu of a greeting.

"You're Mr. Psychic?"

~

George's son stood, his face red and angry, as he stared at his big flat screen TV. A laptop was hooked up to it; the Monsieur Psychic video was stopped on a close-up of George II's disguised and ridiculous face.

"In so far as I went on TV, disguised as a French man, offering my psychic powers... yes, it's true," George answered, sitting down in expectation of hearing more of his son's anger.

"It's not a joke?" demanded George III's voice through the phone.

"It is not, though I'm sure that we'll look back and laugh at this... some day," George replied.

"Be serious, Dad," George III said, frustration and anger in his voice.

"You told us you were a business consultant. We can't believe you were so... deceitful. Acting so noble, so... righteous. What else have you lied about, all these years? Because if you lied about mom," and George III's voice broke down. Then he spoke again.

"If she never left... or if you got rid of her or made her leave and then you lied about it..." The younger man's voice broke, and he gave a small cry.

"She left us," George II said, and his voice broke, suddenly stricken by the raw pain in his son's voice, "And she never came back."

How had things gotten so off track? How was he going to fix this mess?

"I don't know if I can believe that. I don't know if I can believe you. You're such a liar, Dad. You were so vague… not sharing any details, and we really feel it's the self-righteous lies and smugness —" George III sounded as if he might go off on a tirade.

George II didn't want his son to say things that he might later regret, so he chose to be rude and interrupt the boy.

"I'm sorry you feel this way, son," George answered, not allowing his hurt to come to the surface.

"I wasn't trying to harm you or anyone in any way. Who's this "we" you keep referring to? Do you mean you and Jenn?"

"I just got off the phone with granddad. We had a long talk."

"You told them about the videos?" George asked, the mention of his father triggering some alarm within him.

"No, he called me. He got e-mails from everybody he knows, apparently. Oh, and their anniversary party? They said to tell you not to bother to come."

Before George could respond or even process what his son had blurted into the phone, the call went dead.

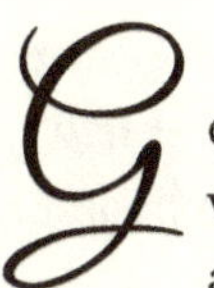

George held his silent cell phone to his ear as if not wanting to admit to himself that his son had called him a liar and subsequently hung up on him. Did George II just say that he was disinvited from his parents' 55th anniversary party?

Was his entire family disowning him? The thoughts of his ever-loving and ever-supportive elderly parents now wishing to cut off communication with him felt too much for him to bear.

He immediately grew exhausted and sick to his stomach with grief and despair.

The day had grown dark. Lying on his bed, fully dressed without the will or energy to switch on the light, George felt debilitating hopelessness, which he didn't know how to shift.

He felt like polishing off the remainder of the brandy, but he knew that alcohol was only a reprieve, at best.

Reaching for his cell phone, he searched for the only name on his contact list that he had any desire to speak to; the single voice that would honestly have the power to make him feel whole and well again.

He pressed the phone to his ear as the call rang on the other end of the line. When George reached reception, he asked for her.

"You've reached the 3rd Eye; this is Mimi. How can I help you?" A soothing wave of relief surfed through George's body the minute that he heard Mimi's voice. Unable to speak, however, his body just as quickly went into a state of panic.

"This is Mimi. Hello?" her voice on his cell phone repeated the greeting.

Emotionally paralyzed with insecurity and weakness, George softly cried into the phone until the line went dead. Feeling sadness he had never felt before, George dropped the phone to the floor.

George woke early. He had nowhere to go and nothing pressing to do, so he was in no hurry to get up. His cell phone beeped with a calendar message reminding him that today was his parents' anniversary.

The thought of them not wanting to share this momentous event in their shared history tore him apart.

Staring up at the ceiling, George took stock of his life. When did he become afraid of things? It seemed clear to him now that at some point in his life, he had begun to live in fear.

He feared things that were coming; they weren't happening yet, but they could happen… things that were beyond his control… things that could hurt him or someone that he loved.

The more he considered his past approach to life, the more he realized the morass of dark fear, near panic, that he had lived up to this point.

Looking at his lifelong thought process clearly, it didn't make much sense. It wasn't logical to be afraid of future negative possibilities, because it didn't make sense to be terrified of things that weren't happening now.

It wasn't intelligent to draw conclusions and make important life decisions based on trepidation that something terrible, something truly horrific, might happen. It had nothing to do with present reality.

His thought process and the mental path it now led him down astounded him. He stared at the ceiling and considered whether he had actually made most of his life decisions based on fear.

He was disappointed in himself to realize that, yes, he had made most life decisions informed by fear-based emotions, including the intense ones, such as terror.

Yet, at the time, it seemed so right and so smart. It was logical to seek to avoid pain, up to a point.

It occurred to him that an underlying rigidity had caused him to be physically, mentally, and emotionally contracted all his life. Words drifted into his mind.

Aite no nai kenka wa denkinu.

It was the Japanese proverb that he had meditated upon months ago after being fired.

"One cannot quarrel without an opponent," George said slowly.

He was dumbfounded to realize that false George, his fearful self, the part that chose to isolate and attempt to control, was his opponent all along.

His dread had reduced him to living as an autobot; he'd been like an automotive robot, a sentient controlled being that acted and functioned but was never truly alive.

Once he tried to remember the moment that he began living from fear, he became aware of how deep the pit of trepidation within him actually was.

He could not only see the ramifications of this unreasonable fear, a pit of terror within him that he experienced as a sort of cobwebby, oily, dark tunnel that seemed to run through the center of his being.

He'd made choices based upon some terrifying nebulous negative "something" that might occur in the future, a future which he or no one could control. The whole malformed and indefinable thought process, and any related notion, now seemed completely ludicrous.

I haven't ever been truly alive, he whispered.

In his mind's eye, George saw soldiers in a foreign land, still hiding out and fighting long after the war had ended. He had really and truly been living in a false reality, all the while believing it was real.

His eyes widened. He focused on his breath. He allowed himself to fully and deeply feel a sense of wonder and shock over his life-long illogical choice process: the epiphany was astounding.

When he heard the thought, "I've been so stupid," he immediately countered it. "You didn't know," he whispered to himself.

You can't know what you don't know, he decided. He wasn't going to castigate himself about an old way of being. Obviously, a person who made choices based on fear of the unknown was terribly scared and trying to avoid catastrophe. There had been no real catastrophe in his life, he realized.

Sure, his wife had left, and it had hurt for a time. In retrospect, he hadn't been a great husband. He was young when they married and had hardly paid her very much mind. He'd ignored her even when the woman indicated that she wanted deep affection and frequent attention.

Work kept him busy. He'd told her to occupy herself. Then, when George III's mother wanted to spend money on herself, for art classes, or whatever, George had always explained why that wasn't possible. She had to stay home, he told her: that money was for retirement, George III's preschool, or to fix something in the house. He'd said she'd have to read library books or entertain herself for free.

He had treated her almost like a pretty object. It was as if she were an asset to bring to dinner parties or family functions. He hadn't really and genuinely cared about her as a person, although he had thought that he loved her. Sure, he'd been young. We all were, he reasoned. He hadn't really known what it meant to really and truly love someone.

He remembered her smile and bubbling laughter; she loved to tease and joke. He recalled her love of vivid colors. He saw an image of her hair aflame in sunlight as she chased George III around the backyard.

Memories of her asking for innocent pleasures, and him happily saying no every time, and her face crumpling with hurt, true sadness, entered his mind. Her disappointment became anger on a few occasions.

George's face flushed hotly. He felt sick, remembering what an insufferable tight-wad that he'd been in his twenties and thirties. Not only that, but he had been self-righteous about it as if he were a superior person.

I was so controlling, he realized. No wonder his wife had left. He wept from shame. It was as if the remembrance and acknowledgement of his shocking behavior and past attitudes were too much for him to bear now.

"Carpe Diem" was never his motto, he reasoned as the tears slowed

Instead, like Chicken Little of childhood storybook fame, he'd lived in perpetual fear that the sky was falling.

He pressed his face against his pillow. His cheeks were wet with tears. His hands were shaking. He felt queasy, thinking about how stingy he'd been and how he'd hurt his young wife.

She'd shut down, eventually. George's wife had given up asking for anything for herself, and he remembered feeling relief.

It had taken her eighteen months, he supposed, to raise the money for the divorce attorney. He imagined her scrimping and saving from the tiny household budget that he allowed her, selling her few personal belongings, things left to her by her dead mother, to come up with a retainer for a divorce lawyer, finally.

He remembered her missing wedding band and how her closet got emptier and emptier. She had sold everything that she owned to escape him. Hot shame flooded his face, body, and being. He wept until he was devoid of tears.

Then, in his darkest moment, eyes hot and inflamed from weeping, his face scrunched so tight that it hurt, he heard it:

"Sir, are you controlling your money... or is your money controlling you?"

He heard Mimi's voice, like an angel, asking him that question that he hadn't before recognized as relevant. As he lay there, emotionally spent, he realized that her philosophical inquiry applied to life areas outside of money and finances. The query was applicable to every facet of his life.

Will I work with my emotions, sitting with, allowing, and processing them, or will my feelings control me? Will I let anything other people's opinions control me, or will I live from my self-opinion? Will I continue down the path of fear that I've travelled all my life, or will I follow my heart? Will I let anything or anyone else control me, or am I going to control myself and my life? He asked himself.

The more he played with the idiom and asked questions of himself, exploring the logic and his feelings, the more confidence he gained and the more his self-worth grew.

I am going to control myself and my life path, George II decided. And on that thought, he jumped out of bed to begin his day with renewed vigor and purpose.

~

It was while shaving and looking at his visage in the bathroom mirror that it occurred to him that he wouldn't let his parents decide whether or not he would celebrate them. He would show up at their anniversary party.

If they were afraid that their son—Monsieur Psychic—would show up and embarrass them, in front of their closest friends, then perhaps those people were not in truth good friends.

He was their son, after all. Would they put their socially "proper" friends and acquaintances before their flesh and blood?

If that were honestly the case, then they would need to tell him so to his face because, family embarrassment or not, he was going to attend their celebration, and nothing, at this point, was going to stop him.

If they truly didn't love him and want him in their lives, then so be it. They could disown him. But they would need to say and do so… in person.

He dressed and then drove toward his parents' home.

~

As George pulled up outside his parents' palatial home, he saw that many classy cars were parked in the street and crammed together in the driveway.

Taking a deep breath, he grabbed his gift-wrapped present and, head held high, strode with purpose and conviction to the front door, which was ajar.

Standing in the hall of the large house, he watched as party guests mixed and mingled. It wasn't until he stepped more fully into the living room that all talking stopped and everyone slowly turned to look at him.

People stopped eating and drinking and seemed mildly shocked at his presence. They stared at him with surprise. Several people looked over to get a sense of how George's parents would react. Putting a brave face on his party crash, George smiled.

"Happy anniversary, Mom and Dad," he said cheerily. Then he added, "Hello, everyone."

Perhaps not wanting to offend their host and hostess, none of the partygoers greeted him in return.

"Hello, George," his mother finally said.

"Can we have a word with you in the study?"

She stood, as did George I, and walked toward the front hall. George II followed.

Behind her, conversation babble, the sound of cutlery and glassware tinkling, and laughter among the guests resumed.

~

George closed the study door and braced himself as he turned to confront his parents.

"What are you doing here, son?" his father asked.

"I'm your son, your only child in fact, and I came to tell you that I love you both and I wish you many more years of happiness together... even if you don't want me here," George replied firmly.

"What are you talking about?" George's mother asked.

"I got your message loud and clear," George explained.

"If I'm not perfect, if I embarrass you in any way, then I'm not good enough for you or your friends. I get it."

George's parents looked at each other as if they did not understand. George noticed how fragile his parents appeared today; perhaps for the first time, they seemed their age.

They were in their eighties and reasonably active, yet George knew that everything passes in this life.

They would eventually be gone. I love my parents so much, George thought.

"I think there's been a misunderstanding, Georgie," George's father finally said, after a lengthy silence.

"Honey, you've got it all wrong," his mother added helpfully.

"I've always had it all wrong, apparently," George responded. Expecting a war of words, he uploaded his brain with a version of the speech that he had mentally practiced while driving to their home.

"I'm sorry if what I did was a cause of embarrassment and distress; it obviously was, but in my defense, I lost my job. So I panicked. I had no one to turn to. I made some bad decisions. You didn't have to exclude me from this moment... this happy celebration. What are you going to do, disown me?"

Completely taken aback, George's parents looked at each other, and back at George, with open mouths.

"I know appearances are everything to you..." George continued, but his father interrupted him.

"George," he said abruptly. "That's not true... nothing of what you're saying makes any sense. What in the heavens are you talking about, son?"

Puzzled, George suddenly felt very unsure of himself and began to feel a bit foolish.

"George the third said that you said for me to... stay away," he said, his statement ending more like a question than a statement.

"We told him that perhaps it was best for you to stay away until we got rid of our friends. We didn't want you to be embarrassed by them if they were judgmental or rude," his mother said.

"But you're always worried about what they think," George answered, not fully processing.

"That may be true, George, that we're conscious of what others think. After your internet video thingy, people did call to gloat... and we let them. We didn't say anything except, yes, that's our George. And you're correct that it was a huge surprise and what some people might describe as embarrassing. But you are wrong about one thing. We care about family first."

"I understand if you want to disown me; it's why I came... to have it out and get it over with," George said. He stuck with his interpretation of events, despite their words to the contrary.

"George, don't be absurd," George's father eventually said, "You're not listening to your mother."

George II flushed bright red. He felt his face. It was hot to the touch.

"We care deeply for you, George. You're our number one concern. We thought we'd get rid of the guests and then spend family time with you and Georgie and his family after," George's mother added.

"Oh," said George, deciding now that it was a good time to sit down.

"I guess I got the wrong end of the stick, so to speak." He wondered if he had misinterpreted George III or if his son had purposefully misled him.

He tried to remember their conversation in detail. His son had been terribly upset about his mother. He'd even wondered if his father had lied about her leaving. It must have been very confusing for him to realize that his father had told him an enormous lie and had been lying for months and months about a few things.

George found that his memory wasn't entirely clear. He was so in the moment now, more aware of his emotions and physical feelings, that it was harder to remember the words that George III had said.

He realized that his throat was hot and scratchy, and he felt like crying. How would his parents react if he cried, he wondered.

At their anniversary party, all their guests are being ignored, and I'm about to cry in the study. Dear Lord, George thought.

"Will I make some tea?" his mother asked sweetly.

"Yes, please. In a little bit," George answered, still coming to grips with his new view of reality.

"You do care about me?" he asked quizzically.

"I'm not a disappointment to you… an embarrassment?"

"Of course not," his mother said. Sitting down beside him, she took his hands in hers.

"You must know that we care for you, sweetheart."

"I don't remember you ever saying so... very often," George said as if thinking hard to try to remember.

"Was I a normal kid?" he then asked. His throat was scratchier than ever.

Surprised by the question, George's mother looked to her husband.

"I don't know. I guess," George I answered. George II felt his eyes grow a little moist.

"I didn't display any... I don't know... weirdness? At all?" George probed.

"You were a sensitive child, not like the other kids. But then at some point, you changed," she said.

"In what way was I changed?" George enquired. His parents exchanged a glance and then looked at George II.

"You hardened up," George's father answered, "we were really worried about you there for a while."

"It was after we sent you to summer camp that one time," she remembered. George II stared in shock. Summer camp?

"You came back changed..." his mother added.

"Something must have happened," George's father interjected, "some kind of incident. We never did figure out exactly what. No one would tell us anything. We had to let it go."

"We thought maybe that someone hurt you," George's mother remembered more.

"But you wouldn't tell us. It was as if whatever had happened to you... You never wanted to talk about it."

"So from then on, we kept you at home with us… to protect you," George's father explained.

"You were an empathetic little boy," George's mother repeated.

"I don't remember any of it," George said, racking his brain.

"You liked to paint and write poetry," George's mother said, smiling at the memory.

"I did?" George II asked with wonder.

"You were a bit of a dreamer," his mother said with great love, "You would talk to flowers and butterflies. You told me they had souls."

"You really loved me," George thought to himself, but ended up saying it out loud.

"Of course, we did and still do—" George's mother insisted.

"But you never said it," George interrupted, grumbling. His mother stared at him, and he stared back.

"As far as I can remember… You never once said that you loved me," George added mournfully.

George's parents look at each other, quizzically. Cut from the same cloth, they spoke at the same time:

"Our parents never told us that they loved us. We didn't know we should do that."

"We can tell you now if you need to hear it," his mother said in a quiet voice.

"Son, we brought you up as best we could," George's father said firmly yet softly.

"We raised you the way that we were raised. The right schools, the right clothes, the right everything," his mother added.

"You sent me to that camp. It was horrible. I was alone," George II retorted.

"Just the one time," his mother said. "After that, we kept you home every summer instead of sending you away to camp… like our friends did with their children. We wanted you safe at home with us."

"Sure, we made mistakes. We tried to bring you up better than the way we were brought up. My father ruled the household with a leather belt. Ran us kids, my siblings and I, like he was an army general. We didn't want any of that for you," his father finished.

"Do you need to hear it?" Meredith asked George II quietly. He looked at her, throat tight, and his eyes welled with tears. He nodded.

"We love you, George. We've always loved you," his mother said, squeezing his hands tighter. George gave a tiny sob.

"I love you, George," she said softly. He stared into his mother's eyes, and he felt her deep, abiding love. He looked at his father.

"I love you, son," his father croaked out. George felt and heard that the old man's voice was thick with deep love and affection.

"Do you love me as Mr. Psychic?" George asked, noticing that his voice sounded like that of a little boy, six years of age or so.

"Monsieur Psychic, Mr. Psychic, or Mister Silly, you'll always be our George," she smiled.

"We love you. I love you… no matter what," George's father said with an air of finality in his voice.

"We're behind you all the way, son… whatever course you set for yourself. Okay?"

George leaned forward and embraced his mom while gesturing to his father to join the group hug. With a hint of awkward emotion and a bit stiffly, his father did.

George II's shoulders shook as he wept silently, overcome with love for his parents. His being buzzed with molecules of emotion and energy. He felt wondrous.

"I love you, Mom," George II said and embraced his mother. Then he hugged his old man.

"I love you, Dad," he said, and he meant it with all of his heart and soul. "Happy Anniversary."

George went home. He didn't feel the need to stay at the party, or even to seek out George III, Jenn, and little Georgie.

Naturally, his son was hurting and very upset about being deceived. George decided to give them time to deal with their feelings. He would work things out with the boy later.

~

eorge sat in bed, not yet tired enough to sleep. Realizing that something was weighing on his mind, he determined to figure out precisely what was bothering him.

Twice in the past few days, the subject of summer camp had come up in conversation.

The very same summer camp, of which he had little or no memory, had been the topic of recent conversation with his neighbor. Some childhood experience had scarred Ed terribly, and it had to be significant.

And then George had flung a mention of it at his parents today, as if it were an accusation. Why was that? And why had his mother said that after that one time he went, that they had kept him home with them each summer? What was the word she had used? It was "safe," that was the word that she had used. Even though all of their friends sent their children there because it was the right summer camp, they kept him home.

Was there a reason that he couldn't remember what happened while attending a summer camp when he was ten years old?

Did something terrible happen that his memory had repressed, as it was too upsetting for his conscious mind?

He decided to employ the technique Mimi had explained when he first met her, the tool she used to help her remember things from the past.

He gave a "command" to his unconscious mind that, during sleep, he would remember an incident from his past, specifically the time that George attended summer camp as a child, if he were now able to face it comfortably.

Expecting little from the exercise, he felt that he had nothing to lose from trying it. He had been growing so much recently, especially emotionally and as a person. Whatever this was, the past incident or experiences, George hoped that he was mentally and emotionally capable of facing it now.

Despite her unusual, and possibly New Age, demeanor and sensibilities, Mimi had wisdom, and he respected her opinions.

"I want to remember what happened in summer camp when I was ten," he repeated dreamily as, fatigued from the day's events, he turned off the lamp and drifted off to sleep.

 *I*n the dreamscape of his mind, George shrank until he was small: he became a young boy. Young George's eyes were wide with fear.

The environment, the inside of a bunkhouse in the woods, was distorted, like a horror movie in a funhouse.

From his position on a top bunk, George observed strange, tough-looking boys watching him and some other kids with a mixture of malice and disdain.

The boys seemed to be whispering about the weakest members of the small herd of male children.

George didn't like being so far away from his family. For the very first time in his little life, he interpreted their sending him away, his mom and dad's choice to place him in this alien and obviously dangerous place, as some kind of punishment.

Figuring that he had done something wrong by accident and was being punished for it, he was able to avoid acknowledging his most profound dread.

In the darkest recesses, at the back of his mind, lurked a genuinely horrifying thought: that his parents didn't really love him, after all.

He felt vulnerable. Terrified of the mean boys grouped, who seemed to enjoy picking on boys just like him, he calculated the odds.

Watching them tease and hit a kid, trying to pick a fight, he wondered how he could escape their vicious attention.

How likely was it that they would leave him alone for over six weeks?

Watching the clowns surround a fat kid, he realized the odds of being left alone were very slim indeed. If summer camp were to be an exercise in survival, it would be safer to be in a group.

Noticing that they picked on the boys that they perceived to be unlike themselves, the quiet kids, the awkward ones, the loners, he decided that, to evade their wrath, he would need to fit in.

He would pretend to be one of them. Without a doubt, he must join the group that was the source of the threat. He must become part of the tough crowd to survive until the end of the summer.

He made friends with some of the group members on the periphery. They were boys who were a bit like him and had joined the group also as a means of self-protection, or boys who didn't take pleasure in harming others but did so to fit in. Somehow, he just knew these things.

He tried to stay anonymous and avoid sticking out. He developed an unspoken understanding with some of the other kids as he knew instinctively that the minor members of the gang were just as terrified as he was of the core group of toughies.

What little George was not expecting, however, was that being like them was not going to be as easy as merely pretending to be one of them and faking being tough.

"Hey, you!" a rough ringleader called out to little George, one beautiful summer morning.

The older kid was standing beneath the bleachers of the empty baseball field, surrounded by his usual crowd. George thought that maybe they had been smoking or pretending to do so.

"Me?" responded an already terrified little George, who was walking to get his lunch. His heart sank. He had stupidly allowed himself to be caught alone.

"Yeah, you," the tough little wannabe gangster said and pointed at him. "Come here."

Little George hesitated and swallowed hard. What could this mean? He wondered. Was he about to get beaten up, or something worse?

"Are you scared?" the tough boy teased.

"No, I'm not scared," George replied, adopting a mean walk as he approached.

"Whatcha want?"

"See that skinny kid over there?" the little toughie directed with a tilt of his head. George looked toward the lake.

A thin kid was sitting on the dock by himself. The kid was singing. Sheesh, George thought. How foolish could that kid be? This wasn't the kind of mob that you could sing around.

"Yeah?" answered little George, "What about him?"

"He called you names. What you gonna do about it, Georgie?" the toughie sneered.

Having an idea where this was going, little George thought quickly. The kid was skinny and more fragile-looking than he was; he probably wouldn't put up much of a fight or be hard to beat. Not that George wanted to beat him up physically.

Perhaps if he acted tough and intimidated the skinny kid, enough to make him cry, then the rough kids, the thugs and bullies, would back off and consider it a victory.

"Well?" the kid challenged little George.

"Whatcha gonna do about it? Are you a wuss?"

"No, I'm not a wuss," answered little George, walking towards the skinny kid determinedly.

"No one calls me names and gets away with it," he added, as he spat meanly on the ground.

"Hey, you!" George called out as he got closer to the skinny kid.

"You got the nerve to call me names?"

Sensing an impending fight, kids from all over quickly gravitated towards little George and the skinny kid. The kid stopped singing and stood up. He looked at George.

George motioned for the kid to come toward him. He didn't want to do this near water, as somebody could get hurt or worse.

"I didn't call you names," the skinny kid said, his body tensing up in terror.

"Yes, he did," insisted one of the tough kids.

"I heard him. We all heard him, didn't we?" the toughie leader challenged his gang. George looked at the group. They all nodded and sneered.

"Yes," the tough kids all agreed. "We all heard him calling you names."

"Do you have a problem with me?" little George asked. He got into the skinny boy's face. The kid was tongue-tied then.

"I don't like being called names," George said with almost gritted teeth.

"I didn't call anybody names," the skinny kid denied, looking like he was close to tears.

"Then apologize," little George said. A tearful request for forgiveness would end this. He could return to the gang victorious. Surely the kid knew where this was going and would apologize.

"No," answered the skinny kid.

"I won't apologize because I didn't do anything wrong. I didn't call anybody no names."

The kid had gotten a bit of courage from somewhere. It embarrassed George. He could hear the ring of truth in the kid's words; his lying, being part of this, made him sick.

The kid's refusal to save his neck and just go along with the act of apologizing surprised George.

"What do you mean you won't apologize?" young George asked.

"You're sitting down here, singing songs, after calling me names. And now you won't apologize. Do you want to get a beating?"

By choosing the word "beating," little George expected the kid to choose a mock apology rather than a bloody nose. His intention backfired, however, as the word seemed to rouse the blood of the tough kids who now began chanting the word like a mantra:

"Beat-ing, beat-ing, beat-ing…"

The skinny kid's silence and defiance confused little George. He was stuck on what the next move should be. The impasse was short.

One of the tough kids pushed George in the back, forcing him to collide with the skinny kid.

Instinctively, as an act of self-defense, the skinny kid swung his arms wildly, his right elbow connecting hard with George's nose, causing it to start bleeding.

The sight of first blood intensified the gang of kids, and they screamed for blood and increased the tempo of their chanting.

Little George looked at the evidence on his hand after he had wiped his nose. He stared in shock at the blood on his palm, and his nose stung.

The faces of the gang of boys leered, grotesquely, as they chanted for a beating and blood.

George gazed around wildly and realized that the die was now cast; there was no going back. The tough kids wouldn't let him walk away from this. If he did, they'd pick a fight with him later, and he might get a severe beating from one or all of them.

It was the skinny kid's fault, too. He was an arrogant little punk and wouldn't take the way out that George had thought of and offered to him. He wouldn't help George save face for everyone.

Pow! Little George struck out and caught the kid with a blow to the side of the head. Thinking that now the skinny kid would finally cry and run away already, he wasn't expecting to get a blow in return.

Maybe the kid felt like a trapped rat, being entirely surrounded by an angry mob, because the skinny guy fought for his life.

Like it or not, George had just entered his very first schoolyard brawl.

What happened next was a discombobulated and fractured blur of activity and madness. Intense anger, fury as surprising as it was savage, took over George's little body.

Swinging his fists and flailing his arms like an out-of-control person, little George was no longer pretending to be mean and rough. The former "sensitive" kid was furious. He pummeled the skinny boy like a berserker warrior.

Fueled by intense emotion and encouraged by the rapturous

mob, little George hit and hit and hit. He finally had to be pulled away by the toughies.

A camp counselor had seen them. Adults were on the way.

The skinny kid was bruised and beaten, his nose bleeding profusely, and he sobbed. The toughies gave congratulatory cheers, shouts, fist-pumps, and other group displays of victory.

The camp supervisors arrived and questioned the boys about what had happened; whether out of respect, fear, or admiration, not one kid would rat on little George and the gang of toughies and reprobates.

The skinny little kid, to the surprise of the toughies, also refused to divulge the names of those involved or even to admit what had happened despite the threat of expulsion from the camp. He was a scholarship kid, and despite camp counselor threats to call his parents, he wouldn't say how he got injured.

All of the other boys cooperated, George included, which is to say they lied unanimously. Most of them claimed to have seen nothing.

George was questioned next to last. Looking at his small hands and feeling very young, George said that the other kid had fallen on the dock and hurt his nose. Little George said that the thin boy was a clumsy kid.

The skinny kid would not offer further explanation for his injuries. He was summarily dismissed from the camp due to his stubbornness and unwillingness to answer questions or participate in the "official" enquiry.

The rest of the summer, the toughies joked and laughed. Whenever anyone got into a scrape, they called him a "clumsy kid."

For the rest of summer camp, George, to his great shame, was treated like one of the gang.

~

George woke with a start. He stretched his arms out and looked at his hands and fingers. They were the usual hands of a grown man. It had been so real. It was hard to believe that he wasn't a child again.

He remembered now. He'd been a loner, to begin with, then much, much more so after the summer camp experience. He had kept everyone, especially his peers, at a distance after that summer.

He opened his eyes and tried to breathe out the last vestiges of his nightmare. He was surprised that he wasn't in a cold sweat, with a terrified and rapidly beating heart, since the dream had been so scary.

He noticed that his breathing, pulse rate, and body temperature were all normal.

Unlike in the dream, which had been fraught with emotion, at this moment, he felt nothing. He felt as emotionally disconnected from the world of feeling as if he imagined one of his netsuke figurines, tightly packed in a small box surrounded by many layers of cotton wool, would. He was entirely and utterly numb.

He knew enough about dreams and their skewed versions of reality to see that he needn't pose questions to himself about whether the dream was something that actually happened, exactly as presented, but rather to know that what he'd experienced had validity.

It alluded to something significant, and it was a clear indication that this event was relevant to his personality change. From that moment on, after the end of that summer, he was much more concerned about safety and control.

One thing he felt no uncertainty about was the identity of the skinny kid in the dream. There was zero doubt in his mind that the little kid, the kid that he may or may not have beaten up, was Ed, the man who grew up to be his next-door neighbor.

That conclusion, he reasoned, despite its horrible reality, made perfect sense. Are we all so close to and yet so far from the other souls whose paths have crossed with our own? He wondered.

Feeling sick, he sat up and got out of bed.

~

While making his morning coffee in the kitchen, George heard a car pull into his driveway. He was not expecting anyone, but more strangely, the engine sounded familiar. He left his house to investigate. George could barely believe his eyes as he stared at his beloved roadster, Miss Betty.

She looked radiant and positively resplendent in the golden morning sun. Smiling like an unhinged person and receiving serious satisfaction from the astonished look on George's face, Ed got out of the parked car.

He dangled the car keys from his fingers, extending them toward George.

"She's all yours again, neighbor," Ed said in a smooth and cool tone of voice.

George continued to stare at the car, taking in its sheer beauty and the sweet lines of its design. Turning to a still-smiling Ed, George's mouth opened to form the word that had entered his mind.

"LuckyPlucky?" George said, putting it all together.

"And don't even think that you have to pay me back. I practically stole it from you. Plus, I got a promotion from my father-in-law. Apparently, he had some kind of weird dream about me last night that has caused him to see me, everything, in a new light. It was so weird." Ed got lost in thought for a moment with an expression of shocked disbelief on his face. He spoke again, "So, anyway. This is my way of saying… I'm sorry for ruining your career," Ed said, and he sounded as if he genuinely meant it.

"Of course I'll pay you back," George said quickly, but his brain was still not yet up to speed.

"Ever do something you thought was right at the time, then you look back and realize how insane it was?" Ed asked.

"Sure," George said sadly.

"I was an idiot, and guess what? It wasn't even about you. When I heard myself the other day, talking about being the poor kid at summer camp? How off the wall was that?" Ed asked, forcing a laugh.

"It was really peculiar for me, at first, Ed," George answered thoughtfully and respectfully.

"But… you know what?"

"What?" Ed said, almost defensively. He grinned, trying desperately to understand what was happening.

Even though he genuinely felt sorry for tricking George and maybe causing him to lose his job, Ed didn't fully understand his compulsion to give this guy the car. However, Lindsay's ultimatum had definitely encouraged him to stick with his decision.

～

*H*e and Lindsay had talked for hours the previous night. Ed had been feeling guilty, remorseful, and very, very confused. Remembering his horrifically lousy time at summer camp when he was nine years old, he cried.

Lindsay was sympathetic, but her religion and her inner sense of right and wrong would not tolerate her husband's lack of morals and ethics. Giving him an ultimatum, she told him that he either had to give the car back or give her a divorce.

Ed had been angry at first, but as the night wore on, he became more and more of an emotional wreck, and it was then that he broke down into fits of uncontrollable sobbing.

Lindsay didn't understand what was happening to her husband. Still, after floating between fear, anger, and genuine compassion, she finally comforted him with a soft heart.

~

*"Y*ou were a little kid. We were both little kids. And it hurts to feel left out. It's scary being in a new place, a place that doesn't feel safe, and a place where you aren't entirely safe. I know that I made you feel bad then... I hurt you, and I'm sorry."

George looked at Ed in such a deliberate and meaningful way, it made Ed feel respected, yet uncomfortable all at the same time.

"That means a lot, George," said Ed, his usual false grin and subsequent look of uncertainty slowly became an expression of genuine respect now that George was acknowledging his emotional pain.

It was such a mind flip. The guy was apologizing.

"It'll sound weird, Ed, but I dreamed about summer camp," George said sadly.

"Oh," Ed replied, really not wanting to go back to that place.

"Yes, and I was horrified. Those kids, what I did, I think I never really recovered after that," George said. Ed tried to take this in.

"I forgive you," Ed said as he looked into George's eyes.

"And those guys weren't my friends," George explained.

"I was their slave that summer. That camp experience was torture. I thought I had to do everything they said. I believe that included physically hurting you, and I'm truly sorry. It was the worst childhood memory of my life. I was so... massively scared..."

"Oh," replied Ed, surprised and confused.

"I didn't know that. I just lumped you in with the rest of the A-holes. I'm so... sorry," Ed added.

"And the worst part is that you were singing happily on the dock. And I believe that summer was the last time that you sang for the joy of it. And so, I ruined your life. I'm the one who's sorry," George said. Ed patted George's arm lightly.

George and Ed smiled at each other.

"Thanks," said George, extending his hand in friendship, which Ed duly and meaningfully shook. After an awkward pause, Ed handed George a brightly colored paper notice.

"What's this?" asked George.

"I joined a band almost two months ago," Ed said proudly.

"This is an announcement of a kind of jam session, in front of a live audience. I'm gonna sing. Will you come hear us play?"

"Sure. I'll be there, old boy," George said and smiled.

"Sweet!" said Ed and waved happily, then he headed back to his own house. George watched him go and then couldn't help himself as he ran his hand down the side of his old roadster.

~

Heads turned with surprise and curiosity as George, confident in himself in a way that he'd never before experienced, walked past the busy cubicles of the 3rd Eye.

Dressed in a beautiful Irish linen shirt and crisp blue jeans—a down-to-earth male mystic—he finally, after all his adolescent and adult years of self-doubt and confusion, felt like, well... himself.

George popped his head into Burton's office, where Burton was busy working behind his desk.

"Burton, got a minute?" George asked.

"George? Come in, old buddy," Burton said, greeting him warmly.

"What can I do you for?"

"What do you need to hear, or what do I have to do to get my job back?" George asked.

"What happened?" Burton asked, putting George's question on hold.

"The job with the suits didn't work out?"

"I didn't fit in," George said, smiling, prompting a giggle from Burton.

"Of course you can have your job back, are you kidding?" Burton said, all smiles.

"Call volumes dropped after clients realized that you left. But I shouldn't be telling you that before we negotiate your returning salary, should I?" Burton said, only half joking.

"There's no hard feelings ?" George asked hesitantly.

"No. Mimi did a tarot reading before you got hired and gave me a heads up. We knew you were leaving before you even began," Burton said and smiled at the quizzical look on George's face.

"We also knew you were coming back," he added, preempting George's next question.

"You knew I was coming back? She knew?" George asked, wondering to himself if Mimi had really been anticipating his return all along.

"Nah, I'm just joshing with ya," Burton admitted, "There was only a seventy-thirty chance of that, or so we believed. If we knew everything that was going to happen, we wouldn't be working here, now would we? Nor would we be on planet Earth, would we? We'd be enlightened."

George tried to work out the logic of those statements. Burton gestured for George to take a seat.

"But then again, we were pretty sure we'd be seeing you again," Burton added, and his voice trailed off.

"Mimi will be happy, for certain," he winked.

"Oh, good," George said, playing down his anxious enthusiasm.

"Will you be reprising Monsieur Psychic?" Burton asked, his tone growing more business-like.

"Naw," replied George, almost blushing from embarrassed memory.

"This time… It's all George."

"When can you start?" asked Burton.

"As soon as a desk becomes free, I guess. I'm available now."

Burton smiled and got to his feet. He took George by the arm and led him to the back.

~

George smiled and waved at his colleagues as he took a coffee back to his old desk. George smiled at Mimi as he passed her cubicle.

She smiled uncertainly back while talking to a client. She looked like she'd had no idea whatsoever that he would be returning to work. In fact, seeing her blush and turn away almost nervously, it looked like she had feared that he would not return.

He couldn't think about this for long as, in moments, George II got a call. The blinking red light signified an incoming video chat line call.

Smiling to himself (because he once dreaded such calls and would scramble to make sure that he was entirely disguised), he casually put on his headset.

Without checking to see how he looked in the mirror hanging by his desk, he looked straight into the webcam and pressed the "call answer" button.

"Hello, and thank you for calling the 3rd Eye. This is... George," he confidently said.

A young lady popped up on George's screen.

"I don't know if you remember me," she began. "I wanted to call you to apologize."

George, indeed, did not recognize her and wondered where he might have known her from.

"Apologize for what?" he asked.

"The things you said to me the last time we spoke... they were so hard to listen to, much less to hear, to comprehend," she explained.

"What was your name?" George asked. He hoped that her name would jog his memory.

"Oh, I'm sorry, you obviously don't remember. My name is Doris. I called in a few weeks ago."

George now remembered Doris. She was his very first call, and she had hung up on him in apparent disgust and intense anger.

The parts of the conversation he did recall involved telling her that she hated men because they reminded Doris of her daddy, whom she must detest. He had hurt her terribly.

She had called him a name, sworn at him at the end of the call. The memory of the session sent cold shivers down his spine.

"I'm so sorry, Doris," George said."You were one of my first—"

"Don't be sorry," Doris interrupted.

"Thanks to you, I got a life coach. I've lost forty pounds, and I feel great!" she exclaimed.

"Really? I mean, you do?" George fumbled. He breathed and tried to relax, to soften the tightness in his chest area and let the energy flow. It wasn't hard: Doris was thrilled with him.

"What you told me was life-changing. It was all true. I did hate my dad... and men. When I got over myself, I did an anger work-shop and spent a few months doing inner work... Then I met someone," Doris paused. Tears of joy seemed about to fall from her eyes.

"That's terrific, Doris," George said with great relief.

"I'm so glad that you…" George began, but he soon got lost in his thoughts as happy images of Doris and her guy appeared in his mind's eye.

"He looks like a good guy and… I can see that he must make you happy."

"It's tough," Doris said, her tears now flowing. George said nothing and waited for the client to continue speaking.

"I don't mean… Roger is his name... and you're right, he's great. It's tough to let someone love me. Hurt and love, and pain are all mixed up for me. Sometimes I feel disgusted when I should, or could, be feeling close or loving. It's hard, but I'm sorting it all out. The minute I stopped BSing myself about what was going on inside of me, my life began to change. And it was you who helped me cut through the BS."

"That's wonderful," George said, "I can't thank you enough for calling back and letting me know. To be honest, I was feeling horrible after that call. I'm so happy for you. I can see that you have had some profound heart healing. Keep up the good work."

"Yeah," agreed Doris, wiping her eyes with another tissue.

"I stopped eating crap to block feelings. I'm working on loving myself and letting someone else love me... and I have you to thank for that. Not even my friends could or would be that honest with me. Sometimes we need a swift kick, I guess. And I'm so grateful that it was you. So, thank you, Mr. Psychic."

"You are so welcome, Doris," George said. He was shocked yet terribly happy at her news and new attitude.

"I appreciate the call so much. Thank you." Doris said a few more things, and then they said their goodbyes.

As George hung up, Mimi popped her head over the partition.

"That was a wonderful call to get to commemorate the return to… my calling," George said, making Mimi smile.

"Welcome back, then, Mr. Psychic," Mimi said.

"Thank you, Mimi. It's just George now, and you, you sparkly woman, taught me all I know, you know," he said, and it warmed his heart to see her smiling at him. He prayed that she would forgive him.

He'd made so many mistakes since meeting her. He knew that she was an exceedingly kind and loving person, but how much could anyone take?

"I know that's not the truth, George, you have unique wisdom… but I appreciate the compliment," Mimi finally replied.

"If you're free for lunch, I know a lovely Japanese restaurant nearby," George said carefully, studiously casual, careful not to show how important it was to him to have her say yes. The best surprises are always unexpected, he thought. Mimi thought for a few moments, then smiled broadly.

"It's a little early," she said.

"I know," he replied, "So I ran it by Burton, and he was cool with it."

"Sparkly," she said, and grabbed her purse.

George and Mimi sat on the floor at the raised, traditional table of their favorite eating establishment. They had finished their meal and sat drinking green tea.

Holding hands and looking into each other's eyes, it was as if they were communicating on some different level than mere speech.

George noticed that the Japanese restaurant had regained the magical luster that he remembered from his first visit. It was as if the glow of love lit up their dining area.

"You are a fantastic woman," George said, kissing her palm.

"Thank you, sweetie. You're an amazing man, yourself," Mimi purred. Her cheeks grew pink in a way that made him feel soft and warm inside, and excited at the same time.

George fumbled to take a small netsuke box out of his pocket without drawing her attention to his actions.

"Have you forgiven my idiocy?" he asked humbly.

"You weren't an idiot, Georgie boy. I like to think that you were suffering from, shall we say, growing pains," she smiled.

"Growing pains, huh? I do feel different, but do you forgive me?" George asked.

"I do," Mimi said softly. Finally getting the netsuke box out and open, George prepared to give it to Mimi. Inside, a little intricately carved figurine wore a ring on its head like a crown.

"We've been together many lifetimes. I love you, Mimi," he said and managed to avoid cracking himself up. George held out the open box with the figure in it, and the surprise ring inside.

Mimi looked down and saw the netsuke figurine and failed to see the ring.

"I love you, too, George," she said happily.

Heart in his throat, George wondered how he could draw her attention to the ring without being an idiot. He gazed into her eyes. She was such a magical and beautiful woman. Maybe she didn't feel exactly the way that he did.

Stop second-guessing yourself, he said to the fearful voice inside his head.

As such thoughts flittered through his mind, Mimi finally noticed something sparkling inside the box. She decided to look closer at the item that George was holding out.

Noticing the ring, at last, Mimi blushed like a teenager.

"Oh, uh," Mimi stammered and blushed deeply. She was startled and overcome with emotion.

"I, uh, don't know what to say..." she said, ever so gently lifting out the sparkling diamond engagement ring.

"What does your heart say?" George asked in a low tone, praying that her heart would feel the same way that his heart felt.

He held his breath for a long moment, waiting for her to speak.

Absolutely beaming with joy and happiness, Mimi slid the ring on her finger with George's gentle help. It was a perfect fit.

"Yes! Yes, yes, yes, yes, yes!" she squealed, practically jumping up and down and kissing his face all over.

George pulled her tightly to himself and kissed her ardently; his heart burst wide open.

She was warm and wiggly in his arms, cooing and squealing with delight, and he almost couldn't believe his good fortune.

George had found someone, and he hadn't even been looking. Finally, after decades of flying solo, he was about to marry for the second time.

This time, he thought to himself, it is going to be so much different: I am going to be so much different.

~

Two weeks later, on a Saturday morning, George pruned the roses in the back garden and enjoyed the early morning sun. He noticed the light and shadow made by the peachy silver morning light shining through the hedge onto the wall behind.

If someone had told him several months ago about this scenario, he would have said to them that they were out of their minds. It would have been utterly unthinkable to him that, in a matter of hours, he'd be standing here marrying a beautiful woman. That it would be a woman that he had known through many lifetimes, as it turns out, would be even more improbable advance news.

The idea that he and a woman would be exchanging vows before a minister, while his family and closest friends witnessed the ceremony, well, he would have thought that anyone who suggested such a thing was some kind of mental case.

He had spent many splendid hours in this garden, pruning and landscaping, self-righteously isolating and focused entirely on the wrong things.

It was a miracle to stand in his place of solitude and join his life to another person, a profoundly beloved woman, someone who understood him, saw his soul, and knew where he'd been and where he was going.

He laughed at his former naiveté; he had thought that he knew everything and had everything.

He had been in denial of so much. How controlled and rigid, tight and contracted, and utterly hollow he and his life had been.

He'd been terribly lonely, and he was too terrified to admit it, much less face it.

George watched a Zebra Swallowtail, with its distinctive and brightly painted wing shapes, its long tails colored marvelously by nature, land on the green leaves of a rose bush.

He remembered, having collected butterflies as a child, one of his solitary pursuits, the Latin name of the butterfly. It was Protographium Marcellus.

He had never caught, killed, and mounted butterflies for his collection.

He had purchased his butterflies or, on extremely infrequent occasions, had found an intact deceased specimen in the wild.

He remembered being nine years old and thinking that he would rather die than pin a live butterfly or put one into a kill jar.

For the last few weeks, he'd remembered moments from his childhood. Most of those moments were precious memories. Some of those recollections were more painful.

From the time he was young, George had thought himself content with his own company, had trained himself to isolate, had told himself that he didn't need anyone.

In actuality, he'd been terrified of getting close to people. He'd felt different.

As a young boy, he'd felt delicate, like a fragile butterfly, perhaps. It was as if his brilliantly colored iridescent wing scales might come off if some person got too close and rubbed them.

The curious part was that he hadn't been consciously aware of any of it; his fears had been safely tucked away below the threshold of his consciousness.

He had only been conscious of a general desire to avoid people.

He laughed at the way his rational, logical mind had fooled him. He used to think that the job he was being paid to do was all that he needed to achieve a future life of well-being and contentment.

In retrospect, he had carefully constructed a life of controlled isolation. Losing his job had been absolutely devastating.

Dealing with the anxiety-ridden suddenness of a financially bleak and uncertain future was about all that he could bear, at times, and something that he wouldn't wish upon anyone.

He hoped not to experience anything like that again in his lifetime… but it did save him.

In retrospect, what appeared to be an utterly devastating event at the time had turned out to be a most fortuitous occurrence. A Japanese saying occurred to George.

Shippai-wa seikou-no moto.

George's Japanese proverb book's translation read:

"Failure teaches us what actions we should change in order to achieve success."

In his case, it was very true. Perhaps he was a bit long in the tooth, yet rest assured, he would forever look upon unforeseen disappointment as a message heralding required life change.

George II finished with the back garden. George III, who had agreed to be his best man, and Jenn and little Georgie were inside getting ready for the wedding.

Star Child, Sacred Rainbow Feather Walking Man, and Burton, along with other new friends from The 3rd Eye, had arrived.

George was nervous and excited. His bride-to-be, Mimi, and her bridesmaids were getting ready at her place.

George leaned close to a rose bush, its lush green leaves and gorgeous crimson silky blooms, so sweet-smelling and fragrant.

The scent made him momentarily dizzy, as it always had. He closed his eyes. Breathing in the perfume, Mimi's face appeared in front of his inner eye.

George knew that soon he would be looking into the sparkling and love-filled eyes of his beloved Mimi.

He thanked heaven for all of the travesties and for all of the goodness that he had been granted in his life, equally.

For whatever events were necessary to get him here, to this miraculous point in his life, a man happily working as a psychic, about to marry his soul mate, he gave heartfelt thanks.

###

DERMOT DAVIS

Irish writer Dermot Davis splits his time between Ireland and the US. An award-winning author, playwright, and screenwriter, his creative work encompasses varied genres and focuses on human themes and characters transformed by life experience. His published work includes a satirical novel, *Brain: The Man Who Wrote the Book That Changed the World*, which was a GREADER'S FAVORITE INTERNATIONAL BOOK AWARD Gold Medalist Winner, a SOMERSET AWARDS FIRST PLACE WINNER, a USA BEST BOOK AWARDS 1st Place Winner, and an INTERNATIONAL BOOK AWARDS Finalist. As a playwright, Dermot is a recipient of the OZ Whitehead Award (co-sponsored by Irish Pen and the Society of Irish Playwrights). In 2025, he won both best Irish play and best play overall in the fifth annual International One-Act Playwriting competition. His plays have been produced at Theatre Banshee, Burbank, the Celtic Arts Center, Hollywood, and Playwright's Platform, Boston, and he has directed his produced work on occasion. As a founding member of Laughing Gravy Theatre, he toured the East Coast of the US. Laughing Gravy was subsequently invited as a resident theatre group at the prestigious Piccolo Spoleto Festival, Charleston, SC. Dermot is an Irish Writers Centre Members' nominee to the IWC Board. Follow Dermot on Goodreads, Twitter, or Facebook.

Find Dermot online at:
https://dermotdavis.com/ or
https://www.facebook.com/AuthorDermotDavis

H RAVEN ROSE

H Raven Rose bleeds star-dust tinted ink and writes story worlds from beyond the stars. Her MFA and PhD are in creative writing, and she is an award-winning screenwriter/director, author, poet, playwright, and creativity researcher; her poem painted in film —— *Sacred Birthday, Sacred Wales - Pen-Blwydd yn Gysegredig, Cymru Sanctaidd* —— won the 2021 Wales International Film Festival Illustrated Poem Jury's Award Special Prize. In 2018, her Super 8 short film *Sleep Disturbance* was shot in Bristol and screened at The Cube Microplex, UK. Her play *Dark Eros*, adapted into a suspense novella of the same title, was staged as readings in Los Angeles, one starring Jessica Biel in the lead role as Leila. An excerpt of the play version of *Sleep Disturbance* was staged as readings at the Taliesin Create Space. Recent publications include creative nonfiction, 'Waking up Wild' and 'Snow', published in *Tofu Ink Arts Press*, the ecopoem '23 Species from 19

States lost to extinction' published in the Winter 2022 edition of *In Parentheses*, and 'Mars or Bust: How Science Fiction Films will Promote Mars Colonization Reality' published in the newly released *The Book of Mars: An Anthology of Fact and Fiction* edited by Dr Stuart Clark (presented initially at The Mars Society 21st Annual International Convention in 2018 in Pasadena, CA). Follow H on Goodreads or @hravenrose.

Find H online at:
https://hravenroseauthor.com/ or
https://www.facebook.com/hravenrosemfaphd

NEWSLETTER SIGN-UP!

Love to read?! Sign up for the eXu Publishing newsletter to learn about new fiction releases by Dermot Davis, H Raven Rose, and other authors.

https://www.exupublishing.com/

PS. If you liked *Mr. Psychic*, it would be stellar if you'd leave a positive review and recommend the book to your friends! 

BOOK PREVIEWS

BUGOCALYPSE EXCERPT

*L*ove *Mr. Psychic?* Then you might like *Bugocalypse: La Cucaracha V1* written by H Raven Rose alone. It's about a young Los Angeles actress who survives an alien invasion from the DNA level and then must escape from LA.

⭐⭐⭐⭐⭐ Excellent. A fresh, funny take on the end of the world as we know it., March 25, 2015

By **Sherwin**

Verified Purchase (What's this?)

This review is from: **Bugocalypse (La Cucaracha Book 1) (Kindle Edition)**

Just finished Bugocalypse. Nearly passed it up; I've had my fill of dystopias. Realized it isn't a mysterious virus, zombies or vampires/werewolves, so I got it. IT IS TERRIFIC! The plot is fresh and fascinating, the hero(ine) is believable, admirable, and funny, and the dialogue is realistic. And the menace! I didn't think anyone could revive the creepy crawlies after what the movies did to them in the1950's (I'm 80 years old, man; I watched those things), but H. Raven Rose has reinvented the genre, and done it just right. Get it, read it, get the sequels, and enjoy!

Bugocalypse tells the story wannabee actress Lacey and the unusual events that occur the week of Halloween. The story is very much a classic alien invasion bug war of a bygone era.

Please enjoy the following excerpt from BUGOCALYPSE!

PROLOGUE

BEFORE EVERYTHING WENT to H E double toothpicks, I so had not been making it as an actress.

Sure, I'm skinny and have long blonde hair. Girls with those attributes are a dime a dozen, or at least no more than non-union rates, in La La Land.

I go to auditions when I can motivate myself. I have an agent, of sorts, though I think the skeeze ball may just want to bang me.

I take classes when I can afford them. I study acting and improvisation, elocution, dance, and even fencing.

I have my platinum blonde hair re-colored; I touch up before the darker roots get so bad that I'm shamed into it. I get regular manicures and pedicures because my friend and I trade them. I get spa treatments rarely.

I am yoga-obsessed. I do yoga, often instead of having hobbies, to maintain a perfect skinny size "O" body and butt.

Less is always more in La La land, where I live.

None of my efforts have helped my career take off. So, between the odd, rare acting gig, I tend bar and always have just enough money to get by.

I just manage to pay my bills, including my SAG-AFTRA union dues, but that is all. Maybe it is because I am from the Valley. Maybe it is because I didn't grow up in an industry or entertainment-connected family.

My dad, Avi, was in pest control. Don't laugh. I'm serious. Then he retired and moved to Florida. Although he invited me, I wouldn't leave La La Land with him—later, I will regret my obstinacy. It's sad, but I never knew my mom well. She died of breast cancer when I was an itty-bitty girl.

All I have left of her is stuff. I have photos and a super-fab copy of a screen test she did for a B movie (she got the role, one of several). I also have her funky, fabulous rhinestone costume jewelry and clothes from the '60s and '70s. Plus, I have her new-age crystals, spiritual books, and rad pink Cadillac.

My mom would have had a great career as an actress. The camera loved my mother. She lit up the screen. My dad never got over her. He has been alone ever since her death. He always says:

"You can't replace the love of your life."

My dad is sweet that way. I miss her, too.

Her final resting place is in Hollywood Forever, the cemetery. When my dad was here, we went to Cinespia together. We went to the movie screenings, visiting my mom beforehand.

My dad told the best stories about my mom and her career. He loved recounting every detail of every audition and each role that she had gotten. My father thought she would have been a huge B-movie star if she had lived.

She was fearless. My dad always skirted the details of her bodacious success, me being his daughter and all.

The gist was that she could heave her ample bosom and toss her long blonde hair, screaming and running from beasts, with the best of the celluloid sirens. She was beautiful, sexy, and strong. She was top-notch at surviving in the end. She still lives in celluloid, in her onscreen roles, after fighting off a terrifying giant ant or another horrible monster, insect or otherwise.

Sometimes, I visit Rudolph Valentino at Hollywood Forever, but only after I visit my mother. With my dad gone, I sometimes go to HF at other times. Then, if a movie is showing, I head over to the Fairbanks lawn with my picnic hamper full of wine, cheese, fruit, and chocolate. I lie on the grass and dream about how I will somehow get screen time someday.

Sometimes, I think that, unlike my mother, maybe I am failing because I lack something. Perhaps I wasn't born with or never found the fire to pursue my creative goals and dreams relentlessly. Until recently, I seemed to lack drive.

It seemed that I was always late to or missed auditions, but even if I made it to the cattle call, I often learned that I was:

"You're too blonde," "too young," "too old," "too thin," "too tall," "too busty," or "not busty enough."

I live with Marisol, my best, best friend in the whole world. We've known each other since the fourth grade. While I spectacularly fail at life, at the ripe old age of 22, Soli is totes bad-ass.

Soli is a teacher. She's almost finished her Master's in Education coursework and student teaching. She has uncanny, bad-ass ambition. She did dual enrollment while still in high school.

Her parents are still together, hard-working, and devoted. They always treat me like a daughter. Marisol loves me. Always supportive and non-judgmental, she is the best girlfriend a girl could have. She always tells me:

"Lacey, you have a gift, something that you were born to do, and it comes from God. Life will reveal it to you."

And, although I hope that it is true, that everyone has a God-given gift and that I will discover mine, my fear is that it's not true. I may be in the wrong place at the wrong time because nothing ever seems to work out for me.

Little do I know it, but Marisol is right.

I do have a gift—something I will excel at and was born to do—and I will find it, to my surprise. By the time I make the discovery, I won't be the same person at all.

Almost everything I have known and believed in, all ordinary reality, is about to fragment.

My God-given life purpose is about to become all-consuming. Allow me to re-introduce myself:

"I'm Lacey, Stellar Pest-Control of Los Angeles. I hear you have a bug problem."

CHAPTER 1

FOR MOST LOS ANGELENOS, when the fit hit the shan, it was the end of the world. It was Judgment Day, as they knew it, and the worst thing that had ever happened to them. For me, it was the best *and* worst thing that ever happened to me. The horrid part was everything went to H E double toothpicks really rapidly. I mean, LA totally went to the devil, but the wonderful part was discovering my life's purpose.

By providence, when the mind-blowing cosmic events began, I wasn't really even all that disturbed as I'd recently begun reading New Age books that had belonged to my mother. They were half doom-and-gloom-conspiracy-theory and half it's all love and Light, and a couple included detailed, if contradictory, info about the coming apocalypse.

So, when the stars fell from the night sky and the other weird stuff started going down, watching reports of shooting stars and meteors on the news or reviewing footage caught on amateur video and posted on Facebook, YouTube, or elsewhere didn't really frighten me or fill me with awe at first.

It was one thing to hear about or watch reports of shooting stars and meteors streaming across the night sky just before villages, towns, and cities were struck down with the Black Death. It was quite another thing to see a flaming ball of orange and yellow-white fire, larger than a building, fly through the blue-black sky.

It happened the day of the earthquake.

I'd had a not-so-great audition that afternoon, even though I had spent hours preparing physically, mentally, and emotionally. My hair was freshly colored and highlighted, washed and flat-ironed, and looked as much like golden wheat as I could get it.

I had my line, a sentence really, about how great this one type of tampon is—it's "so comfortable, I forget I'm wearing it!" As if that would be a selling point?! What girl or woman wants to forget she's on her period and needs to check her tampon? Whatever...

I just wanted the gig. I needed an influx of cash; it takes beaucoup d'argent to pursue the creative life, plus my car requires mega quantities of gasoline. If the commercial played a while, I'd get residuals, and I'd heard that the director was getting into features... that meant if he liked me, maybe he would use me in something bigger. So, I put a lot into nailing the role.

I did a few hours of yoga and meditated on being one with the character in the commercial.

I'd never tried that before; I figured it couldn't hurt.

Before I got ready for my audition, I cleaned up the apartment and then took out the trash because I preferred to clean when I was already sweaty.

I went downstairs with a bag of trash in each hand. I hoped neither bag would break since Marisol insisted we use cheap trash bags. I slowly approached the dumpster outside of and behind the apartment building. I sneezed from the funky smell.

I was about to heft the two bags and toss them into the green rusty metal bin when, to my disgust, I noticed a cockroach, at eye level, staring at me. Why was this critter out in farqing broad daylight? Bold, it was a ginormous cockroach, too.

I hefted the full garbage bags, and the entire bin rattled as the bags thumped and fell in. To my satisfaction, I noticed that the sound and movement had gotten rid of the weirdly huge roach. I went back inside the building to get ready for my audition. I took my time.

I mused about a recent incident where Marisol and I were at her parents' home, and a bug got in the house. We were watching a movie, and Roberto got up to kill the bug while I watched. Then Marisol freaked.

"Take it outside. Take it outside," Marisol screeched.

"Marisol and her 'bugs are living creatures, too,' sentiments," said her father. Then, he said some things in Spanish, and the boys laughed.

Marisol pouted while her mom tried to soothe her.

Roberto rolled his eyes but didn't say anything. Instead, he grabbed an empty plastic cup and napkin off a nearby table and scooped up the insect. Then he did, in fact, take it outside.

At home, I was the designated debugger, that chick creeping downstairs at 1:00 AM with a cup or some random piece of Tupperware with a piece of paper or cardboard over a spider-moth-ant-beetle-whatever to release into the wild.

And I really don't mind, I do love bees, butterflies, ladybirds, bumble bees and such. But, I admit, that stuff gets old, and by stuff, I mean standing barefoot at some ungodly hour, helping another insect escape. Still, I love a great many insects and wish to save them, when and if I can.

In this instance, I was happy to watch Roberto and his muscles in action.

Marisol was happy that the bug lived. I didn't like to kill insects unnecessarily, yet my best friend was entirely against killing them.

After getting ready for my audition, I got in my car and drove to the location. Maybe it was because of the cockroach, but to raise my spirits and get my energy up, I floored my vehicle and sang 'La Cucaracha' as I drove to the production offices.

I couldn't really remember the lyrics to the song, so I kept screaming the chorus at the top of my lungs.

'La Cucaracha, la cucaracha,' I sang, as my pink Cadillac crested a hill, with a dip just after, and sailed through the air. Bump. Bump. I loved the funny feeling that I got in the pit of my stomach when I accelerated and took a hill with a drop just over it super fast.

I checked my appearance when I parked and got out of the car. I was freshly coiffed and showered, lightly made-up with a fresh French manicure, and looked exactly like the especially sweet and clean blue-eyed blonde girl-next-door cheerleader type.

That type of chick would obviously use the best tampons, so I figured that's the look they were going for... but then I didn't get the role. They gave it to a short, plumpish girl with dark hair and big boobs wearing a black leather mini-skirt and dark glasses.

They said I was too groomed, tall and blonde, for the role, so I didn't even get to read for it.

When I saw the other girls on the cattle call, I wondered why my agent had even sent me out. I'm all classic chic blonde doll, but all the other girls were edgy, dark, modern, hipster, grunge, cool chicks. I was totally wrong for the role and the audition.

I felt terribly sad. I needed to make money, and I was increasingly worried that this audition failure was yet another sign that I would never make it in Hollywood.

My only consolation was that I had plans for later.

I tried to focus on the positive as I hiked back to the Pink Lady, which I still thought of as my mom's car, named after the all-girl club from the movie *Grease*. Whenever I approach my gorgeous pink vehicle, I hear the sing-song of the Pink Ladies in my head:

"Ba-Ba-Bum-Bum. Ba-Ba-Bum-Bum."

Thank goodness Marisol and I have a Halloween party to attend tonight; otherwise, I'd spend the evening obsessing about yet another career failure. Instead, I thought about the bash.

I looked great, and my hair was perfect. I'd already done my yoga for the day, but the best part was that I had hours and hours to plan and make the perfect Halloween costume.

Unlike most girls, we don't use All Hallows' Eve as an excuse to wear skimpy slutty lingerie and high heels.

It's not that we don't believe in cute or sexy costumes; adorable and hot are not enough for us. We like to show our sass, not our unmentionables.

Ever since the fourth grade, Marisol and I always make or assemble our costumes. We never buy them. It's one of our things.

We've been characters from literature, film and television, Egyptian goddesses, super heroines, everyday objects (such as a teapot or a bag of jelly beans), animals, insects, plants, food, planets and other celestial bodies, extra-terrestrials, magical creatures (a mermaid and a unicorn), professionals (a police officer, nurse, and so on), or even abstract ideas.

So, we had a tradition to uphold, among our friends, of being annual eye candy that was often food for thought. Naturally, my roomie determined what she would be and created her costume weeks ago.

She was going as Madame Curie. I'm a little miffed that I didn't think of that myself, being as Marie Curie is my all-time favorite real-life heroine. She was, along with her husband Pierre, obsessed with research and was the first female Nobel Prize winner.

Renowned for their discoveries in radioactivity, they both received Nobel Prizes. They had a small laboratory, a rehabilitated shed, and she, ultimately, got sick and died from years of radiation exposure. Now, that dedication to one's art and craft was something that I needed to emulate.

I'd been considering and discarding various costume ideas for weeks. Happily, thinking about Soli's guise and Madame Curie's discovery of a chemical element, polonium (which she named after Poland, her home country), led me to a brilliant thought.

I would go as the element gold. I'd dress in shimmery gold clothing or tights and a leotard and then use gold body paint and glitter on my skin.

I was watching the heat haze, the heat shimmer. The late afternoon sun blurred and created a shimmering effect above the hot parking lot asphalt.

The sunlight beat down. Gazing at the pavement, I was increasingly excited by my Halloween guise concept and the idea that I would soon be shimmering myself as the sparkling, fabulous element gold.

Then it hit. I only had time for one thought: earthquake. Then the whole world shook, and I was slammed onto the ground as the parking lot pavement roiled and rolled, unable to stay on my feet. I hit the ground hard and stayed down there for several seconds, dazed. Everything stopped.

Earthquakes are common in California—the state sits upon the San Andres Fault, the tectonic boundary between the Pacific and North American Plates—so Californians experience thousands of earthquakes each year;. Some of the tremors are so tiny that they're virtually imperceptible.

But a big one, which this obviously was, is felt.

I was about to sit up when strong shaking began again. I realized belatedly that the first one was a foreshock.

My thoughts occurred in slow motion as intense shaking occurred for over half a minute. I heard a boom in the distance and knew it had to be a gas main. I lay there on the ground, shaking and afraid, and rode the parking lot up and down. Then, finally, everything stopped.

I lay still, feeling numb and unable to move, and listened. Emergency sirens wailed in the distance. Buildings and vehicles shifted, twisting metal screeched, and window glass shattered.

The whole of creation cried out, from popping noises to small explosions, dogs barking, and hard and sharp things shattering and breaking.

Finally, things seemed stable, and the cacophony of noises subsided to a nearly inaudible din, or maybe I'd grown numb to it all. I, very tentatively, sat up.

Both of my arms were fairly scraped up from elbow to palm from trying to grasp onto the parking lot. I felt hot, dizzy and overwhelmed but not so besieged that I didn't get to my feet and make my way to the car. I wondered about the epicenter of the quake.

Then concern for my best girlfriend, Marisol, and thoughts of my father flickered through my being. I realized that I wanted to call her and make certain that she was all right. I also needed to call my dad in Florida ASAP and tell him I was okay.

I was almost at the car, using a pink cardigan sweater to wipe trickling blood away from my left elbow, when the first aftershock hit. It wasn't as strong as the foreshock or actual quake, but the movement and the stress of the situation made me feel very ill.

My mind skittered about a million miles a minute, and my heart beat a staccato rhythm as I sweated and rubbed tears from my eyes. I considered whether or not to get into the car or find somewhere else to go.

People ran out of the production office location, some pulling others along, headed to cars, obviously upset, trying to make or already on cell phone calls.

Screw it, I thought and jumped into my beautiful Pink Lady, my bubble gum pink Cadillac. I figured I should go right home or go and get Soli. I wasn't sure if I should take surface streets or the highway and decided I'd figure out the best route on the way.

It turned out that there was no rush. I made the mistake of getting onto the freeway and, after a couple miles of driving at a snail's pace, there I sat.

I flipped on the radio and listened to various radio show hosts describe the damage and take calls from "survivors." I felt sad when I realized that people had lost their homes or businesses and that some people had actually died in the quake.

I sat and listened and tapped the steering wheel and felt anxious and sick and fought off despair.

A moment of overwhelming gratitude swept over me. I knew that my father would be deeply happy that I was fine, except for a few scrapes.

Traffic was apparently backed up for miles due to damage to streets and roads, so, no longer bleeding, I dug through my purse until I found my cell phone.

~end sample~

Will Lacey manage to evade capture by giant, man-sized cockroaches? Can she escape from LA?

Read more of Lacey's story in *Bugocalypse: LA Cucaracha V1.*

~

*V*isit eXu Publishing at https://www. exupublishing.com/

ENCOUNTER EXCERPT

*L*ove *Bugocalypse*? Then you might like *Encounter*. It's a light-hearted science fiction comedy about escaping your cubicle (wherever you are in the universe).

★★★★★ **This is Sci-fi-tastic! I loved it!,**
May 14, 2014

By **AJW**

This review is from: **Encounter: A comedy about escaping your cubicle... wherever you are in the Universe. (Kindle Edition)**

From the quote at the very start of this book to the very last line I had a smile on my face. Simply put: This book is hilarious. The story is engaging, humorous and well written. The on-going dialogue between the main characters N & his clone N2 is simply superb, I can only imagine the authors had a blast writing it. The underlying themes in the book are thoughtful and brilliantly interlaced with humor. I especially liked the portrayal of humans, which is both familiar and introspective. A great novel worthy of five stars.

Co-written with Dermot Davis, *Encounter* tells the story of two ET watchers who aren't supposed to interfere with humans under any circumstances.

Just how far would you go to escape your cubicle? *Would you risk your life and break Intergalactic Federation laws to do so?*

When N and N2 interfere and positively transform the consciousness of a slothful, depressed human man, they discover, too late, that they've inadvertently set up planet Earth and humanity for total annihilation.

Please enjoy the following excerpt from ENCOUNTER!

ENCOUNTER

Two things are infinite: the universe and human stupidity; and I'm not sure about the universe.

— ALBERT EINSTEIN

THE EARLY SUMMER SKY, outside the cottonwoods, an hour or so northwest of Santa Fe, New Mexico, was the ethereal tint of robin's egg blue. On Cerrillos Road, south of I-25, a brontosaurus family—a mother, father, and a baby, their dusty green-gray, leathery, and scaly skin dappled with sunshine—appeared to graze amidst woody brown and green desert trees and shrubs.

It was late afternoon. The sun beat down, and the light and desert were hot, dusty, and golden. Lizards, snakes, birds, and insects moved among the cactus, ocotillo, creosote bush, brittlebrush, perennial, and annual desert grasses that grew in the semi-arid landscape.

The green and dried stems, trunks, branches, leaves, and spines of cacti created a subtle palette of rich colors and textures in green, brown, peach, and lavender. Silvery mica glinted in the sand and dirt of the desert dust.

A beat-up 1967 blue Ford pickup, once ultramarine blue but now pathetically faded, roared past the three life-sized dinosaur sculptures. Going about 90 miles an hour, the pickup truck left shimmering dust motes glistening in its wake.

The truck barreled down the road. It managed to turn right at the very last possible minute. Tipping a bit sideways, it just managed to make the turn into the Los Alamos National Laboratory parking lot.

Barely avoiding crashing, the truck skidded and slid sideways into a parking spot. The faded blue and heavily dented driver-side door opened, and Hank Walsh emerged.

A forty-something, run-down, bloated excuse for a man, he was one of those men who could be handsome... if they weren't severely depressed, apathetic, overfed, frequently intoxicated, unkempt, and entirely lacking in ambition. He drained a beer, crushed and threw the can into the truck bed, where it joined several others, and belched. He then walked toward the building.

The hallways of the über clean, high-tech, high-security national laboratory were silent. Periodically, scientists and geek types would traverse the hallways—the hallway floors so clean and shiny they were reflective—as they made their way to meeting rooms, offices, or laboratories throughout the complex.

At the end of a hallway outside a nuclear physics lab, Hank apathetically trooped past Dr. Blake and Dr. Delaware, two clean-cut, excitable, professional nuclear physicists.

They were holding research papers covered with marks and diagrams and quite obviously comparing notes angrily amid an intense discussion.

Deep in conversation with his colleague, Dr. Blake was surprised when an unexpected stench assaulted his nose. He covered his nose and looked around.

He saw Hank, who had clocked in, now wearing coveralls over his street clothes, pushing a high-tech floor cleaning device down the hallway.

"What the..." Dr. Blake asked, his tone of voice making it clear that his question was rhetorical. Then, interrupting himself, he looked at his watch and then at Hank before turning to Dr. Delaware.

"Can you believe it? It's not even 9 AM. What a seriously—"

"—misunderstood genius," whispered Dr. Delaware, interrupting his colleague. Dr. Blake stared at his coworker with incredulity. He raised his eyebrows as if to emphasize his skepticism. Dr. Delaware nodded at Dr. Blake.

"—I was thinking drunken bum," Dr. Blake said softly, partly as he was now alert to the propriety of being polite and, more importantly, to ensure that the brute would not hear, take offense, and beat him up.

"Ever look into linear perturbations?" Dr. Delaware asked in the conspiratorial tone of a man thrilled to know factual information that others do not know.

Dr. Blake shrugged as if to indicate a) of course he had, but b) what did that have to do with the drunken bum adjacent who was now stinking up the corridor?

"An approximation scheme set to describe a complicated quantum system in terms of a simpler one to convey the under-lying structure?" Dr. Delaware continued, as if Dr. Blake might not know.

"Of course," Dr. Blake said, somewhat defensively, as if his associate had called into question some core aspect of his basic intellect.

"He wrote the book on it," Dr. Delaware said with great satisfaction.

"He's working on perturbation theory here at the lab?" asked Dr. Blake, with disbelief in his voice.

He looked at Hank. True, sometimes scientists were terribly quirky; a scientist might engage in an odd exercise to stimulate his mind and work through a scientific problem.

Dr. Delaware frowned. Hank stared upward at the far end of the hall as if focused on something compelling only he could see.

"Sadly, no. He's a janitor now, but he used to be something really special: one of those rare minds with a gift for theoretical genius with serious application potentiality. It's a pity that he's devolved; I could truly use his mind… if only there were some way, some way to—" Delaware continued.

"To what?" Dr. Blake said, laughing uproariously, "To rewire his brain? To jumpstart his scientific genius? That's a good one," Dr. Blake said and grinned, as if now he had the intellectual upper hand over Dr. Delaware.

Dr. Delaware frowned. He was obviously a little miffed by Dr. Blake's clear implication that he was incorrect in thinking there was something worth redeeming in Hank or Hank's capacity for critical thought.

"There's a huge correlation between depression and high intellectual potential," Dr. Delaware finally responded, almost huffily.

"You build a device like that in your spare time, which we don't have, my good man, and I won't use it on some dude like that guy," Dr. Blake said, jerking his head in Hank's direction. "I would use the thing on someone with real potential."

Dr. Delaware looked at Hank for a long moment and then turned to face Dr. Blake. "The greatest darkness has the potential to reveal the greatest light," Dr. Delaware said sagely.

"Ah, now, don't go getting all Kabbalah on me, Delaware, not unless you wish to jeopardize my opinion of *your* mind," Dr. Blake said and then looked down at the research papers in his hand. "Now, where were we?"

~

*B*illions of dazzling stars shimmered in the vast black darkness of the outer space void. With a flash of light, a space vehicle decelerated from lightspeed and penetrated a fraction of space.

A bizarre, other-worldly space station came into view.

The orbital space station complex was constructed of sub-atomic particles, contributed by alien civilizations from many universes, galaxies, and planets orbiting.

The elemental particles were loosely bonded to create a strong yet flexible rainbow iridescent colored material that shimmered and appeared to materialize and dematerialize alternately. It was, for beings that possessed the ability to breathe, breathtaking.

Inside the mammoth spacecraft, the size of which would be incomprehensible to humans, life forms from all creations and realities rushed about their duties and lives.

Inside of a hallway, which led to an intergalactic meeting room, late arrivers, diverse and curious-looking life forms, from differing planets of origin (and some from realities which contained nothing that could be described as planets even, failing to be solid or have mass at all), opened doors and rushed into a large meeting room.

Strange sounds and shouting could be heard from within the closed doors. Inside the intergalactic meeting room, significantly dissimilar intergalactic space federation council members faced off in a heated debate.

"Despite opposition and ongoing debate, we must weigh and carefully vote on the fate of planet Earth," said Xerb, the Intergalactic Space Federation Council President, carefully and slowly.

"Huguw-huguw, huguw-huguw," a Draconian council member laughed. His laughter squeaked and grated like large pieces of broken glass emitting a low, ragged pitch as they were dragged across a chalkboard.

"It's a simple vote for a situation that, however upsetting for various factions, has an obvious solution," the Draconian council member said when it could finally contain its mirth.

The Zeta Reticuli Grey council member stared at the Draconian with cold rage.

"Obvious? The Zeta Reticuli Greys have billions of ZeRe invested in licensing rights and ongoing experiments on planet Earth's life forms. Our contract won't expire for three more secundi," the Zeta Reticuli Grey council member said.

An obviously peaceful, loving being, the Arcturian council member exuded good vibes. It patiently lifted its appendage, indicating a desire to speak. The Intergalactic Space Federation Council President nodded for it to go ahead.

"Some of these so-called life forms are earthlings. Although primitive, some of them do possess a self-aware consciousness.

Surely they should be given due consideration... protection and rights?" the Arcturian council member asked.

Before anyone else could respond, Q, a Zycorp Spokesperson and special consultant to this council meeting, spoke:

"Those 'earthlings' are subjects and have been genetically engineered by us to be exactly as they now exist. As such, we carry the patent for their modified DNA." Q stared everyone down.

"Our company has been farming these life forms for deons, which have become very valuable resources to the corporation's bottom line. They may have an inferior consciousness, but their biological, etheric, and physical attributes—carefully genetically modified by us—were designed to be exploited."

~

*D*eep inside the space station, buried deep within hundreds of thousands of offices, within a suite of research labs, various types of alien beings, hundreds of thousands of them, worked in identical cubicles.

N and his clone N2, an alien being and his first genetic copy, alone in their work cubicle, watched many human subjects on a bank of monitors.

"Man—" N2 said.

"Don't call me 'man' or dude, N2," N interrupted, his voice filled with irritation.

N2 rolled his many eyes.

"Whatever, N. Anywayz, we've been doing this for a while... we should get to experiment on some of these subjects. Maybe help 'em live an interesting life, for a change. Whaddya say?!" N2 asked with great enthusiasm. N2 twitched with excitement and curiosity while N looked at him in horror.

Then N looked around, terribly nervous over N2's bold statement. Shaking with fear, he checked to see if N2's statement might have been overheard.

None of the other beings in any other cubicle were paying the slightest attention to the two of them. N sighed with relief and turned to face his genetic copy.

"Get off the crazy. We observe and evaluate subjects and make reports. What are the first three words in our job description manual?" N asked N2 pointedly. N2 looked like he was thinking, but his source copy knew him better and wasn't expecting an answer anytime soon.

"Record. Data. Only," N said flatly, with the slightest hint of menace in his tone.

"Get off the crazy," N2 said in a wicked falsetto tone, mimicking N's words. Then, pointing at the vast array of highly technical equipment before them, he spoke intently in a serious tone: "Don't be such a fraidy cat. What else have we got going on? Seriously, I'm bored out of my skulls."

N stabbed his appendage toward the equipment. Hank was now on screen. "What's this?" N2 asked. "What happened to the Jeffrey specimen?"

"The Jeffrey subject passed in his sleep," N answered. "You were right. Sleeping for five Earth days was not normal. This is our new research subject." N2 looked at Hank, on screen, getting out of his pickup.

"You've got to be kidding me. See, this is what I'm talking about. Another pea-brain earthling chump," N2 said sadly.

"Is there any other kind?" N asked with contempt.

"Don't be that way. Some of them are geniuses... Like Elvis and Tesla," N2 said as he watched Hank with a mix of resignation and sorrow.

"Elvis Ann Tesla? What'd she do?" N asked, his voice dripping with hatred. N2 was horrified by N's hatred of and for humans as well as his ignorance.

"You are freaking unbearable," N2 said. "If you applied yourself and got some promotions, we'd be observing interesting earthlings that... live interesting lives."

"Oh, sure," N scoffed. "Firstly, you'd have to define what you find 'interesting.' Secondly, by my definition of 'interesting,' no earthling I've ever seen did one interesting thing in their entire lifespan."

"And you're okay with that? See, that's exactly my point. You criticize primitive life-forms for being boring when all you do with your life is watch primitive life-forms be boring. What interesting thing have you ever done?" N2 challenged.

Appearing unfazed, N continued to study the monitor that featured Hank.

"I see," continued N2 when N refused to engage. "Let's watch this new subject until he sleeps and doesn't wake up. That sounds like an exciting way to spend our lives."

"Subject approaching alcohol store," N said into his voice recorder and enlarged the monitor view.

The cubicle immediately transformed into the extraterrestrial equivalent of a 360° theater in the round.

A high-definition image surrounded the pair near-instantly.

It was as if the two extraterrestrials now stood together outside a New Mexico convenience store.

~

Hank slammed his pickup truck door. Crickets chirped in the night. Bleary-eyed, he ambled toward the storefront and entered the tiny convenience store.

The convenience store was jam-packed with processed food and drinks, alcohol, cigarettes, and cheaply made curio items. Hank knew exactly what he wanted and where to find it.

Slamming down a 12-pack of beer, Hank faced the Native American store clerk. He grabbed a pack of Smoky Chipotle beef jerky from a counter shelf, grunted, and pointed toward the cigarettes and lottery tickets.

"Same old, same old?" the clerk asked.

"Uh-yuh," Hand said.

The clerk grabbed two packs of locally made native smokes, removed five Area 51 Alien Abduction scratchers from the lottery card display, and laid them on the counter.

"Five, right?" the clerk asked.

"Uh-yuh," Hank said. Tap, tap, tap. The clerk rang Hank's items up on an old-fashioned silver and wood punch-key cash register and bagged Hank's purchases.

"That'll be $10 for the Area 51 Alien Abduction scratchers plus $35.52 for the rest... for a grand total of $45.52. That it?"

"Uh-yuh," Hank said and slapped down some cash.

~

Oblivious to the glittering stars that had slowly begun to light up the cobalt blue night sky, Hank drove his pickup home.

Steadying the steering wheel with his knee, he popped open a beer and guzzled it down.

The pickup barreled down a deserted road, made a hard turn into a side road overgrown with weeds and brambles, and finally pulled up outside his beat-up house trailer.

Hank put the pickup truck in park and switched off the ignition. He sat for a few moments in silence, broken only by the sound of crickets and the distant howl of a lonesome coyote.

He finished his beer and tossed the can into the back of the cab, through the open truck cab rear window, and belched hugely. He popped a new beer before getting out of his vehicle.

The house trailer was rusty and old. Knocking back his drink and carrying his sack of treats, Hank ambled toward his broken-down, none-too-clean abode.

He stepped over metal junk and overgrown plants to finally reach the front steps and door. He tromped up the stained cement steps and wrenched open the door.

Inside the trailer, the barely furnished and tiny, cramped space was littered with empty beer cans, used Area 51 Alien Abduction scratchers, empty cigarette packages, cigarette stubs, and other trash. Old filthy shag carpet covered the floors.

Hank flopped into his barcalounger and dropped his paper sack on the floor within easy reach. He grabbed the remote control and clicked it. His ancient TV—a bent hanger functioning as his antenna—came on.

The picture was fuzzy and snow-filled. At times, it was difficult to see any picture at all, but that did not appear to bother Hank one bit. He sank back with a grunt of contentment.

Hank slurped on his open beer. Then, with lethargy, as if it almost took more energy than he could muster, Hank used his teeth to rip open a pack of jerky. He took a bite and chewed slowly. He grunted and then farted. His slow, bovine chewing emphasized his resemblance to a cow chewing its cud.

After eating all his jerky and guzzling all his beer, Hank smoked and stared at the set. Periodically he grunted and farted some more.

Later, watching what appeared to be the evening news, challenged to keep his eyes open, Hank scratched off his lottery scratch cards and seemingly had no reaction when he did not win.

The local news went off, and the almost indiscernible blurry color images of a modern TV broadcast became the almost indiscernible blurry black and white images of an old movie. Hank's apathy did not change, though he grew increasingly sleepy.

Still watching the snowy screen of his old TV, Hank's head began to snap forward periodically as he almost fell asleep.

Each time, at the last moment, before his head fully fell onto his fat-swollen abdomen, Hank would fart and grunt as he jerked back awake.

Finally, unable to keep his eyes open, Hank fell asleep sprawled in his recliner. He snored, and the tiny, static-filled TV screen flickered.

*I*nside N and N2's tiny cubicle in the remote space station, N2 adjusted a control. The flickering, static-filled image, a duplicate of the image on Hank's old broken-down television screen, on their monitor screen became a wide shot of Hank in his trailer. "Look at this... this... lump of..." N2 said.

"Humanity?" N said in a fake-helpful tone of voice.

"I can't watch this anymore," N2 said unhappily.

N2 surveyed the other alien beings and various life forms at adjacent cubicles.

They were a mishmash of the curious, bizarre, and outlandish. None of them, including Beetle Blatt, a tiny, dark, almost evil-looking Zygon with an oversized membranous egg head, paid them any attention. N2 turned to face N once again.

"Aren't you sick of this?" N2 asked, his voice filled with despair.

N looked around. The extraterrestrials around them fervently watched their assigned human subjects on their monitor banks and used strange, mysterious electronic devices to compute and/or record human behavior data.

Just like desk-jockeys on Earth, they mostly appeared supremely bored.

"It's our job. Our activity," N said calmly, as if he were entirely at peace with their daily endeavor.

"Our job? Oh, yes, siree, Bob. It's our task, assignment, bother, burden, business, calling, charge, otherwise known as the daily grind, activity, all right. But, N, there's a million other activities in life. This galaxy is ginormous," N2 declared slowly yet fervently in a sing-song voice.

N was not impressed by N2's line of reasoning. He looked around at the clean, safe, compact, highly technical environment that was their shared workspace.

"What would you know about the galaxies out there, N2? All you've ever seen in your life is the inside of a test tube, the canteen, and this workspace," N replied.

"Besides, I'm just a glott away from retirement and my pension. A single glott. If I can hold on 'til then," he said logically, being careful to sound as positive as possible.

N2, knowing that N was equally bored with their gig, narrowed his many eyes.

"Retirement?" N2 sneered. "They put you on a ship and dump you off in that freaky retirement outpost on the periphery of the galaxy where you eat, shit, and sleep... and then you die. And that's something you're looking forward to?"

"You're forgetting something," N replied. "I won't have to do this... anymore."

"Yippee," N2 mocked.

"Besides, how can you retire? You don't have any memories to retire with. It's like you never even existed," N's clone added.

"I have memories," N said defensively.

"Memories of what? Watching earthlings drink beer, watch TV, and scratch their rear ends?" N2 continued. "You do know, doncha, that the fewer memories retirees have, the shorter their lives once they do retire? It's a scientific fact; look it up."

"I have memories," N insisted. "Besides, I still have time."

"That's right! You do have time, so make it count," N2 encouraged. "This is why it makes perfect sense to..." N2 discreetly looked around. Seeing it was all clear, he lowered his voice and whispered the rest into N's ear.

Enraged, N jumped up, his many eyes widening with a combination of rage and fear. Fiercely grabbing N2 by a tentacle, he hustled him from their shared cubicle and into the space station hallway.

~

Will N2 convince N to do something daring before they retire? A complete, quirky sci-fi read, the story of how two aliens mess up their day job has been called "laugh-out-loud funny."

Buy *Encounter* and read the rest of N and N2's story.

Visit https://www.exupublishing.com/.

BRAIN EXCERPT

*L*ove *Mr. Psychic* (co-written by H Raven Rose and Dermot Davis)?

If so, you might like *BRAIN: The Man Who Wrote the Book That Changed the World*. Written by Dermot Davis alone, the story is about an author who faces the classic dilemma of the writer.

Do you write what's in your heart, or do you write what sells? In this modern age of publishing, there is a huge chasm between the best-selling authors who are rich beyond their dreams and... well, everybody else.

Reviewers say fantastic things about *Brain*.

> *...an entertaining farce about modern society, a deft, fast-paced tale that will leave self-aware readers giggling.*

— PUBLISHERS WEEKLY

★★★★★ **You Have a Brain - laugh with it!**,
June 21, 2013

By **John Reviews**

Verified Purchase (What's this?)

This review is from: **Brain: The Man Who Wrote the Book That Changed the World: A Satire (Kindle Edition)**

Brain is a must read for all authors trying to make sense of the world of publishing.
It reminded me of Bonfire of the Vanities and Tom Sharpe's work.
Essentially a comedy and satire, Brain is a modern fable about the power of imagination and marketing with unforeseen consequences.
It also includes some great set pieces and observations about life which resonate with this reader.
I loved the story and I believe it would make a great comedy film in the right hands. Monty Python would be a great touchstone for the tone and humor.
Roll on the follow-up.
Oh and I'd love to see You Have a Brain - Use it! published!

Award-winning *Brain* tells the story of Daniel. He's an author struggling to make a living. His agent won't accept his latest masterpiece, which he poured his soul into: apparently, it's not commercial enough. In a final act of desperation, Daniel decides to write - not what's in his heart but - what he thinks will sell. What follows is bound to make you laugh!

Please enjoy the following excerpt from BRAIN!

BRAIN: THE MAN WHO WROTE THE BOOK THAT CHANGED THE WORLD

It was graduation day at the University of Tollston in Illinois. Before the assembled students and their families, Dean Reynolds stood at the podium to announce the recipient of the prestigious Marcus and Imelda Rogerspoon award for the student showing the brightest promise for a future literary career.

Although the majority of the persons in attendance didn't give a whit about the prestigious award, or who that year's recipient might be, the handful of literary types present knew that it was short-listed to just two people: the intense intellectual, Daniel Waterstone and the artsy, anti-establishment, outspoken radical, "Crazy" Mary McIntyre.

The Dean spoke into the microphone, the incorrect placement of speakers producing a faint echoing effect. "Founder of the campus publication, *Superior Review*, and the student deemed to be most likely to succeed in the art of storytelling, the award goes to... Daniel Waterstone."

Daniel jumped to his feet with glee and was only half successful in suppressing his impulse to punch the air with a clenched fist. He energetically shook the hands of several disinterested students, who just happened to be sitting in his row, and made his way to the raised platform. Perhaps, in his head, he equated being the recipient of this obscure award with winning an Oscar, so, to the accompaniment of very modest applause, he summarily shook the hand of each of the male faculty and kissed the cheeks of each of the indifferent females he met on his way to the podium.

He then bear-hugged the impatient dean who did not see the hug coming and who subsequently failed, in an awkward way, to complete the hug from his end. Beaming with pride and self-confidence, Daniel received the award in his left hand whilst vigorously pumping the Dean's hand with his right. Expecting Daniel to return to his seat, the Dean replaced his reading glasses and checked his notes to move on to whatever was next on the agenda.

Daniel, however, was not about to let his five seconds of minor fame conclude so quickly and so he proceeded to pull out, from an inside pocket, what appeared to be a prepared speech.

Adjusting the microphone to his desired height, Daniel addressed what was now a puzzled and somewhat bemused audience.

"Dean, members of the staff, ladies and gentlemen, it is with tremendous pride and heartfelt honor that I accept this highly-esteemed and influential award," he began and then looked around to make sure he had everyone's attention.

"We are living in dangerous times," he then said, pausing, for dramatic effect. "Having progressed through the age of reason and enlightenment, civilization is now poised to enter the age of insanity. I tell you, in no uncertain terms that what we are currently witnessing, at least here, in the West, is the decline of culture itself."

Whereas the academically inclined did perk up somewhat to these stark revelations, the majority of the persons in attendance were mentally preoccupied and paid his words of doom no heed. "We live in a time, reminiscent of the declining Roman Empire, perhaps, where style is rewarded over content and where worthy conversation concerning the evolution of our culture is replaced with inconsequential nonsense such as gossip about the lifestyles of the rich and famous. Our literature has been in decline for decades. Loopy fads and fantasy genres, of questionable merit, now clog our once-great literary arteries."

As many in the audience took this opportunity to pay a much needed visit to the lavatories (or to check their email, update their FaceBook and Twitter accounts), Daniel continued his treatise on cultural decline. Mentioning a short list of literary greats, including Faulkner, Steinbeck, Hemingway, et al, he challenged those in attendance to mention even just three contemporary authors who were presently carrying the mantle for—and laudable descendents of—these great literary forebears and legendary authors and who were currently contributing to creating an even greater literary age.

Various authors like Dan Brown, Stephen King and Nicholas Sparks were volunteered by audience members and some jokers shouted out names like Baron Munchausen, Dr. Seuss and Harry Potter. Whether the last three names were said in jest was questionable, as no one was heard laughing in response.

Undeterred, Daniel talked excitedly and passionately about the need for writers and intellectuals to rediscover their passion for the timeless classics and "true" literature. He ranted about the necessity of the re-ignition of "the great quest," (the quest to write the great American novel, that is) and the need, nay, the *urgency* for a renaissance in American literature for which he would lead the way.

Raising his right hand, in a pose reminiscent of a presidential inauguration, Daniel continued: "People before me; fellow citizens of this great nation, to you I make a promise. I vow to be a defender of the hallowed halls of timeless classics, those that make a nation, a culture and a civilization great. With all the innate literary genius and creative wherewithal at my disposal... this is my promise to you. You have put your faith in the right person... I, Daniel Waterstone. Remember that name."

As he paused to take a grand intake of breath, the audience applauded wildly. One got the impression, however, that the rambunctious applause was not so much a validation of his speech and his stated noble quest but more a wild hope that he had concluded and, if not, a ruse to drown out whatever more he might want to say. Many students gave him a standing ovation with mock serious expressions, shouting, "Bravo, Bravo."

Despite her outward show of apathy, a disappointed "Crazy" Mary stood at the rear of the assembled and waited to catch Daniel's eye as he returned to his seat. When he did finally see her and gave her some semblance of acknowledgement, she stuck out her tongue, turned her back, pulled up her weird-looking, homemade, non-traditional gown... and mooned him.

~

It had been ten years since Daniel's graduation and it's fair to say that the intervening years had not been very kind to him, personally or professionally. Despite some early signs of success, where Daniel acquired a literary agent and had two novels published by a small, yet well regarded, independent publisher, his books did not sell well. His most recent book advance was rapidly approaching complete exhaustion.

Encouraged by his agent to move to a larger metropolis, a shift which she sold to him as a necessary career move (to take meetings and, generally, to be taken seriously by the literary establishment), Daniel moved to Beverly Hills. Soon after that he prudently chose to relocate to West Hollywood and then slowly but surely he continued to down-size and move to less affluent neighborhoods as his funds continued to evaporate.

Upon his final move to a poor and quite noisy neighborhood in the San Fernando Valley, he tempered his self-disappointment with the justification that he was a true artist and like the then unknown and struggling literary expatriates of Paris (Sherwood Anderson, John Dos Passos, F. Scott Fitzgerald, Ernest Hemingway, et al), at the turn of the twentieth century, he too only required a bed, a desk and a typewriter.

His light brown wavy hair made curlier by the heat (and his failure to shower immediately upon waking), Daniel stood over his printer as it printed the remaining few pages of his latest novel, *The Impossible Dream: Part Two*. Bought at the local thrift store, his once-reliable printer was now on its last legs and white streaks were beginning to run down the freshly printed pages.

Daniel wiped his sweaty brow and, with excited satisfaction, watched his document print.

Excited about his imminent luncheon appointment with his agent, Suzanne, he was confident that she would not judge him for the poor quality of the manuscript but instead would, once she had read the initial few pages, revel in the prose. In fact, Daniel was one hundred percent sure that the quality of his brilliant writing would obfuscate any short-comings with the print and toner issues in the document. As his new novel was a sequel, he expected it to be a highly desirable property. It answered many questions which were left tantalizingly unanswered in *The Impossible Dream: Part One*.

He didn't want to second guess the publisher's marketing rationale for not having *Part One* out in print yet but he assumed that it was because they were waiting for him to finish *Part Two* so that they could better strategize promotional and marketing opportunities for both books. The publishing and marketing of books was a foreign country to Daniel; one that he didn't know nor truly care to understand but he did appreciate that it was sure to have its intricacies and indeed, for himself and other authors, its necessity.

Like his printer, and most other mechanical and electrical items which he owned, Daniel's fifteen year old car was also on its last legs. As he sat behind the wheel, with ignition key in hand, he made a silent wish that it would start up and without incident transport him to his meeting with Suzanne, on time. Having untold trouble with the vehicle in the past few weeks, he finally had taken it to a mechanic. He had hoped to get a free estimate of its laundry list of issues. Then, he could prioritize repairs and determine what he could afford to have remedied. To his shock, the low ball estimate of the mechanic required a great deal more money than the actual car was worth.

As well as a change of residence (and the repayment of a slew of personal loans, bank and other debts), Daniel needed a new car, or even a new, used one. Back in Illinois, Daniel drove so little that he didn't even remember the model name of his hand-me-down Ford that his father gifted him with. Now living in Los Angeles, where a car was so necessary to one's successful navigation of the sprawling city, Daniel had gotten to know his Toyota Celica more intimately than he had wanted to or was even comfortable with.

Thankfully, with the imminent publication of his new novels, he would at last begin to see some financial daylight. He was sure that when the new novels finally hit bookstore shelves, they would be considered revelations in print and reader interest would re-ignite sales of his other two back-list books, *All Alone in an Insane World* and *Heartache*. Financially, things were dire. Yet he was certain that he just had to hang on for a few more weeks.

Daniel turned the vehicle ignition key. The starter motor engaged but the engine didn't turn over. He tried again. And again. On the seventh nail-biting attempt, the car eventually roared into a loud and smoky state of reluctant engagement. The more he drove the vehicle, in its current condition of disrepair, the more he understood the car's dysfunctional state. He knew that if he turned the starter motor repeatedly, for short bursts only, that the car would eventually start up. Once started, he knew that as soon as he took his foot off the gas that the engine would slowly fade and die. Therefore, it was imperative that he keep his foot on the gas.

His challenge, once he got the car moving, was not to let the engine die when he had to slow down or come to a stop. Luckily, the car was a stick shift (which, he was sure, was the reason he got it so cheaply in the first place) and he could depress the clutch while still keeping his foot on the gas pedal, thus preventing the engine from dying. At the very first stop light that Daniel encountered (despite his feet being securely planted on both the clutch and gas pedal), the engine sputtered and died.

Unfortunately, just like life, no amount of planning and understanding is foolproof and with the declining state of the vehicle's overall health, it was getting harder for Daniel to anticipate the car's behavior. His ignition theory was being put to the test and to his chagrin, each and every time he turned the key, his understanding of what worked and didn't work, was found wanting. Despite the number of quick turns of the ignition key, the car would just not start.

In a controlled state of panic, Daniel didn't know what else to do and turned the key so many times without result that the patience of the drivers in the cars stuck behind him began to wear thin and much honking of horns was heard in the otherwise quiet intersection.

Daniel pushed his car to the side of the road and opened the hood more as an act of desperation than as a show of competence. He knew that if he took a good hard look at the wires and coils and tubes and sundry parts of the interior and didn't see something, something which was obviously disconnected or broken or a part that was leaking liquid or protruding smoke, then he had no idea what he was looking at or how to go about fixing.

Sure enough, save for a minor leak in a radiator hose, which he already knew about (and carried a five gallon container of water in the trunk for constant radiator replenishment); he failed to see anything overtly amiss. This was not the first time he had stared cluelessly at the inner sanctum of his increasingly familiar, personal Rubik's cube of an engine. Taking a cloth in one hand he proceeded to tighten and secure everything that looked like it should be tight and secure: wires, tubes and connections of all shapes and sizes.

Having performed the task to his satisfaction, he once again got behind the wheel and turned the key… again and again. After several attempts, the car started. He had no idea why.

Waiting for him at a Beverly Hills adjacent restaurant, Suzanne sipped some imported sparkling water and, on her smart phone, caught up with her emails. Working as a literary agent in a town like Los Angeles, for all these years, Suzanne knew that so much counted on appearances. Meeting clients in restaurants frequented by studio executives, and industry people, in general, was a way of showing that she was busy making deals and that she was in the game. She knew that by being seen she was reinforcing her brand recognition and through her constant presence, advertizing her services. Seeing and being seen meant that she might get a call sooner than a competitor who relied on the telephone directory alone, for new business.

When Daniel finally made it to the underground parking garage, he was shocked to remember that there was no option for motorists to Self Park: everyone had to pull up to the valet stand. As he did so, a Hispanic valet, Carlos, opened his door with a friendly greeting. Daniel, however, did not move from his seat.

"If the engine stops, it won't get started again," Daniel explained, "You need to switch with me."

"Yes," said Carlos, not understanding. He held the door open wider and stood in puzzlement as Daniel remained seated.

"I can't take my foot off of the accelerator," Daniel said more animatedly, realizing that English might not be the valet's first language. "I need you to switch with me to keep the motor running. Understand?"

"Oh. Yes," answered Carlos as he fixed his eyes on Daniel's right foot which remained pressed on the gas pedal, "I put my foot on gas or car die."

"That's right," said Daniel. "I'm sorry but I didn't have time to go to the mechanic."

"Understand," said Carlos, as he gamely extended his foot to replace Daniel's on the gas pedal. In order to do so, he was now practically sitting on Daniel's lap as Daniel tried to slide out from under the valet and scoot over to the passenger side of the car.

"Is your foot on the accelerator?" asked Daniel, masking his embarrassment.

"Yes. Yes, you go," answered Carlos with good sportsmanship cheerfulness.

Leaving Carlos sitting in the driver seat, Daniel grabbed his manuscript and awkwardly opened and then slipped out of the front passenger door. Then he ran around to the other side of the car and, reaching behind the driver's seat, pulled out a large rock which he had kept for this express purpose. He held the rock up to Carlos.

"Okay. When you park it, put this on the gas pedal. If the engine dies, then I'll have to get a..." Daniel didn't finish the sentence because he didn't have any money to call a tow truck and he didn't want to implant the idea into the valet's head that a tow truck was an option.

"Please don't let the engine die. I won't be long."

"Yes, yes, understand."

Daniel watched tensely as Carlos drove the car away. From Carlos' friendly response to the embarrassing episode, Daniel got the impression that Carlos did indeed understand.

"Suzanne, I'm so sorry," Daniel apologized as he approached Suzanne. Slightly out of breath, he sat and immediately placed his manuscript in her hands. She awkwardly juggled it and then made room for it, placing it on the table.

"Your car broke down," Suzanne said calmly.

"Yes. How did you know?"

"Mechanic's hands," Suzanne said, referring to his somewhat blackened, grease-stained hands. Daniel stared at his hands in embarrassment.

A friendly, yet no nonsense, efficient waiter appeared and smiled as he addressed Daniel. "Can I start you off with a drink? A glass of wine, perhaps?"

Daniel managed to hide his panic and pretended to casually browse the menu. As he looked at the menu options, he was mentally computing what he could order with the nineteen dollars and fifty-two cents cash which he carried in his pocket. As it turned out, what he could pay for, tax and tip included, was not very much. Yet, if he ordered a green salad and a glass of tap water only it would be all too obvious what his pathetic financial situation was.

After a moment's contemplation of etiquette, he decided that it didn't matter. Since the restaurant luncheon was at Suzanne's invitation, he was sure that the accepted, non-written protocol was that the onus to pay was on the inviter and not the invitee. Suzanne was likely to pick up the tab. Then again, he felt that he had to consider the gender factor. If the waiter served the man with the check, which they still tend to do in this day and age of supposed sex equality, then things could get very embarrassing indeed. The waiter hovered, still smiling but looking a tad more impatient. "Do you need a minute?" he asked.

"Yes, please," responded Daniel in a gentle, yet commanding tone. As the waiter shuffled off, Daniel kept his eyes on the menu and mentally wondered how best to ask Suzanne if she was actually paying for this meal.

"Have the steak," Suzanne helpfully suggested. "They're known here for their steaks."

"You're having steak, Suzanne?"

"Can't decide between the tenderloin and the filet mignon. I had the tenderloin here last time and it was exquisite."

"Nice," said Daniel, as he looked at the exorbitant menu prices for both.

"If we both order one of each, we can split them," Suzanne suggested.

"We could do that," Daniel replied unconvincingly. "Don't know if I'm in the mood for steak, though."

The waiter returned and again beamed a smile at Daniel. "Decided on anything to drink?"

"A glass of water would be great. To start with," Daniel said before realizing that there were already two poured glasses of water on the table, complete with ice and a slice of lemon in each.

"Certainly," said the waiter, "domestic or imported?"

"Domestic is fine," said Daniel, wondering what in the heck he had just ordered. At that moment, before his internal panic became external and obvious, Daniel realized that he just had to come out and ask her. So, in as neutral a tone as he could muster, he blurted his query. "How are we doing this, Suzanne? Is this going on your business card as a business expense, is this a business lunch… are you paying?" Daniel asked, all too quickly, his words jumbled together.

Suzanne looked at Daniel for a few beats before answering but it was unclear to Daniel what she may have been thinking.

"Oh, no, honey," Suzanne said with just a slight hint of human feeling, "I assumed we were going to go Dutch."

Daniel wasn't sure if his agent saw his Adam's apple take an impromptu and uncontrolled leap into the base of his throat but he knew he had to stall with a thoughtful facial expression as it might be a moment before he possessed the ability to speak again.

"Is that a problem?" Suzanne asked.

What Daniel knew was (as did every rapidly, out of control, vibrating cell of his entire body), that this was terrible news on many fronts; it was not merely bad news as far as the present meal was concerned. This was not the, 'the publishers love your novel and can't wait for the next installment' celebratory meal that he had joyfully anticipated.

In his gut, he now knew that this get-together was going to go someplace so ghastly, someplace so terribly, terribly, catastrophically appalling, that he wasn't sure he could take it and hold himself together as a fully functioning human being; which was probably why his agent chose someplace public; someplace where he couldn't shout and scream and throw things and smash whatever was before him into tiny little pieces.

"I can't sell your novel," Suzanne finally said. "I'm sorry."

As Daniel's world imploded upon itself, the waiter returned with another fixed and friendly smile, "How are we doing here? Have you two decided?"

Daniel didn't hear the questions being addressed to him or, if he did, he didn't show it. He looked frozen in place: his body, his face, his unblinking stare… frozen.

"Give us a few more minutes," said Suzanne to the waiter, who once more, and less joyfully this time, shuttled off. Suzanne stared at her client.

"Are you okay, Daniel?"

Daniel did not look at all okay. In fact, if he were a computer, what would be showing would be the blue screen of death, along with the error message, 'a fatal error has occurred and this application cannot continue,' familiar to all PC users, especially those still using operating systems XP and older.

Suzanne watched Daniel with concern and uncertainty as to what to do next. If he truly were a computer, she could simply press control-alt-delete and have him reboot, perhaps restoring him to an acceptable level of functioning. He was not a computer, however, and in any event, as she was not thinking of him as a machine, the thought did not occur to her. Suzanne did, however, wonder if sprinkling him with some drops of water would do the trick. Perhaps a good splash would get him back to the here and now. Before she could consider whether it was best to use imported or domestic, sparkling or tap water, Daniel's eyes blinked.

"Daniel?"

Daniel's facial expression looked as if his brain were indeed rebooting: his eyes flickered and his eyelids fluttered.

"Are you okay?" Suzanne asked.

"You can't sell *The Impossible Dream: Part One*?" Daniel asked, incredulously and hoping that perhaps he had misunderstood her in the first place.

"I'm sorry, Daniel. The market's very soft right now. Maybe down the road."

"It's my best work?" Daniel said with such incomprehension that his statement sounded more like a question.

"It's wonderful, Daniel. It's… a classic."

"Then… what? It needs work? They gave you notes to improve it? What?"

"No, Daniel. They didn't give any notes. They really don't… they feel that they can't take it out, right now."

"They didn't like it?"

"No, they loved it. Everyone thinks it's terrific, your best work yet. It's a minor masterpiece, no question."

"Then why won't they publish it?"

"Because they don't think it will sell, Daniel. They just don't see a market for it. It's not the kind of work that people want to buy, right now."

~end sample~

Read more of Daniel's story in *Brain*.

~

Visit eXu Publishing at https://www.exupublishing.com/

www.ingramcontent.com/pod-product-compliance
Lightning Source LLC
Chambersburg PA
CBHW021231190726
48289CB00005B/1277